THE INNOVATOR

WATERFYRE RISING 3

NADIA HAN

PROSE CONCEPTS

For those with the "fyre" to open their hearts.

.

.

.

"You have to keep breaking your heart until it opens."

— Rumi

COPYRIGHT

Mom dropped me off at school, but I snuck back home after she left for work. I was now in my backyard, hiding in my tree house because I didn't want to risk Mom suddenly stopping by at home and finding me. She was probably busy working with Uncle Derek today, but it was better safe than sorry. They worked together at Wu Real Estate Solutions. I'd be grounded if she found me here instead of at school.

Hopefully, my sister Audri wouldn't be looking for me at the end of school. I'd tell her I had gone to some club afterschool and come home later.

Nerves played in my stomach like a slinky that wouldn't stop. How could I concentrate on schoolwork after witnessing that murder last week with my friends? We would've died if that man with the slash across his face hadn't told us to run and keep our mouths shut. He was part of the gang—or mafia—but he let us go. It didn't matter. I just wanted to get away from that church. It had been our regular meeting place to discuss our WaterFyre Rising video game, but now it was a crime scene. Remi had a better view of the murder, but I saw enough and heard the gun pop several times.

He gave us a second chance to live that day, and my heart hammered as though it had just happened. Using my backpack as my pillow, I lay down on the floor of my tree house. Uncle Derek helped me build it. If Dad had been alive, he would have taught me.

How were my friends coping? They'd been scared too. We'd all captured something on our drones and saved it to a flash drive. The man with the scar told us to keep our mouths shut, or they'd kill us and our families. We believed him. We would have died if someone else had caught us. That person might not have had the decency to give us a second chance. My stomach twisted at the thought.

I'd never seen anyone murdered.

A car pulled into the driveway, and I peeked out from the window, which overlooked the driveway and garage. Uncle Derek got out of the car and walked around to the backyard.

Shit.

He wouldn't come up to the tree house. I was the only one who used it. My friends often hung out here too. Audri did a few times, but Uncle Derek didn't. I didn't dare move, not wanting him to find me skipping school. I didn't think I could lie if he caught me.

His voice brought on a protectiveness that only parents could offer. Uncle Derek had been the father figure for me ever since my dad died. Sharing my fears with an adult would help ease it, but I didn't want to get him killed by some gang.

So I hid in the corner, trying not to make a sound. The

summer air was warm, and the sun was shining, but I didn't feel bright and cheerful.

"It's all set. You'll get your money soon," Uncle Derek spoke into his phone, walking around the backyard. "That clip you gave me? I can't see a damn thing. It's too dark. If you find another angle from another street, let me know."

I held my breath as Uncle Derek walked by the tree house and toward the garden. He must have been talking about another real estate deal.

"I'm busy for the next few weeks. Won't be able to join the meeting. I've got to take my nephew to a basketball game this weekend. Reschedule it." He sounded irritated at the person on the other line.

I almost forgot about the Celtics Game. He'd gotten us tickets a month ago. I had been so excited. Maybe that would take my mind off the murder.

"What made him think a cement wall was a fucking good idea? I want him gone. He's just going to mess things up again and jeopardize the larger plan." Uncle Derek's irritation skipped down my spine. I had never sensed this anger from him before. Someone must have ruined an important project at work.

"What tunnel? When?" Uncle Derek cursed again. "Keep me in the loop."

Why was he so angry?

CHAPTER ONE

Huffing out a frustrated breath, I stared at the calendar on my computer, reminding myself that this mundane job was just temporary. Soon, I'd be giving my resignation letter and returning to my former life. No more boring spreadsheets, city council memos, trash recycling questions, and other miscellaneous tasks that came with working for the Department of Public Works and Parks in the city of Providence, Rhode Island.

None of these tasks would serve me after my time was done. *Thank God.*

What kind of person thought about leaving her job when she'd only been there for six months? A person with an agenda. A person who needed to find out why her father had bought her a property in another country and told no one before his death.

Why were you in the States, Dad?

A reminder chimed in my computer alerting me of three upcoming deadlines, including a status meeting I had to attend tomorrow morning.

A headache throbbed in my temple, and I closed my eyes, trying to quiet my mind. For a minute, I became invisible, and my senses honed in on the surrounding noises. I heard fingers flying across a keyboard, a rhythmical *click clack* that could be meditative if I'd been in the mood. Not too far away, a printer beeped, needing a paper refill. Someone stapled papers and slapped them onto a desk, and drawers opened and closed.

My cubicle separated me from my coworker, Penelope, who typed and talked with emphasis. Down the hall were seven coworkers in cubicles, but they hardly made a peep because of Dolores Kennedy, also known as Sergeant Kennedy, who disciplined the office like she ran a military base.

Leaning back in my uncomfortable chair, I released a quiet sigh. I thought my cubicle days were over, but life had a strange way of pivoting. The unexpected twists and turns kept me on my toes.

C'est la vie.

I went from designing luxury apparel and accessories to working in an area in which I had zero experience. My stress level spiked on the first day of work; the anxiety subsided as I learned more about the municipality. There was nothing wrong with an administrative job. It was important to the commissioner, who handled many things people took for granted—water, sewer, trash, recycling, leaf pickup, snow removal, and so on. It was true that a city required a village to run it properly, and now I was a villager.

It's temporary, Natalie. A means to an end.

The career one-eighty shifted my mentality from managing a fast-paced company to dealing with details that moved at a turtle's pace.

I was a quick learner, and that saved my sanity and kept my true identity hidden. People knew me as Natalie Chapelle, the name on my resume that matched all my other documents: credit cards, banks, lease agreement, and driver's license. Money could buy many things, and I took advantage of that. When I told my mom about my plan to go to Providence and investigate Dad's property, Mom almost had a heart attack.

I understood her concern. No mother would want her child in danger. But I needed answers to why my dad was there. Did he have a second life hidden from his family? Though Mom was worried about me, I could see the disbelief and devastation in her eyes regarding the rumor surrounding my dad.

Had there been a second woman? Mom never spoke the thought out loud, but I knew. My luck with men had been anything but fortunate. The unknown was often worse than the facts. But I needed facts, and I'd do anything to get them. My family deserved closure.

The new residence and job gave me a reprieve that I didn't expect. An ocean separated me from responsibilities that weighed heavily on my shoulders and a relationship that kept resurfacing even though it had ended a year ago. Providence was the new beginning I needed, but I didn't share this with Mom, who had a lot to deal with already.

I had wanted a job at the Registry of Deeds, but there were no openings. So I submitted my resume to the DPW, which worked out well. My administrative position made me invisible, allowing me to maneuver around to get information. The city had records of everything, and yet I couldn't find anything on The Prism. Why would Dad purchase an abandoned building? Why hadn't he mentioned it to me and Mom?

I worried someone would find out the truth about me one day. Would I get arrested for ethical violations or for falsifying documents? I had no idea—I didn't have time to worry about that.

I'd tried calling City Hall to request info on The Prism as a resident and not as an employee, but the clerk said there was none available. That should have been a glaring sign that the municipal system wasn't working properly, but she didn't care.

"Dinner at your place? Tonight?" Penelope giggled quietly from the other side of my cube. She was probably talking to her boyfriend, Zach. Ten years older than me, she had a cheerful personality that made her appear younger. Happiness brightened up a person's character and face, making them look more youthful.

Was I happy? *No.* Stress didn't make room for joy or happiness.

Penelope laughed again, and her conversation grew louder.

I cleared my throat and whispered, "Shhh. Sergeant Kennedy might head this way soon."

At sixty-six years old, Dolores Kennedy had been working for the city for thirty years and believed in a strict and quiet working environment. She knew everyone and how the city functioned, and that gave her power.

"Gotta go now. Enjoy your lunch. I can't wait to pinch your butt, babe."

I smiled at her banter with her boyfriend. My ex-fiancé would appreciate that kind of playfulness, not just with me, but with many women. I'd seen videos of him on his other girlfriends' social media platforms. That relationship had been one of my many mistakes from the beginning.

"Thanks." Penelope leaned against the wall that separated my cubicle from hers. She had a lovely face with adorable freckles and curly brown hair.

"You're welcome," I said.

If Penelope got into trouble, Sergeant Kennedy would linger around here more often. That meant I couldn't snoop around for my research. Plus, Penelope had been helpful in showing me the ropes when I first started, so we watched out for one another.

Everything takes time here. No need to rush because no one else is rushing.

That had been Penelope's advice when she saw my urgent email demanding a status on a project. I had to get used to this slow pace that drove me crazy. However, I was playing a role here and needed to adapt. It was like putting on a unique set of attire to portray a specific mood or attitude. Clothes could conceal or reveal.

Right now, I was wearing khaki capris and a pink cotton shirt, casual and simple, with no makeup. I blended in well with my environment. I had to get a new wardrobe because most of my clothes were from my collection or designer brands. One designer dress cost more than the entire wardrobe I'd purchased at Target and TJ Maxx, which had amazing collections. Some designer brands weren't worth the money, especially when the seams tore after one wash. Don't get me started on that.

Quality was important to me. Like clothing, the quality in people mattered.

"Do you want to join me and Zach for dinner tonight?" Penelope asked.

"No, thanks. I'm tired and plan to head to bed early." I almost said I didn't want to interrupt her butt-pinching, but that would reveal I'd been listening to her conversation, which I hadn't done on purpose. She sat on the other side of the wall and she could hear my conversations too.

"Boring."

I shrugged. "That's me."

Boring was exactly the image I needed to portray. Any interest directed my way would cause a distraction. An unseen person was like a spirit that could go wherever she wanted.

"Why don't you wear any makeup?" Penelope gestured to my face. "I've got some products I can give you. I bet you'd look stunning."

"Too much work. I'm lazy. I don't have a guy to impress like you. 'Boring,' remember? Thank you, though."

Penelope was a sweet and genuine person. I wasn't used to girls like her. The women in my circle only cared about themselves. There was constant competition about who looked better, who was engaged to the most eligible bachelor, what the latest trends were in fashion, and where the next banquet to play dress up was. They would never offer me genuine feedback like Penelope did. Their comments were coated with poison or hidden agendas.

"Don't take it the wrong way," she said. "You have a pretty face, but you're wasting it by not showing it off."

"No offense taken. One day, I'll be inspired to wake up early and put on makeup just for you."

"Want to go to lunch now?" Penelope asked, glancing at

the clock on the wall. "Food for Thoughts updated their menu. It's nice out. Come with me."

The July weather was perfect with low humidity.

"Okay. I need to stop by Robert's office first. I'll meet you there."

Grabbing my purse, I swung by the commissioner's office and knocked on the opened door that showed Robert Conner flipping through a stack of folders on his table.

He glanced up at me, offering a warm smile. He had kind eyes and snow-white hair that matched his mustache. I'd met his wife, Linda, once when she came to pick him up from work. The online articles portrayed him as a difficult man, but I found he was a man who got things done. His job wasn't to make friends with the employees, but to get things done in a timely manner. I admired and respected people who had a strong work ethic.

Sometimes you had to be a bitch to get things done. That was required to run a successful fashion empire.

"Robert, you received a call from a reporter at Channel Five News. He wants to discuss the water leak on Main Street. He'll call you back later today. Also, I scheduled a meeting with you and the city manager for a budget review."

He blew out a breath. "Thank you. With so many projects and repairs in the works, it'll be chaotic in the office for the next few months."

"Well, you have a team here to assist you. I'm heading to lunch. Want me to bring you back something?"

"Can you get two extra black coffees? One for me and one for my guest working in the conference room. I've been stuck in meetings and left him working alone there."

Getting coffee for other people was also new to me. The

last time I did that for anyone in a working environment was for my mom and dad.

"Sure."

I didn't know Robert had a guest today. It wasn't on his calendar, but that wasn't abnormal, as he seemed to be pulled into unexpected meetings often.

As I headed toward the stairs, I passed by two women by the copy machine, giggling.

"Grayson's hot, rich, and intelligent," said the girl wearing the plaid skirt.

I didn't recognize her as an employee in the building. I should have ignored them and gone to lunch, but curiosity slowed my pace. Irritation slid down my back at the mention of Grayson's name.

My phone pinged with a text message, and I pulled it out to check in case it was Penelope changing the lunch location. Stepping over to the counter with the office supply cabinets, I checked my message.

Michelle: *Hey! You coming to the martial arts class this week? Vivian's the special instructor.*

Natalie: *Won't miss it.*

Michelle: *Great. See you then.*

Taking self-defense classes was something I'd always wanted to do but never had the time until now. My schedule used to be slammed with meetings, traveling to look for upcoming trends, and choosing colors and fabric for the next collection. In this new role, my life opened to new possibilities.

"You already have a hot and rich man, Jill." Maggie, one of the city's solicitors, flicked her long red hair over her shoulder. "I wonder if he's seeing anyone."

"I don't see a ring on his finger, so you're good." Jill laughed. "Why don't you ask him out?"

"I don't want to get fired if he complains to HR, but I can give him a hint . . ."

"Use one of your legal tactics from the courtroom to get an answer from him." Jill bumped shoulders with her. "You'd make a stunning couple."

"You know what? I'm going to do that right now." Maggie pulled out her phone from her Versace purse and typed as she spoke, "Interested in a 'cock-tale' tonight?" She bit her lip, smiling at the screen, and tucked it back in her purse.

"He'd be a fool to say no to that kind of invitation," Jill said, as though she wasn't in a professional atmosphere that called for more discreet conversation.

Why was I still standing there eavesdropping? I had no idea.

They laughed, and the sound felt like pinpricks on my skin. It was odd because I didn't care if they were interested in the irritating man who had refused to sign multiple documents I'd sent his way. He'd delayed my process, which meant I had more work to do, and he'd been rude in his reply whenever I called or emailed him for an update.

A gorgeous face didn't make up for the ugly character that lay beneath the façade. The fashion industry produced a lot of gorgeous people, but not all of them possessed the personality to match the beauty. I'd learned to look at beauty differently, and I had standards to abide by.

As far as I was concerned, Grayson was just another wealthy, arrogant, and good-looking man who had no regard for others. The glamourous exterior attracted women like

Maggie and Jill, but I knew better. These days, I steered clear of men like Grayson Wu.

"I wonder when he'll reply," Maggie said, twirling a lock of red hair around her finger.

Sergeant Kennedy emerged with a straight posture, squared shoulders, and stern face, wearing a navy jacket over gray pants with a folder in her hand. She had short gray hair that came to her chin.

"Girls, this is not Gossip Hollywood. Please keep your voices down. If you must gossip, please head downstairs to the cafeteria or go outside, where the birds and bees would be more interested in your conversation. You're blocking the copy machine." She squeezed between the girls and started making copies.

Maggie whispered something to Jill as they walked away, sneering at Sergeant Kennedy's back.

Sergeant Kennedy looked over her shoulder at them, then at me. "You part of the Gossip Girls Club too?"

"Nope. Going to lunch now."

I couldn't help but smile as I headed down the stairs and almost bumped into Robert's wife. She had dark brown hair, an oval face, and light green eyes.

"Hi, Linda," I said. "Robert's not in his office. He's at a meeting."

"I know. I'm just dropping off lunch for him since I was in the area."

"He'll be happy when he returns to his office. Enjoy your day."

"You as well." She smiled.

As I walked on the sidewalk, Grayson Wu's face intruded my vision as though he knew I'd been spying on a conversation about him. Why wouldn't I be curious about the man who had made my life difficult for the past few months? I should be used to unpleasant billionaires with massive egos by now, but none of them got under my skin the way he did.

Stress had been piling up on me, and Grayson's attitude didn't help. Thinking about him soured my mood, so I shoved him out of my head and entered the sandwich shop.

CHAPTER TWO

GRAYSON

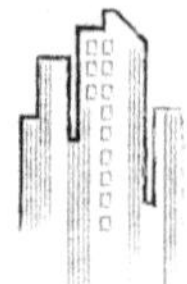

Sitting at a long, rectangular desk inside the conference room with not enough sunlight, I stared at the documents needing Commissioner Conner's signature. I should have been here months ago. The blueprint for the Three Point Park project was finally ready, and I could start the construction without further delay. For the past few months, obstacles had piled up, preventing me from getting anything done, including the renovation of a property that Derek had fucked up.

Derek—I now addressed my uncle by his first name—had been business partners with my parents at Wu Real Estate Solutions. But then he murdered my dad and used the properties to run his illegal drug and sex trafficking business. The insanity of last year was something that should only occur on TV shows.

I'd wanted to demolish the warehouse, for all its ugly memories and negative energy, but didn't want to waste the sturdy skeleton of the building. So, despite my desire to destroy it, I had opted to renovate it. The location had easy access to the highways that would attract businesses. Mom had hired a feng shui lady who gave the property an energetic cleanse with incense, prayers, and crystals. I had no part in that, but Mom believed in that stuff, so I let her do whatever she wanted. That building belonged to her and my dad. I was just the CEO—the shield—who ensured no one hurt my family again.

Though I had reservations about the building, I was a business executive who needed to think objectively. This warehouse was profitable, and if I treated it as such, it would benefit me and my family. Mom's real estate company had recently merged with my Foresight Design Firm, offering design, development, and real estate solutions.

Now that all the lawsuits Derek had brought upon the family business had been all squared away, I could breathe easier, giving me the energy to concentrate on Three Point Park, a project that seemed to evolve, getting more complicated every time I worked on it. I could have delegated more to my team, but I found it difficult to trust people these days —even people I used to trust. It wasn't their fault. This was a weakness I'd been trying to overcome.

Damn Derek. His betrayal destroyed me, and I hated him for it.

Not wanting to think about him anymore, I got up from the table and walked over to the window offering a view of downtown Providence from the fourth floor. I glanced into the distance, toward where Three Point Park would be located, but a few buildings blocked the view. The two buildings had been demolished, waiting on the construction. This unique park would connect three distinctive buildings offering residential and business suites and prime retail space—

My thought was cut off by a figure walking on the sidewalk below. Natalie walked beside another girl, laughing at something. I'd been dealing with her for months. She was like a leech who wouldn't let go of a pending project even after I told her I didn't have time for it. She kept calling and emailing my assistant, who gave the same answers. Unsatisfied, she reached out to me again and again. I could have ignored her, but I hadn't been in a courteous mood, so every time she called, I irritated the hell out of her.

Normally, I admired people with persistence because success required it. I knew this because I practiced it. However, my patience had been reserved for lawsuits at that time. I wanted to kill every damn lawyer who took a hit at my family.

Settling with them had cost millions, but it wasn't the money that frustrated me. The time and energy I had dedicated to it left me hollow, driving me to hate the world. I hated myself and even God.

How could God let so much shit happen? I supposed that was a question even the saints, angels, or Buddha couldn't answer.

Natalie stood in the street chatting with her coworker. I should probably sit down, but I remained at the window staring at her while I wondered if there was a God.

I wasn't a religious man, but I had believed in a higher power at one point in time. But that had changed. I was now a man who had adjusted to life's circumstances. My situation had sharpened my edges.

Natalie disappeared into the building just as my phone pinged. I returned to the table, retrieving the phone.

I need to speak to you. It's important. - D

How the fuck could Derek use a cell phone in prison? I hadn't heard from him since he got locked up—not that I wanted to. But this message begged me to be careful. I glared at the phone as though it were a monster trying to get me.

My chest constricted with hatred, anger, resentment, and sadness. I immediately deleted the text as though the gesture would delete Derek from my life. If only life could be that easy. What people said about family was true—you couldn't pick them.

You played the cards you were dealt with. I didn't want to play shit.

A therapist would tell me to forgive Derek so I could move on. How could I forgive a man who had murdered my father? A sane and logical man would want him shredded. I wanted that, but would his demise make me feel better?

I dropped back into the seat and blew out a breath. I should work and not think about Derek. That text message was an ember from the past, glowing hot and bright, igniting something within me—something I didn't dare to acknowledge because it would only make life worse. Did I need more shit to deal with? Absolutely not.

But you need answers.

I clicked my pen repeatedly, the only sound in the room that lured my mind away from the discomfort brewing in my gut. I grabbed a blank sheet of paper and scribbled an abstract building on it, hoping it would distract me. The scribbles reminded me of the mess in my mind and in my heart.

A slideshow of memories surfaced without my permission. Derek and I at a Celtics game. Playing basketball in the driveway. Poring over calculus homework. Constructing my tree house. Preparing food when Mom was busy.

All those memories were now stained with blood.

Because of Derek, I was stuck in a rut with no way out. I

was an indecisive man with blurred vision. A man without clarity was an incompetent man. At least that was what it felt like for me. Having clarity—a purpose—drove me to success. I'd worked damn hard to become a top-notch architect who demanded a lot of money for my skills.

A knock at the open door ripped me out of my reverie.

Commissioner Conner strode in and grabbed the manila folder from the table. "I'll review these documents while I attend the next meeting." He glanced at my empty cup of coffee. "You need more?"

I looked at the cup, unsure if more caffeine could assist me today.

"We'll get one." Robert decided for me, which I didn't like. It was just coffee, and I was tired, so I didn't protest. "Let's touch base in a couple of days. I need to review the blueprint with the city manager and the mayor. You'll get the green light soon."

"Soon" to the city could mean two weeks, a month, or five months. I preferred none of the above. If they wanted my donations to the city to continue, then they needed to expedite my project.

"Let's make it *next* week." I didn't have the patience to wait any longer.

"I'll do my best."

"Your best is appreciated."

After Robert left, I opened the folder and reviewed copies of the history pertaining to the buildings making up Three Point Park. With my donations, I'd become a friend to the city employees, which gave me access to the archives. I wanted the history of who had previously owned my properties, worked on them, and so forth in case a contractor had added an addition that damaged the infrastructure of my buildings. This old data wasn't retrievable via the internet because some of it had been typed with an old typewriter.

Checking on my other projects, I read an email regarding one of my properties that was being leased by a software company. I cursed at the pending issue. Did I have to do everything myself?

Negotiations had been going back and forth between the company and my financial team about the renewed lease. My assistant had politely told them the contract wasn't negotiable. Nothing was changing from the previous agreement. Sometimes courtesy didn't work out the way it should.

My phone rang, and frustration poked at me.

"What?" I barked at my assistant, Suzanne.

"Sorry to interrupt you, Mr. Wu."

"Why are you calling me mister all of a sudden?"

She'd always addressed me as Grayson before. I hadn't requested that she address me differently.

"Umm . . . sorry. I assumed you preferred it." She inhaled a breath. "Grayson, I just wanted to let you know that the software representative would like to meet with you next week regarding the contract."

For fuck's sake. I didn't want to meet with anyone. I wanted to be left alone. What was wrong with everyone?

"Tell him I'm all booked up. Have him meet with the real estate and financial teams. The terms of the contracts stay as is. If he wants to move, that's his decision. I can replace tenants immediately. That building has a prime location, and he knows it."

"Yes, sir."

"Let me know how the meeting goes." Just because I wasn't present didn't mean I had no interest.

"Will do."

"Reiterate that we aren't budging with the numbers."

"Yes, sir."

Suzanne hung up the phone, and I leaned back into the chair. My body was sore for some damn reason. I hadn't entered the gym in a month, and my body was screaming for me to return. I needed to get my motivation back.

"Why am I surrounded by incompetent people?" I seethed to myself.

The conversation added to my irritation, like a sweaty T-shirt clinging to my already crabby body. I wanted to press a magical button to obliterate the entire world, leaving only a small portion to myself.

Another curse flew out of my mouth.

A noise drew my attention to the doorway. Natalie stood there holding a cup of coffee, an appalled look on her face.

"Oh, it's you," she said. "Someone made you mad by asking questions?"

I could hear the disdain in the forced courtesy. It fascinated me that I could read her mood. Could she read mine? She probably heard me cursing, which explained her disgusted reaction. Or maybe something had annoyed her prior to coming to the conference room.

My frustration had to do with family matters. What was hers?

She wore a pink top with khaki pants and no makeup. The blonde hair piled into a bun at the top of her head made her look like a flower growing out of a crack in the sidewalk—something unexpected, something that didn't belong. Despite that, there was something about her that intrigued me more than women wearing lots of makeup. Maybe it was because of her persistence. Most women—even men—would have stopped bothering me after I told them I didn't have time for them.

But not her. Not this wildflower that seemed to have more to offer.

About twenty minutes ago, I'd declined an invitation from Maggie, the city's solicitor, to a "cock-tale" tonight. A year ago, I might have answered that call, but things had changed now.

Besides, I wasn't interested in Maggie, even if she was a fiery redhead. I didn't want to be in any relationship, which was why I had ended things with Gisele. She'd been the first girl to last six months. Boredom often set in for me, but this time the reason was family drama and my need for solitude.

Right now, Natalie wasn't dressed for attention, yet she had mine. My interest stemmed from her disdain for me. Other women didn't respond to me like she did. But then again, they didn't have to work with me directly. She knew my sharp edges and didn't shy away.

The staring contest between us broke when she walked in and placed the cup of coffee on the table, but not in front of me. She wanted me to *work* for it.

"I should have known you'd demand coffee from the commissioner." A disapproving undertone coated her words.

I can play this game with you, buttercup.

Rising from my chair, I reached over, grabbed the cup of coffee, sipped, and placed it back down. "What's wrong with demanding coffee? A man who knows what he wants *deserves* what he wants, right?"

She eyed me from across the table, and my skin tingled for some damn reason. Maybe this third cup of coffee wasn't a good idea after all. Since when did my skin tingle?

"Did I say there was something wrong with demanding

coffee?" Her blue eyes narrowed. The heat of them singed my skin. "If you must know my opinion—and it's only *my* opinion—I think men who know what they want can *get* what they want on their *own*. Especially if it's something easy, like coffee. Right, Mr. Wu?"

Mr. Wu. How I'd love her to scream that in my bed. How she addressed me provoked an entirely different response than when Suzanne had called me that.

I smirked, loving the slight French accent that made her sarcasm sexy. "Maybe I just wanted to give someone a chance to walk outside for some fresh air."

"How thoughtful." She rolled her eyes. "We're all busy, Grayson. I can open the window and smell the fresh air." She crossed her arms. "Anyway, since you're here and *since* you're a man who *knows* what he wants, show me when you want your warehouse renovation project completed by signing all the documents. Efficiency is a trait for a man who *knows* what he wants. Don't you agree?" She pasted a smile on her face, and I wanted to pull her closer so I could examine those full luscious lips that dared mock me.

I wasn't in the mood for mockery today, but from her, I could entertain it.

"What happened to 'Mr. Wu'? I like it when you address me that way."

"It wasn't meant to be endearing."

"It sounds affectionate to me," I said, studying how her lips formed into a pout and wondered how they would feel around my cock.

Unlike other women, she wasn't mocking me to be funny. She was mocking me because she thought I'd ordered Robert to have her get me coffee. She was painting me as an arrogant asshole who couldn't get his own drink or a man wasting her time when she could have been doing something more important.

I could read between the lines and decode her facial expression.

One, I had my fancy coffee machine in my office where I made it myself and often for others when I felt generous. Two, her preconceived notion of me had roots far older than today, so this poor cup of coffee had been the recipient of her accumulated aggression toward me. Maybe this coffee was the catalyst for our interesting business relationship.

I had no idea why I wanted to explain it to her. Explanation took time, effort, and energy—none of which I wanted to exert right now. It was no one's business, and I didn't give a damn what others thought of me.

Surviving in the business and architectural world, I'd developed a skin as hard as stone. People's criticism of me or my work had no effect. It did in the beginning, but I was no longer young and clueless.

If I was a better man, I'd let her get back to work and forget this conversation ever happened. But at the moment, I wasn't that kind of man.

I couldn't stop myself from taunting her. What the fuck was wrong with me?

Stress, anger, sadness, lack of sleep, confusion, arousal, and a desperate need to escape pushed me to press her buttons. How many buttons did I have to push before she went off the ledge?

I might as well play the arrogant asshole to perfection.

"Have a seat, Miss Chapelle, and I'll sign the documents for you."

CHAPTER THREE

NATALIE

The tension in the room throbbed, and I felt its force skipping along my spine. I straightened my posture in an attempt to shake it off.

It didn't work.

A table separated us, but it might as well not have existed because nothing could stop the powerful energy zipping between us. My stomach quivered from his arrogant smirk that seemed to reach my skin. How could one smirk have so much power?

On a stunning face like his, a scowl would look attractive. Damn him. Maybe everyone in heaven was all drunk on the day he was born and accidentally blessed him with sinful good looks. They missed their mark on his personality, though.

I didn't mean to overhear his conversation earlier. His face had been taut with tension, and his voice sharp like broken glass. It reminded me of my prior phone calls to his office.

I should've sat down and watched him sign those documents. That would've been a miracle and worth the effort of me bringing him coffee. If it were anyone else, I wouldn't have had a problem. People had brought me coffee when they went out, and I'd reciprocated. No big deal.

But this was Grayson Wu. This was a man who had refused to help me. Why should I get him coffee when he couldn't even sign my documents?

That had been the main reason for my displeasure and not the act of getting him a drink. Though if he'd choked on his own ego, then I'd consider getting him a bottle of water without being asked. I wasn't a mean person, but I was adaptable—a chameleon. When someone whipped out rude comments, I'd return them in kind. I'd learned that some people could only understand me when I used their tactic on them. Sort of like rudeness could only comprehend rudeness because kindness was too far from the spectrum, making it appear more like an alien language.

See? I was *helping* his comprehension by being rude back.

You make no sense.

I shoved that inner voice away. Not because there was reason for it, but because I needed to feel this dislike so that it could dull the strange tension squirming in my stomach.

And in my loins.

Sit down.

Why couldn't I move?

The intensity of his eyes anchored me to the floor as though they held power over my feet. For some odd reason, I couldn't breathe. I had no trouble breathing before I entered this room. Was this how he intimidated others? I didn't feel intimidated, but something else—something I couldn't pinpoint yet. My body remained still, as though I was a fit model, letting the designer examine the clothing on me.

We stared at each other like two high school enemies waiting for the other to make the first move. I surveyed him, and he surveyed me.

He sported short black hair, brown eyes, masculine eyebrows, a straight nose, a chiseled jaw, and lips that made me wonder too many inappropriate things. He wore a dark tailored suit with a navy tie that had an allover geometric print, casting him as a stylish panther eyeing its prey. My eyes traced the straight line of his shoulders—strong and capable like the horizon that separated the sky from the land. My designer-trained eyes moved to the powerful arms, the poised posture, and the stable long legs. His casual stance depicted confidence, portraying him as a man with a vision and a mission. Most successful men possessed these qualities, but lacked honesty and kindness.

Which man are you, Grayson?

When my gaze slid to his face and connected to his eyes, my lips parted, releasing a quiet sigh. His eyes raked down my body, and I shivered as I felt his keen observation, like soft feathers skimming all over me, awakening my muscles and cells.

Okay, that was a strange response. I desperately needed some time off from work to recalibrate.

Grayson broke the staring contest, shifted his feet, and gestured with a hand for me to sit down.

I pulled out the chair, not because he asked, but because my legs were wobbly.

He grabbed a manila folder on the table, moved it in front of him, and tapped his fingers on it. "Robert said you'd be working with me regarding the Three Point Park project."

I crossed my legs, trying to remember if my brain had lapsed along with my body. I'd heard about the construction a few blocks away that would become the next tourist site for Providence, but I didn't know the details.

"He never mentioned it to me."

"The city manager will approve it soon. For previous projects, the city would appoint an employee to work closely with me. That person is you."

I considered him. "Is that *your* request or Robert's?"

"It's mine, which will become his." He smiled, and a dimple appeared on his right cheek, transforming his face from handsome to . . . extraordinary. But I kept that thought tucked in a secret place where no one—especially him—would ever find out.

"I'll touch base with Robert later." I looked at the other folders in his pile. "Are you going to sign those papers?"

Grayson didn't even glance at the pile. "I've worked with other assistants from the city, and none of them are as determined as you. Why are you so determined to get these signed?"

"Simple. I'm doing my job. If I don't resolve those issues, more will pile up, and I'll be swimming in issues. I don't have time to follow up on a nuisance when it could be resolved by a quick signature."

"Fair enough." The smirk he tossed my way seemed like a trap. "Just so you know, those documents were signed this morning and already delivered to inspectors. Someone's scheduled to come out and review my warehouse in two weeks."

I blinked in surprise. "How come no one told me?"

"I'm sure you'll be notified soon. Municipal government

isn't renowned for being quick. Besides, I told Robert I want *you* on Three Point Park."

"Why?"

"Why not?"

"You realize we don't work well together, right?"

"Since you like resolving things, this could be an opportunity to *resolve* that issue. Don't tell me you're incapable of this important task."

Incapable? Frustration rose in me. *God, please give me patience so I don't hurt him.*

Grayson pulled out some papers from a folder. "Let me brief you on the project. These are the three buildings that will create Three Point Park." He placed each picture in front of me.

My heart raced as I recognized The Prism—*my* property.

"You don't own this." I jabbed a finger at the printout.

He arched an eyebrow. "Do you know who does?"

Shit. I should rein in my emotions before I revealed too much. This property was the reason I was in Providence. Finding out why my dad had purchased The Prism for me took precedence. I had to clear his name and my family's legacy. Dad wasn't a cheater. He was a good man, and I refused to believe the negative depiction of him in the European tabloids. The images they posted of him looked fake like someone got stock photos and placed his face on the models.

"No." I lifted a shoulder. "I've only heard Robert talk about the other buildings, Sky Tower and Central Tower."

"Those names will change."

"To what?"

"Not sure yet."

"I assumed a businessman like you would have all these details squared away already."

He flicked me an inquisitive look. "Some things take time." He tapped the image of The Prism. "Can you find information about the owner of this property? I can't seem to locate anything useful. There's nothing in the archives. Maybe you know where they hide old files."

"Why do you want this building?"

"Does it matter?"

"I only work well with others when I know the history and the direction of the project."

Curious brown eyes considered me. "I like its location."

He wasn't sharing the entire truth with me, but that was enough for now. I had things I didn't want people to know too.

What was I supposed to do now? Grayson wanted my property, and my job was to help him find the owner so he could buy it. I had no use for the place, but this building held information I needed. If I were in a different situation, I'd sell it to him for an attractive price, but right now, I couldn't.

A man like Grayson wouldn't buy a property purely for its location. His eyes held a different story. He was a visionary, but a cautious one. Or maybe he didn't trust me enough to share everything, which I understood.

I stared at the picture of The Prism for a while, not wanting him to see what was going on in my head. How could I dissuade him from purchasing The Prism and *encourage* him to look at the other buildings in the vicinity? There were several of them that looked more promising than my abandoned property.

My job just got more complicated.

Placing down the picture, I said, "I'll do what I can to dig up information for you. I'll email you when I find something. Can I take these photos for reference?"

Grayson nodded, but still scrutinized me.

The heat in my body shifted to a series of tingles, making me shiver. It was as though the more he focused on me, the more I *felt* him. His presence overwhelmed me. I was aware of his slight movements, even the tilt at the corner of his lips, and the throat motion created by his Adam's apple when he swallowed. The masculine cologne he wore was subtle, yet surrounded me like a cardigan. I swallowed and inhaled a breath, trying to calm my body's strange reaction to him. Why was I reacting to *him*?

I'd been around countless other attractive men—like his friends Forrest and Arrow—since I arrived in Providence, but no one unsettled me the way he did. Not that I'd been around him much. The last time was at the Krazee Tavern with the girls.

Trying to look interested in the images of the buildings, I struggled to regain control of my body. That right there was a major issue. No one had power over my body without my consent, and this man—though incredibly attractive—didn't have my permission.

And yet he affects you.

Grayson Wu and his escapades with women weren't old news. Even his sister Audri spoke about how she never got to know any of his girlfriends except Gisele, his longest relationship.

Was I just lonely? Or was I a woman who fell under his spell? I'd fallen for Rafael that way, but soon realized the horrific truth. Not only did Grayson embrace the same attributes—wealth, power, and stunning looks—he had them on steroids. These were warning signs telling me to stay far away from him.

But a tiny part of me—a *disturbing* part of me—wondered how much he could affect me.

"How about we reconvene in a few days?" he asked.

"I can reach out via email or a virtual meeting." I rose from my seat, gathering the photos.

"You can, but I prefer you see the model I created for the park. You can see the full project on a miniscule scale. I have an office for consultants to work in when they're at my headquarters."

"I prefer to work in my office."

"You mean your cubicle?" He stood up as well.

I didn't like his condescending tone. "Just because it's not a fancy office doesn't mean I can't get work done. If you must know, it's the everyday people who do the simple work that allows people like you"—I jabbed a finger in his direction—"to sit back and make those multimillion-dollar deals." I inhaled, remembering my early corporate days working for high-end fashion brands before working for LaRue. I wanted outside experience and not the privileged one my family could offer me. I didn't want people to look at me and say I got the job because of my family. I had proved my worth.

"Does it hurt?" I asked him.

The smirk on his face turned into confusion. "What do you mean?"

"Does your ass hurt? Because it seems like you have a massive stick up there."

His lips twisted into a half smile. "I didn't know you'd been wondering about my ass."

I rolled my eyes. "Are we done? Because I need to get

back to my 'cubicle' to attend to other matters that have nothing to do with egotistical men."

He slid his ass onto the edge of the table, crossed his arms, and gave me an impassive look that could be described as frigid—so cold that it lacked emotion. "No, we're not done. We're just getting started. Tell me, what do you know about municipal work? What's your experience with architecture?"

Was he testing me? I placed the documents down on the table, slid onto the edge of the table across from him, and crossed my arms as well. If I were an outsider looking in, I'd consider this image of us sitting at the conference table oddly comical. But I was too angry at the moment to care.

"Are you interviewing me for a job?"

"It's a simple question that a dedicated city employee should have no problem answering. I'd like to know who I'll be working with. Wouldn't you agree, Ms. Chapelle?"

"Municipal work pays shit. It takes a village to help the city function properly. 'Architecture is how the person places herself in the space. Fashion is about how you place the object on the person.' That's a quote from Zaha Hadid, an architect and a fashion designer." I narrowed my eyes. "Anything else, Mr. Wu?"

I wasn't sure if that answered his question, but I didn't care.

"I'm thinking." Grayson smiled the way a wolf would smile at its prey, and a tingle zipped down my spine.

Intrigue gleamed in his eyes as though he wanted to continue taunting his prey, to extend its life longer for his sick game. Maybe he wanted to know if the prey dared to bite back.

He didn't know what I was capable of.

CHAPTER FOUR

GRAYSON

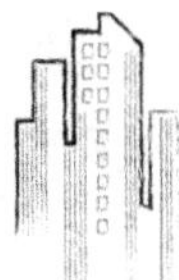

I'd never been turned on by an argument until today. Natalie had somehow irritated and aroused me at the same time, and that confused me. I didn't need confusion. My life was already cobwebbed with issues.

I should let her get back to her cubicle, but I wanted to see how far I could push her.

You're a sick man.

I didn't disagree, but I was too intrigued by this woman.

"Is Antarctica your favorite continent?" she asked.

She had a knack for throwing me off the rails with her odd questions. Perhaps that was another reason I wanted to keep chatting. She could steer my mind away from the various issues cluttering my brain.

"It has interesting ice formations that inspire me. Why?"

"That explains it." She let out a halfhearted laugh. "You look like a cold-blooded person. The frigid terrain suits you."

The more our conversation—or rather disagreement or whatever it was—carried on, the more she aroused me. Was this a new syndrome I'd developed? Stress could throw the psyche from its equilibrium. Was I experiencing that? How else would I explain my swelling cock throbbing for release?

Uncrossing my arms, I reached for the folder on my desk to block the bulge from view. How would she react if she saw what she did to me? But she was too angry to look anywhere but in my eyes.

"I know where you like to hang out—the equator? I can practically see steam coming out of your ears," I said, giving her my best frigid stare.

She flung her arms out, pointing to a corner in the room where a potted plant stood. "Why don't you go hang out right over there in *that* corner?" She scowled. "It'll thaw out your cold blood."

"How so?"

"It's always ninety degrees. Thought an architect like you would know his angles."

I tried not to smile, but one came anyway. Her sass and wit were like beacons of sunshine to my gloom and doom. Of course, I didn't say that to her.

"Well, aren't you *acute* mathematician who knows her angles?"

An image popped into my head and heated my body. She was naked in bed with me, positioned at a very specific angle where I could plunge deep into her. It was her fault for bringing up angles when I was trying to calm my erection.

She bit her bottom lip, and I could tell she was trying to suppress a frustrated laugh.

The struggle between laughing and remaining pissed at me played out on her face. How strange was it I could see that even though I hardly knew her?

This tiff—this unfamiliar thing between us—entertained

me to where I wanted to wipe my schedule free for the next few days just to argue with her.

What did that say about me? A billionaire who had lost his mind? An architect who had lost his foundation because he'd been so sex deprived that an argument got him hot and bothered.

Since she didn't retort, I pushed another button. "I'm an expert at angles too."

"Is that what your ex-girlfriends told you?"

"They admitted that a tilt of a robust column is important. The perfect angle can create powerful pleasures. Have you experienced that kind of bliss?"

Her lips formed into a pout. "You know, I could go to HR about you right now."

"For what?" I loved the way her eyes flashed with heat and dismay. "If you complain, I'll say you've *misunderstood* me. I was referencing architectural terminology that you obviously don't understand. Then I'd suggest to them I can give you some free lessons because I'm a helpful civilian."

"You're such an ass."

"We've already established that, buttercup." I got off the table and walked over to stand in front of her, looking into her heated blue eyes. "I think you're turned on by our architectural conversation."

Unable to resist the seductive pout, I gripped her chin and brushed my thumb across that bottom lip. "If you ever need me to educate you on various angles, just ask nicely. There's no need to start an argument." I leaned in and whispered, "The passion in your eyes makes me think you want me."

She swatted my hand away and licked her bottom lip as though she wanted to taste my touch.

I smiled, satisfied that I'd riled her.

"Dream on." She huffed, whirled toward the door, yanked it open, and stormed out.

My eyes slid to her ass—a very fine one at that—and wondered if she went to her cubicle or straight to HR.

My gut told me she didn't go to HR, because despite our tiff, I discovered that Natalie Chapelle had something to hide. Like me, she had an agenda. She hadn't been fully transparent about her collaboration with me. Well, I hadn't either.

Despite that, one thing was certain: she was as aroused as I was.

CHAPTER FIVE

GRAYSON

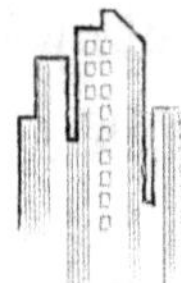

I jerked awake from the most erotic dream I'd ever had with sweat soaking my shirtless body, drenching my bedsheets.

Holy fucking hell.

My heart pounded in my ears like a drum beating to a sexual celebration. I'd experienced this kind of sexual pleasure unconsciously. Heat scorched my body, making my cock hard as stone. I sat up, switched on the bedside lamp, leaned back on the headrest, and blew out a heavy breath.

Natalie must have cast a spell on me with her "dream on" comment. I'd never had wild sex where each position—there were many—fueled my drive even more. I could go on forever and ever. We fucked in every room of a building I didn't recognize. She was a wild vixen, dragging me to the floor, the stairs, the elevator, on the desk, the couch, even at the long window where anyone could see us. I preferred control in life and in bed. But damn, I loved the way she rode me like she owned me.

In the dream, I'd surrendered more than my body to her.

That confused me because I'd never surrendered to a woman before. No one got that close to me, which was why I liked variety. When I sensed a woman wanting more than I could give her, I moved on. The newness kept things exciting and simple.

I couldn't trust myself these days. I didn't know what I wanted, which wasn't like me either. Maybe that was it. Maybe I was a ball of pent-up emotion, repressed sexual energy, lack of sleep, exhaustion, anger, fear, and other feelings I was too tired to name.

I stared at my tented boxer and sighed. *Get down.*

Maybe my sexual energy had been repressed for too long. That would explain the sexual dream. I glanced at the clock on my nightstand—two in the morning.

The fuck?

A groan escaped me, not the kind that came from pleasure, but from the knowledge I'd be paying for this early wake-up later in the day.

I hadn't slept well in months, and I had a board meeting tomorrow that demanded a clear head and my full attention. My employees walked on eggshells when I was in the office. I didn't have the patience for their redundant questions— things they should already know. How long had they worked with me? How long had they been with the company?

Don't ask me the same question twice.

I had a million things in my head, so I needed my team to understand me and take some of the burden off my plate. That was why I'd hired them.

People can't read your mind.

I didn't care.

Stop keeping things to yourself and lashing out when people have questions.

I hated this internal war inside me that resolved nothing.

Grunting, I got out of bed, walked into the kitchen, poured myself a glass of cold water, and gulped it down. The chill traveled down my throat and settled in my stomach, cooling me off.

I noticed dust on the kitchen counter, and annoyance pricked my skin. They missed a spot. Did I have to teach the cleaning crew how to *clean* too? Retrieving a wipe from the container, I swiped at the dust. There. Done.

Shaking off the sudden irritation, I slid onto the cushioned stool, twirling the empty glass in my hand. My mind wandered back to Natalie, and the annoyance subsided a bit. I wouldn't have been at the commissioner's office if I had let one of my team members manage the Three Point Park project. A year ago, I would have. But now, I didn't trust them to do it right.

I had a fabulous and dependable team, but this project was too important to me to let someone else oversee it.

That's not the main issue.

Fine. A part of me was hesitant about the project. There were parts of the project I was uncertain about. It was mostly a feeling that told me I was missing something. And because I hadn't figured it out, I wanted to monitor it every step of the way, hoping the answer would come to me.

But now that Natalie was working with me, I wasn't sure if thinking clearly could happen. Based on tonight's wild dream, I was afraid I'd be spending my time imagining sex scenes with her instead of working.

She probably hated my guts. I'd decided to have her work with me on the spot, and emailed Robert about it after she had stormed away. I told him I wanted her to be my liaison and no one else. I preferred Natalie's different perspective. Mostly, I was curious about what she was hiding.

A memory surfaced, and a laugh burst out of me, echoing through the quiet home. I couldn't believe she told me to go to the corner as though it were my time-out spot. No woman had ever whipped out an angle comment at me like that. The other women I'd dated only asked if I could design a home for them.

Natalie was the distraction keeping my thoughts from terrifying things I didn't want to face yet. Maybe that was why I didn't mind sitting in my kitchen at two in the morning, thinking about how much I wanted the dream to be real.

What would she feel like under me, on top of me? My cock hardened again. I could still feel that sexy mouth of hers on me . . .

You need a woman to resolve your issue.

I got off the stool and placed the empty glass in the sink, thinking about how much my life had changed. Life could turn in an instant, changing everything. When my dad died, I lost parts of myself, but I remained strong for Mom and Audri. They'd suffered more. Derek had helped me cope, but his betrayal shattered my soul in unimaginable ways.

Not only did I not trust others, I lost trust in myself. What if I made the wrong decision and trusted someone who ended up hurting me again?

I was a fool for not seeing Derek for who he was. It seemed like everything that had happened between him and me was a lie. I felt used and stupid.

It was best to separate myself from others until I could figure things out. I stopped hosting parties at my home, declined invitations, and didn't have any relationships. The solitude in my home was perfect for me to wallow in.

I stood in my kitchen, appreciating the darkness. Though dark, I felt like I could see more of myself now than before.

Too wired to fall back asleep, I went to work out so I could stop feeling sorry for myself and wishing Natalie's naked body was still molded to mine. I flipped on the local news station with a replay of the evening news.

Chaos erupts at Rhode Island's Maximum Prison. An unexplained explosion occurred inside the prison this evening, injuring several inmates and correctional officers. They are being transported to local hospitals for treatment. The explosion occurred during a kitchen renovation, which is under investigation. We will update you when we receive more information.

I slowed my pace to a walk on the treadmill. Something told me the explosion wasn't an accident. Derek had been attacked a few times in prison. The secret organization known as The Trogyn had wanted him dead, but failed. These people had a hand in killing my father.

They had to be stopped, but first, I needed to know who the elite members were.

Did Derek get hurt by this explosion? Was it intended for him? What information did Derek have on them?

No longer in the mood to exercise, I walked past my bed, heading to the shower. My phone buzzed from the nightstand.

I need to see you. It's important. - D

Waves of resentment surfaced and made me tense up.

I ignored Derek and went to shower off any feelings tied to him. As the water ran down my body, a face popped into my vision, arousing me again. Natalie seemed to intrude on my mind at the most inopportune time.

What would she think if she knew I was jacking off, thinking of her?

Perhaps today called for an unannounced visit to her office for an update on The Prism.

CHAPTER SIX

NATALIE

I spread out all the images Dad had left me and tried to piece everything together. Nothing made sense.

Grabbing the pocket watch, I ran my fingers over its intricate designs. Dad had this made when I was seven years old. I remembered going to the jewelers with him and watching him discuss it with a man with a white mustache who I came to know as Monsieur Henri Ducasse, a well-established watchmaker. He had passed away several years ago.

What do you want me to see, Daddy?

If he hadn't sent this watch along with the original deed stating I was the owner of The Prism, I wouldn't have believed the letter came from my dad. It came two months after he died. But he didn't send any keys to the property.

Who had sent the package for him? Who was helping my dad?

I was dealing with the tabloids claiming my dad had an affair with several women and making sure House of LaRue functioned properly after his death when this letter threw me another curve ball. In addition, Aunt Estelle—Dad's sister—had taken over as CEO and wanted to sell it to a venture capitalist. She'd been the CFO prior to her new role.

Though Mom told me Dad had wanted to update his will, they never got the chance. Was he planning to remove Aunt Estelle? My grandparents had wanted Dad and Aunt Estelle to run the company, so he had honored their wishes. But over the years, Aunt Estelle had proven she only cared about money and not about the legacy my grandparents had started. That didn't surprise me, as I had encountered her mean streak when I was younger.

"Please let me out, Aunt Estelle! I'm sorry I pushed Nicolette! I won't do it again . . ."

Ghostly sounds surround me, and I tremble as I imagine monsters reaching for me. An icy chill touches my skin, and I scream, scooting farther away.

That terrifying experience had trapped me in a frightening place I couldn't seem to escape. A shiver ran down my body as I remembered the nails poking out from the wooden floor, scraping me, making me think they were skeletal fingers trying to grab me.

I never told my mom or dad. Being young and vulnerable, I'd believed her threat and refused to go to her house when my parents needed a babysitter. Over the years, I let that experience fade into the corner. Now and then, it would surface like an awful cold that came and went.

Aunt Estelle could be the CEO if she wanted. I was still Creative Director and Lead Designer, so creativity was more my forte. The Board of Directors would vote on the sale in four months. LaRue profits had already taken a nose dive before Dad's death. After his passing, it worsened, and the press became vultures attacking him and House of LaRue. I had to clear my dad's name and persuade the directors to vote against selling it. Mom was VP of Marketing and had been keeping me posted while I tried to uncover what my dad had been doing in the States.

If he had an affair, where were the women? I couldn't find any names. What had Dad been up to? I tried my best to remember if there had been anything off with Dad, but nothing stood out. Had he been protecting Mom and me by pretending everything was all right?

So many questions swirled in my head as I looked at the last pictures of us at a restaurant. Mom and Dad looked so happy. They had wanted another child, but Mom experienced some complications so they only had me. My dad loved us, and now I had to protect the business he'd worked so hard to maintain.

The business had started out as my grandparents' small tailor shop. When the men's wives saw my grandmother's custom-made outfits, they requested her business, and a boutique was born. My grandparents used up all their savings to grow the business. They taught my dad and aunt how to design, sew, and run the business since they were teenagers. Within one year, the boutique moved to an additional space with fifteen employees. The following year, they had investors who helped them acquire a five-floor building with an adjacent warehouse. House of LaRue had now been in business for over sixty years.

So I had to fight to keep this legacy alive. I had to honor my grandparents' and my dad's hard work and dedication.

Financial problems had fallen onto House of LaRue months before Dad's death, but he'd had a plan. I'd assumed things were looking up. I should've paid more attention. There was no way he'd want the company to join the

Fontaine and Chalamet Group—a wine company that owned luxury car brands and jewelers and was now trying to gather up fashion labels. The problem with these capitalists was that LaRue would be *one* of many brands, and it wouldn't get the attention it deserved. Having been in the fashion business for a while, I'd witnessed countless companies merged or bought out by another, only to be dissolved after a few years.

I couldn't let that happen to the LaRue brand. LaRue belonged to my dad—our family—and not to some outsider who didn't care about it as much as we did.

Finances had a way of unmasking people. Though Mom was Dad's wife, she wasn't a true LaRue in terms of bloodline, and therefore didn't have the power to block Aunt Estelle from selling it. I voiced my thoughts vehemently, but again, the will stated Aunt Estelle would become CEO and oversee the company if something should happen to Dad. She couldn't make any major decisions without my approval. But she'd been ignoring that statement. I could only take over if Aunt Estelle stepped down, viewed unfit by the members, and so forth. But she couldn't sell the company unless the Board of Directors approved it. Mom and I were members, and we'd definitely vote against it. The will was outdated, long, and complicated.

Despite all that, Mom and I could influence the Board of Directors and sway the vote. So the battle was now between my family and Aunt Estelle. People usually assumed that glamor and money shielded people from family drama. But the truth was, no family was immune to that.

Had I made a mistake by not going to the authorities when I received my dad's documents? I wanted to, but intuition had told me not to. What if going to the police would escalate the drama already being played out in the public? The tabloids would twist things to attract as many eyeballs as possible. I didn't know why, but I knew there was something not right about this entire scenario.

I held the picture of The Prism in my hand. It was a twenty-floor brick building with a lot of windows. There was nothing extraordinary about it. I'd seen more unique buildings.

Why did you buy me this property? Was there something you wanted me to find out? Did you cheat on Mom? Please give me the closure I need. Please show me how I can save House of LaRue from falling into the wrong hands.

It would take a lot of money to buy out Aunt Estelle and all the Board of Directors who had a portion of the stocks. I didn't consider myself poor by any means, but I was no billionaire. The accumulated assets of House of LaRue barely touched a billion dollars, but we owed a lot to the banks too.

I had thought my ex-fiancé, Rafael Caputo, was the man who could help me, but I was wrong. Caputo Holdings was a group of European banks, and he was the son of the CEO of that company. If I had married him, he promised to finance House of LaRue. But while I was engaged to him, he dated three other women. He didn't even keep his escapades discreet. His support would have saved my family, but at what cost?

I felt used, dirty, betrayed, and worthless. The relationship had been wrong from the start. I had dismissed those signals that something was wrong. The late hours at work, the long weekend trips alone, the sudden calls at night— these were signs the universe had given me, but I was too blind to see them. Rafael only wanted to be associated with me because it boosted his persona to be with a fashion designer of a luxurious brand. He didn't love me. At least not the way I wanted or needed to be.

A man who loved variety could never settle for one woman. He'd get bored and move on. But I wasn't a woman who settled for less than what I deserved. Terrible experiences with men had taught me that, so now I was more careful.

When I admitted to my mom why I'd agreed to marry Rafael, she was furious.

Don't sell your soul for money. Whether House of LaRue fails or succeeds, it won't come at the cost of my daughter's happiness.

As I stared at The Prism, Grayson's face appeared in my mind, and my heart raced. I didn't understand this odd reaction to him.

It's not a reaction, it's an attraction.

Was it an attraction? Why was I attracted to men who could hurt me? Like Rafael, Grayson preferred variety. Why couldn't I find a decent man who wanted to be with me and only me? Was that too much to ask?

How did these men juggle so many women, anyway? Women could be demanding—especially women who knew what they wanted—and keeping everyone in check would be difficult.

My reaction to Grayson was a simple aspect of human nature. He was a handsome man, and I enjoyed looking at beautiful things. So that was natural. There couldn't be anything more between us. How could I be attracted to someone who irritated me? Plus, he probably had a girlfriend, maybe multiple girlfriends. I had to stop this absurd attraction before it got out of hand.

I didn't have the energy to patch up a broken heart again. My energy was reserved to uncover the truth about my dad.

I searched for other properties near The Prism. There were two buildings for sale. Maybe he'd be interested in those. What was his vision for Three Point Park? Perhaps if I knew, I could help him find a more suitable building as a replacement.

I wasn't an architect, so I looked at the aesthetic differently—from a fashion perspective. Maybe the interior and the structure of The Prism made it a gem. Maybe I should sneak inside one of these days. Then I'd be breaking another law here in the States. If I had keys, that would solve a lot of problems.

I'd already broken a couple with my fake ID, lying on my resume, so adding another crime would officially make me a criminal.

Shit.

If this came to light in Europe, my career would be over and House of LaRue would be destroyed.

Fear made my stomach cramp.

Don't fail. Don't fear. Breathe.

I leaned back on the couch and concentrated on my breathing. When the cramp subsided, I focused on my goal: find out the truth about my dad, restore House of LaRue to financial stability, and work on my own collection. Dad had a great skill for designing novelty trims. Customers had always commented on the unique buttons, belts, and cuff links. I'd learned a lot from him, and I'd do whatever was necessary to protect my family's legacy.

Though I worked for the City, I hadn't found any useful information regarding The Prism in the archives, which Grayson had also looked into. All I found were a few papers about electrical and sewer pipe installation misfiled in another cabinet. It was as though someone removed everything regarding the Prism.

Was someone at City Hall hiding information? Had I met this person? It could be any of my coworkers. Was I being paranoid? There were other properties that had missing files too. So maybe the files got damaged or were misplaced by someone. That could happen.

Back at House of LaRue, I'd uncovered missing files in another department's drawer when the assistant was reorganizing.

My phone pinged with a message from the girls.

Kiera: *Wanna go to a fashion show in Boston? It's for charity. The designers for Marchesa and Valentino are going.*

Natalie: *Thanks, but I'll pass.*

If I went there, they'd recognize me. I'd attended trend and fashion shows with these designers before. They were in my circle, and right now, I wanted to exist under the radar.

There was comfort and security away from the limelight. I craved that kind of peace. It allowed me to breathe, to be myself—wear no makeup, be silly, do nothing—and not have to worry about what the tabloids would say or how it would reflect on the brand.

Glamor and wealth could be a prison too.

Michelle: *Kiera can introduce you to some of her male model friends.*

Kiera: *Yes! I have a few in mind who might suit you.*

Natalie: *Thanks, but I'm not interested.*

Audri: *Are you okay? You sound sad.*

Natalie: *Not sad. Just tired and stressed.*

Vivian: *Sex can solve that. Lol.*

I shook my head and smiled. These girls cared about me, and I appreciated them. But I also feared the closer I got to them, the more I had to hide my true self. And what would happen when they discovered I wasn't Natalie Chapelle, a municipal employee?

Natalie: Sleep will help just fine. I'm boring.

Michelle: You are not! But I get it.

Kiera: She's only pretending because she has someone else in mind! You can tell us your dream man! Lol. Eggplant emoji. Cucumber emoji. Wide smile emoji. Wink emoji.

I knew she was teasing, but why were nerves swirling in my stomach?

Audri: Have you met anyone interesting lately?

Grayson's face intruded my mind even though I didn't want it to. He was more of an irritation than an interest. Why would any woman be interested in a man who stressed her out even if he could make her body feel all kinds of things?

Perhaps Kiera was right about me needing some release. But I wasn't going to sleep around to achieve that. There were safer ways.

Natalie: I have a big project at work, and it's overwhelming. Send me pics of hot guys. If one of them stands out, I'll let you know. Smile emoji.

That would settle their curiosity and give them something to work on.

Kiera: You got it! I'll send tons of hot guys your way.

Natalie: Make sure they have a brain too.

Michelle: Yes. Women want substance.

Audri: Intelligence.

Vivian: Depth.

Kiera: _A working stalk. LOL. Cucumber emoji. Eggplant emoji._

A laugh burst free, making me feel better. Yes. These were my girls.

Natalie: _You know me so well. Thanks, babes._

I spent the next thirty minutes chatting with them about nothing in particular and discovered that Grayson hadn't been seeing anyone for a year.

Somehow I didn't believe that. Maybe he hid the truth from his family and friends. And if that were the truth, I was curious about what inspired such a profound change in him.

CHAPTER SEVEN

GRAYSON

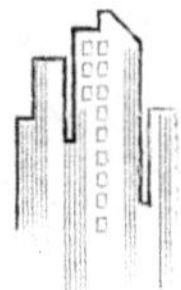

Even with a packed schedule that didn't leave room for a detour, I headed downtown to see Natalie when I shouldn't have.

"Is Commissioner Conner available?" I asked Marge, a silver-haired clerk who had been with the city for twenty years.

I already knew the answer because he had told me in an email that he'd be taking time off to spend with his wife in Texas. But I didn't want to show up and just ask for Natalie. That would make it seem like I needed her. I didn't need her. I just had a question for her.

Stop lying.

Since when did I need to explain why I had to do something?

Since Natalie. For some reason, I couldn't stay away.

"Sorry, he's out of the office for the rest of the week, Grayson." Marge recognized me from all my visits. "Do you want to leave him a message?"

"No. Where's Natalie?"

As though on cue, I saw her walk down the hallway.

Marge said something to me, but I didn't listen. Instead, I walked away to catch up with Natalie.

She wore a gray skirt, which fell below her knees and outlined her ass beautifully, and a light blue top, which brought out the colors of her eyes. The scent of her fragrance dragged me along as though she yanked at my tie. It annoyed me. I couldn't stop the pull. I'd always been the one in control, but around her, my self-control wavered.

"What are you doing here?" she asked, surprise wrinkling her eyebrows. Her face was like a breath of fresh air, no makeup, yet so perfect.

This was what I needed to see—something different from my gloomy world.

Most of the women I'd dated dolled up for me, but it was Natalie's natural beauty that stilled my senses. The rawness of her features was the honesty I'd been waiting for. I didn't want anything covering up the truth. Natalie delivered that to me without knowing.

"Do you have any information regarding The Prism?" I asked, trying to regain my self-control.

A man who lacked control was a man on a ship without a steering wheel. Or he could be a building with rotting beams that could collapse at any moment. I didn't appreciate anyone threatening my character. But Natalie was doing a lot more to me than threatening my self-control. She tugged at a deep place within me that even I didn't know existed.

Your life fell apart before Natalie showed up. True, but I didn't like her poking at my vulnerability.

And yet, you're here allowing her to do exactly that.

I swore sometimes I wanted to kill my other self. Maybe I'd developed a multiple personality disorder. People who experienced that psychological syndrome did some illogical shit.

She paused in her steps. "No. I have other responsibilities too. Things don't work that fast here. Don't you have other projects pending? Maybe you can focus on those? It's only been two days since we last spoke."

"But Three Point Park *should* be your priority."

"Says who?" Blue fire flickered in her eyes, and my cock twitched.

"Says the man who donated millions of dollars to the City of Providence. I'm basically paying your salary. Three Point Park is going to be a staple in Providence. The city knows this." I stepped closer, inhaling another whiff of her scent. "The faster the project moves along, the sooner the city will get to show the world how great it is."

She searched my face, but didn't reply. I'd give anything to see into her mind.

"If you need me to tell Robert to delegate your other projects—"

"I don't need you to meddle. I can manage my schedule. Thank you." She continued walking, and I kept up with her.

Following a woman around was an abnormal routine for me. In the past week, irritation had crawled all over me like a colony of ants staking claim on my life, biting me from all angles. I needed sleep and a month's rest without thinking about work or my issue with Derek. An unexpected storm rolled in last year and destroyed my stability. I went from living a carefree life to one that trapped me in this odd loop of repetitive confusion and unhappiness.

You're doing it yourself.

I tried to break out of the loop, but failed. I tried to ignore

Natalie, but my feet followed her as she turned down a hallway and into a kitchenette.

She whirled around, glaring at me. "Don't you have work to do? You came here for an update, and I gave it to you. Why are you still here?"

I didn't know why I wanted to taunt her. I was no gentleman when it came to certain things, and Natalie Chapelle lured my inner troublemaker.

That wild dream of her still gripped me. It had been a long time since a woman affected me, but I wasn't sure if her influence was beneficial to my sanity. She was the perfect distraction, and life was too short to ignore beauty like this.

She lifted an elegant eyebrow when I leaned against the wall of the kitchenette, watching her grab a reusable water bottle from the cabinet and filling it with water.

"Is there something you still need help with? The exit is *that* way." She pointed to the other end of the hallway.

How long could I goad her before she snapped?

"I know where the exit is, just as I'm aware how much you don't want to work on this project." I tucked my hands in my pockets and studied her.

Average height, an alluring face with flawless skin, eyes that looked like gems, sensual lips that made me yearn to taste them, a perfect chest that promised softness to my eager hands, and long legs I wanted to run my fingers down.

She gulped her water and closed the lid. "Do people usually line up to work with an egotistical man? Last I checked, it's safer to stay away from men like that."

I pushed myself away from the wall and stepped closer, inhaling her floral scent. It pulled at me as though it gripped the lapels of my suit, showing me who was truly in control.

It wasn't me, but I didn't want anyone to know.

"You're afraid of me?" I asked, loving the defiance on her face.

Lifting her chin, she said, "I'm not afraid of you." She looked into my eyes.

A strange sensation swirled in my stomach. Something new, sharp, and exciting like an invisible compass had drawn an unexpected blueprint within me. At the moment, I wasn't the architect. Natalie Chapelle had drafted something inside me, and I was afraid of what it could be.

"It looks like you're afraid of me." Conviction showed in her smirk.

No woman had ever claimed I feared her. "That's a bold statement with no proof."

"Maybe you're scared I'd prove you wrong. Maybe you're not used to 'capable' women who could succeed. Are you the kind of man who tears people down to make yourself look better?"

The biting words stabbed me unexpectedly. She thought I was disparaging her? I never cared what people thought of me. Their misconception was their prerogative, just as my opinion mattered to me.

So why the hell did her statement cut me? More importantly, why did I care?

Natalie didn't show fear or defeat as she glared at me. The energy pumping off of her was of someone who was used to the competitive arena where she had to prove her worth to survive.

Who are you, Natalie? What kind of world did you dwell in before working here? Did someone chase you into Providence?

I'd encountered two versions of her—the simple woman defending her integrity and the dolled-up and sophisticated woman who spurred my desire from a single look at the Krazee Tavern.

Which one is the real Natalie? What was she hiding?

Why should I care? I had things I didn't want the world to know. Everyone had secrets, but I was becoming more intrigued by this woman who thought I feared her.

A smirk grew on my lips as I gripped her chin. "No fear here, buttercup. The only fear I see is the one lurking inside you, telling you that I make you uncomfortable."

She gripped my wrist, held it, and laughed. "You're an overconfident man, Grayson. Your charms may work on other women, but don't waste your time on me. We're more like enemies than friends."

In a quick move, I shifted my hand so that I was the one holding her wrist. "Since when did we become enemies?"

"Since you called me 'incapable.'"

"I never said that."

"You insinuated."

"You seemed like you don't want to be part of Three Point Park." My voice grew hoarse as I held her wrist, letting the warmth of her skin seep into mine.

"I never said that." She threw my words back at me.

"You insinuated." I smirked.

The volley of words between us aroused me more than I expected.

She tried to retract her hand from my grip, but I held it in place, loving the smoothness of her skin.

"Remember this," I said, rubbing my thumb against the pulse on her wrist. "I'm a man who loves a challenge." Her pulse quickened, and it fascinated me that I was aware of her body to this degree. "The more daring, the better. Sometimes, I have the enemy in my grip without them knowing. I enjoy winning, and I'd do anything to ensure my victory, my beautiful buttercup."

She blinked at the nickname.

"Is that what you call the women around you?" She narrowed her eyes at me. "Are they 'flowers' in your massive garden where you get to pick one for the day and toss it aside when you're done?"

I loved women. There was a time in my life when I had viewed them as nothing more than flowers. They were pretty and fun to look at, but nothing more. I didn't want to get close to anyone because that meant I had to reveal parts of myself to them too.

When she summarized my past, I appeared tainted and shallow. Was that how she saw me? I didn't like this image she had of me.

"A buttercup is a stunning flower with over three hundred species. It symbolizes enchantment, positivity, and joy. It also has medicinal uses such as treating arthritis, nerve pain, and swelling . . ." The bulge in my pants grew on cue.

She arched an amused eyebrow as though she'd read my mind.

"Swelling of what?" she asked, waiting for my admission.

"Of *bronchitis*. What were you thinking?" I smiled. "So when I address a woman as buttercup, I consider it the best form of endearment."

She looked at me suspiciously, still not trusting me. "And how many women have been the recipient of such a 'swelling' endearment?"

I loved how she always used my words against me.

"Just you. The others had different nicknames . . . like dandelion, grass, and other weeds."

She laughed, knowing I was lying. The dandelion, grass,

and weed were a lie, but buttercup was hers—the truth. She brought a positive energy that cut through the grayness I'd been dealing with. Would she believe me if I told her that?

Maybe someday, but not right now.

Her facial expression showed she was trying to grasp my words, weighing the truth against the lie. But her struggle told me something important: she was attracted to me. If she hadn't been, she would have ignored me and left the kitchenette. But she stayed and continued this tug of war between us.

She got under my skin, and maybe I got under hers too.

If life had taught me anything, it was that betrayal had destroyed my family. I'd been ignorant, putting trust where I shouldn't have. Life was full of deception, and I had to play the game as though I were the most skillful deceiver.

That sounded awful, but life was full of awful things. I wasn't a saint, and I was certainly no hero. I wasn't out to save anyone but myself.

Egotistical. Her words boomed in my head. I had a sizeable ego, but every competitive person possessed one. According to Carl Jung, *"The ego is the workshop where the self is made."* I was remaking myself in a workshop that was taking its damn time, but at least I acknowledged the need for reconstruction.

I watched as two men strode towards the kitchenette, one carrying a pile of yellow envelopes. "Oh, here you are. These are for you, Natalie." He held out a stack of mail. "Two are for Robert."

"Thanks, Neil." She smiled warmly at him. The man had brown hair and a friendly face and wore one of those bright neon green jackets that city workers often wore.

"You got it." Neil gave me a nod and turned to Paul

Greene, the city inspector who would review my warehouse renovation soon. "You saved me a trip." He gave Paul two yellow interoffice envelopes.

Paul stood a few inches shorter than me and wore a white shirt with an orange tie matching the color of his hair. "Leave them on my desk. I'm getting coffee, then heading to a meeting."

Neil nodded and left.

Paul grinned at me. "I'll be over at the warehouse next week. Thanks for moving this along."

I'd met with him a few times when I needed the city to approve my building projects, and he'd done his job well.

"I'm happy to help."

Natalie rolled her eyes at my comment.

Paul glanced at her, and her expression changed, but I couldn't read it.

"Excuse me, I've got work to do." Natalie looked at me, but didn't offer the warm smile she'd offered to Neil. She walked away, and my eyes followed her as though they had no control.

Paul did the same, but I wanted to gouge out his eyes for looking at her.

"What day are you planning on coming to my warehouse?" My question drew his attention to me—away from her. I didn't wait for his answer. "Send me an email."

I walked out of the kitchenette, wondering if Natalie was thinking about me.

CHAPTER EIGHT

NATALIE

Changing into my knit top and pants, I strode out of the locker room of Martial Arts Studio, trying to release some tension. Today had been an interesting day, where my body experienced a full spectrum of sensations—annoyance, anger, sexual desire, wonder, frustration, and something I couldn't quite comprehend. No man had annoyed and enthralled me at the same time.

I hadn't stopped by the gym in over a week. It was more welcoming because of the warm atmosphere. The cream-colored walls with daylight bulbs brightened up the atmosphere. The plants scattered all over the studio added a delicate touch and fresh air to the space. I adored the boutique-style gym and loved the massage services they offered in the backrooms. The muscles in my body relaxed as though they could sense the massage chair.

I desperately needed this workout to release my mounting anxiety. My quick meeting with Robert the other day outlined my responsibilities, which included my presence at Grayson's office when necessary. Apparently, his massive donation had put the city at his beck and call. The power of money and prestige never ceased to amaze me.

One good thing that came out of this additional responsibility was access to any information I wanted. Usually, as a worker for the Department of Public Works and Parks, I could only access data pertaining to those areas. But this Three Point Park project involved all departments. This was my opportunity to dig up information on The Prism from a different angle. Another department could hold the key to what I needed. There had to be breadcrumbs somewhere. I only had four months before the Board of Directors voted on the fate of House of LaRue.

"Hey! You're early." Michelle tapped me on the shoulder. She wore a pale-yellow top and brown pants. Her curly brown hair was tied in a ponytail.

Meeting Michelle on a plane on my way back from Iceland had been an incredible happenstance. I hadn't wanted to attend the bachelorette party for my cousin Nicolette, but family duties called for representation, and I delivered. Even though Nicolette and I were the same age, we weren't friends. We hated each other as kids because she was a bully. When I fought back, her mom punished me. Now, as adults, we were cordial to each other because she didn't want to taint her persona. She'd married into a wealthy family, and I'd moved on. But I would never forget her part in making my life hell that day in the closet. There were certain traumas you'd never forget no matter how much you tried.

"Yeah, I left on the dot. Time to kick some butt tonight." I stretched out my arms and legs.

"Who do you need to kick?" Michelle asked, doing stretches of her own.

"An irritating man." I spotted Audri exiting the changing room and heading toward us.

Though Grayson annoyed me, I didn't want to put Audri in an awkward position by hearing me speak ill about her brother. Michelle and Kiera had mentioned that he was protective of his younger sister, so despite how I felt about him, I'd spare her my opinion.

Michelle bumped my shoulders with hers. "Deets, please."

I rolled my eyes. "It's not like that."

These girls had become my good friends, and they loved discussions about relationships. My frustration had nothing to do with that kind of relationship—well, sort of. It was both business and personal. I didn't like mixing the two. It complicated things, and I needed simplicity to focus on my goal. Plus, I didn't know if my body's reaction to him was just a temporary phase that would disappear in due time.

My friends didn't need to hear about my dilemma.

Audri approached us in a blue outfit with her black hair in a French braid. "Ready to sweat?"

"Born ready!" I bent down and touched my toes, stretching out my legs.

Kiera entered the room with a group of girls and walked toward us. "It's packed tonight."

Michelle glanced around the room and nodded. "It's always packed when Vivian's the guest instructor. Did you know she's also a dentist?"

"Really? I'm due for a cleaning."

"Yup. Her office worked on my cavity last month. She's a pediatric dentist, so I don't qualify to be treated by her."

"I think she opened her practice a year ago."

Relief settled in when the discussion turned to Vivian's

occupation instead of the "deets" Michelle wanted to know. That discussion could lead to things I wasn't ready to entertain yet. It was also the reason I needed the workout. The events of today confused me. Grayson made me want and hate him. How could that be possible? How could I have opposite emotions pulling at me? I'd never experienced it before, and I didn't know what to do about it.

I needed clarity to focus on the one reason I was in Providence: to find out the truth about why Dad had bought me The Prism and if he had an affair. If so, who was this woman?

Vivian entered the room, wearing her loose cotton pants and a fitted knit top. She had a beautifully toned figure, which resulted from hard work and dedication.

She came up to us, offering a group hug. "Thanks for coming tonight, girls."

"We wouldn't miss your special class," Kiera said.

"I'm excited to see what you have planned for us," Michelle added.

"Make us sweat!" I twisted from side to side.

"Do you guys want to get drinks after class?" Audri pointed outside. "We could try out that new bubble tea place in the plaza. It's Gisele's new shop. I heard great things about it."

"Grayson's ex, Gisele?" Kiera asked.

"Apparently, she wanted her own business." Audri lifted a shoulder. "I didn't get that when they were together. But I didn't know her well."

"I'm game," Michelle said.

"Sorry, I've got to pass. I have a private session after this class. Next time, I promise." Vivian tightened her ponytail and walked up to the front of the room.

I wouldn't miss the chance for a peek at his ex-girlfriend.

We all spread out on the wooden floor, making sure there was enough space between us. Vivian stood in the front of the classroom, and I saw my reflection in the mirror behind her. I'd taken her class before, and she was a fantastic instructor. She knew techniques that catered to women's needs.

"Thank you for coming tonight, ladies! We're going to sweat! You'll be sore tomorrow, but the pain will be worth it. I promise. We're training your muscles and sharpening your good reflexes. Let's begin."

She started us out with an easy warmup of stretches and running in place.

"Muscle memory is important. We need to help the body remember what to do so it doesn't freeze up in tense moments." Vivian threw out a punch, and everyone followed.

After the warmup, I spent the next thirty minutes kicking, punching, and learning techniques from the various animal poses. The tiger stance was fun, allowing me to visualize clawing out my enemy's eyes.

Grayson appeared in my mind. I envisioned my hand connecting with his face, erasing that taunting smirk. Maybe I could create a dimple on the other side of his face. But that would probably make him more irresistible. Too dangerous. Dimple or no dimple, Grayson stepped on my nerves today and I had to force him out of my system.

I punched to the right. *Stop making me think about you!*

I kicked to the left. *Stop making me yearn for your lips on mine!*

I curled my fingers into sharp claws. *Stop thinking about his nickname for me! I'm not his buttercup! I'm not his joy!*

Sweat streamed down my face and neck. My heart hammered as I continued mimicking Vivian's moves. How come she wasn't sweating like me?

I had to stop this attraction to Grayson. Why was I even entertaining that there could be anything between us? All we did was argue when we were together. That wasn't the relationship I dreamed of. How was I going to survive working with him? I needed to keep a suitable distance between us for my well-being. The closer I stayed, the more difficult it would be to not want him.

Mimicking Vivian's powerful moves, I imagined Grayson lying on the floor, surrendering to me and begging me to release him from his misery.

A smile crept onto my face, making me feel a lot better. He said he liked to win, and I enjoyed seeing the look of defeat on his face. What would it be like to spar with him? I'd probably lose in no time, but it was still nice to imagine I'd beat him.

I had a long way to go before I could actually beat anyone. Not that I wanted to, but I needed to ensure I could react appropriately if my enemies attacked. Huffing, I took a quick break and toweled my face before finishing my bottle of water.

Despite the workout, nerves still churned in my stomach. I couldn't tell if they were from anxiety over my family situation, my false identity at work, or my hesitation about working with Grayson. Maybe it was a combination of everything. I felt like I was walking through a maze strewn with booby traps that could explode at any moment, killing me.

Overanalyzing was never good, but I had to do that so I didn't miss important details.

An hour later, I was showered, dressed in a T-shirt and

jeans, and sitting with the girls at Sweet Bubbles. I got a milk tea with jelly bits.

"Grayson needs a break from work, so I'm throwing him a surprise birthday party. You're all invited." Audri sipped her Thai iced tea. "It's not a big thing, just close friends."

"He used to have people over all the time," Kiera commented as she used her straw to poke at the sweet boba balls at the bottom of her drink.

"He used to do a lot of things." Audri sighed. "Mom and I are worried he's working himself to death."

"Have you talked to him about that?" Michelle asked.

I absorbed every word about him, letting it marinate in my brain. What had changed him?

"Yup. We spoke to him several times, but he always dismissed it. He claims it's just work. But I know something's wrong."

The man who aroused me with a wink of his dimple didn't appear like he was struggling with anything. Of all people, I should know that others often disguised their true selves. Some hid with makeup and clothing, while others masked the truth with a beaming smile that told the world all was well when in reality, they were going through hell.

Hearing about his internal struggle added another intriguing layer to him. Maybe there was more to him than his good looks, intelligence, and creativity. Yes, I googled him and browsed the buildings he'd designed all over the world. I liked his architectural style, ranging from elegant skyscrapers and modern villas to innovative structures that appeared geometric or even futuristic.

He was a man with a unique sense of style, and I was a woman who appreciated a distinctive flair. Maybe that was it —maybe our common creative thread was the reason behind my attraction to him. My previous boyfriends were entrepreneurs, lawyers, or doctors. I'd never dated someone in the creative field. But Grayson wasn't just an architect, he was a successful businessman as well. So that added texture to his façade.

What kind of monster are you dealing with, Grayson?

"Men don't like to admit they have issues," I said.

"That's for sure," Kiera said.

"Maybe he just needs time." Michelle shrugged.

Audri let out a heavy sigh. "I'm afraid there's stuff lurking beneath the surface, and if he doesn't get rid of it, it could fester and develop into something worse."

Those words hit me hard. I'd ignored my childhood trauma for so long that it often crippled me. I had thought the closet incident would disappear on its own, but I was wrong. It was too late to do anything now. I was an adult, so I could deal with my fear better. But I understood what Audri was saying.

A part of me wanted to help Grayson, but I didn't think he was ready to accept help. The first step in healing had to be made by the patient—the person had to want it. I didn't want my healing back then because I didn't know I needed it.

Three people knew about my trauma. The person who shoved me into the closet and locked the door, the person who taunted me from outside the door, and me.

"Maybe the party will help him relax," I said, unsure why I felt sad for him. "Do you need help with anything?"

Though he annoyed me, it didn't mean he didn't deserve a wonderful birthday party.

The door to the café swung open and a bubbling sound boomed in the store. A gaggle of people walked in, and my heart hammered in fear at the sight of the man behind the group. Why was Rafael's bodyguard here in Providence? Was he here on vacation? Bodyguards took vacations too.

I pretended I didn't see him and listened to Kiera's latest encounter with a German fashion model she'd met.

"There's a guy staring at you, Natalie," Kiera said. "Three o'clock by the wall with the fake Van Gogh painting."

I glanced in that direction even though I knew they were referring to Adonis, an olive-skinned man who probably worked out every second of his life to maintain his bulky physique.

I couldn't let him spoil my disguise. I'd tell my friends my real identity on my terms. Had Rafael sent Adonis here? Why?

Had something happened to my mom or House of LaRue? Fear knotted my stomach. If something had gone wrong in Paris, Mom would've alerted me. Her assistant would have reached out as well.

"Oh, yes, I know him. A former acquaintance. I'll be right back." I wandered over to his table and sat down. "Adonis, what are you doing here?"

Gray eyes glinted. "To bring you back to Rafael."

I snorted at the ridiculous notion. "For what? He and I are over. The engagement ended a year ago."

"Boss changed his mind. He wants you back."

"I'm not his property, and I'm not going anywhere."

"You're coming back with me tonight."

Anger surged through me. "No, I'm not. You and your boss have no right to demand I do anything. My life is here now."

His lips thinned. "I have a job to do, Natalie."

"Even if it means kidnapping me? Because that's the only way you'll get me to leave. What's wrong with Rafael? Is he bored with his harem of women? I'm not his property, and he has no claim over me." I rose from the table. "You should leave before I call the police."

Adonis stood up, towering over me. "We're going home." He gripped my arm hard.

"No!" I tried to yank my arm away, but failed.

"Let her go." Grayson appeared out of nowhere and shoved Adonis's hand off me, nudging me behind him. "She said no. Do you understand the meaning of that word?"

The calm in his voice reminded me of the killing calm before a storm. But it was the way his eyes were trained on Adonis that frightened me more. Grayson just transformed into an unrecognizable man—dangerous, unpredictable, and ready to kill. It was as though something dark and dormant had switched on in him.

Adonis glared at Grayson. "Who are you?"

"Someone who won't have a problem breaking your bones if you touch her again." Grayson gestured to the door. "Leave."

Adonis surveyed Grayson. "She belongs to Rafael."

"No, I don't," I interjected. "He needs to remember I'm no longer his fiancée."

Grayson flicked me a curious look, but he didn't say anything. He turned his attention back to Adonis. "You heard her."

Adonis flared his nostrils as people stared at us, and the tension billowed in the store with every second. My friends had surrounded Grayson and me, eyeing Adonis like a pack of wolves.

"You're making my job difficult, Natalie." Adonis looked at me pointedly.

"Maybe you should stop working for Rafael, and life would get easier." I forced a fake smile. "Tell Rafael I have a new life now. I don't want to be with him. He should leave me alone unless he wants the media discussing negative things about him: 'Rafael Caputo demands his bodyguard to force his ex-fiancée back to Paris when she refuses to marry him.' The European media will eat that up, and I know how his family will react. You remind him I don't want to be with him, and that 'no' is a complete sentence. He should learn that."

Adonis straightened his posture, gave me a once over, sneered, and stalked out of the shop. When I'd been with Rafael, Adonis had respected me, but now, he viewed me as his boss's property, and he wouldn't have hesitated to hurt me if Grayson hadn't intervened.

I didn't realize my hand was trembling until Audri gripped it. "Are you okay? Who's the asshole?"

"My ex-fiancé's bodyguard."

Grayson stared at me with eyes that held a hundred questions. At that moment, I wanted to hug him for not asking any of them.

Rafael had never behaved this recklessly before. Sending Adonis to another country to retrieve me like his lost luggage? What prompted him to cross the ocean for me? He didn't love me. It didn't make any sense, and I didn't have the energy to analyze further, especially when concerned brown eyes intensified on me.

"Thank you for helping," I told Grayson.

His gaze flicked to my arm. "Did he hurt you?"

I rubbed the spot with my hand. "No, I'm fine."

"Grayson!" A pretty woman who looked more like a supermodel waved at him from the counter. That must be Gisele.

He nodded at me, then returned the gesture, walking toward her. Despite the slew of emotions stirring in me, I couldn't help but acknowledge the seed of jealousy rooting in the pit of my stomach. Something was wrong with me. I wanted him, and I didn't want him. How despicable was that?

Make up your damn mind, Natalie!

"The drama is over! Nothing more to see!" Kiera waved at the nosy crowd still staring at us.

We all sat back down at the table, but I was too unsettled.

"If that jerk stayed another second, I would've called the police," Michelle said.

"What if he comes back for you?" Audri asked.

"He won't. Rafael won't want his family's name dragged through the mud. They don't like the bad press. Image is everything to them."

I tried my best to convince them Adonis wouldn't return, but I feared he might. If only I knew what he wanted with me, then I could ensure I didn't have it so he'd leave me alone. I didn't need him to become another obstacle in my life.

I sat half-listening to my friends and half-wondering what Grayson and his ex-girlfriend were talking about. He turned and leaned against the counter, crossing his arms, and met my gaze while still chatting with Gisele. My body shivered, sighed, and shivered again as though it was having some weird conversation with him from a distance. A tingle slithered down my body, making me aware of its movement like a seductive whisper against my skin.

I broke the gaze because my body couldn't take it anymore.

A few minutes later, Grayson brought over a tray of various drinks and a plate of pastries. "Enjoy."

Audri looked up at her brother. "Why are you here tonight?"

"Supporting a friend's business." He took a mango tea drink and offered it to me. "Heard this was delicious."

"Thank you." I took the drink from him, and our fingers touched. A zap of energy raced down my fingers and straight to my center. Maybe the event had heightened my senses. Everything he did to me, I felt it in the extreme. "I'll take it home to try."

Grabbing my bag filled with dirty clothes, I got up and prepared to leave.

Gisele strode over and stood right next to Grayson, beaming. "What do you think of my drinks?"

"They're wonderful. I'll definitely be back." Kiera smiled.

"I agree." Michelle finished her drink and took another from the tray Grayson had brought over.

"I'll take this home for Remi to try." Audri chose a melon drink. "This is a fantastic shop, Gisele. Congratulations!"

"It's a lovely place, and your drinks are delicious." I lifted the mango drink to her.

"Thank you!" She placed a gentle hand on Grayson's arm. "I'm so happy you made it."

"Congratulations on your venture, and I wish you all the success," Grayson said.

While the girls and I discussed our next meetup, Gisele leaned into Grayson and whispered. "You busy tonight?"

"I'm busy." Grayson offered her a warm smile.

"How about tomorrow?"

"Don't you have this shop to manage?" he asked.

"I can always make time for you."

His lips tightened. "My schedule is packed for the next few months."

"When your schedule frees up, call me and we can catch up."

He neither accepted nor declined.

Everyone said their goodbyes, and I left the shop, walking toward my car.

"Where are you parked?" Grayson strode beside me.

I looked up at him, surprised he wasn't still chatting with Gisele. "Just over there in the lot."

"I'll walk you to your car."

"Why?"

"Because I want to."

"Don't you have things to do?" I couldn't help myself. "Don't you have a packed schedule?"

The corners of his lips lifted, knowing I'd heard his conversation. I was too exhausted to care, and this jealousy was growing more intense by the minute.

Stop it.

"It's my schedule, so I can make changes when I need to." When we got to my car, Grayson said, "If that guy bothers you again, I want you to let me know."

"He won't."

"It's better to be careful."

"Why are you being so nice to me?"

"Because I need to protect the only woman I enjoy arguing with."

"Is that what this is? You enjoy pissing me off?"

He skimmed a hand down my cheek. "Something like that."

As I drove off, I saw him watching me from the rearview mirror. Though he didn't say it, I knew he'd escorted me to my car because he was concerned about my safety.

At the stoplight, my phone pinged with a message. I checked the text message from Grayson and grinned a bit too much.

Drive safely. Don't you dare think about me.

CHAPTER NINE

GRAYSON

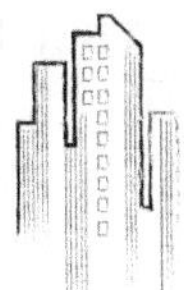

I was still burning with fury as I arrived home, kicked off my shoes, and walked into my office.

Natalie had been engaged. I didn't like that thought at all.

Who the fuck was Rafael? He sent his bodyguard to retrieve her like she was his damn dog.

I'd debated on visiting Gisele's café today, but decided to go so she'd stop asking.

She was a good time while we were together, but my interest in her died along with other things in my life. Any other man would jump at the opportunity to be with her, but I wasn't that man. Not anymore.

I wanted something I didn't understand.

I wanted Natalie. She could touch me in ways no other woman had. The surge to protect her had overwhelmed me when I walked into the shop and saw her frightened face and his hand on hers.

At that moment, darkness spiraled from the depths of me, pushing me to pummel him.

Though he was built like a tank on steroids, I knew exactly where to hit on the body to be effective. My years of martial arts training had taught me shortcuts to hurting my opponent.

I logged onto my computer, preparing to review the pending issues from the day, but I couldn't concentrate. I needed a drink.

Walking out to my kitchen, silence welcomed me. More than a year ago, silence had bothered me. I liked noise because it drowned out things I didn't want to think about. But now, silence was my preference.

Who are you?

I passed a mirror on the wall and stared at my unrecognizable self. Though the person staring back looked the same, I felt different.

I was lost somewhere, and I was trying to find my way back. The journey had made me angry at the world—and at myself. But recently, I'd found an unexpected spark in the darkness. The beam of sunlight peeking through the clouds, calling me, enticing me.

Natalie Chapelle had piqued my interest, making me forget my issues momentarily.

She triggered something in me, and I wanted to find out what it was.

The sensors turned on the recess lights as I made my way through the hallway into my kitchen. I loved the open floor plan, which represented possibilities rather than restriction. I used to prefer a lot of lights because they enhanced the interiors of my space. These days, I didn't care for them. The darkness became my salvation, and I didn't mind dwelling in it.

My phone rang and startled me. I fished it from my back pocket and sighed at Gisele's number.

"She should move on," I said out loud, ignoring her.

Shrugging off my suit jacket, I draped it over the office chair.

My agenda for the day had been to get home to work on WaterFyre Rising and let the outside world crumble. It took too much energy to care and things could backfire unexpectedly. I didn't want to waste my energy.

WaterFyre Rising gave me hope. My friends and I had been working diligently on each level of the game—a distinctive world that represented the creator. Remington had finished the demo for Level One, and Royce completed his demo for Level Two. Once the demos for all the levels were done, we could see the overall universe connecting the various worlds. From there, we could tweak it before moving it forward. This video game had been a passion birthed when I was a teenager, hanging out with my friends. We'd been young boys with big dreams.

That dream had helped groom me into a man, even if that man had been stalling for over the past year. I'd been cruising along, living a successful life until one incident destroyed my world. In video games, that event was the turning point when the hero had to decide whether to fight or surrender.

I did neither.

That infuriated me. How could I let one event have this much control over me? But then again, reality was no video game.

Blowing out a frustrated breath, I walked over to the bar, filled the shaker with ice, added vodka and vermouth, and stirred. Unlike the British spy who preferred his martini shaken, I liked mine stirred. Shaking it risked the dilution of the vodka and changing the temperature by a few degrees. Everyone knew a perfect martini was best served at a chill twenty-eight degrees.

Right now, I needed that exact chill to diminish the fire in me. It wasn't a huge fire, but it could be if I didn't put it out now. That was my method these days: squash anything that disrupted my day.

Except for this flame for Natalie. She was the exception.

I slid into my bar, enjoying my drink and my solitude. Glancing around my bar, which was on the side of my spacious kitchen, I evaluated my situation—the past, present, and future.

My internal infrastructure had been shattered. For me to feel again, I had to find those pieces and start rebuilding myself. Where were those missing pieces?

Searching required too much energy, time, and motivation. It was easier to just let them be.

Lazy ass.

Lazy wasn't the appropriate word. Laziness hadn't described me since elementary school. I worked damn hard. Perhaps the proper word was avoidance.

My body was still tense from my conversation with Natalie earlier in the day, and only escalated when I discovered she had a fiancé. Too wired to rest, I finished my drink and returned to my office to work on Level Three. This had always been an escape from reality for me. The world I had envisioned consisted of sci-fi elements that allowed the players to enter a different dimension through portals. But I'd been stuck on my portal design. Every artist—every creator—encountered this kind of block, and I supposed mine took longer to overcome.

Since I couldn't move forward with my game tonight, I entertained something else.

Who are you, Natalie Chapelle? Why did you run to Providence? What happened to you and Rafael?

My Google search for Rafael offered interesting information that I'd review later. I was more interested in Natalie because her name came up with nothing. The only social media account she had was on the popular platform ChatNow with the alias Nadda and the name Natalie C. on her profile. There were three images on her page: one of downtown Providence, another of a cloud in the sky, and a third confirming it was her. A picture of a buttercup posted a day ago.

She followed a lot of fashion brands and magazines but had no followers. The profile showed it was only created a few months ago.

Why weren't there more pictures?

Because she knows you'd be spying on her, you creep.

Natalie was a young professional, and I expected to find more about her. The women from my past all had accounts on several platforms, showing off pictures of them and me.

Even I had a few social media accounts to keep up with the fast-paced world. Though I wasn't active on them, I often used the platforms for research. Many of the international design companies and architectural magazines I followed were on social media.

Maybe Natalie liked keeping to herself or thought social media took up too much energy and time. Still, something nudged at me.

I followed her, becoming her first follower.

Then I accessed DarcNett, a website that I'd frequented after my uncle betrayed my family. Access to the website cost a lot of money, but it was worth it. Most people wouldn't get access to it, but being a successful billionaire with connections to people in the gaming business, I'd acquainted myself with hackers who had various websites for all manners of services.

I typed in her name and came up with some interesting information. Natalie Chapelle was born in Paris, worked at a bakery for three years, an administrative assistant for two years, and that was it. No other history showed up for her, and that was a red flag to me. This website collected data from everywhere. A few other names showed residences in Canada and California.

Their pictures revealed they weren't my Natalie.

Since when did she become mine?

She had me on an invisible leash.

Since that unforgettable dream.

There was no history of her education or birth certificate either. There were just receipts of credit cards and a bank card.

I glanced at a copy of her lease. *No fucking way.* She lived in *my* luxury high-rise and drove a Mercedes. How could she afford the lease and the car with her salary? Maybe I should show up at her place unexpectedly and demand to know how she could pay rent.

The mystery around her just got more interesting.

My phone rang, and Audri's name flashed on my screen.

"What's up? Isn't it a bit late for you to call me?"

"It's nine-thirty." I could imagine my sister rolling her eyes.

"What do you need?"

"Are you busy two weeks from now? I want to add an

addition to the library, but I need your expertise to ensure it'll work."

"Another addition?" I leaned back in my chair, trying to envision what my sister wanted to do this time.

Remi truly loved her, letting her change up his entire home. I wasn't sure if I'd let any woman alter my home like that. My space was sacred. There hadn't been a woman who could make me change anything, never mind giving her free rein. Even my mom didn't have that power.

"You just added a spacious room to your already massive jewelry studio, *Moy Moy*."

That was how I addressed her as my "little sister" in Chinese, a language I didn't speak as well as I should. I knew enough to converse with my mom, but I wished I'd spent more time learning how to write and read it. My grandparents and my dad would've been disappointed in me. They were stricter in carrying out traditions. Academia and honoring the family name were important to them. And since I was the male, that responsibility fell heavily on me.

You're not worthy of the family name.

"That was different, *Gor Gor*." The way she emphasized "big brother" in Chinese told me she wanted something. "My business is growing, so I needed the extra room. Speaking of which, I need to find a nice office space. Remi wants to buy a building for me, but I told him no."

Man, my best friend would do anything for her. At first, I was hesitant about them dating because I knew him. He wasn't the type to date, never mind settling down with one girl, but Audri changed him. I supposed love had the power to heal a man who had been deeply wounded. I couldn't be happier that my best friend loved my sister.

I'd never known what love was. Had never experienced

it and never would. I didn't have it in me to want it. With my shattered soul, how could I even feel love? Would I even know what that felt like?

My trust radar was too unstable these days. I didn't trust people. And wasn't trust a major requirement?

"Good call," I said. "Normally, Remi is a savvy entrepreneur, but for you, he might purchase something that doesn't turn a profit."

"Are you saying I'm not profitable?"

Women and their ways of twisting things drove me crazy.

"I didn't say that. If you're looking for an office space to work, I suggest you seek a location you want and lease it for a while. And if you like the space and location, you can purchase a property close to it. As far as the home expansion goes, I need to look before I can give you some ideas."

"Great! Show me two Saturdays from now."

"Why not this Saturday?" I asked.

"Because I'm busy. I've got plans with my girls."

"Well, I've got plans too."

"I asked Remi, and he said there's nothing planned," Audri retorted.

"Dude, I hang out with other people too, you know," I said.

"Please come two Saturdays from now? I'll make you some wonton noodle soup."

I snorted. "Is that a bribe?"

Since she'd been with Remi, her skills in the kitchen had improved. She'd learned to perfect the wonton noodle soup to where it was better than my mom's.

"You're my favorite brother."

"That comment means nothing when I'm your *only*

brother. You're really trying to bribe me. Fine, I'll take the noodle soup and dumplings. I'll be there in two weeks."

"Stop by around noon, please. Thanks," Audri said.

"I should be able to stop by whenever it's *convenient* for me. Who's doing who a favor?"

"But I'm busy in the morning. Noon, please?"

"Fine." I didn't have anything planned for the next few weekends, anyway. Maybe I could use the opportunity to show Remi what I'd done so far for Level Three.

"By the way, loosen up a bit." She huffed a breath. "Don't be an ass."

My eyebrows furrowed. "What are you talking about?"

Audri huffed out a breath. "I shouldn't be intruding, but I have to say something. I don't want to see my friend stressed because of you."

I thought I was an intelligent man, but I had no idea what my sister was referring to. "Come again? Are you sure you're talking about your amazing and very handsome big brother?"

She snorted. "Natalie is my friend, and you've been making her life . . . difficult."

I opened my mouth to protest, but remembered how I'd acted every time she had called to inquire about documents. She was persistent, which I admired and hated.

"*My schedule is packed. I don't have time for an inspector.*"

"*If you want your building renovated, then make time.*"

Her words had surprised me. No one from City Hall had ever dared speak to me that way.

That challenge in her voice—that spark of fire—had hooked me. But too much fire could burn me. Still, that didn't mean I couldn't enjoy pushing her buttons.

I never said I was a gentleman. The things I imagined doing to her had reserved a seat right next to the devil. Hell was a place I often frequented these days. The change in me was inevitable, and I wasn't surprised people noticed. I was still walking through misery, through this darkness I'd encountered. No one knew this, and no one would.

I remembered reading all these depressing books in high school and college that described a person's journey through life where he questioned his existence. I'd never understood those books until now when I questioned the meaning of my life. I was like the zero point on the X and Y axis, not going forward or backward, up or down. I was . . . stagnant.

Stagnation was the worst. For the first time in my life, I felt trapped and had no clue how to free myself.

"Hello? Earth to Grayson." Audri's voice yanked me out of my reverie.

"Did she tell you I was difficult?"

"No, Natalie's not like that. She won't complain about my brother to me because she *knows* it would make me feel awkward. I can see it in her eyes whenever your name comes up, though."

Was that a knife piercing deeper into my gut? Why did it bother me that she saw me in that way?

"Why are you and your friends talking about me?" I asked, keeping my voice even to hide my discomfort. "The conversation must have been amazing because my ears didn't itch."

Audri sighed. "She's just trying to do her job. Just be more considerate, okay? She's new in the area, and we've welcomed her into our little group."

"The gossip group?"

Audri snorted. "I used to think you were a cool brother, but you're turning into a bigger ass every day."

"I don't need to be cool because girls love me."

"Well, where are they? You haven't brought a girlfriend home in a while. You chased Gisele away."

"No, we broke up." Gisele wanted more out of the relationship, and I didn't have the energy to give her what she needed.

"Natalie is just trying to do her job, Grayson. She seemed stressed the past few times we went out. I hope it's not because of you."

It couldn't be me. Could it?

I flipped through my memory and couldn't remember anything except the sexual desires she sparked in me. Perhaps I had been demanding and rude, but that was the nature of business.

Christ.

Just thinking that I had been responsible for her anxiety irked me. "I'll try to remember to be nice to her."

"I think you need a vacation. You've been working so much that you've forgotten how to be human."

I laughed. "Is that what you say to Remi when he works late? Because we both know he's a workaholic too."

"Yes, but he takes breaks. And you don't."

"Okay, sis. Are you done lecturing your big brother? Because I've got stuff to do, like maybe plan a getaway."

"Good. I'm done. Just don't forget to come over to review my renovation ideas. You're the best!"

Shaking my head, I placed the phone on my desk, scrubbing a hand over my face. I needed a vacation, but only after I delegated the Three Point Park project to various departments in my company so they could start the renovation.

Despite all the things bouncing around my head, Natalie's anxiety came to the forefront. A notification banner popped up on my screen, signifying I had a new follower on ChatNow.

I opened it and grinned like a fool. Natalie C and I were now friends. We were each other's followers.

CHAPTER TEN

GRAYSON

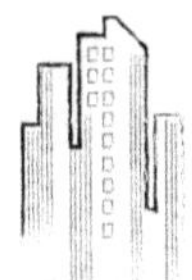

On Sunday, I spent a couple of hours at the office to get some work done. Lunchtime came, and the nice July weather called for a walk. I shouldn't be working, but I'd been behind on several projects, so it was catch-up time. Especially since I'd planned on taking a much-needed vacation.

As I headed to the sandwich shop, I bounced ideas around my head. What should I create as the focal point at the center of Three Point Park? I had some ideas, but nothing truly stood out. Hopefully, it would come to me soon.

After picking up a roast beef sandwich, I took a different route back toward my office. Something made me glance into a window, and my heart leaped at the sight of Natalie sitting by a wall inside a small shop called The Plot Twister. She was looking at something on her laptop. A stack of books sat next to her mug of coffee or tea. She wore a light blue dress where the wide neckline slid off one shoulder, revealing her smooth skin.

Something warm spread across my chest as though an

internal sun had risen in me, making me warmer than I already was in a T-shirt and torn jeans. I could stand there and watch her all day, but that would make me a creep. Besides, I wanted to be closer to hear her voice and inhale her scent.

And to see if she still suffered from anxiety. After that call with Audri, I made a mental note not to call her for an update on The Prism. I glanced at my watch. My conference call wouldn't start for another three hours, so I had plenty of time for a chat.

Yanking the door open, I stepped inside and surveyed the cozy bookstore with only two tables. Natalie occupied one, while an older couple took up the other. They offered me a pleasant smile, and I returned the gesture.

I pulled out the empty chair at Natalie's table and sat down, placing my takeout bag on the table.

She jerked, closed the laptop, and blinked in surprise. "What are you doing here?"

"It's Sunday, so I'm out and about." I studied her face. She wore some makeup today and dressed up nicer than when she was at work. "Are you waiting for me?"

"What?" She furrowed her eyebrows, grabbed her mug of coffee, and sipped.

I gestured a hand at her dress. "You look like you're dressed for a date."

"Just because I'm wearing a dress doesn't mean I'm waiting for anyone. Women like to dress up when they want to." She gave me a once-over. "You look like you're getting ready to do some yard work."

"I have a landscaping service for that. I'm actually working today. On a break before a meeting in a few hours." I leaned into the table, and my elbow touched her arm. "I haven't seen you in a dress or wear makeup." My eyes went to her lips, which had a slight pout. "I love that you're all dressed up for me."

"I'm not dressed up for you, and I'm not waiting for you." She stared at me for a long moment. "You must be used to women doing both."

"I am."

"Sorry to disappoint, but I'm not that woman." She grabbed a book from her stack and flipped to a page, pretending to read the copyright text.

"But you will be," I said with conviction and shifted my seat closer so my thigh brushed against hers. She didn't pull away, and my thigh became the happiest flesh on my body.

If my boys discovered my desperate act, they'd never let this go. Maybe Remi and Royce would be more under-standing about my foolishness because they were in love.

She gave me a disbelieving look with a hard flip to a new page. "I think Gisele is waiting for you."

"She'll be waiting forever." I studied Natalie and couldn't see any anxiety on her face. "I don't want her."

"What do you want, Grayson?"

My thigh pushed against hers. "A mysterious woman who loves to argue with me."

"I'm not mysterious."

"Did I say it was you?"

Her lips twisted and blue heat flared in her eyes. "Why are you playing games with me?"

"It's not a game."

She let out a sigh and flipped to another page. "It sure seems like it."

I heard the anxiety in her voice. Was I the reason for it? Or was someone else to blame?

Was I playing a game? The game was more in my head. The indecisiveness, the skepticism in me, had nothing to do with her. It had been my internal struggle for a while.

But Natalie had brought out potent desire in me, adding to the mix of my emotional struggle.

I wanted her, but feared that it could spiral out of control. What if we ended up hating each other? That would put a wedge in my Three Point Park project and make Audri and her friends hate me. I didn't need to work directly with Natalie on the project, but I wanted to use that opportunity to be closer to her—to understand this attraction between us.

The attraction was undeniable. We were both dodging it in our own way, ducking behind the façade of our disagreements, smirks, and teases. The connection we shared was like an invisible framework that held a building together. Unseen from the outside, but it was there, strong and supportive.

"I don't know what this is, Natalie." Honesty slipped out of me before I could stop it. "I just know that I like seeing your face and making you mad."

A laugh burst from her. "If that's your pickup line, you need help. No woman wants a man who makes her mad."

"Blue fire brightens up your eyes whenever I irritate you. It's fucking irresistible. It turns me on."

She blinked, and I knew I'd slipped something sacred into her mind. Maybe she'd dream about me tonight.

"Did you know I had the most erotic dream about you? Somehow you made me surrender to you—"

Holy fuck. I hadn't meant to share this dream with her.

Her eyes widened, but she didn't say anything.

"You make me do things I don't normally do, buttercup."

The smile that appeared on her lips would make a man give up ten years of his life just to see it every day.

My stomach growled, and I glanced at my takeout bag. I'd gone out for lunch and found something else more enticing. Despite that, human needs kicked in. "Want to share my sandwich?"

"No, thanks." She studied me.

I got up from my seat, and my thigh didn't like the separation from her touch. I could sense it sighing with disapproval. This was when I knew I'd lost all of my brain cells. I'd never had a thought as cheesy, sappy, and syrupy run across my mind like that. This woman resurrected me from the inside out, and I became a new man. I had to be extra careful around her.

"I need to get a drink. Do you want anything?"

"No, thanks." She looked at me with keen interest.

I stood beside her, tapping her nose gently with my finger. "Did I make you speechless with my dream admission? Do you want to hear more details? I'm not shy about sharing them with you since you're the star of the show."

My cock swelled just at the mention of that dream.

"No, thanks."

I grinned and tapped her forehead. "Are you okay? What happened to your vocabulary?"

"It got lost in a . . . dream." She smirked and closed the book, revealing the title, Sartre's *Existentialism*, which completely surprised me. "I'd like another croissant, please."

"That's more like it. When I get back, I want to know why you're reading Sartre."

CHAPTER ELEVEN

NATALIE

Today had to be one of the most interesting days of my life. Wanting to decompress from stress, responsibilities, and the sense that something awful was about to occur, I had dressed up to go out to make myself feel better. I needed to do something for me, so I didn't end up wallowing in depression. A clear head was the only certainty that could help me continue.

The incident with Adonis shook me a little. Knowing Rafael, he'd take my rejection as a slap in the face. For a pampered man protected behind the walls of wealth and power, he wouldn't stop pursuing me. But why?

Our engagement had ended a year ago. Why now?

If I'd been home, I wouldn't have been able to concentrate on work, anyway. So here I was inside an adorable bookstore where I didn't expect to run into familiar faces.

I'd been switching back and forth between checking up on the status of the upcoming collections for House of LaRue and my private line, when Grayson interrupted, startling me. Concern stirred in me knowing I didn't have a lot of time before the Board of Directors voted on the fate of the brand, so I had to work extra hard. But when I switched my attention to my private collection, there was a peacefulness that reminded me about what my heart desired: to create from a place of no stress and expectations.

Before I left Paris, I'd turned in the next three LaRue collections for my team at to handle. They could take care of the minute details like choosing buttons, ribbons, appliques and so forth. But I'd given them a wide selection and palette as my preference for them to work with. I'd been prepared for this long trip.

Turning, I watched Grayson standing at the counter talking to a brunette who offered him an inviting smile that reminded me of Maggie, the city's solicitor. For a man used to women surrounding him, would he be satisfied being with only one?

That caution played out in my head—as it would in any sane woman's head.

Sergeant Kennedy strode by and lifted her coffee cup to me. "Enjoying your weekend?"

Why was I meeting everyone in this tiny bookstore? "I am, thanks. You?"

She nodded and saw the book on the table. "You're a fan of Sartre?"

"I admire his genius, but it takes a lot of focus to read his work."

"Sure does. I studied philosophy back in the day. Anyway, enjoy your day." She left the bookstore.

She didn't seem uptight like she did at work. But work was a place that demanded people be a certain way. For instance, I played a role to ensure no one knew my real identity. So far, my mission in Providence hadn't yielded any helpful information.

I returned my attention to Grayson, who was still at the counter. Electricity had zinged through me from the moment he sat down. My body was still warm from all the wild images that had popped into my head when he mentioned his dream. The attraction between us throbbed in my body, especially when he pushed his thigh next to mine. Being with someone like him was entering a dangerous territory that would lead me to heartache, and yet, I couldn't stop myself from wondering about the "what-ifs."

What if being with Grayson was the anomaly I'd been waiting for?

What if he crushed my heart to where it could no longer be salvageable?

What if I lost myself if I gave in to this need?

I couldn't let my desire distract my goal.

Focus on why you're here. Forget about the pleasure. Forget about how he looks at you and thinks he knows what's under your clothes.

Grayson returned to the table with a chocolate shake and a croissant for me.

"Thank you," I said. "I'll pay you back."

"Just answer my question, and we're cool. Why Jean-Paul Sartre?" He gestured to the book on the table and began eating his sandwich.

Something had changed while we sat in this bookstore. Our conversation had shifted to a friendly discussion about philosophy. That was something I'd never expected. Rafael used to roll his eyes every time he saw me reading one of my self-help or philosophical books.

"Because he appeared at a vulnerable moment in my life and saved me."

"How?" His eyes sparked with interest.

I shiver as I scoot away from the awful screeching. My hand touches the cold metal surface and sharp edges of what feels like a lantern. I find a switch and flick it on. Soft light glows just enough for me to see old books in random piles around me. One book sits beside me, Being and Nothingness. It has dust and a fat stain on the cover. I need something to keep the fear away, so I flip the book open and read.

I tapped at my croissant. "This is a being in itself. It can't make decisions. It is what it is." I placed a hand over my heart. "*This* is a being *for* itself. It has choices. The will to survive." I met his eyes, and his genuine curiosity opened my heart. I couldn't stop the tears from flowing down my face. My voice broke. "That first time I stumbled on the book, I only read a paragraph, but I connected with it. It showed me I had a choice to fight back."

Concerned, Grayson offered me a napkin for my tears. "Sartre has a way with revelation."

"I'm sure Sartre meant something much deeper, but for a frightened eight-year-old girl, I molded the meaning to suit my circumstance. After that, I was drawn to philosophy because it helped me make sense of things that usually didn't, you know." I dabbed away the tears. "This is so embarrassing. I don't even know why I'm crying."

He cupped my face with both hands, catching more tears with his thumbs. "It's the damn croissant, isn't it? Too much onion?"

I laughed, appreciating his attempt to lighten up the mood. "Yeah. Definitely an overdose of onion and other spices." I glared at the plain croissant that had somehow become my savior.

"I'll demand a refund and get you a dozen plain ones. No more crying, okay?" He tapped my chin, holding my face a little longer, before releasing it.

At that moment, my heart moved a little closer to him, wondering who this man was. He had a caring side I hadn't seen before.

His cultured voice, the sound of his laugh, the glint in his eyes, even that damn dimple—everything about him had shades and textures. They caressed my body like the serrated edge of a knife, teasing my senses enough to make me crave danger.

Something was seriously wrong with me for being turned on by that.

I knew I had to stay away from a man like him. So why was I closer to him now than before?

Questions swam in his eyes. "I want to know what happened to you."

I'd never shared that experience with anyone, not even my parents.

"Maybe someday, but not today. I'm not ready."

I shifted in my seat, tugging at the hem of my dress as though I could tug my thoughts into place. I felt lost, but also very found. That made no sense at all. Having this serious conversation with Grayson wasn't supposed to happen. We were supposed to be discussing the Three Point Park project or disputing something, but somehow, the conversation took an unexpected turn and made me cry in front of him.

Something about him made me feel safe and taken care of. I could be myself and not pretend. Pretense took so much energy. I felt like I didn't have to hide anything from him, which was silly because we didn't know each other that well.

He nodded. "I'm ready whenever you are."

"Thanks."

"Want to go see the model display for Three Point Park? It'll give you an overview of the entire project. Maybe you can give me some insight on a few pending issues."

CHAPTER TWELVE

GRAYSON

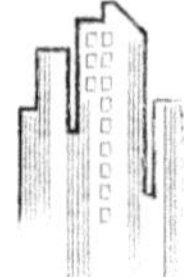

Natalie twisted her lips, thinking. "I can check it during the week."

"Don't tell me you fear me."

"Why should I fear you?"

She pulled her thigh away from mine, letting me know she knew my intention all along. "I'm not afraid of you, McDimple. But you should be frightened of me."

"How so?"

"Because I just made you miss your multimillion-dollar meeting."

I grinned at her accuracy. She was right that I should be cautious of her. What she didn't know was that I'd canceled the meeting when I went to order my drink and her croissant. I'd already decided her company was all I needed today. Nothing and no one could stop that. Not even a multimillion-dollar construction deal that had been postponed too many times. I was surprised the guy hadn't gone with another architectural firm.

Money could buy many things, but not this joy she

offered me. I felt like I was sitting in an oasis of Natalie where everything was bright and cheerful. I liked knowing she believed I feared her.

"Then it would be nice of you to help me recover that loss."

Twenty minutes later, I led her past the security guard at the entrance and up to my office to a display area with miniature architectural models of my current projects. The largest display was the Three Point Park landmark, the project I monitored while my design team focused on smaller projects.

Natalie sucked in a breath. "Wow. This is spectacular." She dropped her purse on my leather couch, walked over to the display, and examined the models. "Did you make the buildings all by hand? Look at these little people, trees, and benches."

Standing behind her, I took in the sight of her ass. I was a man, after all, and when beauty stared me in the face, I'd be a fool not to appreciate it.

I walked to the other side, where I could see her face. "I used to. But these days, I use a 3D printer. They save time and achieve so much more."

"There are fashion designers who use 3D printers for wearable art. Technology is changing everything. Like anything, new inventions can be used to good or evil ends." She walked around the display and stood beside me.

"Yes, it's all about the person and not so much the technology itself." I looked at her. "You understand the design concept. You see things through a creative lens. Why are you working as an administrative assistant?"

"We all do what we gotta do."

"If you ever want a design job, let me know. I have several openings at my company."

"I'm good, but thanks." Amusement gleamed in her eyes, and I wanted to dive into them and know all her secrets.

I should ask her how she could afford my luxury apartment, but I didn't want to scare her. She had built a barricade that prevented the world from seeing the real her. I had my barrier, so I respected her privacy. But dammit, I desperately wanted to know what was beyond that wall. In due time, she'd open her door and welcome me in. That was my mission.

Still studying the miniature landmark, she veered back and angled her head. "I see why it's called Three Point Park. The three locations create a triangle. It's more obvious from a bird's eye view. Why a triangle?"

"Because it's the strongest shape. When a force is applied to the triangle, the tension is evenly spread to all sides. But I like it because of the way it looks."

"What's going in the center? There's too much empty space." Her hand gestured to the area.

I rocked back on my heels, loving this creative discussion with her. "What do you think it needs?"

She crossed her arms, and the wide neck of her dress slid further down her shoulder, revealing more smooth skin. My mouth watered as I imagined my lips skimming over the elegant lines of her shoulder and down her arm. She had two tiny freckles on her shoulder that seemed to be calling me.

Her voice yanked me back to reality. "Something that matters to you. The essence of the project. Everything is connected to the center—the heart—that gives life to everything around it."

My heart flipped from that statement. No one had ever

articulated my vision so clearly until her. She saw me in ways no one could. Her clarity and comprehension just made the project more important to me. Before this moment, it had just been an idea still forming in my head. But she solidified it as though she'd snuck into my head—my heart, my soul—and arranged the scattered pieces into their proper place. She was reconstructing me in unimaginable ways.

What if she could adjust other parts of me without my knowledge? That frightened the hell out of me. I didn't want anyone to have that kind of power over me.

Her phone buzzed, and she glanced at it. Fear splashed on her face, and all other thoughts in my head vanished.

"What's wrong?"

She inhaled a breath, and her hand shook, but she didn't reply.

I took the phone from her, glanced at the screen, and fumed at the threatening text message that came from an anonymous caller.

Come back to Paris or you'll regret it.

I knew who it was. He'd pay for the terror on her face and the dismissal of my threat.

"Has Adonis reached out to you prior to today?"

She shook her head. "No."

The muscles in my arms tensed. Perhaps a show of faith from me would prove how much he should heed my warning. I didn't give out threats often, but when I did, I meant every word.

"Adonis needs a reminder." I memorized the number to relay it to my PI.

Natalie grabbed her phone back. "It's okay. Don't make this thing into a big deal. It's not your responsibility to intervene."

I gripped her defiant chin and bore my eyes into her. "It is *my* business. You're working on *my* project. A threat to you is a threat to me. And this *thing* is a big deal, Natalie. Men like Adonis or Rafael don't take rejection well. They need to deal with someone who's not afraid of them." I stalked over to my desk, retrieved my phone, and sent the PI the number.

Grayson: *Get me everything you know about this number.*

A few seconds passed.

PI: *Will do.*

I looked at Natalie, who glared at me with her hands on her hips. She should be pissed at her ex, not at me.

"If you get another message from any unrecognizable number. I want to know." I walked back to the miniature display. "Now, let's resume our discussion on what you think belongs at the center of Three Point Park."

I didn't want any fuckers ruining my time with her. I had skipped out on my multimillion-dollar meeting for *her*—did they think I'd let this threat slide?

In the business arena, one didn't succeed by being nice. I didn't give a fuck how much money Rafael's family had. I could influence Caputo Holdings and ensure they lost a huge chunk of wealth. A hole in their wallet would inject enough panic.

I preferred to stay in my lane because my enterprise took enough energy and dedication from me. But when assholes believed they could trespass into my territory and mess with me, they deserved all the panic and fear I could deliver. I didn't give a damn who Natalie had dated, or who she'd been engaged to. Right now, she was mine. Period.

Perhaps I'd been repressing my pent-up anger, and this incident provoked my release. My moral compass was flexible, and these assholes just ensured I trained my direction on them.

"I don't want you meddling in my business." She huffed out an annoyed breath.

"I'm helping you."

"If I ignore him, he'll just go away." She folded her arms, her lips thin with tension.

Not him. *Them.* But I didn't correct her.

"People like Adonis and Rafael don't just go away, Natalie."

Indignation surrounded her and me. Her storm had become my storm.

How could she believe people like them followed society's rules? They wouldn't leave her alone.

Was there something else she didn't want me to know? Did she owe Rafael something? Was that why he wanted her back? Whatever it was, I wanted to know.

I crossed my arms, matching her stance. "For someone smart, you're missing the mark."

She jabbed a finger at my chest, digging in for emphasis. "Oh, I missed the mark by coming here. I'm leaving." She whirled away from me.

Her face was inches from me as I wrapped an arm around her waist. "I never miss the mark." I crushed my mouth to hers, taking what I'd been craving.

The anger between us was like fire attracting fire. I couldn't stop myself. My lips absorbed her mouth, wanting to devour the frustration from her. She moaned, and her lips softened, molding to mine. I slid a hand down to her ass and claimed it. I discovered her body's shape, loving all her curves. When my palm claimed a breast, she gasped, and her mouth opened wider for me. My tongue dove in and met hers, and a new fire exploded between us.

The kiss was fueled by passion, irritation, and a pounding need that intensified to a level I'd never experienced.

Natalie was fucking perfect, meeting my tongue with every stroke. My cock throbbed uncomfortably in my jeans as I took in her decadent flavor, her scent. She tasted sweet and wholesome, like an intoxicating drug I didn't know I needed until this moment. She smelled like secrets, sex, and sin, wrapped in a cloak of honey that made me want to lick it all away from her. Cupping the back of her neck, I slanted my mouth for a deeper kiss.

Desire slammed into desire, sparking this inexplicable need that turned us into two desperate people wanting release.

She sucked my tongue, gripping my hair with her fingers. I loved the way her nails scraped my scalp while her body pressed into mine. She tasted better than the dream. I broke away from the kiss to nibble on the junction of her neck and shoulder. I dropped kisses along her elegant shoulder and down her smooth arm—the exposed area that had aroused me earlier.

She moaned, and it was like a command calling me. I answered by returning to her mouth, offering another wild kiss.

My hunger for her overwhelmed me, and my hand adored her breasts, kneading and making them mine. I sensed the change in her body as she broke for breath, then pushed me away. Her chest heaved as she stared at me with lust darkening her blue eyes. The sweep of her tongue over her lips almost made me burst in my jeans.

"Stay away from me and my business," she said with a tremulous voice.

She didn't realize that I took orders from no one. However, my body had a way of disobeying me for her, but I wasn't going to disclose that.

"I just made you my business, buttercup. The next time we kiss, it'll be in my bed. I can show you other dimples in my body. We can have a discovery session. I'll check out yours and you can check out mine."

Amusement splashed on her flushed face. "That's not going to happen. It already went too far today."

"It *will* happen."

"It won't."

"Wanna bet?"

She considered me for a long moment, and I could see the pros and cons weighing on her scale. "That depends on what we're wagering."

This conversation—this dispute—had just turned into something more interesting. There was no negotiation about me having her. It was only a matter of when. I just had to make sure I didn't let her get too close. It would be sex and nothing more.

I stepped closer and pressed the pad of my finger to her swollen lips—swollen because of me. "If you kiss me first, you lose. If I kiss you first, I lose."

I'd do anything to have her kiss me.

"You know this is ridiculous, right?"

"It's been a ridiculous day. Nothing else will surprise me."

A challenge gleamed in her eyes. "Fine. If I win, I want to choose a replacement for The Prism. I've got ideas."

Now *that* surprised me. "Why?"

"Why not?"

I doubted she'd tell me the reason, but I intended to find out. Had I made a mistake in assuming she wanted to wager something else? Did I already lose a game that hadn't even started?

"Don't dream about me tonight, McDimple." She flicked a gaze down at my bulge, trying to burst free from the fly.

With her curious fingers, she traced it, outlining the shape slowly and seductively like a vixen who knew exactly what she was doing. She was trying to kill me. My cock pulsed, begging for more.

"I can imagine the dimples you have on your body." She smirked, already trying to make me lose. Straightening her dress, she strode out of my office, leaving me alone with her scent, the memory of her kiss, and the pounding need to release the pressure within me.

That night, I received a reply from my PI confirming Adonis had sent Natalie the threat.

Grayson: *I also need info on Rafael Caputo.*

PI: *From Caputo Holdings?*

Grayson: *That one.*

PI: *Want me to prioritize him or Derek?*

The PI had been working a few projects for me, mostly Derek and his associates.

Grayson: *Rafael, then resume on the others.*

Though I'd lost confidence in people, I forced myself to trust the PI that Remi and Royce had vouched for. So far, he'd been effective with any requests I'd tossed his way. He'd delivered everything efficiently, and I appreciated that.

There were certain things he could do effectively that I couldn't. Despite that, I was aware of how much faith I'd placed in him. He hadn't failed me yet.

After my conversation with the PI ended, I called my bodyguard, Andrew. "I need you to do something for me."

"Whatever you need, boss."

Andrew had worked for me for several years. He was head of security at one of my buildings, but he was dependable and flexible when I needed him to carry out a job discreetly.

Society was a treacherous place. In order to survive this perilous terrain, I had to be several steps ahead of my enemy.

I made my move. Now, I just had to wait and see how things would develop.

CHAPTER THIRTEEN

NATALIE

"Is everything okay at home, Mom?" I asked as I slipped on my silk nightgown.

"Yes, why?"

"Oh, just checking in, making sure all is well. I've been away for months, so I miss the fast-paced environment." I slid into bed and placed my phone on the nightstand with the speaker on. "The marketing campaign for our next collection is intimate and effective. I love it."

"The new model is perfect for LaRue. You prepared everything for us before you left, so there's no need for you to keep checking in. How are you doing? I'm worried about you."

"I'm fine. No need to worry, Mom. You just concentrate on making sure Aunt Estelle doesn't decide anything without you knowing. Have you been talking to any of the board members?"

"My darling daughter. I love you, but I don't want you stressing out more than you already are."

"I'm not stressed."

I could hear the stress in my voice.

Her laughter brought a smile to my lips. "You're not a good liar. I can sense your anxiety all the way over here."

"If there was no deadline for the company vote, I wouldn't be as anxious. The pressure is on, and I can't ignore that House of LaRue could belong to someone else other than our family. I can't let that happen."

Mom sucked in a breath, and tears were probably streaming down her face right now, mimicking mine.

"It won't. Your mom is a smart woman. I've got things under control. You worry about your situation over there. Leave everything here to me. Have you found out anything about that property?"

Mom didn't ask about my status regarding Dad's rumored affair. I'd hired a private investigator to help me, but he hadn't come up with anything useful.

If I discovered information on the previous owner of The Prism, maybe I could find a connection that would lead me to the elusive woman my dad had been rumored to be with. But intuition told me there was no woman. Dad wasn't like that. But maybe I'd been looking at him through rose-tinted glasses because he was my dad. We often didn't see flaws in people we loved. Love made everything pretty, even the ugly things.

I couldn't tell my mom about my intuition. A woman in pain needed solid proof. Dad was her husband, and he'd kept this property from me and her, so it was natural for Mom to suspect dishonesty from him. I would react the same way.

After the threatening text message, I had to make sure Rafael didn't disturb my family.

"No, not yet. Someone's been hiding info on it." I didn't want to share that a billionaire was interested in the property. She'd ask questions, and my reply would probably reveal something I didn't want to acknowledge yet.

"Okay." Mom sighed. "I hope you're taking some time off for yourself. Meet any friends? Are there any cute guys over there? Have you been on a date yet?"

"Mom, I don't have time to date." I pulled the blanket over me as though trying to hide a secret from her. "I've met some wonderful friends here. There are these amazing girls who love fashion, food, and silliness like me. And they're not like the girls in my regular circle. There's no competition with them. I can just be me. No makeup, no expectations. We talk about stupid things." I laughed, remembering all my chats with them. "They care about me as a person and not what I can offer them."

"I'm so happy to hear that, sweetie. Maybe this trip will help you find a genuine group of friends. You grew up wealthy, and sometimes that prevents genuine friendships. It's hard to know who your real friends are and who's just trying to make connections." Mom released a sigh. "If you can't find any information in Providence, come back home. We'll figure things out. I don't want my daughter wasting her life away."

I wasn't going back until I found something, but my mom didn't need to know about my determination. It would only stress her out even more. Between her and me, we had enough pressure to turn us into diamonds.

Yawning, I said. "Don't worry. I've got it handled. Keep me posted on the current affairs over there, okay?"

"Okay. You sound tired. Go to bed. We'll catch up soon. Love you."

"Love you too, Mom."

I leaned back into my pillows and blew out a breath.

Relief washed over me to learn that Rafael hadn't reached out to my mom. Our engagement was to save House of LaRue from its financial debt. We'd been dating for over a year before he proposed. As time went on, I lost myself. He didn't love me. He loved being with a lot of women. The shame and embarrassment that he brought to me and my family were likely worse than the financial problem.

I never imagined I'd marry anyone for money. Rafael had appeared at a time of crisis, and I'd been vulnerable and made a huge mistake.

What could he possibly want with me now?

My phone buzzed, and the message distracted me, taking me from a place of worry to something more delightful.

Grayson: *Don't dream about me.*

Natalie: *I was just dreaming about how you're going to lose to me.*

Grayson: *I don't lose.*

Natalie: *Neither do I.*

I had to win so I could persuade him to pick another building to replace The Prism. What excuse could I give him?

Grayson: *You don't like The Prism?*

Natalie: *Compared to the other architecture on your landmark, that building is too simple.*

Hopefully, that would satisfy his curiosity.

Grayson: *Interesting point. But simple things have deep meanings.*

So there was something special about the building he wasn't disclosing, but if I kept asking questions, he might figure out I had ulterior motives. I had to change the topic.

Natalie: *We never discussed what you want if I lose— which I won't. (Smile emoji)*

At that time, I didn't care because my primary concern was protecting The Prism. But now, I wanted to know.

Grayson: *I like a confident woman. You might be terrified if I told you.*

Natalie: *Rules need to be transparent or the bet is off.*

Grayson: *WHEN I win, I'll fuck you from all angles.*

My body jerked, and I gasped as arousal leaked out of me and soaked my panties. My mouth hung open at the audacity of his admission.

I didn't reply. What could I say?

Grayson: *See? You're scared.*

Hell, no. He wasn't going to make me appear like a frightened woman.

Natalie: *Not scared at all. I'm wondering what kind of 'angles' you have in mind. Because in your head is the only way that will ever happen.*

Grayson: *I'm experiencing ERECTANGLE while thinking of you right now.*

Heat flushed into my cheeks as a wide smile made its way onto my lips. How was I going to win this bet when my body betrayed me with every reply? He made me feel powerful, safe, and horny at the same time.

I could make him want me. I saw that earlier today when he devoured me in his office. The hunger that possessed him also possessed me. That fact made me push him away.

Grayson had the power to make me want him so badly, I almost lost sight of my goal. I couldn't think when he'd kissed me with that much fervor. My body had responded to him on command. It made me feel powerful to have a man desire me that much.

Right now, he was seducing me with text messages. I

could practically see him touching himself while thinking of me.

Our relationship had already shifted beyond business matters.

Natalie: *I'm terrified of this chat.*

Grayson: *Why?*

Natalie: *Because it's making me hot and bothered. I need my sleep for an early meeting tomorrow.*

Grayson: *Go to bed.*

Natalie: *Okay.*

Grayson: *Buttercup?*

Natalie: *Yes.*

Grayson: *I know you're lying.*

Natalie: *About what?*

Grayson: *You're not afraid of this chat but of how I make you feel.*

Natalie: *You're not in my head. You don't know.*

Grayson. *The reason doesn't matter because I'll be the last person you think about tonight before bed. I WIN. Goodnight. (Smile emoji)*

I didn't reply. Because if I did, this conversation would go on all night.

Before bed, his face was the last thing I remembered.

CHAPTER FOURTEEN

NATALIE

Sitting inside my car after work, I breathed slowly, trying to calm my nerves as I patted my roomy purse for my tools. I felt the outline of a hammer, a wrench, and pliers—all the things I needed to commit a crime I never imagined I'd ever do.

I couldn't sit around waiting for clues about The Prism to show up. I had to do something. Nerves wreaked havoc in my stomach, but I willed them away.

I'd never done anything illegal in my life. Breaking and entering had never occurred to me until desperation forced me to make a move. Knowing me, I'd probably do it wrong, but I had to try. What was so special about The Prism that had my dad keeping it a secret from me and Mom?

There had to be something in the building to help me. There *had* to be.

Dad, please guide me.

There was nothing wrong with the owner examining her property, right? The problem was if I got caught, I'd have to prove to the authorities I was Natalie LaRue—the legal owner of The Prism. That would create more trouble than necessary. My job would know I'd lied about my identity, and that crime would probably be worse than breaking and entering.

The tabloids would have a field day with me. *Natalie LaRue—designer for House of LaRue—has started a new trend: lying and burglarizing in the States.*

I quickly shoved the thought away because it wasn't helping my anxiety.

Driving toward the business district of Providence, I parked a block away from The Prism, and walked around, browsing the area. The warm summer weather brought more people out in the streets. Around seven in the evening, I walked toward my property. My heart pounded in my ears. Sweat made my hands clammy, and I wiped them on my gray capris as I neared The Prism. It had been vacant for a while, so there weren't any cars around the building.

The sun was still out, and the sunlight illuminated the building, making it brighter and more beautiful. My nerves were concocting wild scenarios in my head, making me see strange things. When the pedestrians passed me earlier, my mind whispered they were undercover cops and that I should be extra careful. I wasn't good at breaking the law.

You can do it. Your family needs you.

Shaking off the self-doubts, I glanced around, making sure there was no one close by before walking toward the back parking lot. I spotted the back entrance, but there were cameras at the top. I couldn't tell if they were working, but I didn't want to risk getting caught.

Taking another path, I stayed close to the wall, moving farther back until I came to a side door with a shiny doorknob that looked new. Relief settled when I didn't see any cameras around. Praying that God was on my side, I yanked on the door, but it didn't budge.

Shit.

I reached into my purse, pulled out the hammer, and realized it was no match for the metal door. What was I thinking? When things didn't work out for one of my fashion designs, I pivoted. Life was all about adjusting, wasn't it?

If God were watching me, he'd either laugh at my incompetence or admire my stubbornness. I wasn't going to give up. I'd find a way into my property no matter what. Spotting some wooden pallets nearby, I rushed over. If I stacked them high enough, I could climb onto the window ledge, break the window, and get inside.

Excellent idea.

I hadn't planned this act out as thoroughly as I should have. It was more of a spontaneous urge, and I went with it before fear stopped me. Desperation often made people do stupid things. I guess I fell into that category today. It was too late to back out now.

I dragged a wooden pallet over to the window, placing it on top of the one already there. It clunked loudly, and my heart pounded, praying no one heard it. The noise of the city probably drowned it out. As I went to get another pallet, I heard voices coming from inside the metal door. I dropped the pallet quietly, crouched, and listened.

Two men cursed at something as their footsteps approached the door.

CHAPTER FIFTEEN

GRAYSON

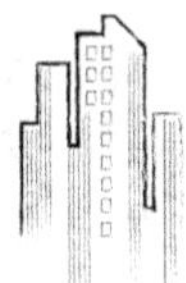

Forrest invited me for drinks at Prime One, a restaurant across the street from The Prism. Since I'd declined twice before, I went after work. I was avoiding the world, not him. It wasn't personal, but my approach hadn't been going well. The world seemed to work against me, with unforeseen obstacles popping up daily.

"How's Three Point Park coming along? What about the renovation of your warehouse?" Forrest drank his Tom Collins, placed the glass down, and studied me.

He had olive skin, a shade darker than mine, and shaggy brown hair I wasn't used to seeing on him. As an immunologist, he'd always kept it short and simple.

"What's up with your hair? Going for a new look?"

He raked a hand through his locks. "I'm helping a friend with a nonprofit project." He patted my back. "Stop trying to change the subject. Since when do you care how I wear my hair?"

"Since you started looking like a GQ model instead of a doctor. Even the clothes you're wearing are different."

Forrest furrowed his eyebrows, considered me for a while, and held up his hand. "How many fingers do you see?"

I rolled my eyes. "Dude, I'm not sick. I'm an architect. It's my job to notice details. And you've been acting strange."

"Me? If you ask anyone, they'd say *you're* the one on the edge, bro." He jerked his chin at my head. "I heard longer hair is the new trend."

I quirked an eyebrow. "You're into trends now? Aren't you spending most of your time wearing scrubs at the hospital, Dr. Navarro?"

"You know I'm only a part-time immunologist. I've been busy, and so have you. I let my hair grow, and you turned into a moody hermit." He shrugged. "That's our lives right now."

"You're going through shit too?"

"Not like yours." He tapped my shoulder. "Mine is manageable. Yours is . . . psychological."

"You're calling me crazy?"

"No." He smirked. "Just on edge. Anyway, what's going on with your projects?"

"There are water and sewer issues at the warehouse, so a city inspector needs to review and approve the new pipe installation before the final renovation can take place. There's not much about the park. I'm waiting for the blueprint approval from the city." I finished my Martini and considered getting another one. "You didn't ask me to come here to inquire about building renovations, did you? Did Audri put you up to this?"

My sister could overbear like a second mom. She wouldn't have asked Remi to check up on me because it would've been too obvious.

Every time Audri or Mom asked how I was doing, I'd tell them all was well, but they didn't believe me. I wasn't lying. Everything was *fine* because nothing was happening. I wasn't moving forward or backward. I was stuck at point zero.

They didn't need to know that, though. No one did.

"I just want to catch up with my boy," Forrest said, not denying or admitting that Audri had gotten to him. "I'm worried about you. You stopped hanging out with us. We all miss the old Grayson."

Christ. I didn't know my friends acted like a bunch of sappy busybodies.

"It's called growing up, man," I said. "I just need time to figure things out. Haven't you experienced a dilemma where you don't know what to do about it?"

"Yup." He looked at me and didn't elaborate.

I didn't inquire about his dilemma because I didn't want to share mine. A mutual understanding passed between us.

"If Audri or my mom ask you about me again, tell them my brain's working just fine. I haven't changed. The only thing I need is time. Suggest that they leave me alone. The more people crowd me, the more I'm going to shut them out. Know what I mean?"

He blew out a breath and nodded. "Family is wonderful, but they can be overbearing sometimes."

"It's because they care."

Sometimes, I wished they didn't care so much. I had to be extra careful not to hurt them again. My mom and sister had gone through hell from the death of my father and my uncle's betrayal. So any new information I got from Derek might churn up painful memories again.

Derek had answers I needed, but deciding when to visit

him had been a struggle. Seeing his text messages stopped me from going. Why should I let my dad's murderer tell me what to do? He had no effect on me. I didn't answer to him.

The rebel in me—even if it didn't make any sense—refused to go. If and when I visited Derek, it would be on my terms.

My indecision swayed like a pendulum, just waiting for me to make it stop. What was I waiting for? I had no clue. The universe was probably toying with me.

Let's see how much we can fuck with Grayson's mind.

Forrest nodded. "If you need to chat, you know where to find me."

A hot brunette and a redhead entered the restaurant. They sat down on the bar stools at the opposite end of the restaurant and smiled at us.

Forrest leaned into me. "Maybe a woman is the remedy you need."

Any woman wouldn't do. It had to be a very specific woman—one who had given me the most extraordinary dream, aroused me to no end with her kiss, and gotten me all horny just with a text message. A woman who had a bet going with me.

Tapping my fingers on the marble counter, I studied the brunette, who offered me an inviting look. In the past, I'd have gone over, started a conversation, and if she suited me, I'd have taken her home for the night. Back then, it never occurred to me I didn't have any standards in women. A nice body, a pretty face—that was all. What else did I need for a good time? I was certain my dates possessed more than those external traits, but I never cared to confirm. Why should I go through the trouble of having standards when it was just temporary?

The only thing I used to work hard at was expanding my architectural firm. Relationships were just accessories to me —like the tree or lamppost accent used for my architectural models. I didn't need those decorative pieces to survive. If one accessory didn't work, I'd pick another.

This brunette had a pretty face, a fabulous body, and a rack that would entertain a man all night. So why wasn't I interested?

Because I want Natalie. But I couldn't kiss her first. Defeat wasn't an option for me.

What used to turn me on no longer could. Was I going backward or transforming into something better?

"Are you referring to *your* needs?" I asked. "Weren't you dating the hot cardiologist?"

"That was a while ago, dude. Like you, I've got stuff going on. No time for women."

I didn't see Forrest with many women, but that was true with all my friends. We were busy men with visions and empires to manage. We also worked on our video games, which didn't leave much time for relationships. But love had changed Remi and Royce. Those guys had found a perfect balance between work and having someone who loved them. I was happy for them, but I couldn't love a woman like that.

I didn't know how to love. It seemed like a lot of work and dedication. Hell, I had to fix myself first before I could understand love. My heart was a mess. My soul was scattered here and there, and my ability to know what I wanted had vanished.

So how could an empty heart offer something it didn't have?

"Ladies, drinks on me." Forrest lifted his finger, getting the attention of the bartender. "Can you take care of these lovely women? Put it on my tab." He nodded at the women. "Enjoy."

Forrest could be such a flirt. The way these women looked at him showed they took "drinks on me" literally. Maybe he'd go home with them tonight. Good for him.

"Thank you," said the redhead. The brunette whispered something in her ear, and they both giggled.

My gaze slid past the giddy women to a figure outside the window, struggling to fight off two men. Was that Natalie? I couldn't be sure, but my gut told me it was her. Somehow, I'd gotten to know the shape of her body from the dream and the kiss we'd shared.

The powerful need to protect her surged again. I didn't understand it and had no time to analyze it.

Forrest said something to me, but I didn't hear him. I shot up from the bar stool and rushed out of the restaurant. My fingers curled into fists as I reached for the guy who clamped his hand on her shoulder. With one hand, I gripped his arm, whirled him around, and threw three punches into his face, breaking his nose.

My intervention caught him by surprise, and the power of my fist knocked him to the ground. Fury blinded me, and I saw nothing but a frightened Natalie. I was a pressure cooker unleashing this repressed rage that exploded from some-where deep inside me.

Anger coursed through my body, pulsing in my veins. Adrenaline roared through me, and I knew what it felt to want to kill someone.

"What the fuck?" screamed Broken Nose as he jumped back to a standing position, almost tripping over a purse on the ground.

Was that Natalie's purse? I didn't have time to retrieve it

because Broken Nose charged at me. A battle erupted in the street between me, Broken Nose, and the bald guy with a skull face tattooed on his cheek.

The stench of alcohol from these guys made me gag, but my desire to destroy them numbed everything else.

Forrest joined the battle and fought Skull Face. A crowd formed nearby, watching and cheering like idiots.

It didn't take long for me to pummel Broken Nose. I hadn't spent all those years learning martial arts for nothing. It had taught me discipline and human anatomy, teaching me where to attack my opponent to ensure my victory. My aggression poured out onto him. Too fucking bad.

"That's enough, Grayson." Natalie's calm voice penetrated my brain.

I looked up at her as she touched my arm gently. "Are you okay?"

Terror still consumed her face. "Yes, thank you."

I glanced over at Forrest standing above Skull Face, who was curled up on the sidewalk, groaning in pain.

Sirens blared in the distance. The cops and ambulance arrived in no time. I spoke to the police officer about the incident, and they checked the surveillance outside the restaurant to confirm my statement. An EMT asked if Natalie wanted to go to the hospital for a thorough checkup, but she declined.

"You should go." I picked up her purse, surprised by how heavy it was. What did women carry in their purses?

"I'm fine. It's just a scrape on my arm." She held out her hand. "I can take my purse."

"I got it. It's heavy for an injured arm." Glaring at the red mark, I wanted to punch the guy again for putting a flaw on her perfect skin.

With confusion, she stared at how I held her purse by wrapping the straps around my fist like a bandage and making her purse appear like a weapon.

"Let me look." Forrest examined her injury and smiled. "You're right, just a minor scrape. It'll heal in a couple of days."

"Thanks for coming to my rescue." She looked at Forrest and me. "Those jerks came out of nowhere."

I had several questions for her. From first brush, it seemed almost like she had run from the direction of The Prism. What was she doing there? Was she there to retrieve info for me? I wanted to know who the owner was, but I didn't need her to go about it like that. It was after work hours for her.

How did she meet those drunken guys? At a bar? The idea of her sitting alone at a bar and men ogling her like Forrest had with those women irritated me.

"What were you doing at The Prism?" I asked.

"What makes you think I was there? Maybe I wanted a drink and bumped into the idiots."

My jaw tightened. "If you're going bar hopping, you need to be aware of drunk assholes. Someone like you is perfect prey for them. You shouldn't be out by yourself."

"I don't need a babysitter, Grayson." She scowled. "You're not my father or my boyfriend. I don't need your permission to do anything."

Forrest cleared his throat. "Those idiots will feel a lot of pain when they sober up." His phone rang, and he fished it out of his back pocket. Glancing at it, he sighed and turned to me. "Gotta go. You okay here?"

"Yeah, I'll take her home."

Forrest picked up the call as he walked to the parking lot where our cars were parked.

Natalie walked off to where I assumed her car was parked. A few steps forward, and she limped.

Stubborn woman.

"Minor injury, my ass." I gripped her arm, assisting her. "Let me help you."

Whipping me an annoyed look, she tried to yank her arm away, but I didn't budge. We stood on the sidewalk, staring at each other. Sexual tension throbbed in my cock, which was inappropriate timing on my part. When it came to her, my cock did whatever it wanted. This "thing" between us needed to be dealt with soon because it was driving me crazy.

I wanted to kiss her, so she'd stop talking back to me and let me take care of her. But that would mean I'd lose the bet. I didn't want to give up The Prism yet.

"I can walk to my car, Grayson," she said. "Thanks for helping earlier. I'm good now. Don't you have somewhere to go?"

"The only place I need to be is with you. You need to get home safely."

She huffed out a breath, appearing calmer. "I'm fine. You can go home."

"I'm going where you're going."

"Why are you so stubborn?" She scowled.

"Not as stubborn as you. I'm concerned about you. I'm not your father, and I'm not your boyfriend, but I'm a man who wants you. So that gives me the right to make sure you're safe."

Something flashed in her eyes before she blinked it away.

"That line isn't going to make me kiss you. You're not going to win the bet."

"This won't either, but it'll take the pressure off your feet." I scooped her up into my arms, carrying her to the car. "I'll go home after I drop you off. You cool with that?"

"Put me down!" She tried to wriggle free. "I can walk."

"You mean *limp?*" I loved having her in my arms.

Her lips twisted. "You're being absurd. Put me down!"

"As you wish." Once we got to the car, I placed her on her feet. "You were wasting time being stubborn, so I took the initiative. I'll drive. Give me your keys." I wiggled my fingers.

"Does your bossiness ever annoy you?" She crossed her arms.

I mimicked her gesture with a smirk. "Does your stubbornness ever annoy you?"

The fire flickering in her eyes sparked a warmth, making me want her beneath me. What the fuck was wrong with me? She was injured and needed to get home.

"Look, the sooner I get you home, the sooner I'll be out of your way, okay? Though I want to win the bet, this isn't the time for any secret agenda. I just want you safe. You're Audri's friend, and she'd want me to help you. And if my sister were injured, I'd want someone to take her home too."

Her expression softened, and she reached for her purse.

"Let me." I used the opportunity to dig into what appeared like the cosmic depths of the universe. I pulled out a hammer that gleamed like new. "Why is this in your purse?"

"I was doing some handiwork and forgot to put it back," she said without blinking.

I knew it was a lie, but I'd play along because whatever

she was doing at The Prism was more than searching for the owner. Either that or my buttercup had a side job I didn't know about.

"Okay." I dropped the hammer back into her purse. "Can I hire you to adjust my kitchen cabinet doors?"

"You can't afford me," she said and told me her address.

Laughing, I drove her Mercedes SUV into the garage of my luxury apartment building. How could she afford the car and the apartment as a city employee? Administrative assistants didn't make enough to pay for this luxury.

Was she a trust fund kid? If so, why would she work there? She should hang with the other trust fund kids. When I spotted her in the bookstore, she'd dressed up like a socialite. But right now, in her casual work clothes, she blended in with the regular crowd.

"You really didn't have to take me home. I've driven with a sprained ankle before."

"Bad idea."

She shrugged. "Sometimes you have to do what's necessary."

"Well, as your landlord, I need to ensure you're well enough to work so you can pay the monthly lease."

She whipped a surprised look at me. "You *own* the building?"

"You have a problem with that?"

"No." Thoughts swirled in her eyes. "You have questions for me. I see them on your face."

"I do, but I won't ask them. I have faith you'll tell me when you're ready."

She twisted her lips. "You suspect me."

"Because you're acting suspicious."

"I'm not." She lied. "I think you're untrusting in general."

That comment lifted a bandage covering my wound, exposing something she didn't even know. "When you've experienced a gut-wrenching betrayal, it's hard to trust again."

She looked at me, swallowed, and nodded. Silence filled the car, and we both let it be because anything else would be too much for the moment.

When we parked in the garage, she asked, "What's going to happen to your car? How are you going to get back home?"

"Don't worry about me. I'll have my assistant retrieve the car and bring it back to my home. Someone will give me a ride back, but thank you for your concern."

Once inside her apartment, I said, "You should take a few days off to heal that ankle.

"I already plan to." She settled on the gray couch and examined her ankle, which wasn't swollen. "Do you want anything to drink? Help yourself to the refrigerator."

"Thanks. Would you like me to get you anything?"

"No, thanks."

"Okay, then I'll give myself a tour of your apartment."

"I thought you owned this building. You should already know the layout." Impatience splashed across her face.

"I do, but I want to see how you've decorated it. Is there some handiwork I need to check on in here?" My lips curled into a smirk from the way her eyes held mine. "Is there something you don't want me to see?"

"I have nothing to hide."

I walked around, taking in the details and understanding her a bit more. Cream-colored walls with abstract printed drapes picked up the gray tones of her furniture. Very few personal items. No picture frames of family or friends. No paintings on the walls. The apartment appeared like a hotel room—a temporary stay. That thought made my chest ache.

I spotted some fashion magazines on the coffee table. "Looks like you're still moving in?"

"I don't have a lot of stuff." She fluffed up a throw pillow.

"Girls always have a lot of stuff."

Natalie lifted a shoulder. "I have to live a simple life to afford rent. Something's gotta give."

Understanding her train of thought, I flashed her a smile. She couldn't steer me away from what I already knew—Natalie Chapelle had something to hide. I appreciated her quick mind. Intelligence in a woman was like silky lingerie—sexy and dangerous as hell.

I dropped on the couch beside her, whispering into her ear, "I don't want you sacrificing your needs to pay rent. There are other ways to pay the landlord." I blew a warm breath down her neck and felt her shiver.

"I'd never sleep with a man to pay my bills."

"I didn't say that, buttercup. An intelligent conversation would suffice."

She shook her head in disbelief. "I'm sure there are other girls out there who would love to chat with you for free rent."

I gripped her chin, turning her face toward me. "No. That offer is only for you."

"I think you're trying to seduce me to kiss you."

"Is it working?"

"No," she said, biting her bottom lip.

I was the Leaning Tower of Pisa, tilting toward something I didn't fully understand—the most beautiful woman who read philosophy for fun, couldn't lie, and looked at things through a creative lens better than designers I knew.

Danger zone. Unstable ground. Every architect knew that instability meant a collapse eventually. If I weren't careful, I could lean too far, which would lead to my absolute destruction. I had to push her away.

The reality check had me brushing a finger down her cheek. "I'll let you rest. Don't stress about getting me information on The Prism."

I rose from the couch just as my phone buzzed and looked at the message from the PI.

"Thanks for escorting me home," she said.

I offered a nod. "Sweet dreams, Natalie."

While I waited for my car ride back, I browsed the information the PI had gotten me on Rafael. Did the Caputo family know that their heir was a sick son of a bitch? He could destroy their name if the world knew what he'd been doing.

CHAPTER SIXTEEN

NATALIE

A few days later, it was August 8th—Grayson's birthday. I arrived early at Audri's house to help with the surprise party, but there wasn't much to do except create a space for the presents. Unsure what to get Grayson for a gift, I purchased a tie in a persimmon color. He'd worn several colors during my encounters with him at work, but the shades of red suited him best.

Audri and Remi lived in a gorgeous home with all the amenities a billionaire and his girlfriend would have. The jewelry studio Grayson had added to their home was beautiful and spacious, with wide windows that would allow natural light to stream in. I couldn't believe Audri told her brother she wanted another addition, using that excuse to make him come to her house today.

Michelle had brought blue and pink balloons with matching streamers and a "happy birthday" sign that Royce hung in the foyer so everyone could see. Kiera brought a fruit salad, while I had picked up some French pastries on the way over even though Audri didn't ask me to.

"You guys didn't have to bring anything. I ordered catering." Audri shook her head at Kiera and me.

Kiera shrugged. "Have you seen those guys eat? They'll finish everything."

"No one ever complained about having too much food," Michelle said.

I looked around at the baby blue and pink color scheme and laughed. "He's going to think it's a gender reveal party."

"Good. He needs a little humor in his life." Audri pulled a metal tray from the refrigerator and set it on the marble countertop. Then she turned to stir the big pot of soup, releasing a delicious aroma that had my stomach growling.

"Wow, you made these wontons from scratch?" I asked, examining Audri's work of wonder on the tray. The yellow wontons looked perfect. "Do you cook often?"

"Didn't use to, but Remi loves wonton noodle soup, so I've been making that and a few other meals my mom taught me. She's fabulous in the kitchen."

"I suck at cooking." Kiera helped take out the soup bowls from the cabinet. "It's just easier to order out or stock up on frozen meals."

"Baking is more my thing." Michelle took out fancy chopsticks from the drawer and looked over at me. "Oh, do you know how to make macarons? Royce and I had the best pistachio macarons when we visited Paris."

"Sorry, cooking and baking aren't my forte." I moved the trays of food Audri had catered to the side table, making room on the counter. She only made the wonton noodle soup. The amount of food could feed over twenty people, and there were only eight of us.

The guys played a video game on the massive TV in the entertainment room.

"Where's Vivian?" I asked while squirting some hot sauce and hoisin sauce into a small condiment dish.

"She's at a seminar in California. Then she's flying over to Vietnam." Michelle chopped cilantro and scallions. "She promises to catch up as soon as she returns."

I hadn't been attending my self-defense classes as much as I should have. Vivian had been my motivator because I liked her teaching style. The other instructors were excellent too, but Vivian understood a beginner like me needed extra time and patience. She didn't make me feel rushed to catch up to everyone.

Though the classes were for both beginners and intermediate students, I didn't want to hold anyone back.

Audri's phone buzzed, and she smiled at the message. "He'll be here in ten minutes! Get ready!"

Ten minutes later, everyone gathered in the foyer. Audri opened the door, and Grayson stepped in.

"Happy birthday!" everyone shouted.

Kiera shot colorful streamers into his hair. Royce threw a fistful of confetti at him.

His eyes widened, then he saw the colored balloons. "What the—"

"No cursing on your special day!" Audri embraced her brother. "Smile!"

"Christ! I should have known." He picked the streamer out of his hair and glared at his sister. "There's no renovation, is there?"

"Not today." She grinned.

"Well, next time you ask, I'm not coming." He turned, saw me, and blinked. It was as though seeing me was more of a surprise than the party itself.

Grayson arched an eyebrow. "Are you part of Audri's evil plan too?"

"No. I'm wicked all by myself. Mom had a trip planned with her friends, so she couldn't make it."

"That explains the weird text message from her—'sending love to my firstborn.'"

Audri laughed. "She shipped your gift to your house."

"Happy birthday, old man." Remi slapped him on the shoulder.

"Yo, I don't have time for parties."

"You gotta eat, don't you? Come eat with us. You don't always get what you want." Royce fist-bumped him. "Besides, we need another player on this video game Arrow just got."

"Check out our competition." Arrow gestured to the couch. He had short brown hair and appeared like he spent time at the gym.

All the guys seemed disciplined with their career and their bodies, which told me they took care of themselves.

An hour later, the soup was ready to eat, but the girls wanted to enjoy a cocktail before the meal. While I sipped champagne, I watched Grayson. The smile on his face and the gleam in his eyes revealed a snapshot of what he used to be like. There was no tension, frustration, or secrets weighing on his face.

We both knew there were things neither of us wanted to disclose yet. That was the silent understanding between us. It was also the thing that kept us apart. What if we didn't like what we heard if the secret was revealed? It could be too much baggage, and who wanted that in their life? Life was complicated enough.

Perhaps in this moment, he shoved the clutter away to be

with his family and friends. Like him, I pushed all my concerns aside for now.

"I whooped your ass." Grayson rose from the couch and faced Royce, spreading his arms victoriously. "Bow to the king."

Royce snorted. "I don't want you anywhere near my ass. And neither does Michelle."

Remi and Arrow laughed from their seats.

"You're right. I hear Viking farts are deadly." Grayson grinned, forcing the irresistible dimple to appear on his cheek. The muscles in my thighs tightened as though the dimple sent a laser beam heating my skin.

The girls and I shook our heads while exchanging glances. Conversations between men were definitely different from women.

"I let you win because it's your birthday." Royce placed the controller on the coffee table. "You're welcome, you old fart."

"We're all the same age. Besides, thirty-three is the new twenty-three," Grayson said.

"Didn't know you watch Hollywood Gossip," Arrow blurted. "They make people feel better about themselves by making things up."

"If you must know, it's the History Channel discussing the change in human behavior, social interaction, and the evolution of the *brain*. Yours is obviously in need of an upgrade."

The dynamics between these men intrigued me. They were billionaires, men of status who exuded power and respect, yet right now, they portrayed a playful version of themselves that others didn't get to see.

Life required us to wear masks as we navigated its intricacies. Genuine friendship offered a safe space to be our true selves. I never had that before. My heart ached knowing that my experience here was only temporary.

Grayson walked over to the refrigerator, grabbed a bottle of water, opened it, and looked at me while he gulped it down. He wore dark jeans with a fitted gray button-up shirt where the sleeves were rolled up, cutting him a man of casual elegance with a subtle edge.

Even though we hadn't chatted since he arrived, I sensed the pulsing energy between us—a quiet storm brewing from within.

We hadn't interacted since he brought me home that day. I didn't dare return to The Prism after my horrendous failed attempt to get inside. I'd learn from the police that those men were drug addicts who had been camping inside the building for a few weeks. I placed my tools back into the toolbox, vowing never to take them out again.

We both needed some space. I had to reevaluate my plan to get info on the property and my dad. The private investigator I hired still hadn't delivered anything useful.

While Grayson stared at me, I felt the sparks he exuded. They flew around the room like the embers of a fire drifting wild and free, affecting everyone in their vicinity. Women couldn't resist this about him. This wild spark was unrestricted freedom, allowing the heart to do as it pleased. I wanted that liberation.

Though I had a charmed life as the heir to a well-known fashion house, that responsibility shackled me. There were certain things I couldn't do because it would affect the brand. Even my collections had to be a certain way to keep true to that brand—to keep it sellable. It was a business, and making money was of the utmost importance.

But in keeping true to the label—to my family—I wasn't being true to myself. So I could see the allure of what Grayson used to offer—unregulated independence and unlimited indulgence. He still had this spark in him. It was cloaked with layers too messy to dig through. I wanted to undress him to find out what lay beneath.

Did he miss that life?

What would it feel like to experience that kind of freedom, even for a second?

Though my character hadn't shifted as drastically as his, I'd become someone different here in Providence. If someone were watching me, would they notice the difference?

"Let's take a break and enjoy Audri's wonton soup." Remi got up and went over to embrace her in an enormous hug.

We all took our seats at a round table. Grayson sat next to me, his elbow brushing mine, sending an electric shock running up my body. Once again, his thigh pressed into mine, but this time it wasn't subtle. He wanted me to feel his presence.

"What's going on with Three Point Park? Do you know who The Prism owner is yet?" Arrow asked.

My knee jerked, and I expected Grayson to toss the question at me, but he said, "Still looking into it." His thigh didn't move from mine.

"It's been empty for a while," Royce said. "You want to demolish it to rebuild? Or just renovate the interior?"

"Not sure yet."

"What exactly are you envisioning for Three Point Park?" Kiera blew at her soup spoon. "The open space in front of those buildings could host a fabulous fashion show or smaller concert. I saw something similar in Milan a few years ago."

"That space has a lot of potential," Grayson replied. "A fashion show would be an outstanding event to bring people there."

When I'd asked Grayson why he wanted The Prism, he'd given me a cryptic answer. Maybe now that we knew each other better, he'd give me a proper answer. It could be the key to why my dad bought it for me.

"Why do you want The Prism?" I asked. "The building beside it is nicer."

Grayson sipped his glass of water and looked at me with amusement. "It's not what the building looks like *now*. It's the potential it possesses." He held my gaze for a beat before reaching for a bottle of hot sauce and squirting it into his soup bowl. "The location of The Prism catches the light at sunrise and sunset in a way that transforms it due to the glass panels on the surface."

"Oh," was all I could muster. I remembered seeing how the sun had illuminated it that day when I wanted to break in.

Did Dad know that about the property?

"Have you always known that? Does it have any other features that would make it valuable? I wonder if the previous owners knew this trick of the light." Too many questions popped into my head, escaping my mouth before I could hold them back.

The aspect fascinated me the way a couture piece of clothing spoke to me. The structure itself wasn't unique compared to the other buildings around it, but this light-reflecting characteristic made it stand out.

What did the interior of the building look it?

Grayson flicked me an inquisitive glance.

Tell everyone you have an interest in it, why don't you?

These people around the table considered me a friend, but I hadn't been completely honest with them. Guilt prodded at me.

"I didn't notice its uniqueness until a year ago," Grayson said.

"I've got to check it out one of these days," Kiera said, wiping her mouth with a cloth napkin. "Thanks for cooking, Audri. Your wonton noodle soup is the best." She got up to put her bowl away, washed her hands, and came back, standing between Grayson and me. "Who's up for a game of Charades to burn off some calories?"

Remi and Royce moved furniture around the entertainment room to create a cozy atmosphere for Charades. Audri transferred a vase of flowers to a side table. Sitting on the couch, Remi dragged her onto his lap. She yelped and pinched his cheek, and he kissed her. Michelle shared an armchair with Royce, running her fingers through his blond hair.

Grayson and Arrow entered the room.

"Are we really playing this game?" Grayson asked.

"Scared of losing?" Arrow arched an eyebrow at Remi and Royce, each with a woman on his lap. He dropped into a brown loveseat, looked at me, and tapped his thigh. "Wanna sit?" he teased.

Before I could reply, Grayson threw himself onto Arrow's lap.

"Man, what's wrong with you?" Arrow pushed him off.

Kiera shook her head, gesturing for me to sit with her on another loveseat. "Girls against boys!"

"What are we wagering?" Michelle asked.

"Winner gets to have Grayson cook for them for three straight days!" Royce cheered.

"Why should I be the one to cook? If we lose, each guy will cook, and vice versa." Grayson jerked a chin at Arrow. "You game?"

"You know I can't cook," Arrow complained. "Let me rephrase that. I *can* cook, but it won't look pretty."

"Dude, there's something called restaurants and gift cards."

"That works! I have to win this, girls!" Kiera clapped her hands, walking to the center of the room. "Let's change things up for this game. We'll make it our own." She handed everyone an index card. "Write something that you want the other team to guess. Be creative."

"Why are you making me think?" Arrow flicked the card against his palm.

I loved the dynamic between these friends. There was this unbreakable bond sealed from a long time ago. I could feel the appreciation they had for one another. As an outsider, I admired what they had. Yes, even though I sat there with them, a part of me still lingered on the outside because I hadn't been truthful.

"Stop watching those gossip TV shows and your brain will function properly." Grayson punched him in the arm playfully.

I couldn't help myself. "Well, sometimes gossip shows have information that the History Channel doesn't—like current affairs."

"Look at that. Natalie understands me. Seems like you

need to catch up, pal." Arrow smiled at me, then got up when his phone rang and walked into another room.

Grayson's facial expression changed with the tight lips, the crease between his eyebrows, and the irritation beaming from his eyes.

Was that jealousy on his face? Joy poured over me like champagne, dripping into every corner of my body. A man who exuded power like him just revealed a vulnerability that made him adorable. And I was the reason.

He narrowed his eyes at me. "What current affairs should I be aware of, *buttercup*? Enlighten me."

Michelle and Audri exchanged glances, but didn't say anything.

I couldn't think of anything except a quote I read the other day from John Milton. "The mind is its own place, and in itself, can make a heaven of hell or a hell of heaven."

Audri elbowed Remi. "Am I your heaven or hell, love?"

"That's a tricky question." He kissed the side of her head. "My answer is always heaven."

"What about you, Viking?" Michelle looked up at her lover.

"You're my heaven too." Royce wrapped an arm around Michelle.

I hadn't meant to put them on the spot with the quote. Grayson just stared at me, the look more intense by the second, and I felt heat pooling at my center even though there were so many people around me.

"These boys know the safe answer." Kiera grinned.

Grayson's phone buzzed and he glanced at it, surprise splashing on his face. "Sorry, I have to go."

"Where?" Remi asked.

"To the police station." Grayson headed out toward the door.

"Why?" Audri's face scrunched with worry.

"What happened?" I asked, following him.

Grayson looked at me. "Adonis is dead. The police want to speak to me. My lawyer is already at the station."

CHAPTER SEVENTEEN

GRAYSON

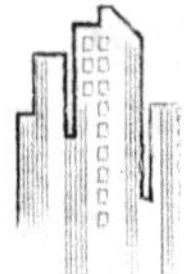

Inside the police precinct, I sat next to my lawyer, Gregory Price. With a head full of light brown hair and sharp green eyes, he looked like he was only thirty years old, even though he was well into his fifties. Gregory had worked with me for the last seven years, and he'd helped me resolve the fiasco Derek had brought into my family.

I didn't really have to go down to the station. The police could have dealt with Greg or come to my home for an interview, but I wanted to know about the case. Besides, I didn't want cops on my doorstep. They carried negative vibes I didn't need or want in my home.

What had happened to Adonis?

"What do you want to ask my client?" Gregory looked over at Detective David Evans, who wore a navy suit. He was bald and had a round belly.

Detective Evans nodded. "Just following procedure, Greg. Mr. Wu isn't in trouble."

"Damn right, I'm not," I said calmly. "Someone killed Adonis, and that person isn't me."

"You're wasting our time." Greg leaned into the table.

I tapped his shoulder. "It's okay, Greg. I'm a helpful citizen. And if my presence can help Detective Evans find the killer, I'll do my part."

Thoughts swirled in my head at who could have killed Adonis. He was an ass, so he probably had enemies everywhere. But I wanted to check the surveillance near Natalie's home to see if he'd been snooping around.

"Can you tell me where you were on this date and time?" The detective pointed to a sheet of paper.

The time of death placed me inside Prime One. "I can get you videos of me sitting at the bar in a restaurant at the time of his killing."

"That would be helpful." The detective wrote something on his notepad.

"Why did you ask me to come down to the station?" I leaned back in my chair. "Am I a suspect?"

"We received an anonymous tip saying you had an encounter with the deceased days before his death. Did you threaten him?"

"I did. He harassed my friend. I was defending a woman who was terrified of him. She works with Commissioner Conner. Her friends and the shop owner can also verify Adonis harassed her, dragging her out of the shop. I *stopped* him."

Detective Evans nodded. "If you can leave their names and number, I'll verify." He pushed the pad of paper over to me.

"I'll have Greg send you the info later. At the moment, I'm too irritated to jot down notes. How did the tip come to you?"

"I can't answer that."

I leaned forward with my elbows on the table, and my fingers tented together. "Detective Evans, I've donated a lot of money to several departments in the city, yours included. Why? Because I want to improve this City. I've got business here, and I intend to keep it flourishing. Do you think I'm stupid enough to ruin my career for some lowlife?"

"The city appreciates your donation," he said. "Consider this interview as a *discussion*, that's all. It had to be done so it can go on record."

He ruined my birthday party with my favorite people to drag me out for a meaningless discussion? I wanted information. That was the only reason I showed up.

"Someone is trying to sabotage my reputation, and I don't appreciate it. Did the tipster call it in? Email it?"

Probably sensing my irritation, he answered. "Via snail mail without a return address."

I understood everything had a process. A tip came into the office about a prominent entrepreneur. Duty called for the office to check out the clue. Still, it annoyed me. Were these cops looking at every detail? Did they look for fingerprints on the envelope?

Could Rafael have killed his bodyguard to frame me? For what? I didn't know Rafael. I had my bodyguard follow him for a few days after that event at the café. Andrew didn't see Adonis anywhere near Natalie's apartment or doing anything suspicious. But he could've been extra careful. Maybe I should have had Andrew survey for a longer duration.

Who had killed Adonis? I didn't care about his death. I was concerned about the person who was framing me.

Another obstacle in my way. I didn't need this fucking shit.

"I'm working on an important project to increase tourism in Providence. I'd appreciate you clearing my name from this case as soon as possible." I forced a smile at him. "You'll get the video and the contact details by the end of the day.

"There's nothing for you to worry about, Mr. Wu."

If only that were true. I wasn't worried about the police finding clues that tied me to Adonis's death. Who was after me? Why?

"All communications go through me." Greg rose from his seat. "My client doesn't need negative publicity. A stain to his name would be a stain to the City of Providence."

Detective Evans stood up as well. "I understand."

My head throbbed, and I needed a damn vacation. All the shit flying around me was too much. I needed to get away for a few days to clear my head.

When I arrived home, I dropped onto my couch and saw Natalie's text inquiring if I was all right. Seeing her message eased the tension in my body. My headache subsided as I replied to her message, telling her not to worry.

Something happened during the party today—my extreme jealously toward her and Arrow. It was pathetic, but I couldn't help it. I'd never been this jealous over a woman. I didn't like her being like that with anyone but me.

What claim did I have to her, anyway?

Something had to change, but I was too exhausted to think about it tonight.

CHAPTER EIGHTEEN

NATALIE

Kiera and Audri brought macarons, brownies, crackers, cheese, white wine, and tea to my place for a mini gathering. Kiera had to leave for her next photoshoot in Brazil in a couple of days. Michelle and Vivian were busy and couldn't join us. The combination of food looked delicious when spread out on my coffee table, but I wasn't sure how my stomach would react.

Kiera and Audri sat on the rug around the coffee table while I chose the couch.

"Is Grayson off the hook for what happened to that bodyguard?" Kiera bit into a macaron, looking at me and Audri.

"He said not to worry about it." Audri sipped her wine.

"When people say that, it makes me worry even more," I said. "I assume this happened or that happened, and before I know it, an entire scenario has formed in my head."

"The female mind is a magical wonder." Audri added Swiss cheese to her cracker. "Remi's getting better at sharing things with me instead of brushing it off as 'don't worry about it.' Men need training. It takes time and patience, but it can happen."

A man in love was inspired to change. Moving a man who wasn't in love would be next to impossible.

Could Grayson be trained? I didn't even know why that thought invaded my mind.

I switched my thoughts back to Adonis. His death had been a shock. I didn't want him dead, but I was glad he wouldn't be bothering me anymore. Would Rafael send someone else to replace him? I prayed Rafael would drop the idea now. Who had killed Adonis? Was the kill a warning to Rafael? Maybe Adonis had enemies who came for him? Or perhaps Adonis went after someone who'd retaliated. I blamed the crime shows I'd watched over the years for making me paranoid.

"Guys think they know everything." Kiera rolled her eyes as she ran her hand through her auburn hair.

"Grayson told me the police received a false tip about him, but he's not in any trouble. He was at a restaurant when Adonis was killed." Grabbing an almond-flavored macaron, I took a small bite and let my thoughts settle.

I didn't tell my friends about the incident at The Prism. The fewer people who knew about me getting injured by those drunken men, the better. If my friends knew, they'd hound me with questions, and I wasn't ready to disclose anything yet.

"He could have told me that, and I would've been satisfied." Audri huffed out a breath.

Kiera got up from the floor and plopped onto the couch next to me. She gave me a strange look with a suspicious smile. "Something going on with you guys?"

"No," I blurted. "We're just working on the Three Point Park project together."

Liar. I couldn't tell these girls about the bet I had with him. How would I explain the reason I wanted him to choose another building?

"Is he making your work life easier these days?" Audri inquired.

I remembered the way he'd kissed me—the way he had *consumed* me. "Yes, things are better. But my anxiety isn't from him. Did you say something to Grayson?"

Audri lifted a shoulder. "I told him to lighten up because he's making people around him miserable. It's not just you, it's me too."

Kiera reached for her purse, dug into it, and retrieved her phone. "I reserved a retreat at this gorgeous place in Vermont, but I have to leave for my photo shoot." She swiped at the screen. "I don't want to cancel it. Do you want to go? I booked it a year ago. It's a heavenly oasis in the woods."

Still sitting on the floor, Audri reached for a fashion magazine from my stack and flipped through the pages. "Are you talking about The Fortress retreat?"

"Yeah, you're the one who told me about it." Kiera typed something on her phone. "I'll go next year."

"You should definitely go. I think it'll be good for you." Audri put down the magazine and looked at me. "It's peaceful there. The hiking trails, pretty hills, and ponds are simply breathtaking. You can't beat the fresh air. It'll help you relax."

"I do need to relax."

"Nature will heal you." Audri pushed herself up from the floor and joined us on the couch, taking the spot on the other side of me. "You've been experiencing a lot of stress lately. Go clear your head."

"You won't regret it. Maybe you'll come back stress-free and have all the answers to your problems."

Wouldn't that be nice?

The opportunity sounded perfect, and God knew I needed an escape. "If it's not a bother, I'd love to take your place. Send me the details, and I'll pay you."

"Don't worry about it." Kiera waved a hand.

If this retreat was as spectacular as she described, then it would have cost a lot of money. I'd been to private retreats before, so I knew the price range.

"What do you mean? I *have* to pay you back. I'm certain this high-end retreat isn't something anyone can sign up for. It sounds niche, and those things are costly. I won't go if you won't let me pay you."

"You know that novelty sweater you wore the first time we met you? The one with the LaRue label?" Kiera's eyes brightened. "Get me one of those sweaters and we'll call it even. Any color is fine."

The price for the retreat couldn't compare to the cashmere sweater, but I appreciated her generosity. I didn't remember the last time any of the girls in my old circle gave me something more valuable than what I'd given them.

I smiled at Kiera and turned to Audri. "Do you want one want too?"

"I'd never say no to gorgeous clothes. Fall and winter aren't too far away." Audri smiled.

"Okay. I'll take care of that. I'll get one for Michelle as well." I tapped my phone to set a reminder.

"You know someone who knows someone?" Kiera asked.

Guilt squirmed and knotted my stomach. I had to tell

them the truth about my identity before I returned home. "Something like that."

It wouldn't be hard for me to get them each a LaRue sweater. That sweater had been one of my early designs that sold well, and the company kept the style on reorder. I'd love to gift my friends something that originated from me.

The friendship with these girls hadn't been on my agenda when I arrived in Providence. They had accepted me wholeheartedly without asking a lot of questions. I supposed true friendship happened naturally, without the need to explain anything. Life often placed you in situations where you met people who would change your perspective. I treasured their friendship more than they could ever know.

This retreat appeared at the perfect moment. I couldn't wait to visit The Fortress. Just thinking about a getaway eased the tension. In the past, when I visited the States, I'd only been to New York and Los Angeles for fashion shows. So this trip into the wilderness was something new and exciting. I had a feeling this vacation was the reprieve I'd been waiting for.

Perhaps Kiera was right about finding answers. A clear mind made room for new ideas to bloom while a cluttered mind hid important things in piles of debris. It was time to declutter.

CHAPTER NINETEEN

NATALIE

August in the Vermont woods offered exactly what I needed. As I drove through the winding roads, I left the windows down, letting in the fresh air that made my lungs rejoice. The summer heat wasn't so bad with so many trees. I felt like I was driving toward a magical place hidden away from the world. The road snaked around and around, finally straightening out and guiding me to a pebbled path.

I arrived at a gorgeous retreat that took my breath away. It was *extraordinary*. A magnificent tree house greeted me with its unique presence. It was like an art installation that some creator placed inside the woods for the lucky few to witness and admire. I'd never seen anything like this.

This wasn't a regular kid's tree house, but an unconventional architecture built meticulously around a massive oak tree. The oak tree was part of the tree house, or rather, the tree house was part of the tree. That was the beauty of it.

I didn't see any cars around. Was anyone here to check me in? I looked at the address Kiera had given me. This was The Fortress, and the GPS had brought me to the right place. Maybe the attendant went out.

I got out of my car and browsed the area. I felt like I just stepped into tranquility. Lush vegetation filled the surrounding area with pretty flowers. The plants didn't appear too manicured, allowing them to grow free and wild. But someone took care of this gorgeous space, though. The variety of stones and pebbles gave it a nice curb appeal.

Manicured lawns seemed too restrictive. I preferred greenery with more freedom. Didn't we all crave freedom?

Walking to a garden, I held a fuchsia-colored rose in my hand. "No one likes to be told what to do or how to grow, right, flower? You're the most beautiful when you can grow however you want."

A butterfly floated by and landed on a leaf as though greeting me.

"Hello to you too," I said, not caring if anyone could hear me.

Talking to myself was one way to help me focus on the present moment, and it was a gentle form of therapy.

I walked to the hibiscus plants, smiled at them, and then wandered to the blue hydrangeas, admiring their limitless beauty. These flowers didn't have any restrictions. They possessed immeasurable freedom—the kind my heart yearned for.

In certain ways, my family's legacy restricted me. Duty kept me bound to what I had to do rather than let me be boundless. I loved my family and the name it represented. My grandparents and my parents worked hard to keep true to the LaRue brand and its mission statement: timeless elegance. Don't get me wrong, I loved what LaRue stood for. But my soul wanted to try something else. It was like a flower seeking the sun and knowing that reaching the sunlight would allow it to grow even more. I wanted to take a detour from the norm. I gravitated toward novelty that didn't fit in with the LaRue brand, but to branch off on my own would be a disappointment to my family. It felt like a betrayal to them. I couldn't let that happen.

You can't always get what you want.

Despite my desires, I couldn't abandon my family at a time like this. My family needed me now more than ever.

Stop thinking about work. You're here for a break, remember?

I pushed all my concerns aside and took a deep breath. The scent of honeysuckle and roses snuck up my nose as I walked behind this modern tree house that was a secret villa in the woods. The tree house was an innovative fortress, indeed. The wooden stairs spiraled around the oak tree that stood like an ancient god. There were several balconies and wide decks that sat on top of sturdy tree trunks. I could imagine myself sitting on the balcony sketching my next collection. There wouldn't be any city noises to distract me, but only the peaceful birdsong to soothe me.

As I stood glancing up at the magnificence, I felt small and insignificant compared to the wise oak tree with the extensive thick branches, looking like arms and limbs welcoming every patron.

How old was it? What had it seen in all its years? Did the visitors treat it well? Did it enjoy the squirrels running up its trunk and across its branches? Did the animal's feet tickle it? Did bird poop annoy it?

I smiled as I entertained myself with silly thoughts.

As a fashion designer, I often tried to put myself in the position of inanimate and animate objects, seeing from their perspective. It made the design process more interesting. What would a tree see if it looked at me?

The thought made me itch to finish my private collection —something no one knew about. It was my meditation, a way to indulge myself while still following my responsibilities. It helped me survive the transition from working in Paris to working in a water and sewer department in a foreign country.

Two different worlds, yet somehow, I belonged in both. There was an underlying connection somewhere here, but I didn't see it yet. I laughed at the contrast of my life, and the noise echoed through the woods.

"What's so funny?" The deep, rich voice was wine warming my stomach after a long day of work.

My heart skipped as I turned to face Grayson, looking stunning as usual. He wore a fitted blue T-shirt that hugged every muscle in his body. I could see the outlines of what appeared to be a six-pack. His shorts revealed muscular legs that reminded me of the sturdy tree house.

When did he get here? I didn't hear a car arrive. I'd been so wrapped up in the beauty of the tree house and my thoughts that I didn't hear him come. I wasn't sure if that was a good thing.

Shock slammed into me, but I was also annoyed. I wanted time alone to think and reevaluate my current situation. I didn't need or want the man who had contributed to my confusion to be present, muddling my emotions.

Was God joking with me? Did he think it would be interesting to toss a few more obstacles my way?

What was I supposed to do? Go somewhere else? Nope. This was a private retreat that couldn't be booked easily. He wasn't going to chase me away.

Maybe *he* should go elsewhere. I was here first. The bet between us hung in the air, wanting me to acknowledge it.

Not right now. Not here where no one else was present to help reduce the sexual energy between us. My body was fully aware of his presence.

That annoyed me too. I just wanted to be alone to think.

Despite that, I wondered if his appearance was an opportunity to resolve my issue with him—the undeniable attraction.

My skin heated and tingled when his eyes raked up and down my body. I wasn't wearing anything provocative. A tank top with a low V-neck and jean shorts with frayed edges.

If he were a model, he'd be hotter than any I'd encountered. The fashion world was full of beautiful people, but appearances were deceptive. Was Grayson a man who only had a gorgeous exterior?

My feelings toward him had changed from when we first met. The undeniable attraction between us begged to be dealt with, especially after that unforgettable kiss in his office. My body had been dying for more, but I needed to win this bet. I had to persuade him to buy any other property for Three Point Park instead of The Prism. I hadn't gotten far in terms of finding out information on the building, but I could only move one step at a time.

"I'm just thinking about where I've been and where I'm at now. Isn't this tree house spectacular?" He would appreciate this creation. Maybe that was the reason he came to the retreat as well. I didn't ask Kiera how many rooms were available, but from the look of it, it could probably fit twenty people.

Grayson walked up to me. "It is."

His closeness made it difficult for me to breathe, but I couldn't make myself step away. He had a magnetism that gripped me like the ribbon on a corset. Every time our eyes connected, the corset tightened, wanting me to release something I was afraid to acknowledge.

We stood there gazing at the tree house, and his overwhelming presence combined with the summer heat, got to me. "I need some cold water."

CHAPTER TWENTY

GRAYSON

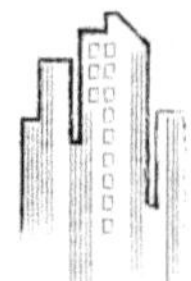

Work, frustration, exhaustion, and confusion had crammed into my brain when I was at the local market. But somehow, Natalie's face snuck through the cracks, making her presence known.

She wouldn't leave me alone. I'd come to my tree house to clear my head of everything—including her. So seeing her in my sacred space was a taunt from the universe. Maybe I should be more open to unexpected coincidences and not focus on controlling everything.

She gulped down the bottle of water she'd retrieved from her car.

"Feeling better?" I asked, watching her tongue catch the water droplet clinging to her bottom lip.

"Yes."

I'd been thinking about her while buying necessities at the local market for my much-needed vacation. So when I returned from my shopping trip and noticed her car, I thought it was a hallucination. This woman had visited me in dreams and every time I had a private moment, so I wasn't surprised if I had hallucinated.

The mounting workload, the bodyguard's death, my indecision on visiting Derek, and this urgent need for Natalie . . . Too much was going on, and I couldn't trust my thoughts.

I needed solitude to think. The Fortress was my place to recharge. To see her appreciating my personal space and mesmerized by my tree house did something peculiar to me. The needle inside my inner compass shifted toward her.

Though the shift was subtle, it was noticeable to me.

She was a spark of newness—an ember in the dark thrumming with potential—an idea that hadn't fully formed yet, but I sensed its power. I'd felt this force many times when I'd been immersed in the zone of creation. I didn't know why, but seeing Natalie admiring my work ignited the ember in me.

Her presence transformed the energy of the place. What had once been quiet and simple had become more vivid. The flowers were brighter, the air seemed cleaner, the birds sang louder. I sounded like an idiot, but I didn't care. It was like designing a room in a house that suddenly offered a new purpose than originally planned. That was the only logical explanation I could come up with.

"What are you doing here?" I asked, admiring her minimal clothing of shorts and a tank top. There was so much exposed skin for my curious eyes.

"What are *you* doing here, McDimple?" she asked, lifting her chin with a slight defiance that made me want to grip it for a closer examination.

I could have told her this was my property and moved

on, but that twinkle in her eyes and the way she addressed me motivated me to hold back.

When I didn't reply, her lips twisted into a wry grin. "Don't tell me you're stalking me. There are laws against that kind of thing, you know."

Desire swelled in my shorts from her challenging smile. I escaped the city—and her—to come here, but it seemed the universe had a different plan for me. Was this fate forcing me to decide? We had a bet going on, and I'd been so close to losing it by kissing her.

To an outsider, the bet may have appeared silly and inconsequential, but to me, it was paramount. I wanted this woman, and for me to hold back this long without having her said something about me—she affected me like no one else. She could control me by not controlling me. That made no sense, but it was how I felt. She didn't force me to do anything, and yet I'd been stretching out this challenge longer than necessary. Did I fear that once I kissed her, I'd no longer have a link to her? It was a stupid concern, but I couldn't help the vulnerability that whispered I wouldn't be the same man after one night with her.

Once again, fear kept me at bay, but I couldn't resist this powerful attraction to her.

Natalie fascinated me like a design concept I'd never encountered.

I stepped closer, looking down at her beautiful face. "It's more like you're stalking me. After all, this is my property. You're trespassing. I should call the authorities."

Her mouth dropped open. "This . . . *this* place is *yours?*"

"Yup. Built four years ago. I was part of the construction team."

"You mean, you didn't just design the tree house but you

built it with your hands?" She walked up to the front door and ran her fingers down the wooden beams supporting the intricate portico. Her fingers traced the length of the wooden beam, and a tingle ran down my cock as though her fingers were on it.

I stepped onto the porch, placing my hand on the support beam just above hers. "This is my sanctuary, my personal space, so I put in the sweat and labor. There was no deadline, so I worked on it whenever I could."

Her pretty pink lips formed into a slight pout, and the memory of our powerful kiss surfaced. I'd been desperate for her mouth, and I wasn't sure if I'd survive the next few days with her near me.

"I've only met architects who designed but stayed away from the hard labor." She glanced up at the metal accents around the porch.

"That depends on availability and what the building means to the architect. I don't usually have time to take part in the construction, nor do I want to. There are skilled men and women who are better at it. But to be a brilliant designer, you must understand how the pieces connect, how they come together. You become the creator externally and internally."

What the hell are you talking about, Grayson?

I hadn't spoken with depth in a long time, and I wasn't giving a speech at some conference regarding my designs. This was her influence on me. Grayson Wu had been a man who saw things with depth, but then he found it easier to skim the surface. Digging deep meant stirring up unwanted memories. Who wanted dirt and debris, anyway?

Her curious blue eyes warmed on me. Something about Natalie made me feel at ease. I was a bundle of chaos, but meeting her here had rocketed me into a whole new galaxy, an unfamiliar territory that terrified and fascinated me.

She broke the gaze and looked at the wall, the floor, and the front door. "A great designer is one who can speak and understand his masterpiece. And you can only understand when you immerse yourself in its journey, right?" She gestured to the surrounding plants. "A gardener who plants seeds without gloves knows the true meaning of growth. He knows the textures, the scent, and the softness of the soil when water is added, the sound of tiny pebbles grinding together, the warmth of sunlight baking the surface—all the things the seedlings need to grow. But a gardener who wears gloves loses part of that raw connection. Do you agree?" She looked at me, and my chest tightened at the truth of her words.

That was an artist's statement. Only an artist, a writer, a creator of things could comprehend the meaning with such eloquence. My eyes slid to her neck, where her pulse thumped against her skin.

Without thinking, I placed my index finger over it. "Creativity is sex with and without a condom. Everyone approaches it differently." I smiled. "There's wisdom in sex."

"There's wisdom in everything."

"Are you nervous?" I asked, loving the beating of her pulse against my finger. It quickened as I moved over it. She had an elegant neck, and I wanted to explore it with my mouth.

"Should I be?" Her voice came out soft and seductive.

Here we go again with the tug of war of a bet.

She could have moved away from my touch, but she didn't. My finger traveled to her smooth chin. "You should be, because you're trespassing."

"Maybe I'm a detective checking out a hideaway. What secrets are you hiding here, Grayson?" She purred my name, and my blood heated several degrees.

"I'll tell you my secrets if you tell me yours."

She considered me for a long moment. "You really want to know?" A slow smile crept onto her mouth as she stepped away, breaking our contact.

"You have no idea."

Blue fire gleamed in her eyes. "I'll be here a week. Since this is your spectacular tree house, want to give me a tour? Maybe I'll be inspired to tell you why I'm here."

I took her toward the outdoor area furnished with cushioned chairs, tables, and a fire pit. To the right was another seating area with an awning and flowy curtains. Trees and flowers in large pots adorned the area.

"Sorry I dragged you into this Adonis mess. I'm glad it's over."

"I have no regrets. No one is allowed to hurt you. I'll be your shield." That was a declaration to her and to myself. The need to protect her was just as powerful as the need to touch her.

She stared at me for a moment, but didn't comment. Instead, she walked over to a wooden bench made from a fallen tree and sat down, admiring the tree house. It was composed of three floors built intricately woven around the old oak tree. No one knew the reason I built this place, and I liked to keep it that way.

"I've never seen a tree house like this. You turned childhood fascination into marvelous architecture. It's cutting-edge design. I could stare at this all day."

Natalie got up, stepped farther back, like an artist

needing extra room to view her painting, and studied the tree house. That gesture revealed she was a designer too.

I hadn't realized I was standing so close to her until she whirled around and bumped into me, sending a surge of lust to my cock.

"When did you build this place? What inspired you? This is more than a simple tree house." She faced it again and released a sigh. "It's a . . . dedication."

The windows to my heart flew open all at once, and something warm and sunny shone in. No one had ever nailed the truth like that. I hadn't known Natalie well enough, or even long enough, for her to know me like this. And yet, she saw the truth as though it were obvious.

"I designed it right after graduating from Harvard, but it took a while for me to get the project going," I said, trying to subdue the spiraling lust.

I wasn't sure if I wanted her to know this much of me. What if she didn't like the mess? What if it was too much for her?

She knew me as an architect, as a businessman she had to collaborate with on a project. But she didn't know why I was here. This was where I stripped myself bare. There was no pretense for the world. I was simply a man trying to reconnect to myself.

The issue with my uncle—and the dangerous organization associated with him—weighed on me. The organization had tried to kill Derek. What info could Derek give me to help destroy this organization? Would he even want to help? Would he dare betray them? These people had killed Royce's younger sister, and their crimes expanded to several continents, ranging from sex trafficking, drugs, and money laundering, to other illegal activities that powerful organizations were capable of. They lived in the shadows, which was why it was difficult to find out who the elite members were.

Would they leave me and my boys alone if they knew we'd witnessed one of their crimes? So far, they had no clue. But what if that changed down the road? What would stop them from coming after us and our families? There was only one way to ensure we were safe—destroy The Trogyn.

That would be a massive task that would take time and careful planning. One wrong move could be the end of all of us.

Why did Derek want to see me now? What did he want from me? But seeing him would only bring up anger and resentment.

What would Natalie see if she got close to me? She could touch me at a core level, and that scared me. I'd dated women from various backgrounds and nationalities with interesting occupations. But none of them pulled at me like Natalie. Maybe it was her wit, her intelligence—her ability to speak and understand the language of creativity.

After Natalie had been attacked at The Prism, I had my PI retrieve videos from the building and the surrounding area. My Natalie had been trying to break into the property. That was why she had the damn hammer. My Natalie wasn't who she said she was.

She was like a complex masterpiece thrown in front of me, and I couldn't resist wanting to know everything about her. What was her life like growing up? What inspired her? What were her fears? What were her dreams?

"It's an inspiring creation," she said, still studying the tree house.

"It's a dedication to my father . . . and my uncle."

Holy.

Fucking.

Hell.

I thought I'd shut off my brain to ensure that truth never made its way out of my mouth.

The muscles in my back tensed. I didn't like this sudden lapse in judgment. What the fuck? That revelation had been one of my deepest secrets. No one knew this.

I glared at her, the temper in my body rising. The anger was aimed at me for not having control of myself, but it was also at her for making me weak. Somehow, she had snuck into my sacred space, pulling things out of me. Her presence had completely changed everything.

Vulnerability was something I didn't want to show anyone.

Unperturbed by my instability, Natalie lifted a finger and pressed it onto the tense spot between my eyebrows, rubbing gently. "Why the frown? It's a beautiful dedication that would make anyone proud."

She had no fucking clue, and somehow, she held the key to unlock me. I didn't want to talk about it anymore, fearing I'd reveal more than I already had.

Though none of this was her fault, I couldn't stop the frustration and sexual need rising in me.

"Let me show you to your room." I led her through the door, up the stairs, and into a hallway that offered access to the balcony.

"Wow, the view is stunning. I love all the trees." She stepped past me and the scent of her perfume tantalized my body, dragging the frustration that had clung to me and tossing it elsewhere.

She could shift my mood with ease. How could I go from being frustrated to feeling lusty in mere seconds? My gaze followed her as she walked to the guardrail, leaned over, and glanced around without knowing her effect on me. My eyes slid down to her full ass and then to her long, toned legs. Legs that would wrap nicely around my body . . .

Christ. I was in deep shit.

She turned to face me, her back leaning against the railing. Blonde hair framed her gorgeous face against the green backdrop of the peaceful woods. She looked like a goddess from a magical world who came to Earth to put a spell on me. Maybe that was it. Maybe I was stuck in a dream state.

If that were the case, I could extend this magical dream by envisioning doing other things to her—

"How many people are staying at your retreat? Are more guests coming? How many bedrooms are in this extravagant tree house?" Her voice snapped me out of my lusty bubble.

I forced my body to behave, but it was a fucking traitor.

My eyes darted to the enticing mounds peeking above the low neckline of her tank top. Touching her would relax me. I stepped next to her, inhaling her scent. If I was going to die of lust, I might as well indulge in it now.

"There are five bedrooms between the three floors. No one comes here but me and a few friends. I didn't build this for public use. It was for me, and since I love having space, I added a bunch of rooms and filled them with furniture. I own fifty acres of the surrounding lands. This property is very secluded."

"I see." She nodded slowly, studying me. "A perfect place for *crimes*." Mischief sparked in her eyes. "I've watched a lot of true crime shows."

"I wouldn't know anything about that." I bent down and whispered into her ear, "But I could make you scream and no one will hear you for miles. You're going to lose the bet. I'll make sure of it." I licked her ear.

She sucked in a breath and turned to face me, her pupils darkening. Our lips were inches apart. All I had to do was kiss her and satisfy this need to taste her, but that would make me lose. I wanted more than a kiss. I wanted to fuck her from all angles. That was the deal—the prize for my victory.

I didn't know where I found the last thread of self-control, but I gripped it tightly.

Straightening up, I said, "There are walking trails over there. Do you want to take a walk later?"

"That sounds wonderful, thank you."

I never imagined being here with her. Now that she was here, a plan formed in my head to win. Natalie was here for a reason. God must have read my mind.

We continued down the hallway to her room.

"Kiera offered to let me take her place. I hope you don't mind."

I'd forgotten I'd agreed to let Kiera use this retreat, but I preferred the sudden change in guests. Kiera would've been here all by herself if I hadn't taken this impromptu vacation.

"I don't mind. We're on vacation, so let's enjoy it. Don't think about work or anything that's bothering us, okay?"

She looked at me. "Okay."

"Have lunch with me, and I'll answer questions about this tree house. Or you can ask me one question about anything."

She arched an eyebrow. "Why do I get the sense that there's something hidden in that offer?"

I grinned. "Now you're being suspicious."

"Because you're acting suspicious."

These had been words we tossed at one another not too long ago.

"I know a few tricks with business negotiations." She touched my face, her fingers emphasizing each word. "I understand process, procedure, profit margins, and creative ways a businessman or businesswoman makes deals. I think you're trying to make a very dangerous deal."

She was my perfect match.

I gripped her hand. "Are you frightened that you're here all alone with me?" I kissed each finger slowly.

Her mouth opened slightly as she watched me adore each finger. When I got to her pinky, I took my time licking, nibbling, and taking it into my mouth.

I expected her to protest or yank her hand away, but she didn't. Her eyes darkened and she let out a whimper. "Grayson."

"This attraction between us needs to be resolved. You're driving me insane." I sucked her finger delicately. "I may do something I've never done."

"What's that?"

"Lose to you on purpose."

"Maybe we should start arguing again so you don't have to think about the bet."

"It's too late. That's not going to work. Arguing with you arouses me now."

The blush on her cheeks deepened. "Where's my room? I need to get ready for lunch."

CHAPTER TWENTY-ONE

NATALIE

I didn't know why I was nervous about lunch, which was in a few hours. Apparently, Grayson had bought a lot of ingredients for the week. When I returned to Providence, I'd have a conversation with Kiera and Audri for setting me up. They knew Grayson owned this retreat and said nothing about that.

After dropping my luggage off in my room for me, he left to prepare for lunch. I unpacked and acclimated myself to the stunning suite. It was cozy, with parts of the trunk embedded into the wall. The trunk went up through the ceiling, which was the second floor to where we'd have lunch later.

I came here to rest and relax, but I wasn't sure that would happen. Especially when I could still sense his lips around my fingers, making me wonder how his lips would feel on other areas of my body. When he sucked my fingers, sensations I'd long forgotten combusted to life.

A few months ago, I detested this man who was rude, cold,

and inflexible. Now, those traits were broad brush strokes, giving him more dimension. There was more to him than sharp edges. I wanted to seek the caverns deep within the mountain of this man. It was as though I could hear his pain whispering to me through the cracks, wanting me to come closer.

Though I told him he should be afraid of me, I was the frightened one—extremely terrified. Being here with him made me want to do something I'd never considered. He'd mentioned something similar earlier. We were both inspired to do the unthinkable.

Spontaneity called to me. This was my chance to be free —free of responsibilities, free to listen to my heart, free to take what I wanted.

I wanted him out of my system. Someone would lose the bet before the vacation was over. I'd make sure it wouldn't be me.

After a quick shower to wash off the early morning sweat, I put on a new pair of pink shorts shorter than the denim ones. They had metal studs decorating the back pockets. I was fully aware that if I bent over, he would see a large portion of my ass, but I didn't care.

I was a single girl who hadn't expected to see him here on my vacation, where I had planned on being alone. My wardrobe satisfied no one but me. He'd have to deal with my shorts and low-neckline tank top. Plus, the hot weather called for appropriate clothing, so I was merely complying with Mother Nature.

A mischievous part of me wanted to test him, torture him. In design, I loved stretching the limit. How else would I know what worked if I didn't experiment?

The seduction excited me. What could I make Grayson

do? How many layers did I need to peel off to get to the real and raw man?

Feeling free as a bird, I walked up the wooden stairs to the second floor. The steps had metal bolts that matched the masculine railing. Beautiful wooden floors greeted me as I surveyed the spacious room furnished with comfortable couches, uniquely shaped tables and chairs, a TV sitting on an abstract wooden stand, a wide bookcase, unique art, a cozy rug, and a mini bar tucked in the corner. An adorable swing with a round back hung near the balcony, facing the backyard.

A seed of jealousy sprouted in my stomach. I placed a hand over it, rubbing it gently. Why should I have been jealous? Why should I have cared how many women he'd brought here? This tree house was a peek into the Grayson beneath the layers, and I didn't like that other women had gotten to know him first.

Stop asking irrelevant questions!

Jealousy was a natural human emotion that everyone experienced. I wasn't immune to it. It didn't matter if he had women lined up at his other homes or tree houses—I had men asking me on dates in Paris, Milan, London, and so forth. The problem was, I hadn't felt a tinge of jealousy with them.

Was I getting sick? This surge of jealousy was abnormal. I placed a hand over my forehead and didn't feel a fever.

I forced myself to focus on the intimate ambience of the space. This cutting-edge tree house was a combination of the masculine and feminine parts of nature—the hard and soft edges blending together. Metal and wood, dark and light— the opposites that somehow completed each other. It was a superb design, a reflection of who he was and how his mind connected things. I understood why people wanted to hire him.

A noise drew my attention to the left, where Grayson stood in a fancy kitchen that shouldn't belong in a tree house. He wore a printed apron that read Hot Stuff Coming Up, and I couldn't help but smile. His height, build, and magnetism filled the space beautifully.

Would he model for me? I could see him wearing one of my menswear ensembles from my private collection. No, he'd probably prefer the well-known brands like Armani, Gucci, and Balmain.

He moved around the kitchen with precision, speed, and dangerous sophistication—a panther with determined focus that mesmerized me.

Grayson was making lunch for me. No man had ever done that. They'd taken me to elegant restaurants, but had never put in the effort to show I mattered.

I didn't have time to cook and didn't enjoy it when I did. So this was extra special.

He transferred something from the stove onto plates, washed his hands, and removed the apron, hanging it on the hook on the wall. Then he stared at the plates of food as though they were artwork. If a man could grin without smiling, he just did it.

I sighed, and his eyes cut to me. The galvanized look made me suck in a deep breath that probably shifted an organ out of place.

"Ready to eat?" he asked.

CHAPTER TWENTY-TWO

GRAYSON

How long had she been wandering around this floor? How long had she been watching me? I'd been immersed in cooking and wondering if she'd enjoy the meal when her sigh broke my trance.

Natalie walked up to me, wearing a new top that gave me a peek at her chest and a sexy pair of shorts that made her legs appear longer than before.

She viewed the plates of salmon and turned her attention to the two bowls of salads. "I'm impressed."

"About what?"

"That you can cook." She gestured to the plates.

"I grill, not cook."

"Way better than me." She sniffed the salmon. "It smells so good."

I brought the plates over to the table and she followed with the two bowls of salad.

She stood next to me, her bare arm brushing mine. Just looking at her shoved all other thoughts aside, leaving only her in my mind. My eyes flicked to her neck. That damn pulse on her neck called me again.

Looking up at me with appreciation, she said, "This looks delicious."

Her gratitude broke my resistance. "So does this." I bent down and nibbled her neck, skimming my lips over the pulse that galloped even faster. "This is a nibble, a taste, not a kiss. So it doesn't count as a kiss."

A soft laugh followed by a moan escaped her. "You're improvising."

I had to get creative. The need to touch her was too much, and I'd burst if I didn't listen to my body.

"Creativity makes the world a better place." My tongue drew shapes on her neck.

"Is this your unconventional way of trying to make me lose?" she purred.

"No. It's an innovative way to sample a craving." I sucked lightly at the junction of her neck and shoulder.

"Grayson," she moaned.

"Yes?"

She palmed my cock and squeezed. "Seems like someone is causing trouble."

"I wouldn't dare." An obvious lie.

She looked at me with molten eyes and pressed her finger to my lips. "But a dare is what your eyes are revealing and what your raspy voice is saying."

"Is that so?" I stared at her hand, still gripping my length. It was fucking hot, and I could stand there all day letting her do whatever she wanted. Forget about lunch and dinner. Forget about everything.

I was starving for her.

Nodding, her eyes gleamed like a seductress who knew exactly what she was doing. "You know why I'm drawn to you?"

"Why?"

"You make me feel comfortable . . . at feeling dirty."

Pride spiked in me.

My grin stretched as my mind jumped to extremely filthy things. "Then I suggest we experiment on how dirty we can be together?"

She shook her head. "Not yet. Right now, I'm hungry . . ." She squeezed me once, twice and then released me. ". . . for salmon."

A wicked smile flashed on her face, making me want to toss her over my lap and spank her. God. I wanted to do so many things to this woman.

"Let's take things slow, McDimple, otherwise we might burn down this peaceful retreat, including this spectacular tree house that I want to explore."

CHAPTER TWENTY-THREE

After dinner, we planned on taking a walk around the surrounding trails to digest our meal, but then Grayson's phone rang.

He arched an eyebrow at the screen. "I need to follow up with something."

"For work?"

"Something like that."

"I thought this was your vacation."

"It is. But this call isn't an issue per se. It's something I've been waiting for. Do you mind if we postpone the walk till later?"

I understood his position. Though he was a billionaire on vacation, his phone was always on for emergencies. He had an empire to oversee. Things could go wrong at any moment, and he needed to be at the ready. He probably had several projects going on simultaneously, and they each progressed differently, needing his attention at different times.

My phone was on in case my mom needed me. "Of course. Go do what you need to do. I've got things to work on as well. We can walk later or even tomorrow. There's plenty of time."

He tipped up my chin. "I'll see you soon."

After he left, I went to my room, inspired to create a few sketches for my collection. I hadn't thought of a brand name yet. It would come to me at the right moment. There was no deadline. I was working on this at my own pace. That slow pace allowed creativity to flow naturally. As I began sketching, Grayson's face wavered in front of me like a taunt. Dripping with charisma, good looks, brilliance, and sophistication —all with a luxurious edge.

A few sketches later, I took a break to check my email. The private investigator had sent information he'd gotten about my dad's presence at the Rhode Island School of Design. Dad had been a guest judge there many times. He'd given presentations and donations to the fashion departments at RISD, MassArt, and FIT. He'd even invited me to go, but something had always come up and I couldn't make it.

I didn't need the investigator's help anymore. He wasn't as effective as I'd hoped, and I didn't want to waste any more money.

From all the information he provided, one thing stood out. My dad had attended a talk at RISD on the last trip he made to the States—the trip where his plane went down and changed my life forever. As far as I knew, Dad had been on a business trip to New York to meet up with a few vendors. It wasn't unusual for him to use his time well to network while he was in town.

An ugly thought popped into my head. Was his mistress at RISD? Was she a professor there? I didn't like the way my mind spiraled out of control. For the next hour or so, I researched RISD and all its professors. I didn't recognize anyone's name. Maybe I was being paranoid. Maybe my dad's visits to the college had just been to educate students wanting to join the fashion world. We had a well-paid internship program that was always looking for eager fashion students who wanted first-hand experience in the industry.

But something kept nudging me to continue investigating.

"Dad, is that you trying to tell me something from the other side of the veil?" I asked out loud, knowing full well that he wasn't going to answer me.

I remembered the day I got the call from my mom, telling me Dad's plane had crashed into the Atlantic Ocean. She'd been hysterical. Life could change in one instant. I'd plummeted into depression and trying my best to understand the misfortune placed upon my family. It had been surreal, and it took a long time for me to learn how to cope with his death. Though he was the CEO of the company, he always included me in all of his decisions.

It's going to be yours someday. I want you to know about House of LaRue inside and out.

He'd caught me sketching an ensemble that didn't fit in with the LaRue brand, but he didn't dismiss it.

It's a fantastic design, but for a different label.

My dad was right, but I never stopped creating for myself. I had several sketchbooks containing all of my designs, not knowing when or if they'd ever come to fruition. I needed an outlet to collect my ideas, and the sketchbooks served that purpose.

Though my dad recognized my heart desired something else, he didn't force me to abandon my dream to focus on the family's business. He kept the communication open and even asked me about my sketches when we spent time together. When I showed him a sketch of an asymmetrical dress, he smiled and said, "For another brand—the other Natalie."

I missed him so much.

Walking over to the balcony, I stared out at the woods, which had darkened from the setting sun. Tears slid down my face. Had my dad been frightened during his last moments? Had he been in pain? Did he think of me and Mom?

Life consisted of sacred moments strung together. Some were happy, some brought lessons along with them, while others shocked your system wide awake. Images of my childhood flowed in front of me. Then images of Grayson joined in, and my heart went from pain to a burst of joy.

I was flowing on a wave of momentum.

Momentum.

I repeated the word softly, then loudly, as though I wanted the earth and the sky to know. A thrill skidded down my spine, and I knew Momentum was the name for my label.

CHAPTER TWENTY-FOUR

GRAYSON

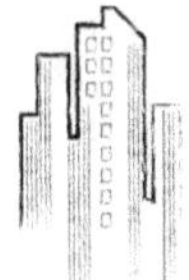

Inside my office, I sat at my desk and logged in to my laptop. The PI had uncovered information regarding the woman I couldn't stop thinking about. So I had to postpone our walk to see what he'd found.

Images of Natalie LaRue flooded my screen. I studied each image of her as though it was my first time meeting her. It was sort of like that, though. I was being introduced to Natalie LaRue, an elegant designer who was familiar with the tabloids and gossip.

I didn't know how to feel about this discovery. A part of me felt betrayed. She hadn't been honest with me. *Fuck.* It wasn't as though I'd been upfront about everything, either. We all had secrets. But why did Natalie feel the need to keep her real identity hidden?

What kind of trouble are you in, buttercup?

This powerful need to protect her kept resurfacing. Was she hiding from her ex-fiancé, Rafael? He'd found her already, so why keep the identity hidden? She was Creative

Director and Lead Designer for House of LaRue, a high-end fashion label in Europe. No wonder she understood the design concept. Not only that, she was the heir to this fashion house.

I read her profile. She was an only child, went to college for fashion design and business, but worked at other corporations before being employed by her father. She worked her way up from the bottom, learning from different companies. That made me smile.

That tenacity—that versatility—was what made her adapt so well to the City of Providence. She fell several steps on the corporate ladder by working for the municipality. Most wouldn't survive the fall. She went from a powerful role to working an administrative job, dealing with unattractive things like water, sewer, and trash recycling. Why? What was the purpose? That was a drastic change in her life. It wasn't just the salary difference—the whole mentality shift must have been uncomfortable and stark.

Audri's comment about Natalie's anxiety echoed in my head. I had added fuel to the surrounding fire. She was probably struggling to fit in, trying to learn her way around the new job, when I thought it would be fun to annoy her with my delays and rude remarks.

Fucking asshole.

With each new image of her, I got to see her from a different angle. One video showed her preparing for a fashion show in the backroom. She fixed the lapel of a male model before going to a female model to adjust a wide belt. Details. She paid attention to the little details. The big picture was important to get an overview of the project like I did with my miniature landmark. But details gave life to the masterpiece.

She didn't know it yet, but she was my perfect match—the feminine to my masculine creativity. Together, we could achieve unimaginable things.

I had never been more excited to lose to someone than losing to her.

CHAPTER TWENTY-FIVE

GRAYSON

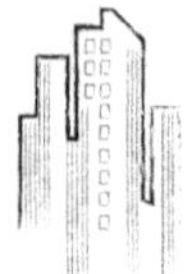

After staying up most of the night learning about Natalie's real identity, I still had questions for her. But my admiration for her tripled. I admired people who did the unthinkable. She could've stayed in Paris and lived a luxurious life. What motivated her to abandon that lifestyle to move to Providence?

Last night, we both stayed in our rooms and didn't get to walk. So today, I made it up to her by taking her on a splendid hike on several trails. Despite my desperate need for answers, this was our vacation. I didn't want to make her feel uncomfortable by asking questions she probably didn't want to answer. Besides, I didn't know how she'd react to me investigating her. How could I not? I couldn't resist the mystery surrounding her. But that discussion with her could wait.

After a day of hiking, we returned to the tree house. The cloudy weather allowed us to hike farther than usual. My lovely companion, along with low humidity, made the adventure in the woods one of the best I'd ever had. There wasn't a minute I didn't think about her comment from yesterday.

You make me feel comfortable . . . at feeling dirty.

What filthy things did she have in mind when she thought about me?

Despite the sexual attraction between us, I appreciated her friendship as well. We talked about everything, even the frogs, lily pads, moss, rocks, and the texture of the tree bark. Everything became more interesting because she was with me. The girls I'd dated before preferred the city life, fancy restaurants, shopping centers, boutiques, and all the parties I could take them to.

I could see the city girl in Natalie, but I also saw the yearning for serenity and simplicity—the desire for something beyond the external.

"I'm going to hop into the shower, and I can help you prepare an early dinner."

She didn't know I'd already placed an order for delivery. "Can I join you?"

"No." She smiled.

"It'll be fun."

"No."

"I'll let you sleep in my cozy swing," I bargained.

She snorted. "My paperwork states that anyone staying on the premise has access to *everything*."

"Except my suite."

"Do you have illegal stuff in there?"

"You'll have to find out."

She rose to her feet and wiped the sweat from my forehead with her hand. "You need a shower too, but in your suite."

"I thought you liked me dirty." A single rivulet of sweat trickled down her neck, and I bent down to lick it.

She let out a moan. "Grayson."

"Yes, buttercup?" I pressed my lips to her racing pulse. "I love your flavor. Want to shower together? We can save water."

She laughed. "I'll pass."

"We can get creatively dirty."

Right now, I didn't expect her to say yes to me joining her in the shower, but she would soon. The sexual energy between us could topple this very tree if I didn't do something about it. The sooner I resolved it, the sooner my life could return to normal.

"I know we can." She left it at that and walked up to her suite.

My eyes darted to those enticing shorts that revealed enough to make a man want to see the rest. Was she wearing underwear?

The bulge in my shorts ached. I should probably go shower to cool myself off, but I was inspired. A familiar spark ignited in me, and I grasped it.

Heading to my workshop on the ground floor, I retrieved the toolkit from the shelf and pulled out the chair I'd started a year ago but never finished. It needed two more legs and some sanding. The maple tree that had fallen over a year ago had been used for multiple purposes. It became the abstract stools and a bench around the grill area, a nightstand for a suite, the railing on the deck, and this chair.

I attached one leg and then the other. I set the chair down on my work table and shifted it around. I examined it, remembering the joy that had started this project. I'd wanted to make a unique chair that was both functional and stylistic.

It was finally finished. The only thing it needed was the final touches, which were as important as the assembly itself.

Standing at my work table, I got lost in the process of creation. It was just me and the chair. Everything else disappeared. As I sanded the roughness from the wooden surface, I was symbolically removing the dirt and unnecessary things clinging to me. The motion of sanding—of refining—was my meditation. It had been a long time since I could connect to this meditative state again. Before I knew it, I was finished and whistling. I couldn't remember the last time I'd whistled.

The modern style chair was done. I placed it down on the ground and studied it. I'd stain it another day.

Maybe Natalie would like to help me pick out a stain color for it. Now that I knew she was a fashion designer, she'd be wonderful at choosing colors.

CHAPTER TWENTY-SIX

NATALIE

After my shower, I went to look for Grayson, and noises drew me to his workshop. The door was left open, and I didn't want to interrupt his concentration. His eyes were fixated on the modern chair that looked almost animalistic—a clue to another aspect of him.

He was in the creative zone—a magical place that allowed creators and inventors the freedom of expression. It would be wrong to distract someone from that creative flow. I understood it because I'd experienced that every time I worked on my creation. The mind shut everything out, allowing the heart to take over.

He moved his whole body while he worked, and I couldn't keep my eyes from the muscles that flexed on his shoulders, back, arms, and legs.

I stood in the doorway, admiring him and his masterpiece. "It's beautiful."

Grayson whipped his attention to me and smiled. "You look fresh, clean, and stunning."

"Thank you. I didn't know you made furniture."

Grayson walked over to stand next to me, looking hotter than before in his now sweat-drenched T-shirt.

"I make furniture when I have time. Just for fun."

I walked around the chair, studying it. "You're very talented."

"I know," he said, rocking back on his heels, watching me.

"And very arrogant."

"It's confidence."

"The abstraction makes the chair look like unique architecture." I ran my fingers along the curved backing and tilted the chair. "From this angle, it also looks like an animal, some kind of fantastical beast."

"You see that too?" He grabbed the chair, turning it upside down and sideways. The way he held the chair and how his hands and fingers touched it showed a man who cherished his work.

Would he examine me the same way?

Did I want him to?

Yes, I do.

"It's a unique piece of furniture. Are you going to stain it?"

"I'm hoping you can help me pick out a color tomorrow."

I smiled. "I'd love to."

This was my link to Grayson: my ability to comprehend his creative side. But I also admired his business acumen because he'd succeeded whereas I had failed. I was struggling to keep House of LaRue afloat. Could I have done something different to prevent our financial downfall? I should have paid closer attention to the finances even though the CFO, Aunt Estelle, should have taken care of everything. Numbers weren't my forte.

"Sounds like a plan." He gestured to the chair. "Have a seat. You're the first person to test it out. Give me your thoughts."

Joy leaped in me. "Are you sure? Don't you want to sit on it first?"

"I want to see *you* sit on it." His eyes flickered with heat.

His high sexuality demanded I comply. I sat down on the wide seat, leaned back, and then turned to meet his gaze. "It's strong, sturdy, and ingenious."

"The unfinished chair had been sitting in storage for over a year." He held out his hand, and I didn't hesitate to place mine in his. He pulled me up flush against him, molding me into the hardness of his body.

I sighed, and his eyes dipped to my mouth. I didn't know it was possible to smell hard work, discipline, and determination on someone. But right now, his body offered that scent. God, it was sexy as hell.

I enjoyed looking at him in a powerful suit, all business and demanding, but now I devoured this handyman version of him—the soul beneath the expensive suit. How could any woman resist a man with a brilliant mind and extremely skillful hands?

"You helped me finish it, so you get to sit in it."

"Me? How?" I turned to the chair. "I didn't do anything."

"You sparked my desire to work on it. I wasn't inspired to complete it until today."

His comment blew at my heart, causing it to twirl like a dandelion puff that sent florets of joy flying through me.

"Maybe it's all the hiking we did earlier," I replied. "Nature and a good heart rate are healing essentials."

He smiled, but didn't offer a retort.

Was anyone ever ready to face something that could change them forever? The way he excited my body, how my heart raced at the mention of his name, and my muscles tightened at the sight of his face revealed the power he had over me.

I should have known from the beginning he would play a major role in my life, even when our connection started out with disagreements. But those weren't normal disagreements —at least I didn't think they were. Did people have disagreements where sexual innuendos were peppered in like condiments?

Fly like a dandelion seed and see where it takes you.

There were moments in life when you knew there wouldn't be another opportunity like this. Tonight was that moment for me. I was ready to change my life. I didn't know where it would take me, but I desperately wanted to know.

This man could speak to me without using words. He used his delicious food, his unique furniture, and his marvelous tree house to show me who he was. I was ready to discover more of him and of myself tonight.

My body shivered in fear and excitement.

CHAPTER TWENTY-SEVEN

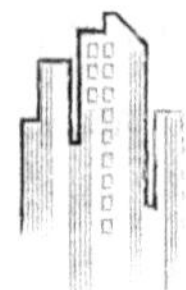

After a quick shower to wash off the sweat and dirt, we settled down for dinner that arrived early from the delivery service. When we finished, Natalie helped me clear the table. We chatted and acted like a couple who had been together forever.

"Want to go for a quick walk? The fireflies will come out in about an hour or so." It was seven in the evening, and the sun had descended, creating a pink hue in the sky. "Or we can watch the sunset from the balcony of the top suite."

A glint of mischief glittered in her eyes. "I'm going to read for two hours, then I'll meet you in the backyard by the outdoor furniture."

Two hours? She'd rather read than watch the sunset with me? What was she up to?

"What book are you reading?"

"Something I want to learn."

Intrigue rose in me. "What do you want to learn?"

"Something innovative."

"Like what?"

"Like something . . . *dirty*." She emphasized it with an exaggerated French accent that made it sound even dirtier. My cock perked up like a cat on alert. Now I was desperate to find out.

"Do you need help?" What the fuck happened to my voice?

She smiled. "You can help by relaxing and making sure we have snacks for our evening under the stars."

"Are we watching a dirty movie?"

Her eyes gleamed with amusement. "I'm going to *architect* a bedtime story for you. You'll have the sweetest dreams tonight."

Fuck. This woman knew how to negotiate. She knew about the erotic dream I'd had of her, and now she wanted me to experience it again? Who would decline that kind of offer?

"Since we've been collaborating on the Three Point Park project, you've learned about properties and real estate."

She nodded. "I have. It's all about location, location, location, right?" Her eyes went to the bulge in my shorts.

"That's right."

"I'll make sure to craft a compelling bedtime story for you, McDimple."

Natalie could arouse me by simply tempting me with a bedtime story. What the hell was wrong with me? The only person who had ever told me a bedtime story was my mother. But I had a feeling Natalie's story wasn't my mother's kind of story.

I'd never been more excited about a bedtime story until tonight. I'd been willing to lose the bet to her. Now that I knew her real identity, I was more curious why she wanted me to replace The Prism. Was that the main reason she was in Providence?

I cupped her face with both hands. "You have two hours to show up, buttercup. If you're a second late, I'll come find you and punish you."

CHAPTER TWENTY-EIGHT

NATALIE

Once I got inside my room, I locked the door, giggled, and danced around like a fool. Spontaneity had its own high, and my body thrummed with excitement. My heart wanted to jump out of my chest as I improvised a plan to seduce Grayson. This man needed something wild and outside of the box.

What had I never done before? I had an idea, but I flipped through my mind in case there was a better one hidden somewhere. Nothing compared to the insane concept swirling in my head. It made me nervous just thinking about it. Tonight was the perfect opportunity to try something new. It could fail miserably. Or it could be the most courageous idea I'd ever acted on. Sometimes too much planning ruined the joy.

Opening the drawer, I pulled out the only negligee I'd brought with me. It was made of soft red lace that was partially see-through. Ribbons tied the bra together at the center. Being in the fashion industry, I had contacts at facilities that produced garments for other brands. House of

LaRue didn't make super sexy lingerie. Ours had an elegant and classy appearance. But I was often in the mood for something more risqué, something edgier. This mini vacation was time for myself, so I brought it along on my trip. Wearing it made me feel sexy, even though I hadn't planned on anyone seeing me in it.

It was the perfect outfit for the act I wanted to perform for him. Doubt whispered into my ear. What if I didn't do it right? What if Grayson didn't like me in this lingerie dancing for him?

Stop it. If he doesn't like it, it's his loss.

I just needed one night with him to satisfy this aching desire burning inside me. I didn't know where things would go after tonight, but I didn't want to taint the moment by thinking about it. My time in Providence was limited, which meant my time with Grayson was also temporary. I had to use the time wisely and take advantage of every moment I had with him.

After changing into my lacy bra and panties, I studied myself in the standing mirror and admired how the lace enhanced my breasts and butt. Yoga wasn't just for the mind; the results showed in my body. I had to keep up with that and self-defense classes before my muscles turned back to mush.

I sat down at my desk, searching for how to do a proper lap dance for Grayson. I had no idea where the courage to do that came from, but I wanted to please him. This moment would change things between us. But then again, things had already escalated to where all I had to do was think about him, and I'd need a change in panties. It was inevitable.

After scrolling through a few options, I chose a video and followed the instructor. The girl was a fitness guru with an amazing body, making the moves look easy. I didn't bring any high heels, so I walked on my tiptoes, pretending I had them on. I followed her moves, strutting my hips as I walked around the chair, imagining Grayson sitting on it.

On my second round, I tripped and stumbled to the floor. *Oh, my God.* Embarrassment flooded me even though no one was around. Laughing to myself, I got back up and resumed the practice. The bedtime story I wanted to tell him was how I would seduce him. I prayed I wouldn't fall because that would be an unforgettable plot twist—not the kind I'd want anyone to remember. He'd probably gotten a lot of lap dances. Insecurity crawled up my spine, but I shrugged it off.

I was a fashion designer, dammit. Creativity flowed in my blood. I could do this. I could design my own lap dance.

I blinked at the thought. Why didn't I think about this earlier?

Because you've been too frightened to fail. Fear clouds judgment.

This was unfamiliar territory for me. I'd never wanted a man like this or planned a seduction where I had to learn a new skill.

A designer shouldn't fear anything. A designer took risks. It wasn't that I didn't take risks; I did to an extent. But this was different. Being with Grayson wasn't like designing a garment. A garment didn't have feelings. I could only assume his feelings for me. What if he didn't want me the way I wanted him? Relationships were a risk, and I'd made bad choices in the past. The last thing I needed was a repetition.

After watching a few more videos, I sat on the bed to let my body absorb all the moves from the various instructors. I got up, shook my muscles loose, and strutted around the room like a runway model, pausing and resting on my hip. Then I tossed a provocative look over my shoulder, slinking around the chair. I didn't fall this time. Points for me.

I had an imaginary conversation with an invisible Grayson in my head and laughed until the alarm on my phone beeped, reminding me it was time for my bedtime story.

CHAPTER TWENTY-NINE

GRAYSON

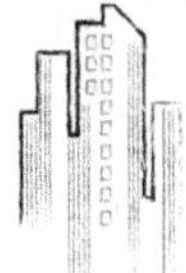

Sitting on the long bench beside the stand with a plate of fruits, cookies, a bottle of wine, wine glasses, and napkins, I looked up toward Natalie's suite. What was Natalie doing up there laughing like that? Was she on the phone with one of her friends? Was she reading a humorous book?

She probably forgot The Fortress was secluded in the woods, and any loud sound she made echoed. The genuine joy in her laugh put a smile on my face. The night had gone dark, and the surrounding lights automatically turned on, offering a soft glow around the tree house. Fireflies flew around the bushes, making them appear like stars swimming in the dark. I turned off some lights so she could see the stars better.

I checked my watch to see if I could go up and disrupt her, but I heard footsteps. Rising from the bench, I turned toward her, and my heart swelled, followed by my cock. She had on makeup and wore a summer dress that stopped just below her knees.

"Hello," she said in a smoky voice as she walked over,

pulling the chair I'd recently finished closer to the bench. Then she placed her phone on the bench.

"Wow." I twirled her around. "Did I miss the memo? You said a bedtime story at the bench and not a date in the city, right?"

"Just a date here at this beautiful tree house with the unique chair."

"I'm underdressed. I didn't bring anything fancy with me."

She placed a hand on my chest. "It's okay. You won't need clothes for this story, McDimple."

"Show me." I yanked her closer, clasping a hand to her firm ass. "What kind of filthy fairytale are you telling me? I'm dying to know."

"The kind that will make this chair come to life." Smiling, she nudged me down to the chair that she had inspired me to finish and stood between my legs. My cock tented my shorts.

My throat dried when she bent down, hovering over my lips like a feather, tantalizing me. "Do you want to strip me, Grayson? Are you willing to lose the bet to have me tonight?"

Fuuuck. She had no idea I'd already planned on ravaging her, regardless of the bet. No property could compete with my desire for her. I'd give her any building she wanted.

I pressed my face to her bosom, inhaled her perfume, and reached back to unzip her dress. It pooled to the floor to reveal a stunning body adorned with fuck-me-now lingerie. Red just became my favorite color.

"You're trying to kill me, aren't you?" I didn't recognize the raspy voice that escaped my mouth.

My throat tightened. Her skin glowed from the soft lighting, making her appear like a moon goddess.

Unable to resist, I reached for her, but she stepped away. "Not yet. Story, remember?" She pressed something on her phone, and music played—the kind of music piped into a strip club.

"I don't need a story, Natalie." Could she hear the desperation in my voice?

Ignoring me, she strutted around the chair, forcing me to follow her with my gaze. I took in her full breasts, lovely curves, and marvelous ass as she walked and posed in front of me, pausing at various intervals to give me that sexy look as though she were a model. She was better than any model I'd ever encountered.

Natalie was giving me the most alluring dance under the stars, and I wanted to remember every single detail of it. Tonight would be ours. I may lose the bet willingly, but I'd already won the one thing I wanted most: her.

She stopped in front of me, braced her hands on either side of my shoulders, and shimmied her breasts. "Once upon a time, there was this crazy woman who was attracted to a crazy man who kept arguing with her." Then she turned, bent over, and wiggled her ass. When I saw parts of her center, I forgot how to breathe.

I grabbed her buttocks, loving the smoothness of her skin against my palm.

Moaning, she whirled to face me, sat on my lap, and looped her arms around my neck. "Touching will cost you, McDimple."

Cursing, I fished out my wallet, pulled out my black American Express card, and slid it into her panties. "All yours, buttercup."

Looking down at the card that peeked through the lace, she gyrated her hips against me, following the rhythm of the music. The friction intensified the heat, and my cock pleaded for release. I'd never been this aroused.

"Let me show you the pin." My mouth nipped at her neck, kissing down to the top of her breasts. With my fingers, I traced the invisible numbers on her skin, followed by my tongue. I drew digits over the impeccable mounds that rose and fell. "Did you get the numbers?"

"No," she breathed.

"Then I'll have to show you in other ways."

"I need to finish the story . . ." She trailed off, watching my movement.

I dragged an open mouth over the see-through bra, hovering at the peak that begged for attention.

"The crazy woman didn't want to like him," she continued.

"Why not?" I asked as I kissed my way back up her neck.

"Because he seemed dangerous," she breathed, her lips centimeters from mine.

"How so?"

"She feared he might not want her the same way."

One hand clasped over her breast. "Oh, baby, he *wants* you bad."

"How bad?" Her eyes dared me.

"So bad, he's willing to lose the bet."

She smiled. "Prove it."

My lips crushed to hers, and the restraints that held my desire in check broke free. An explosion of need poured out of me. She moaned, opening her mouth, and my tongue dove in. Her eager tongue slashed against mine, showing how much she wanted me too. Her passion made me feel alive.

The vicious heat that burst in my blood screamed for more. More of Natalie. More of this power surging through me as though my life just got a jump start. I wanted to devour all of her—her heart, her dreams, her wishes, her soul—and make her part of me. It didn't make any sense, but it felt right.

Her hand fisted into my hair, tugging while she kissed me wildly. The passion in her fueled my need. Her reckless response drove my hands to the ribbon at her bra. I yanked at the bow, and the bra fell open. Nudging it off her, my hand clasped over a breast and played with her pointed nipple. She purred, sucking on my tongue. This was better than the erotic dream I'd had of her.

If I could taste a dream, it would be her—sweet, addictive, and powerful. The taste of her raged through me. Needing to see her, I broke the kiss and stared into her passionate blue eyes that contained the mysterious deep sea and the bright sky. Two kinds of blues swam around her pupils. If the eyes were windows into the soul, then hers invited me in. She was a mystical goddess, coming to take me elsewhere. I'd go wherever she wanted.

I wanted to gorge myself on her in greedy bites until this craving subsided.

My gaze found her gorgeous breasts. "You are absolutely beautiful." I captured a nipple and suckled it like a desperate man finally finding his salvation. But the more I took, the more I craved.

"Grayson," she cried, arching her back, offering me whatever I wanted. Making out on this chair was something I didn't imagine, but it was sexy as hell, and I'd make sure no one would touch it except for us two.

"Make note of my pin, buttercup." I adored her breasts, suckling slowly so she could register numbers.

"I don't want it." Her fingers dug into my hair, holding me in place.

And that made me cherish her even more.

I looked up at her and loved the wash of pink over her face and the sated eyes meeting mine. So much desire radiated from her. I pulled at the ties on her panties, tossing them aside. My credit card thudded to the floor. I'd get it later. My palm found her center. "I'm giving you a happy ending to this bedtime story."

She whimpered when I shoved two fingers into her wet center, pumping slowly. Her body became malleable to my touch.

"Is this proof enough, buttercup? You're mine."

She didn't respond, looking down at my hand, claiming what belonged to me.

"Grayson." More juices poured onto my palm, and I fucking loved it.

Her body glistened with sweat, and I was still fully clothed. I didn't know when the music on her phone stopped. The only sounds that I heard were her moans, her sighs, and the wetness of my finger exploring her.

I removed my fingers and let her watch me lick them. "I'm going to fuck you from all angles as promised."

Even though I lost the bet, relinquished The Prism, and had no right to claim what I wanted, she didn't object to my demands. The desire in her eyes burned my skin. She wanted me just as much.

I scooped her into my arms and brought her over to the cushioned cot. Her naked body glowed as she propped on an elbow, watching me strip off my clothes in swiftness. She sat up and gaped at my arousal. Her mouth opened, and her pink tongue snuck out, licking her bottom lip.

"Oh, my God. He's a beast." She clasped a hand over me, stroking gently.

"He thinks of you a lot."

A seductive smile formed on her lips. "Then I have to show him my appreciation." Her mouth came over me, and all thoughts from my brain vanished.

Sensations blazed through my body as her warm mouth welcomed my cock. Her exquisite tongue did amazing things, sending fiery blood roaring through my veins.

I knew she was creative, but fucking hell, the way her tongue maneuvered along my length with proficiency and around my crown with mastery earned her top-notch seductress.

CHAPTER THIRTY

NATALIE

I'd never felt freer as I did tonight. Seeing his desire for me turned me on more than I realized.

His beautiful cock filled my mouth with heat and passion. He throbbed in my mouth, and I loved that I was responsible for his desperation. It made me feel powerful. Even though I'd won the bet, I wanted him to fuck me as he promised.

I couldn't deny my desire for him. My body wouldn't allow it.

"Baby." Grayson moaned and placed a gentle hand on my cheek.

I gazed up at him. "Yes?"

"Slow down. I have a lot planned for you." He nudged me back down onto the cushion, shifting one of my legs to the side at a forty-five-degree angle.

I pushed onto my elbows and bit my bottom lip with anticipation.

He dropped to his knees beside the cot and slid a hand

under my butt, lifting my center. "Let me show you the various angles an architect is good at. This is a straight angle." He lowered his mouth and swiped his tongue straight on my folds, then moved it up and down.

An electrical current raced up and down my body.

He moaned as he adored me. "You should already know the right angle, but let me remind you." His tongue slid into me, and I had to grip the sides of the cot to stabilize myself.

"Oh my God!" I cried out his name and begged, "More!"

"You're fucking glorious." He smiled against me, delivering my request with urgency.

I half-heard him saying reflex, obtuse, and acute angles as I floated into a well of bliss. My moans echoed into the night, and I didn't care if anyone heard me. I'd never experienced pleasure like this. No man had ever wanted me this way.

The hunger in his eyes held my heart, and I was falling toward something I didn't want to admit. So I focused on how he had my body at his command. I yielded to his mouth, surrendering to him, letting him discover me. There were no secrets left on my body for him. He knew every crevice, every sensitive part of me, and he honed in on them.

Tension rose in waves, and my body bowed, and burst in a powerful explosion. Pleasure rippled through me, forcing my face toward the night sky where stars twinkled.

"That's right, buttercup. I want tonight to be the best night you've ever had." His tongue fluttered intensely over me, sending another wave of pleasure that had me shouting his name.

"My name sounds like a god on your lips."

I let out a laugh, wanting to retort with something that negated his arrogance. But I'd be lying. "You're so good."

I felt the smile against my inner thigh as he nibbled his way up to my mouth. "I love how your body reacts to me." The tongue that had just adored my innermost parts traced over my lips. "And I especially love the way you taste."

He kissed me possessively, and then flipped me over so I was on all fours. My body was relaxed and pliable, ready for whatever he wanted next. I heard him reach for his shorts and rip open a condom.

The tip of his cock teased my entrance as his body pressed down on me. "Are you ready for another right-angle fuck?" He slapped my ass.

The way he talked aroused me. "Show me what you've got." I lifted my ass to him, taunting him.

He plunged into me hard. "You like that?"

I gasped as my muscles expanded, welcoming his massiveness. "Love it."

"You're so tight." He drove in deeper, faster, and groaned out dirty words that turned me on. "I've wanted you for so long." The soft words sounded like a private thought had escaped his mind and wasn't meant for me to hear, but I was glad I heard them.

Grayson straightened and gripped my hips with both hands, slamming into me. I loved every moment. My heart pounded as he thrust, the friction between us growing uncontrollably. My fingers dug into the cushions as a chill skipped along my spine. His body stiffened, and I smiled at his impending release.

With one mighty plunge, he groaned a loud, "Natalie!" His body trembled against me as liquid heat filled me. I sensed the throbbing of his cock inside me and knew I wanted more of him.

I thought this one night would remove him from my system, but all it did was intensify the need for more.

He lowered his chest to me, his warm breath on my ear. "That was unforgettable. And I loved your bedtime story style. I want one every night."

He removed his cock, reached for a roll of napkins, cleaned himself off, and tossed everything into the trash. Then he gathered me into his arms as we lay on the cot, staring at the stars.

We didn't speak for a while. Our breaths, our heartbeats, and the sounds of crickets created a peaceful melody that added magic to the night. I wondered if he was thinking the same thought I was.

I turned, studying his face. "This changes everything."

A part of me feared what he would say. What if it was just an impulsive statement when he said he wanted more of me? People said things when they were high on pleasure, making promises they couldn't keep. Once that adrenaline subsided, their minds could change. I'd experienced this with previous relationships, so it was natural for me to doubt his words.

He met my gaze with seriousness. "I know."

A sharp pain speared through me, tightening my chest. "No one has to know what happened here, Grayson. It's just one night. Things can return to normal tomorrow." I tried to extract myself from him, but he wouldn't let go.

"Hell, no. I'm not returning to a time without you." He tightened his grip on me. "'Normal' is being with you. I meant what I said. I want this every night, Natalie. We're dating from this moment on. You're mine starting now. I won't have it any other way. Does that work for you?"

I didn't know what to say, so I nodded.

He shifted, tossing one leg over my body, entrapping me in his embrace. "You're the only woman who's able to spark life into me again."

My heart leaped. "But you lost The Prism."

"And gained Natalie LaRue."

CHAPTER THIRTY-ONE

NATALIE

On the balcony of his suite, I sat and enjoyed breakfast, wondering how he knew my real identity. Last night, when he blurted out my name, I'd wanted to inquire, but he prevented that with his kiss and another wild sex session that carried on into his bedroom. My brain and body had been too exhausted to chat after that.

But now, with a clearer mind, I needed to know.

Sitting across from me in his T-shirt and shorts, he sipped his coffee and peered at me over the rim of his cup. "My day is complete when you're the first thing I see in the morning."

My cheeks flushed even though that comment was nothing compared to all the insane things he did to me during last night's marathon. His stamina was admirable, and my body was quite sore. He was a sex god, and I was the fortunate recipient, but I'd keep that thought to myself for now.

"When did you find out about me? Why didn't you say anything?"

"Just recently. I like to know the woman I'm attracted to. You had mystery written all over you from the beginning. It was only a matter of time until I found out."

I poked at the blueberry muffin. "What else did you find out?"

"How about I let you tell me *your* story when you're ready? What I know is irrelevant compared to what you want me to know. Information can be skewed. The truth comes from the individual, right?"

The sincerity in his eyes told me I could trust him. Moreover, it was how he didn't pressure me into doing anything. I had the option of when I wanted to share. That spoke volumes to me. With Rafael, he demanded with threats. With Grayson, he demanded indirectly, which still gave me free will. My power was never taken away from me, and I appreciated that more than he could ever know.

Maybe it was this quiet place that thrummed with serenity, or maybe it was the intimacy we'd shared last night where I surrendered to him, or maybe it was how he made me feel special that pushed me to trust him. It was a risk, but if I didn't take it, I'd never know what would happen.

Perhaps sharing my problems with someone else besides my family could help ease the stress.

"House of LaRue is having financial issues," I began. "There's a board meeting in a few months. The members will vote to sell the company to the Fontaine and Chalamet Group. They know nothing about fashion. I'm scared they'll dissolve all the hard work my parents and grandparents have put into the label." I blew out a breath, looking out at the sturdy trees against the gray sky, wondering how they stood against inclement weather. They survived, and so would I. But right now, I felt a bit lost.

"What caused the financial trouble in the first place?" he asked, his eyes steady and calm on me.

I shrugged. "Some poor investments. I'm not really sure. My focus was always on design. I didn't have time to ask my dad. He passed away over a year ago." I told him about Aunt Estelle and how she was the CFO who didn't get along with my mom and me. Before I knew it, he knew why I was here and more. "I'm sorry. I didn't mean to overload you with my family drama."

He reached across the table for my hand. "Don't ever apologize for telling me what troubles you. I want to know. You're my girlfriend. Don't forget that."

It felt surreal to have him address me that way. So much had changed in only a few days, and it scared me. Despite that, being with him made me feel safe and grounded, which was what I needed.

"My dad bought The Prism for me, but I don't know why. I can't find anything on the property." I looked at him. "That's why it can't be part of Three Point Park. I don't know what my dad's intention is for the building, and I need to find out."

"I'll help you."

Three unexpected words dropped into my heart like coins into a wishing pond. Warmth rippled out of my heart to everywhere in my body.

I flicked a gaze at him. "You don't have to. It's my problem, and you already have a full plate."

"But I want to. I'm good at delegating, and I can free up time to help the woman who tells me sexy bedtime stories."

I rolled my eyes. "Is that what I've become? Just a woman who tells you bedtime stories?"

"You're very talented, and you've incorporated that

talent into wonderful storytelling. I love the sexy plot twists you do with your mouth, buttercup."

"Shut up." Grinning with embarrassment, I broke off a piece of my muffin and whipped it at him.

Laughing, he dodged the attack, and a bird flew in and snatched the crumb away. Thunder boomed, and the sky darkened quickly.

"Let's go back inside. It's going to storm." He got up and extended a hand to me.

I placed mine in his, and the gesture illustrated something I didn't see until now—I wasn't alone anymore.

"What did the weather forecast say?" I glanced out the windows where the angry wind and rain had already begun to pound the trees.

"Thunderstorm with powerful winds."

Like life, Mother Nature brought on unexpected things, and all you could do was make the best of it.

After sharing my problems with Grayson, I felt the heavy load lift from my shoulders as though he'd taken half or even all of it. I had a few more days left at this retreat, and I wanted to enjoy them with him. I never expected to start an actual relationship with Grayson, but now I loved being his girlfriend.

I'd still need to go back to Paris, but maybe we could have a long-distance relationship . . . I didn't want to think about that now.

Lounging on the couch with him, I grabbed an architectural magazine and flipped through it. "You know things about me. Now, I have questions for you."

"Ask away." He draped an arm around me as I looked at interesting buildings around the world. "I know each designer has their signature style. What's yours? You have an eclectic style, but that could've been influenced by what your clients wanted. Is there something about your buildings that makes them *yours*? Like if you could design something with no restrictions, what would be your signature?"

He smiled. "Frank Lloyd Wright loved the fireplace. It was the center of the home. He had one in every building he designed. Sometimes he had a fireplace in every room." His eyes looked into me—into places I didn't even know. My stomach quivered from the intense gaze.

"Everyone loves a fireplace. It brings people together," I said.

Nodding, he continued, "Windows are my thing. I love them. They let in the light. Metaphorically, they allow me or the person in the building a peek at the outside world. In doing so, the outside world has a view into me—into the building. The more windows, the better. I like innovative designs where I can incorporate high-tech materials that haven't been used yet. I'm working with an MIT professor on a product that's similar to plastic, but it's organic and flexible. It's a fusion of materials from Earth and products manipulated by machine to replace glass and plastic. It's still in the works, but this is the direction of the world. We have to think outside the box to help the Earth."

I stared at him, absorbing the passion in his eyes, in his hand gestures, and his excited voice. I was thrilled for him. He had so much depth—a master who understood his mastery. And he had every right to be confident and arrogant about his work.

I asked more questions that turned the conversation to his WaterFyre Rising video game. "What inspired you to start the game?"

"We all have something we're passionate about. For my

friends and I, WaterFyre Rising gave us a way to create our own reality. That was our escape. Water and fire are opposite elements, but when you find the perfect chemistry between them, magic occurs. The 'waterfyre' is the life force in the game. With each new level, you gain new versions of waterfyre, giving you more power and opportunities."

I felt the love and the dedication vibrate from him.

"Let me show you." He grabbed a piece of paper and drew an abstraction of the portals he created in his Level Three game. "My theme is the power of illusion. The windows are portals. They're all different, and each one leads to a different world. Once the player enters the new world, it becomes a replica of their reality, but skewed. Some are upside down and others are parallel universes."

"That sounds incredible. I want to play."

He angled his head in surprise. "Do you play video games?"

"No, but this sounds interesting, and since you created it, I want to learn. I can give you feedback on the attire for your players."

His face brightened. "You read my mind. I'd love your thoughts on the clothing and accessories."

A vicious boom shook the ground as a flash of lightning sparked outside the window. The electricity went out, and darkness surrounded me. I dropped the magazine as panic mode set in.

Shit. Please, no.

My breathing became difficult, and I trembled uncontrollably.

I tried to breathe in and out, attempting to calm myself, but nothing worked. Why did I have to panic right now? In front of Grayson?

Embarrassment and shame flooded me. Of all things, they should be the least of my worries, but I couldn't stop the emotions. I didn't want him to see me broken and weak like this. I wanted him to see me as perfect.

"What's wrong? Are you okay?"

Curling into a ball, I wrapped my arms around my legs, pressing my face into the couch, and closing my eyes tight.

"Natalie, what's wrong?" he asked in a calm voice. "What do you need?"

"Light," I whispered. "Please turn on the light."

"Okay. I'll get some candles." He stroked my hair before he left.

I kept my eyes closed as I heard him shuffling around. Though the eerie sounds that used to overwhelm me weren't present today, my body remembered the trauma. I hated myself for not being able to fight it.

Seconds later, Grayson returned. "You can open your eyes now."

CHAPTER THIRTY-TWO

GRAYSON

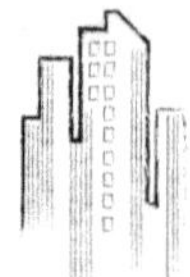

Concern overwhelmed me as I gathered Natalie's quivering body into my arms. I felt helpless, and I hated that. She looked pale and vulnerable, and I desperately wanted to know what triggered this panic in her.

Natalie opened her eyes, glanced at the three candles illuminating the room, and extracted herself from me.

Embarrassment flashed over her face. "Sorry about that."

"What did I say earlier? Never apologize for something that's troubling you."

She blew out a breath, still looking distraught.

"Can I get you anything to drink?"

"Water, please."

Trying to hold my emotions in check, I got up and studied her for a moment. There was more to her story, and she didn't trust me enough to share everything. That bothered me.

Patience, Grayson. You have things you haven't told her either.

"I'm going to turn on the generator too. Be right back."

It didn't take me long to activate the high-end generator I'd installed a couple of years ago after experiencing a similar situation. It had also been a thunderstorm that day, but I'd been alone. Now, I had Natalie.

Uncapping the water bottle, I offered it to her and sat down.

"Thanks." She took a sip and looked at me, tears brimming in her eyes. "I've been trying to fight this trauma for a while. It's not that bad today. I've experienced worse."

"Want to talk about it?" I didn't want to pressure her, but dammit, I wanted to know.

"You might see me differently after I tell you."

I gripped her chin with my fingers, turning her to face me. "Buttercup, if that's what you're worried about, scratch it. We all have flaws, including me. I'm not going to judge you. I care about you, and I want to know everything about your life."

CHAPTER THIRTY-THREE

NATALIE

Needing something to grasp, I reached for a throw pillow, holding onto it. I would've reached for Grayson's hand, but I was hesitant about his response to what I had to say. He said he wanted to know about my life, but the truth would paint me as a weak person. Would he still want to be with someone still struggling with a childhood trauma?

Maybe I was overanalyzing or being overly sensitive about things, but Grayson mattered to me too. I'd told no one my story, but the look in his eyes showed me he truly cared.

So my heart opened for him, and my past poured out.

"This will teach you to never touch my daughter again!" Aunt Estelle yanks my arm so tight it hurts.

"I'm sorry, Aunt Estelle. I promise I won't push Nicolette again."

It's her fault. She bullies me all the time. I can still feel the pain in my scalp when she pulls my hair and think it's funny. She calls me names and steals my sketchbook, scribbling all over it even when I beg her not to. But this time I couldn't stand it anymore. I fought back, but she fell and scraped her knees. Now, I'm in big trouble.

Hot tears stream down my face from fear and the pain from Aunt Estelle's grip. She digs her manicured nails into my arm. Where's she taking me?

Aunt Estelle is nice to me when Mommy and Daddy are around. But they're traveling for work. Aunt Estelle always offers to watch me, and Mommy thinks it's better to have family babysit than a stranger.

She yanks my arm, dragging me to a section of the house I haven't been to.

"Ow. My arm hurts, Aunt Estelle. Please stop."

When she looks at me, I know she hates me. Smiling, she tightens her grip. I don't know why she hates me.

She opens a door, and all I see is darkness. My body immediately trembles.

"No! No!" I shout. "Mommy! Daddy! Help me!" I try to break free from her, but she's a lot bigger than me. I'm only eight years old.

Aunt Estelle shoves me into the closet so hard that I fall on my back. She slams the door shut, and I hear a click. It's so dark, and I'm so scared. Mommy and Daddy know I'm afraid of the dark. They always leave the two nightlights on when I sleep.

My heart races as I squeeze my eyes shut. My body won't stop trembling as more tears run down my face. I pray this will be over soon.

Mommy and Daddy will come get me. I see them in my vision, and they make me feel better. After a moment, I gain some courage and open my eyes. Maybe there's a window or something. I let my eyes adjust, but I still can't see anything.

Then I hear a scary movie. Nicolette loves watching

horror movies, and she's playing it outside the door from her computer. "That's what you get for pushing me, brat!"

I cover my ears, not wanting to hear the terrifying music and the screams for help from the movie characters. Terror heightens in me.

Warm wetness fill my pants, and my stomach curl as shame overwhelms me. I haven't peed in my pants in so long, but I've never been this scared before. Why is it so hard to breathe? To move? The darkness starts shifting around me, forming terrifying shapes that look like scary faces. I close my eyes again, trying to shut them out.

"They're not real." Mommy's words echo in my head.

Keeping my eyes closed and imagining my parents are with me, I force myself to crawl away from the noises until the sounds become faint. My hand touches a wall, and I lie against it.

Grayson draped an arm around me, pulling me close. My head rested on his sturdy shoulder, and my hand felt the beating of his heart. I lifted my face to his. He looked like a man ready to hurt someone, and my heart opened a little more.

"You were only eight years old," he seethed. "I've never been physical with a woman, but right now, I want to kill her. She's the adult who should've protected you."

I took his hand in mine, squeezing it. "Growing up, I was always scared of the dark."

"Most kids are."

"But they grow out of it," I said as exhaustion weighed on me.

Every time these memories surfaced, I relived the trauma again. I should've been able to stop them by now, but I had a long way to go.

"I was getting better with the nightlights during bedtime. But that event cemented me to the fear. I couldn't escape it after that day. It comes and goes." I let out a laugh. "It's embarrassing, Grayson. I'm a grown woman, and I'm afraid of the dark."

He didn't reply right away. Instead, he rubbed circles on the top of my hand while his gaze fixated on the flickering candles. I loved the contemplative look on him. What was he thinking?

"Don't be," he said. "I don't think the darkness is the main reason for your trauma. Maybe it's part of it, but I think it's the culmination of everything you've experienced. A normal childhood fear together combined with the bullying and being locked in a closet, formed into a trauma. Your aunt failed you. She's family, but she mistreated you. Your body recoils and tries to hide because it remembers the terror, even now, after so many year. The darkness just reminded you of a time when you were scared."

I considered his comment for a moment. His explanation made sense. I'd never looked at the issue from that perspective before. But I guessed it was difficult to see clearly when it was your own problem.

"Maybe you're right. I never told anyone about what happened. Not even my parents."

"Why not?"

Sighing, I told him the rest of the story.

After reading Sartre's Being and Nothing *for a while, my eyes drift shut. But then I hear voices. Aunt Estelle is talking to someone. My skin tingles from her mean voice. I scoot closer to another wall, trying to get away, but she talks so loud. So demanding.*

"Ten million dollars isn't enough for what you want me to do. Twenty-five million."

"Done."

I don't know who she's talking to, but it's a man's voice. They keep talking business stuff and it's too boring. I don't know how long I've been in the closet, but I'm getting tired.

Mommy and Daddy are coming home tomorrow. I'll be brave and wait for them. I'm going to tell them everything.

The fantasy of being elsewhere relaxes me and I drift to sleep.

The bright light startles me. "Wake up, Natalie. Your parents will be here in two hours. Let's get you washed up."

Aunt Estelle carries me out, checks me over, and pats my hair. "I'm so sorry I forgot you were in here. Please forgive me." Her smile is fake, just like her daughter's.

I step away from her. "You left me there."

The smile fades. "You tell your parents this, and I will make sure you will never see them again. You understand me?"

The look in her eyes sends a chill down my body, and I believe her.

Grayson inhaled a slow breath as he tightened his arm around me. "No one will ever hurt you again."

CHAPTER THIRTY-FOUR

GRAYSON

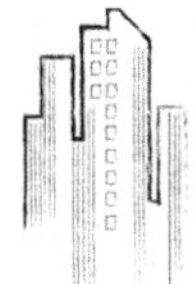

Estelle LaRue was an evil woman. She'd threatened her eight-year-old niece, who had been locked in a dark closet. No wonder Natalie was traumatized. I remembered the day Slash had warned me and my boys. If we mentioned anything about the crime we'd witnessed to another soul, the crime organization would come after us. I had been terrified for days, but I'd been fifteen years old. Natalie had only been eight.

My fingers curled into a tight fist. Her aunt needed to be punished.

I kissed her head. "I can help you overcome your fear. Have you thought about therapy?"

Trauma often blocked a person from healing. It had done that to Audri, with her fear of fire. She had thought fire was her phobia, but it was the guilt that crippled her: she was alive while my dad and her pet had perished.

She nodded. "I tried for a few years when I got older, but it didn't help."

"Maybe they were diagnosing it incorrectly. I can help you."

"How?"

"By experiencing the dark with you."

Natalie had to understand that the dark wasn't the main reason for her fear, but she had to acknowledge this on her own. I'd be there along the way to help her.

For the last few days of our vacation, Natalie and I spent time in the dark before bedtime. We turned off all the lights and lay in bed chatting. The darkness cocooned us, and there was a peacefulness to it. At first, she stiffened, but I held her against me.

"I find the darkness peaceful. It's a retreat into yourself— a place where secrets are stored. I think most people fear the unknown, and the darkness is sort of like that because you can't see anything. But not being able to see allows you to *feel* more, you know?"

She touched the stubble on my chin. "I didn't know you were so wise."

"Well, I had to upgrade my mind since I'm with a woman who reads philosophy."

Minutes turned into hours, and she relaxed as we talked about random things. I behaved in bed, knowing that she needed my help more than my sexual desire for her. She told me about her high school days, and I told her about mine. We discussed our previous relationships, and jealousy made me grunt several times. But her kisses soothed the irritation.

"Do you have something that's crippled your mental state?" she asked.

"Yes." I shifted on my side to twirl a lock of her hair between my fingers, loving its softness.

"What is it?"

"My uncle, Derek."

She was the first woman to hear about my trauma, my betrayal. How could I not share it with her, when she'd spilled her family's dirty laundry to me? We all had shit to deal with.

I told her a brief version of my unforgettable story, and how I'd been struggling with facing Derek. She didn't need to know all the details because there was already too much darkness around her. I had to protect her.

"It's time you face him too. Avoidance doesn't solve anything. It's just a temporary bandage. Peel it off so you can move on."

I tapped her nose, but didn't reply. I wondered if she knew she was peeling off her bandage by immersing herself in darkness with me.

We talked until she fell asleep in my arms. That was my version of therapy for her. She experienced the darkness in a way that was nonthreatening. With my presence and our conversations, she forgot about the fear. Perhaps the repetition would become a habit, and the habit would help her realize that the dark wasn't her enemy. It could be her salvation, like it was mine.

While she slept beside me, I flicked on the light to look at her. I couldn't believe how things had changed between us. She was now sleeping in my bed, looking serene.

No one would hurt her again. That was my pledge to the earth and the sky. Helping Natalie had pushed me to make the first step toward my healing.

Tucking my arms behind my head, I planned on visiting Derek. It was time for me to face my wound.

CHAPTER THIRTY-FIVE

NATALIE

It had been three weeks since our vacation in Vermont. I hadn't mentioned my relationship with Grayson to my friends yet. They had a gazillion questions for me, but I also had questions for them. They could have easily said The Fortress belonged to Grayson, but nope, not a peep. We planned on meeting up soon, and I couldn't wait to share my retreat experience with my girls.

Yes, they were my girls.

I had to tell them about my real identity. There was no need to hide anything any longer. After getting back, I immediately put in my resignation and was now officially unemployed. There wasn't much I could do to retrieve information on The Prism there. I'd rather spend the time exploring other avenues. I had to get out of city employment before someone discovered who I was and got me arrested for lying. I preferred to leave quietly.

With the extra time on my hands, I'd been spending it with Grayson at his place, understanding him more. It felt normal, natural, and cozy to be with him.

Last night, I slept over at Grayson's place because I was accompanying him to a charity event today. I walked into his dressing room as he adjusted the French cuff on his shirt. I wore his oversized T-shirt, which stopped at my thighs. If only he could see what I wore underneath his shirt. Friskiness was in the air, and I was going to do something about it.

"Why aren't you dressed yet?" he asked, looking at me as though he could see through the T-shirt.

"We've got time." Since he caused the friskiness in me, he'd have to resolve it. "Would you like me to pick out a tie for you?"

"I was just going to ask you." He'd worn the red tie I'd gotten him for his birthday several times, but he needed more simple designs.

Walking around his massive dressing room, I surveyed how his clothes were organized into sections.

"Do you have a stylist? The color schemes are well thought out." I browsed the racks of dress shirts and casual shirts that made me think of the Pantone booklet I received yearly for the color trend forecast. A good stylist could transform a person's appearance. He had a fabulous one.

"Bianca was great."

Jealousy squirmed in me. "Well, these corduroy and denim jackets belong over there with the casualwear. What else did she do for you?" Annoyance crept into my voice, making my words come out like sharp knives.

Grayson remained quiet, so I whirled around and found him grinning at me. He was wearing a crisp white shirt that cut him as a dashing, cultured man with a brilliant mind and skillful hands that made magic happen. He could bring fantasy into reality. That was what I'd learned at The Fortress. That was where we'd bared ourselves to each other, literally and figuratively. He knew my flaws, and I knew some of his.

His grin widened as he swept a gaze over me.

"What?" I asked with a pout.

"You're jealous." A cocky smirk appeared on his lips.

I rolled my eyes, even though he was right. "These casual jackets don't belong with the suiting. Every stylist should know that." I moved them over to their appropriate section.

He came up behind me, wrapped his arms around my waist, and dropped a kiss on my shoulder. A sizzle zipped through me.

"Don't dodge the topic. I love that you're jealous." He nibbled my skin. "I'm looking for a new stylist because Bianca moved away with her *girlfriend*."

"Oh." A smile crept onto my lips as I turned, looping my arms around his neck. "I'm not for hire, McDimple, but I can assist you for a price."

"You have my credit card." His eyes flickered with heat. "Do you need me to remind you of my pin?"

My body shivered, remembering how he had given me the code, which I didn't remember. I had my own cards, but I loved that he trusted me.

"I've got it memorized." I lied. "You should be more careful about giving out your pin number like that."

"You're the first woman I've offered it to, and you haven't used it. Why?" He tucked a lock of hair behind my ear.

"Because I have my own." I poked his dimple playfully. "I know most women would have gone on a shopping spree."

"But you're not most women. You're *my* woman—smart, creative, and tenacious. You constantly surprise me."

You inspire me to surprise myself.

"The unpredictable stuff keeps things exciting. That's

true for your architectural designs and for fashion as well. If you can make people accept the unexpected with ease, then there's power there, correct?"

He tapped my chin. "Absolutely. Power isn't always about how loud or strong something is. Sometimes, subtle things speak louder."

Like how my heart hums for you. Like how my stomach flips when I think of you. Like the nerves dancing around in my body, preparing to do something unpredictable.

"You weren't afraid I'd take advantage of you? Or was that number fake?" I asked.

I didn't want anyone taking advantage of me. Rafael wanted to marry me because my family's name made him look good. Appearances mattered to people with money and status. And I had thought about using him to help my company recover. Things that twist the truth never worked out well. I'd never wanted Grayson to think I was using him.

"It's real, buttercup. Like I said, you're the first woman I offered the card to." He cupped my buttock and squeezed. "You make me lose my mind. I can't think straight when I'm with you."

The urge to please him skipped down my spine. I loved this new side of me. The feeling reminded me of the thrill I got when I created an ensemble that spoke to my soul.

"I suppose we both lose our minds when we're together." I turned to the drawer filled with neatly displayed ties, all organized according to color, from solids to patterns. He had a varied selection he probably received from ex-lovers as gifts, but I didn't inquire. I was here now in his dressing room, and *I* was the one choosing his accessory from now on.

My fingers skimmed past the tie I'd bought him and stopped at another tie that suited him.

"This one." I held up a red tie with slim silver lines running across it, reminding me of his architectural style.

"How did you know I was thinking of that one?"

I shrugged. "A wild guess."

He watched as I looped the tie around his neck, creating a unique knot.

"I could never master any fancy knots. My normal is just a Windsor. What's this one called?"

"The Natalie knot." I grinned. "It's a twist on the Eldredge knot."

"You're tying me to you? It's an eternal link, love. You can't get rid of me now." He placed his hand on my lower back, pressing me to him.

"Being tied to me comes with a fine print."

"Like what?"

"Like becoming my model when my menswear collection is finished." I ran a hand over one of his shoulders. "You have the perfect build, the height, the face to be the ambassador for my collection." My lips hovered over his. "Most of all, you have this deadly dimple that could sell underwear like hotcakes."

He laughed, deepening the dimple. "What do I get out of it?"

"Free clothes." I smiled.

"You're some negotiator, buttercup. I'll sign up for anything except modeling underwear. I'll do that *only* for you. My mom might have a heart attack if she saw me in a magazine wearing nothing but undies. Hell, my friends would print it out, tape it all over my house, and give me a copy on my eightieth birthday. I know this because that's exactly what I'd do to them."

Speaking of Mrs. Wu, I hadn't met her yet. She'd been

traveling with friends, but I spoke to her over the phone when Grayson mentioned he had a girlfriend. She wanted to meet me as soon as she got back. I didn't know why, but I was nervous about it.

Grayson had a nice package that would sell. However, I was too selfish to display him to the world. I wanted him to be my sinful secret.

He narrowed his eyes at me. "Whatever is going on in your head must be dirty because those sexy lips and lust-filled eyes are telling a very interesting story. Are you imagining me as your naked model?"

"How did you know, Monsieur Wu?" I clasped his hand, dragged him over to the armchair across from the three-way mirror, and pushed him down into the seat.

His eyebrow arched. "What are you up to, Mademoiselle LaRue?"

I walked across the room to my phone, searched for the instrumental song, and hit play. Remaining there, I looked over at him sitting in his armchair like a king with a powerful red tie, all hot and bothered.

"I'm wondering how I can repay your generosity. You gave me your black American Express card to use. So I'm returning the favor with a Natalie Express card." I placed a card I'd made with the cardstock on the table and stripped off the T-shirt, revealing the black lingerie he'd gotten me.

His gaze perused my body, heating me up as though his eyes were his hands. From across the room, his desire pushed me to my knees.

"You're fucking hot," he groaned. His face transformed into that of a predator.

"There are six digits to my pin." I crawled over to him like a lioness ready to devour her mate.

He leaned forward, watching me.

"Pay attention to the six ways I'm going to love you." I reached the armchair, kneeled between his legs, unzipped his pants, and wrapped my fingers over his burning hot cock.

"How often can I use the Natalie Express card?" He breathed heavily, gripping the armchair.

"Whenever you want. It doesn't expire."

CHAPTER THIRTY-SIX

GRAYSON

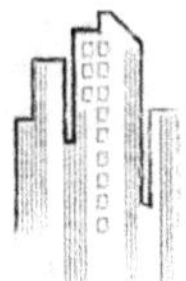

A half-hour later, I tucked the Natalie Express card into my wallet with every intention of using it nightly. That woman's creativity was unparalleled.

While she went to change to get ready for the event, I moved my clothes around, making more room for her. There was plenty of storage space for her belongings in any of the other four bedrooms, but I wanted her things in my dressing room. I'd never made room in my closet for any woman. The previous girlfriends left their belongings in the guest bedrooms, but I'd never offered or attempted to shift things around for them.

Natalie was the magnetic pull on my compass. I did things because of her.

I took out my sweaters and knit tops, placing them on the marble counter. I'd put them in another drawer later. Or better yet, I could ask if she wanted to help me reorganize and update my wardrobe. As I placed my favorite sweater—which I'd never worn—aside, Natalie strode in, siphoning the breath out of me.

She left me not only speechless, but bewildered. I'd seen beautiful women. They surrounded me, and I had easy access to them, but the captivating woman standing before me came from elsewhere.

I had seen the red dress hanging on the door, but she brought it to life. Natalie was a walking masterpiece in sexy straps with a tailored bodice and a skirt that accentuated her curves. Her blonde hair was swept to the side with a sparkly accessory that matched the simple moon-shaped studs in her ears.

She walked up to me, and my heart melted. I didn't know what that phrase meant until this moment. Warmth oozed from the center of my chest, spreading to every part of my body.

"You okay there?" She touched my face, and the gentleness added more warmth and something else.

What the hell was happening to me? For a moment, I stepped outside of myself.

Stepping back in, I yanked her to me, letting her feel my arousal. "If you keep turning me on, we're going to be late to the event."

"I'm glad you approve of the dress." She smiled, turned to the marble counter, and gasped. Her gaze fixated on a garment, and she broke away from me and walked toward it.

"Where did you get this?" Her lips trembled.

I came up beside her as she unfolded a sweater that had cost me three hundred thousand dollars. "In Paris at a silent auction. One of my clients invited me. The sweater caught my eye. There's no label on it. I'd never seen anything like it. It looked like a unique piece of architecture."

Tears glittered in her eyes. "That's *my* sweater. I knitted it for the auction anonymously. I didn't want people to know it was me in case no one bought it." She held it close to her body, closing her eyes for a moment before opening them to look at me. "But *you* did. Have you worn it?"

How had I not seen her at the auction? At that time, I had eyes on many things, including several women. Even if I saw her, would I have noticed the zing in my body? Probably not. I was a different man back then. My emotions had only skimmed the surface. But now, my feelings came from a deep place.

"No. I was afraid I'd ruin it. I didn't see you at the auction."

I didn't remember it being crowded, but I'd been in a rush to catch my flight back.

"Once I saw the sweater on the mannequin, I left. I was too nervous." She ran her fingers over the gray yarn. "This sweater meant so much to me. I'd always wanted to branch off and create a new collection from LaRue, but I feared no one would like it. That's something every creator fears. But deep down, I had to do it."

"You listened to your intuition." I offered her a tissue.

"Thanks." She dabbed at her eyes carefully. "I don't want to redo my makeup."

"Don't. You're beautiful with or without makeup."

She smiled. "I don't want to look like a monster walking beside you." Her fingers hovered over the masculine buckles that secured the asymmetric collar on the sweater. "Out of all the people in the world, *you* purchased it."

"I connected with that masterpiece because I understood the mastery that went into it."

"That means a lot to me, Grayson." She looked at the sweater the way a mother adored her baby, with love, devotion, and wonder.

My jaw tightened. "Who crushed your confidence? Was it your aunt?" I wanted them to feel the pain they'd bestowed on her.

"No one in particular. Aunt Estelle doesn't know about my passion. She couldn't care less. It's more about responsibility. I couldn't detach from the LaRue brand because it's my family. There's duty and legacy there. But I wanted something for myself, even though I wasn't sure if it would be well received."

I tipped up her chin. "You're a spectacular designer, and I'm glad you made it. It's my favorite piece of clothing. I'm not just saying that because you're mine. I'm giving you an objective critique. This sweater has design features I love. The various stitches—not sure what they're called—create unique textures that beg to be touched." I tugged up the collar. "The asymmetrical collar drew me to it. The buckles give it a military look—power, vision, intellect. You portrayed a story with a sweater."

She smiled, and my world brightened. "How can it be your favorite when you haven't even worn it?"

I kissed her temple. "I'm fond of its exceptional creator, so everything she creates will be my favorite."

She folded the sweater back, and I made a mental note to wear it as soon as the weather cooled off.

"I've always wondered who bought it. You left an anonymous donation at the auction and took it that day. There was no shipping address on record."

"After spending so much on it, I had to make sure it came home with me. I didn't want to risk it getting lost during delivery."

She embraced me. "Thank you for keeping my dream alive."

"No one is allowed to crush your dreams. Not even me."

"Ditto." She narrowed her eyes. "Give me the name of anyone who wants to destroy yours. I'm very handy with scissors, needles, and other sharp tools. I'll tear them apart and stitch them back together so that they won't even recognize themselves."

The conversation took on a whole new trajectory. "Remind me not to piss you off."

Laughing, she gripped my hand. "That's a nice reminder that just because I've struggled internally doesn't mean I'm weak."

"No, buttercup. Weakness is when you surrender and bury your dream. Courage is when you drag that dream through the mud to make it real despite what the world tells you. You have admirable courage."

"Let's get to the event before I strip you out of that gorgeous tux and show you how courageous I am."

I stopped in my steps. "That sounds more interesting than a visit to the museum. How about we stay home?"

Her laughter sent joy ascending like a superstructure inside me.

CHAPTER THIRTY-SEVEN

NATALIE

Grayson and I browsed the Mount Centauri Museum, which wasn't as large as the Metropolitan or the Guggenheim museums in New York or even the MFA in Boston. The Mount Centauri Museum was spacious and cozy and not quite as intimidating as the larger museums.

"Is there a special exhibit this evening?"

"There's Egyptian art on display for the next few weeks, but this event is for the Keeping the Vision charity. Aiden Kellwood's wife, Tasha, is passionate about this. I've heard wonderful things about this charity focused on women. He's also one of the investors for the WaterFyre Rising video game."

I read up on the cause and loved that there was a place to help women in need.

After Grayson introduced me to some acquaintances, we headed toward the Egyptian art exhibit. A handsome man with dark hair approached us and offered a hand to Grayson. He held a stylish cane and walked with a slight limp. "So glad you made it tonight."

"Attikus." Grayson shook his hand. "It's a fabulous event. This is Natalie."

"Very nice to meet you." He gripped my hand firmly.

"Do you have a minute, Grayson? I'd like to discuss a project with you." Attikus turned to me. "It won't take long, Natalie. I'll return him to you in less than ten minutes."

"No worries. I'll give myself a tour."

"I'll come find you." Grayson pulled me close, kissing me on the lips as though marking me in front of other men. He whispered, "I've canceled on him too many times. The last time was at the bookstore with you."

Smiling, I placed a hand on Grayson's cheek. "Take your time."

I walked into the spacious room where Egyptian sculptures, jewelry, and artwork were displayed on the walls and stands. Figurines of Egyptian goddesses caught my attention. I didn't get far when a chill ran down my body, warning me.

"Natalie, darling. I've finally found you."

I stiffened at the familiar voice.

Rafael stood next to me and placed a hand on my lower back. The touch stung my skin. I tried to step away from him, but he clasped my waist tighter, nudging me out of the room. His dark hair had grown past his ears. The brown eyes still harbored contempt and deception. His face had gotten thinner, and he looked stressed. He wore a white tuxedo, which always made him stand out in the crowd, but he couldn't measure up to the man who held back the dark so that I could heal.

"What are you doing here? I'm not going back with you."

"You're coming with me if you want to save your family. You *will* marry me." The commanding tone and the tense face portrayed a desperate man. "Your dad's plane crash wasn't an accident, Natalie. Come with me, and I'll tell you everything."

What was he talking about? The knots in my stomach tightened on top of one another. I had to know about my dad's death.

"Fine."

Rafael took me out to the Egyptian room and down a hall to a room where no one was in sight.

"What do you mean his plane crash wasn't an accident? How do you know this? Are you lying just to get me here? There's nothing between us. I've moved on, and so have you."

"You're going back to Paris with me. We're getting married, and you'll be saving your husband and your fashion brand. I've got an event next week. The paparazzi will be there. It'll boost our personas and businesses. Our union will benefit both of us."

I flicked him a disgusted gaze. "You don't get it, Rafael. I'm *not* marrying you. The engagement was a mistake from the beginning. I'm not interested in a business transaction. We don't love each other. Go home. Find another girl. You don't have a problem with that. How about Elise or Chloe?"

"I want *you*."

"Let's be clear. You want the LaRue name, not me."

He raked a gaze down my body. "I want you too." He gripped my ass, and I slapped him, making my way out of the room. He reached for my arm, whirled me around, gripped my throat, and pushed me against the wall with his body pressing hard into mine. "Don't you walk away from me! You need to learn how to—"

Rafael's body flew away from me, and Grayson's fist connected with the creep's face. Rafael regained his composure as embarrassment coupled with anger flashed in his eyes. "You're the fucker who killed Adonis."

"No, you did." Grayson's voice was calm, but lethal, like a cobra surveying its prey. "You killed him and framed me. I've got a solid alibi. I heard he died from a gunshot wound. The cops are closing in on you."

Rafael's chin ticked with dismay. "I didn't kill him, but yeah, I framed you." A sly smile formed on his lips. "Anyone who touches my property deserves to be punished." He looked at me.

Grayson stood between Rafael and me, his fingers flexing for battle. I sensed a dangerous storm erupting, so I interlaced my fingers with his, hoping that would calm him.

"Natalie is my girlfriend. It's in your best interest to stay away from her."

Rafael glared at our joined hands, then at me. "Slut."

Grayson released my hand and charged at him. They fought with their bodies, fists, and legs. Grayson dodged a long arm and swung an uppercut that connected to Rafael's chin. He punched him again before shoving Rafael against the wall with his forearm at his throat.

"Call her that again and I *will* kill you." The violence in Grayson's voice chilled me. "You as much as speak her name, walk into the same room as her, or even think about her—I'll kill you. I'll make sure everyone at Caputo Holdings knows how sick you are with young kids. Do you understand me?"

What was Grayson referring to?

Rafael's eyes widened, but I wasn't sure if it resulted from Grayson's threat or if he was struggling to breathe.

"Do. You. Understand. Me?"

Rafael nodded, trying to yank Grayson's forearm away.

Fearing Grayson might kill Rafael, I said, "I'm okay, Grayson. Let him go."

Grayson released Rafael but kept his glare on him. If there was ever a glare that sliced like swords, this was it. My skin crawled from the promised threat.

Two security guards arrived, surrounded by four people who probably went to get help after witnessing the altercation.

"Is everything okay here?" The tall security guard walked up and examined the artifacts and paintings, probably making sure nothing was damaged.

I hadn't realized I'd been trembling until Grayson wrapped his arm around my waist. "Everything's fine with me. Check on him."

"Are you okay, sir?" asked the shorter security guard with the bald head.

Rafael rubbed his chin, face, and neck before straightening his tuxedo. "Fine." He shot Grayson a look before leaving the room abruptly. Image was important to Rafael, so he'd want to exit as fast as he could, fearing bad press. Had something happened to him? I hadn't seen this kind of desperation in him before.

How did he know I'd be attending this event? What did he know about my dad's death?

After speaking to the security guards and Attikus, who owned the museum, we could stay for the rest of the event.

Grayson led me to a private washroom, locked the door, and surveyed me. "Are you okay?" The tense lines between his eyebrows and his taut jaw showed he was still reeling from the fight.

I took his hand in mine, examining his fingers. "I'm okay. How's your hand? Does it hurt?"

"Yeah, it's throbbing to kill him. He hurt you." His fingers touched the marks on my arm. "What did he say to you?"

"He wants me to go back home and marry him."

"Fuck, no."

The lethal look in his eyes would make most men cower, but there was something about it that attracted me. Something was wrong with me for finding that flash of heat—the danger—alluring. I wasn't afraid of him.

I sensed his anger and placed my hand on his chest, rubbing gently. "He also told me my dad's plane crash wasn't an accident."

"He could've been lying to lure you away from me. But I'll look into it."

Several emotions swam across his handsome face. A war between possession, lust, and fear battled within him. He was in pain because of me. Somehow, I could sense his pain, and I wanted to ease it for him.

He should know I had no intention of leaving him for Rafael. Grayson was the only man I wanted.

"I'll replace the button for you." I ran my finger over the spot where the button should have been. It probably flew off the tuxedo during the fight.

I had questions about my dad's plane crash, but that could wait. This troubled man with the tense face needed my reassurance.

GRAYSON

I clasped her hand. "I don't care about the fucking button. I have other suits."

Natalie had no idea what had transpired within me when I found her in that room with him. At first, I had thought they were being intimate, so I stood there watching them. That horrible mistake cut me to the core. If I had intervened sooner, I would've prevented him from hurting her. If I had trusted her, I wouldn't have had to witness the fear on her face. It had been Rafael's threats that snapped me out of my stupidity.

I cursed at myself for being an idiot.

Not everyone will betray you.

Rage boiled inside of me, seeing her helpless. The level of violence I wanted to enact on the fucking asshole was something new to me. I'd never felt it before. It was a high-voltage current that singed my blood. I became someone else —something else. The monster in me unleashed.

A protectiveness—a possessiveness—stormed through me like a typhoon. Violent, raw, and relentless.

Right now, I didn't care about anything but her. I needed to touch her, taste her. She was the only one who could subdue this raging storm.

I cupped her face and devoured her mouth. She returned the kiss with the same urgency. Then I whirled her around so her back rested on my chest, allowing her to see herself in the mirror. I yanked up her dress, palmed her center, and slipped my fingers under her tiny thong, claiming her. My buttercup was already wet for me.

"You're mine." I shoved two fingers into her, pumping fast.

"I'm yours. Do as you please." With her dress bunched on her back, she bent over the counter, taunting me with her gorgeous ass.

I dropped my pants and boxers, releasing my cock. "Fuck, I don't have a condom."

"It's okay. I'm on the pill, and I trust you."

I. Trust. You.

Those words were my salvation. I should have trusted her earlier.

Gripping her ass and yanking her thong aside, I plunged into her, letting out a loud groan as her muscles contracted to welcome me. The rawness of my cock in her core was the best thing I'd ever experienced. No more condoms from now on.

I drove into her fast and hard, watching her reflection in the mirror as I possessed her. With each thrust, she moaned my name. She met my gaze, and the lust in her eyes spurred me on. Natalie could make me want so damn much.

I could listen to her moans all day.

"Grayson!" She looked at me when she came, and it was the most beautiful sight.

Tension coiled so tight that my body trembled for release. A massive eruption and then liquid heat filled her. "I love being inside you."

"And I love having you inside me." She squeezed her internal muscles and showed me what she meant.

I extracted myself, smearing my cum on her thong and inner thighs like a signature.

I placed my pheromones on her so every man knew she belonged to me. I removed her underwear and swung it in front of her. "It has me and you on it. I'm keeping it."

Her mouth dropped open as she stared at her soaked thong. "That's one of my favorite pairs of underwear."

I straightened out her dress. "I'll buy you as many as you want."

That night, after Natalie fell asleep, I went to my office and gave the PI more assignments. Even though I'd threatened Rafael, I knew he'd retaliate sooner or later. A man like him wouldn't let the embarrassment from the museum slide.

I had to ensure I was steps ahead of him.

CHAPTER THIRTY-NINE

NATALIE

I spent the morning speaking to my mom, maneuvering my way by asking her about the plane crash without giving her details. I didn't know if there was any truth to Rafael's claim, so I'd save her the heartache. The last thing she needed was a rumor dredging up all the old hurts. Mom only knew Dad had gone on a business trip, and that was it. From our conversation, Mom didn't remember anything out of the ordinary.

I'd stop by RISD or call them to inquire about my dad soon. Maybe they'd remember something that could help me solve his case.

Noon came, and I prepared the sweaters that had arrived yesterday, placed them in a large shopping bag, and prepared to meet up with the girls. I had to tell them the truth about my identity. What if they hated me for lying?

Audri had reserved a table inside the Krazee Tavern. As Remington's girlfriend, she got the best services and ate for free. As her friends, we got similar treatment.

I placed the shopping bag at my feet, waiting for all the

girls to take their seats. Vivian was at another seminar, so she couldn't make this luncheon. I'd give her the sweater later.

Glancing at my friends, I crossed my arms, giving Audri and Kiera—who sat next to me—the evil eye. "You guys knew."

"Knew what?" Audri bit the sweet potato fry, chewed, swallowed, and flicked an innocent look at Kiera. "Do you know what she's talking about?"

"Color me confused. I have no clue." Kiera finished a tortilla chip.

I rolled my eyes.

Michelle furrowed her eyebrows. "Did I miss a memo?"

Audri elbowed her. "You know that 'retreat' I told you about?"

Michelle twisted her lips, thinking. "Oh . . . *OH* . . ." Her eyes sparkled. "How was it? I wanted to text you so bad, but decided you needed time alone."

Audri leaned into the table. "Did you like the tree house? It's one of a kind, isn't it?"

Kiera wiggled her eyebrows. "How's the *wood*?"

Audri's mouth dropped open. "Oh my God, Kiera! That's my brother."

"What? I'm referring to the quality of the wood he chose to build the magnificent tree house." She sipped her iced tea as though it wasn't obvious what she was truly aiming at.

I bit my bottom lip, stifling a laugh.

Michelle's shoulders shook from laughing. "Kiera's head is always full of sexual innuendos."

"Hey, I'm a wealth of information, and you should consider yourself lucky I'm sharing this knowledge with you. It's not my fault I have high sexuality." She turned to me.

"By the way, is 'penisse' pronounced like 'finesse' in French? Your language has a way of making things sound elegant."

"No." I shook my head, never having heard anyone pronounce the English word like that. I placed a hand on Kiera's forehead. "Did you catch a virus? Are you in need of a 'penisse' fix?"

Everyone laughed, even Kiera. "We're talking about *you*, babe. Besides, I'm just saying what you guys are all thinking."

Audri protested by lifting a hand. "I'm not thinking that at all."

"Neither am I," Michelle said.

"Grayson is a hot guy, but I'm not attracted to him. But I know who is." Kiera narrowed her eyes at me.

Curiosity sparked in me. "How do you know?"

"Anyone who witnessed the two of you debating at his birthday party knows." Kiera picked a grape tomato from her salad and popped it into her mouth. "The way he got jealous of you and Arrow was quite cute."

"He kept staring at you. I felt the heat rising in the room. The guys didn't notice, but we did. We're good at these things." Michelle bit into her chicken wrap.

"I'd never seen Grayson like that," Audri said. "You put the spark back in his eyes."

"We knew something was up." Kiera lifted a finger. "And we also knew you weren't ready to make a move. So when I had to go on that work assignment, it was the perfect opportunity for the two of you to hash it out." Her eyes glittered. "So, did you 'hash' it out in bed?"

Despite knowing they'd set me up, I couldn't help the smile that stretched across my face. I was one of them.

They'd accepted me into their group, and I became the recipient of this comradery I'd never experienced.

"We inducted you into the SSG group." Michelle winked.

"What's that?" I lifted an eyebrow. "Sounds interesting."

"Super Spy Girls. It used to be SSG 003, but we dropped the digits since there are more of us now. You and Vivian are new members. Our spy group is growing."

"What exactly does the group do?"

"Whatever we want," Kiera blurted.

She told me about Audri's mission of License to Kill and Michelle's From Iceland With Love.

"You girls are really something. I can't believe you set me up!" I loved these girls and wished I'd met them earlier. "What was my mission?"

"You need to name it," Audri said. "We don't know what happened at The Fortress that turned you into his girlfriend. Must have been something profound."

Memories swirled in my head, and my cheeks heated, remembering all the decadent things he did to me. He was magnificent at possessing me from various angles.

"My mission is The Man with the Golden Angle." I smirked, thinking about how I got the title.

Audri almost choked on her drink, laughing. "Oh, boy."

Michelle fanned herself with her hand.

"I assume the mission was successful?" Kiera asked.

All eyes were on me. I'd never shared anything about my relationship with anyone, but there was something about these girls that made me want to share.

"It was . . . *innovative.*"

After we finished lunch, I looked at them, nerves churning in my stomach at the other reason for meeting up.

"What's wrong?"

Michelle placed a hand on my shoulder.

"I have something to confess." Below the table, I interlaced my fingers.

The girls exchanged a confused look.

"You have ten kids in Paris?" Kiera asked.

"No." I smiled.

"Are you a serial killer?" Michelle inquired.

"No."

"Are you pregnant?" Audri eyed me. "You know 'golden angle' and all."

"No." I shook my head as tears rolled down my cheeks.

"You girls are the best. I've never had friends like you." I paused and inhaled a breath. My hands trembled under the table. "I'm so sorry I haven't been completely honest with you."

Audri gave me a clean napkin for my tears.

"My real name is Natalie LaRue." I dabbed my tears away.

Kiera held up a hand. "Wait a minute. LaRue, as in House of LaRue, the fashion brand?"

I nodded and told them the story of why I was in Providence.

"Sweetie, you should've told us sooner. We would've helped you," Audri said. "But I understand. You didn't know us well enough to trust us then."

"Are you mad?"

"Of course not," Michelle and Audri said simultaneously.

The knots in my stomach loosened.

"I am." Kiera flipped her brown hair over her shoulder, looking angry. But then a smile formed. "I'm mad you didn't tell me sooner so I could get a discount on that label!" She clapped her hands together, laughing.

I shoved at her playfully.

Reaching for the gift bag at my feet, I pulled out sweaters for each girl.

"Oh, wow. I *love* it." Audri held up the aqua-colored cashmere sweater made from textured yarn. "I can't wait to wear it."

Michelle got a lilac sweater, and Kiera got a meadow green one.

"Thank you, Natalie!" They both shouted.

My phone buzzed with a message from my mom. She hardly texted me. It was usually a phone call. While the girls reviewed their gifts, I replied to my mom.

Natalie: *Everything okay?*

Mom: *Can you make a trip back to Paris? It's urgent. Call me when you can.*

CHAPTER FORTY

GRAYSON

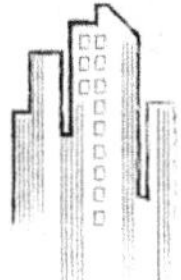

Natalie was leaving for Paris tomorrow, so I was spending as much time as I could with her today. I wanted to come with her, but she told me to remain here. I had several projects that needed my attention, but I wanted to go with her. She had become more important to me than my enterprise. Before Natalie, I'd always prioritized my projects. But things had shifted. That was something to think about later.

Rage had boiled in me seeing Rafael's hand gripping her throat and the unforgettable fear on her face. I had asked the PI to send an anonymous tip to a few investors I knew at Caputo Holdings. They saw an image of Rafael with two young kids. He looked unconscious in that photo, but that was enough to create chaos within the company. Investors didn't like anything that could tip the scale the wrong way in their business. The stocks on Caputo Holdings had been declining, which made me smile. Rafael was probably staying under the radar for now.

No one fucked with me or my woman.

Inside my office, I walked over to my desk and picked up

the model for The Prism that sat next to a blueprint I'd taken home for review. The mini model wasn't needed on the landmark display at work because it wasn't part of Three Point Park any longer. I planned on giving the model to Natalie for a keepsake because The Prism belonged to her.

I still needed to find a replacement for it. Two other properties showed potential, and I could offer the current owners a price they couldn't refuse, but I had to reevaluate my vision for the project.

Sitting at my desk, I checked my schedule on the computer. In two days, I'd visit Derek. If Natalie could face her fears, then I had to face mine.

I logged into Level Three of WaterFyre Rising and checked out the apparel Natalie had designed. One of the outfits was made from a high-tech fabric that adapted to the environment, allowing the characters to survive harsh terrain. In the water, the outfit grew gills so the character could swim and breathe underwater. In the air, it became lightweight wings. On land, the fabric acclimated to the character's body temperature, allowing the characters to warm up or cool off. After giving her a snapshot of my world, it was eye-opening to see what she created. I'd never shared my video game with anyone except my boys.

Natalie had made this game even more special to me. She was part of it now. I couldn't wait to show her the complete demo.

"Dinner's ready." Natalie popped into the doorway and gestured for me to follow her.

She wasn't a cook, but she'd brought prepared food where all she had to do was toss the components together onto nice plates. She was acquainting herself with the kitchen because of me, and that made all her meals exceptional.

"Come here." I crooked a finger at her.

"Why?" She looked at me suspiciously, but entered the office and plopped onto my lap.

I pulled out a small gift box. "For you."

"Why?" Her eyebrows furrowed as she stared at the box.

Most women would just open the damn gift box without question.

"Stop asking why. I can give my girlfriend gifts whenever I want. Open it."

Smiling, she lifted the lid and gasped. "Grayson . . . this is gorgeous. Is this a red diamond?" She touched the pendant with a gold rim around it.

"There are only about fifty red diamonds in existence. It's very rare. Let me put it on you." I placed the gold chain around her neck, admiring it on her.

"It must have cost a fortune." She examined it.

I shrugged. "Only the best for you. I want you to wear this and think of me when I'm not around. Don't take it off. It'll keep all those European men away from you."

She laughed. "Did you put a spell on it or something?"

"No, but that's not a bad idea. Do you have a spell book?"

Laughing, she looped her arms around my neck. "No, I don't. There's no need for any spells. I love the necklace. Thank you. I'm going to miss you, even though I'm only going for a few days." She kissed me hard, and we christened my office while she wore my necklace.

Dinner occurred two hours later.

CHAPTER FORTY-ONE

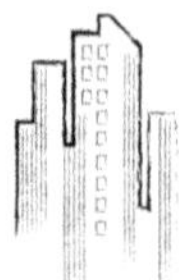

I stared at the pathetic man who had once been someone I had admired. Derek had gotten thinner, his cheeks hollower, and dark circles appeared under his eyes as though hell was sucking the life out of him. Had guilt been keeping him up at night? Or the fear that someone from the crime organization would sneak into his cell at any moment to end his life?

Sitting in front of Derek in prison with the glass panel between us symbolized many things for me. Despite our relationship growing up, there was now a wedge separating us. I stared at the man I once looked up to—the man I used to ask for advice.

Our eyes connected, and an onslaught of memories flooded my brain. I let them come to the surface so I could face them—get rid of them forever.

"You need to be careful with that." Uncle Derek points to the hammer in my hand. He's been teaching me how to build this tree house in the backyard. Audri prefers making weird jewelry and has no interest in building anything.

I hammer the final nail into the ladder that leads up to my tree house. I step back, admiring the workmanship. "It's awesome!"

Uncle Derek stands beside me, draping an arm around my shoulder. "You did a wonderful job, buddy. Better than some men I know. You have a great talent for interpreting concept." He ruffles my hair. "This brilliant brain of yours and your skillful hands will help you succeed in the future. You'll go far, kiddo. Don't let anyone stop you."

I smile at his belief in me. He's right—I enjoy building things. All the Lego collections I've had over the years help me build structures. Being able to see my idea come to life makes me so happy.

"Thanks for the cool birthday gift, Uncle Derek. It wouldn't have been finished so soon without your help. If Dad were still alive, he'd be so happy." My dad promised to help me build a tree house, but he died before that could happen.

"I'm sure he can see you from up there." Uncle Derek points to the sky. "And he's super proud of you the way I am."

I've done it, Daddy. This tree house is for you, too. I can show you all my building sketches when I'm done. I'm going to be the best architect!

"Now I'm a twelve-year-old with an awesome tree house that I helped build. My friends are going to be so jealous." I embrace him, appreciating all the time he spent teaching and showing me how to construct from my simple sketch. "You're good at building too. Why didn't you become an architect?"

"Nah." He shrugs. "My interest is in finance."

I laugh. "You love money."

"Who doesn't?" He sighs. "But there's a dark side to money. Just don't get yourself caught in it. You'll be trapped forever."

I scratch my head. "What do you mean?"

He smiles. "You're too young to understand, kiddo. When you're older, you'll know that money has a dark side."

"Like the guy in the black helmet from that sci-fi movie? He was good, then turned bad."

Uncle Derek nodded. "Yeah, something like that."

I supposed he taught me a few life lessons back then. There was a dark side to money. I'd seen how it corrupted people easily. There had been opportunities for me to make three times the money on projects, but I'd declined. I chose projects that aligned with my interests and didn't push me toward something I didn't resonate with. Growing up with a mom and a dad who taught me the value of money made me realize it should be respected, that it couldn't buy everything, and it couldn't make everyone happy. They always preferred to do things the right way and believed that hard-earned money had a special power all on its own—it attracted more of its kind and opened opportunities that weren't available to others.

Karma will always demand justice. That was what Dad used to say. He believed that karma would come when you least expected it to take away what mattered most to you. *So live life as though it's your last day.*

Being cautious didn't mean being stupid. I knew how to negotiate, and I made sure I was paid my worth.

Derek was in prison because of the dark side of money.

"What do you want from me?" I asked, trying not to show any emotion.

"To tell you the truth." He muttered and looked down at the table as though preventing the cameras from seeing his face. "My time here is limited."

I snorted. "You seem to be lasting longer than I expected." Leaning closer to the panel, I whispered, "The Trogyn's getting to you?"

"Shut up." Derek grunted, and his eyes showed he didn't like my comment.

I was going to tell him to fuck off, but then he lifted a finger, moving ever so slightly to the right of his shoulder. From the corner of my eye, I spotted a camera. Someone from the organization could be watching us.

Shit. I'd let my anger cloud my judgment. The last thing I needed was for the crime organization to connect me to him. Though I'd paid some guards to keep tabs on Derek, I didn't fully trust them. I made a mental note to request the PI hack into the prison's computer system to delete my visit.

Crossing my arms, I said, "So tell me the truth. I'm all ears."

"I made a huge mistake. I was blinded by money, greed, power, and jealousy." He swallowed, and his expression appeared genuine.

But I couldn't believe his words. Everything he'd said before had seemed genuine until the day he confessed to killing my dad. So no, I took his comments with more than a grain of salt.

"Money has an evil side. You warned me about it."

"I did." He nodded. "It consumed me. I got involved with extremely bad people—powerful people—and I couldn't get out. They're everywhere." He glanced down at his hands again.

"Why?"

I'd asked him that question on the day he confessed his crime, but his answer hadn't satisfied me. So now I inquired again, looking for closure.

Why would he kill my father—his biological brother?

"Because if I didn't, they were going to do it." His eyes hardened. "They'd have killed you, your mom, your dad, and your sister."

Those words were like blocks of ice in my stomach. "You placed my family in danger."

He pressed his lips into a thin line. "So I made a decision."

My voice went calm. "Don't make it sound like you saved us. You were part of the organization for a long time. What happened that made you kill my dad?"

"Someone tipped off the members, saying I was stealing money from them. I had to prove my loyalty. I was running my business, becoming a direct competitor to them. They didn't like it. I needed money to escape, but your father didn't want to get involved."

"What about loyalty to your family?"

Derek didn't answer me. I didn't need his answer. My question told him my feelings.

I sat up straighter, remembering the other reason for my visit. "Who are they? Where can I find them? I can't live my life constantly looking over my shoulder, wondering when they'll come at me."

I didn't dwell in their world, so they shouldn't have anything on me, but Derek was my uncle, so maybe that placed me on the radar.

"Do these people have information on me?" I asked.

Derek met my eyes. "They had videos of you, but I destroyed them."

Unable to reply, I blinked in surprise.

"A few days after the crime, a member discovered some recordings from nearby streets. The videos showed some teenagers flying drones. Some were blurry, some weren't. I was responsible for reviewing them." Derek looked at me, and for the first time since his betrayal, I saw the uncle I used to trust. It was the conviction glinting in his eyes. "I deleted them, told him that the videos were corrupted."

Fuck. He had known all this time?

Emotions churned in me, confusing me. I didn't know what to feel or what to say.

"And you didn't share this with anyone?"

He scrubbed a hand over his face. "No."

"Why?"

"I had my reasons."

That wasn't the answer I wanted. "You've sent me messages wanting to speak to me. Why?"

"Because it's time to right some wrongs." He leaned in and whispered. "If you want to destroy them, focus on the elite clubs. Like how you and your friends gather at the abandoned church, some of these members meet at elite clubs. Start there. You can't destroy them all at once. There are too many of them. You and your friends will fail. Attack one club at a time. Deflect. Create chaos. Continue on. Attacking from the shadows is how you'll win."

"But they dwell in the shadows."

"Then you find an abyss to work from." His jaw tightened as though he'd been planning this for a while. "If you plan on destroying them, you must keep those you love far away." A smile curled onto his lips. "That beautiful woman could get hurt in the crossfire."

I didn't even bother asking how he knew about my personal life. If I could keep tabs on him, he could do the same to me. How much money did he have left? I thought the authorities had taken everything from him.

Something flickered in his eyes. "There's a tunnel in the city—"

An explosion erupted somewhere in the prison, and the ground shook as though an earthquake had occurred. The lights flickered, and dust rained down on us from the ceiling tiles. A fluorescent light bulb shattered to the floor. Something crashed in the nearby room, and alarms blared. Then lights went out in half of the room. The guards emerged shouting with some carrying extinguishers.

"That tunnel is one way to attack them," Derek said.

"You need to get back into your cell." The guard yanked him away.

I rose from my seat as another guard came to escort me out.

"What happened?" I asked.

"Not sure. There's construction on a recent addition out back. Maybe they hit a gas line or something. It's not the first time." He shook his head. "It's best you leave, just in case."

I drove for a while before pulling over to the side of the road and texting the PI to delete videos of me visiting the prison, including any videos of me traveling to and from there. It was obvious someone was watching Derek, and I didn't want to be dragged into his shit.

CHAPTER FORTY-TWO

NATALIE

Wearing a floral dress and always looking fashionable, Mom led me to an unfamiliar café packed with people getting lunch. We sat outside at a table under a pergola adorned with beautiful vines crawling and draping over the beams like lovely curtains. The crowds of people drowned out the gentle music playing at the café. The ambiance would have been romantic with fewer people. I could take Grayson here one day.

It had only been a day since I last saw Grayson, and I already missed him tremendously. Was he thinking of me right now? I couldn't wait to call him later this evening.

"Why are you blushing?" Mom asked, holding up a hand. "Don't answer, I already know. When do I get to meet this special guy who makes my daughter blush at random?"

Mom had recently started wearing auburn bangs, which I loved on her. It made her look five years younger. Bangs wouldn't work on my face—I'd tried it.

"Soon." I wanted to plan a trip with Grayson so he could meet Mom. He'd been to Paris before, but I doubted he knew all the special shops that only residents knew. I wanted to show him around where I grew up. But right now, we both had too much going on.

"That necklace is beautiful on you." Mom gestured to the multimillion-dollar gemstone that I forgot to hide under my shirt. I only knew its price after googling how rare the red diamond was. I *loved* it, but I didn't want to attract unwelcome attention. From a distance, it looked like a ruby, which I preferred people to assume. Rubies were affordable. Red diamonds weren't. I'd rather keep the identity of the gem a secret.

Fearing my mom would ask more questions about the gem, I looked at my phone and asked, "When is she coming?"

Mom had run into Aunt Estelle's former housekeeper at a market, and Camille had some interesting information she wanted to share. A noisy place to meet was the perfect location to "accidentally" bump into old friends for a friendly chat.

"She'll be here soon."

The waitress came to take our orders. I wanted a *croque monsieur*, which was a delicious ham and cheese sandwich. Mom got the *jambon beurre* sandwich, another version of ham and cheese on a baguette.

Mom's eyes darted behind me. "Hi, Camille!" She stood from her seat and waved.

Camille looked to be in her late sixties, with short silver hair and a pretty face. She wore an adorable long skirt and a simple top with a gold poodle pin.

I'd seen Camille a few times at Aunt Estelle's home. She wasn't around when I'd been mistreated at my aunt's place.

"It's so good to see you. Are you out for lunch?" Mom

extended her hands, welcoming Camille in for a *faire la bise*. Air kissing was a common greeting amongst family, friends, and loved ones.

"Yes, indeed. Now that I'm retired, I look for places to enjoy my time." She looked at me and offered a kiss on each cheek. "You're more beautiful every day."

"Thank you. You look younger every day too." I pulled out a seat for her. "Please join us. What would you like to eat?"

"A strawberry *crêpe* with a side of fries would be lovely, thank you."

When the lunch arrived, Camille grabbed a fry.

Her hand shook a little, and I placed mine over hers, calming her nerves. "Thank you for coming. It means a lot to my family and me. No one will ever know you said anything to us." I squeezed her hand. "I promise."

Mom reiterated the same assurance.

Camille nodded. "I trust you both. It's just nerves." She sighed. "A week before the plane crashed, I overheard Estelle —I hope it's okay to address her this way now that I no longer work for her." She looked at Mom and me.

"Of course, Camille," Mom said.

"You were always nicer to me, Charlotte." Camille smiled and continued, "Estelle was speaking to someone on the phone. She often had conference calls in her office, but that day her windows were open. She had ordered me to replant the herbs she'd gotten from someone into bigger pots, so I was outside in the garden."

Camille paused for a sip of her tea as a nearby toddler screamed for his toy that had fallen to the ground.

"Take your time." Mom bit into her baguette.

Camille continued, "I heard her conversation. She said

something about disrupting a plane's engine. Then she spoke about money. It sounded like a negotiation of millions of dollars . . . I thought nothing about her phone call until I heard about Monsieur LaRue's plane crash." Sorrow haunted her eyes. "It seemed too eerie, and I feared for my safety. I wasn't sure if Estelle saw me working outside that day, so I made an excuse to retire early. It was time anyway."

Nausea gripped the muscles of my stomach.

Mom rubbed Camille's back while her face tensed, probably trying to calm the angry storm within.

Camille looked at Mom. "When I saw you at the store, I knew it was a sign from God. He wanted me to tell you what I knew."

"Thank you," Mom said with a trembling voice.

To lighten the mood, the rest of the conversation was about Camille's grandkids and how they wanted to go to Disney World in Florida. She didn't know it yet, but a family vacation would be my gift to Camille. She had given me valuable information, and I couldn't thank her enough.

This information showed the evil side of Aunt Estelle that I'd experienced as a child. Maybe I should have said something to my parents sooner. Guilt clawed at me.

How could I get the truth about the plane crash? There was no way Aunt Estelle would admit to it. She was a shrewd woman, and I had to take careful steps.

Who had she spoken to on the phone? Who was her accomplice? Why would she do this? For House of LaRue? I was entitled to the company, not her.

Once we got to my apartment, Mom said, "I've set up a meeting with her under the guise that you wanted to know the status of the new vendor who's producing our limited-edition trench coats."

"Are you okay?" I asked.

"No. I need a drink." She went to my wine cabinet and opened a new bottle of red wine. "Otherwise, I might go over there with the first weapon I can find and end that miserable woman. But that would leave you all alone and she'd win. I won't let the bitch win."

I embraced my mom, knowing she was hurt, angry, confused, and didn't know what to do.

"I'll drink with you."

After Mom passed out in my guest room, I followed suit in my room without calling Grayson.

CHAPTER FORTY-THREE

GRAYSON

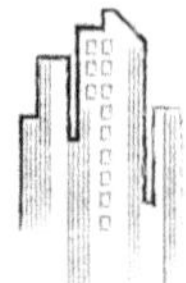

After a brief discussion with my friends regarding Derek's admission, I walked around my home office. Should I believe what he'd told me? After all he'd done, believing his words would be illogical, but instinct told me to trust him. Could I even trust my instincts?

Apparently, my friends and I hadn't been as careful as we'd thought. Who else had videos of a group of boys flying drones? At a glance, those videos would have shown teenagers having fun. But someone who had been present on the day of the crime would've suspected we might have seen or heard something. They could try to eliminate all evidence.

Had someone else found videos of us but hadn't come forward yet? That was a possibility that terrified me. A headache throbbed as I tried to figure out my next step.

Trying to calm myself, I walked to my desk to look at something with more hope. I picked up the mini model of The Prism, which Natalie had forgotten to take. I had to accompany her inside this building soon so she could investigate. Knowing her, she'd make another attempt. I couldn't let her go alone.

The PI had been bombarded with requests from me, including any information he could dig up on the building. That task hadn't been on his to-do list until recently. Hopefully, he'd have some useful information soon.

I stared at the printout of Three Point Park. Geometric shapes played an important role in architecture. As a child, I'd been good at piecing things together. Now, as a man with vision, I'd applied that ability to my life.

However, I'd been ignoring that ability. Why? Good question. Perhaps I was afraid to see the truth—my weakness. No man wanted to admit he had a weakness. Acknowledging that would be an absolute defeat.

But everything changed when Natalie entered my life like an unexpected beam of sunlight, cutting through the muck, going straight to my heart. As I got to know her, the sunray brightened, burning away the darkness, and I couldn't help but *see* the flaw within myself.

Derek had murdered my father; that was a fact. He took away my chance to bond with a man whose blood ran in my veins—the legacy I was supposed to carry. I could never forget or forgive Derek. But I understood what drove him to his demise. Greed. It fed on a man's soul, making him believe money gave him power, which he thought could fill the void in him.

Money carries darkness that can trap you forever.

I now understood that statement he'd told me so long ago.

If money was sunlight, too much of it blinded a man. Too little made a man see only the darkness, thus craving more sunlight.

The difference between me and Derek was that love had given me the ability to step back and look at myself from an objective perspective. I could detach myself from everything. A detached man started at zero—had nothing, wanted nothing. As I scanned the horizon from that zero axis, I knew where I stood and what I wanted.

I inhaled a breath as I faced the frightening flaw: I had loved Derek. He had been a father to me when I needed one. He'd helped me with homework, took me to games, and showed me how to build a tree house—a symbol of hope and a dream for a young boy who didn't recognize his capability. He helped me make the dream—that had also been my father's—come to fruition.

My chest constricted as I faced this revelation. A massive tidal wave washed over me in slow motion as I tried to grasp onto something stable.

Last year, the truth about Derek had crushed me, sending me into a frenzy where I didn't know what to feel. How could I have feelings for a man who had murdered my father? Wouldn't that be a betrayal? A storm of confusion and guilt had warred inside me from that day. I became a prisoner in my own hell.

Life asked no questions as it shifted. It was up to me to adjust, to find my landmark, or to be swept away.

I found my freedom because of Natalie, and that scared the shit out of me—even more than what I'd dealt with regarding Derek. I'd been lingering between acknowledging and dodging the truth for as long as I could. But everything had a catalyst—that one thing with the power to resurrect everything.

Natalie was my catalyst—the change that transformed me. I couldn't hide it anymore.

"I love her." The words flowed around my office.

My heart quickened, and my body jerked as an electrical current raced through me, charging my bodily cells awake. Then the thrill descended to a fulfilling calm, like having a cold beer on a humid day on the balcony of my tree house looking out at the peaceful forest.

That was love, and that was all I needed.

Natalie entered my soul and rebuilt me like she understood the blueprint of my heart. Every time she smiled, every time she kissed me, and every time she looked at me with those yearning eyes, I wanted to be a better man. For her.

But what if I failed?

Before Natalie, I approached life like a business—nothing could fail if I put in the effort and time. But the heart wasn't a business with guaranteed success. It was too precious and priceless.

Derek's warning flashed through my mind.

The danger that lurked around me could put Natalie at risk. The sun gave life to everything on Earth. She taught me the power of sunlight—that everything it touched came to life. She was the sunlight that resuscitated me to life again.

I'd do anything to protect her, but that protection came at a painful price.

CHAPTER FORTY-FOUR

GRAYSON

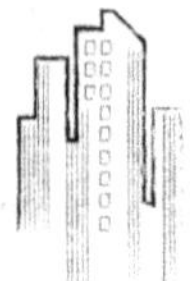

From the data I received, Rafael was staying in the New England area instead of being back in Europe. Tonight, he'd be at a sports bar in Boston.

Sliding onto the barstool by the pool tables, I studied Rafael. Short dark hair, tan skin, around six feet tall. He chatted with two men, dressed in black, probably bodyguards who had replaced Adonis.

I remembered Rafael saying he didn't kill Adonis. He admitted to framing me, so why would he lie about his bodyguard's death? If he hadn't killed Adonis, who had?

Working with the enemy hadn't been my preference, but I had things to discuss with Rafael. He had information I needed. We could benefit each other; this was the nature of business.

Life was a battlefield. In business, the field was filled with greedy people who fought to survive. I survived because I knew how to defend and offend. Tonight, Rafael would understand the meaning of "threat" and "collaboration." He could choose which one suited him most.

A few minutes later, Rafael turned, and our gazes connected. Shock, intrigue, and fear splashed on his face. He should be afraid of me. I knew his secrets.

With disdain on his face, he approached me, with his bodyguards following behind. "What do you want?"

"A chat." My eyes slid over to his men. "Alone."

He knew the owner of the sports bar and led me into a back room.

"You've done enough damage to my image. Caputo Holdings lost a lot of money recently, and my parents are fucking pissed. What's there to talk about?"

"Well, *I'm* pissed. You threatened my woman. You *hurt* her." I made sure he heard the emphasis.

His lips twitched, but he didn't reply.

"You have information I need." I sat down in the chair, gesturing for him to take a seat. "Sit and have a mature conversation with me. I have a business proposal for you. It could make you money."

Rafael's eyes lit up as he folded himself into the chair. "Go on."

"You're obviously tied up with dangerous people. What's up with young kids?"

Shame flashed over his face. "That was a one-time thing, and I was blackout drunk. They took pictures without me knowing and blackmailed me."

"So you know what it feels like to be framed?" A sardonic smile curved my lips. "You didn't kill Adonis?"

"No. He was the most loyal bodyguard."

"Who killed him?"

"No fucking clue."

"Did he have an assignment from you before his death?"

Rafael went quiet.

"If you want me to help you, then I need to know the truth."

"He was supposed to bring Natalie back at all costs." His eyes looked anywhere but at me. "The day he died, he was going to abduct her."

"The fuck!" I slammed a fist on the table, rattling a tray of empty shot glasses and mugs. "Anyone else involved? If there is, you'd best demand they disappear because I'll make sure they'll be six feet underground. Then I'll ensure you lose more than just your reputation."

"There's no one else," he replied quickly. "I didn't want to hurt her."

I snorted. "So why did you?"

He considered me for a moment, but didn't reply.

"She agreed to the marriage because Caputo Holdings was going to finance House of LaRue to help them bounce back. Were you going to help her?"

Rafael grabbed an empty shot glass from the tray and spun it on the table. "I made a deal for her."

"What kind of deal? With whom?" I demanded.

He stopped the shot glass, gripping it in his palm. "Why don't you tell me how you're going to help me? Then we can continue this discussion."

CHAPTER FORTY-FIVE

NATALIE

I extended my stay a few days in Paris to accompany my mom to meet with Aunt Estelle. On Saturday, Mom and I walked into the conference room at House of LaRue. It was the only time Aunt Estelle could see us before flying out to Shanghai. We had to discuss the production of our limited-edition trench coat collection for the next season with new vendors.

I rubbed my mom's back, giving her warmth and courage so she could endure this conversation without attacking Aunt Estelle.

Aunt Estelle looked up from her laptop and smiled. I wanted to run over and slap that look off her face. After hearing what Camille said, she needed to pay for her crime. Aunt Estelle wore a purple dress with her blonde hair in a French twist, looking cold and elegant. Two years younger than Dad, she'd been a widow for ten years. She'd spent her life overseeing LaRue with Dad until he passed. Her only daughter, Nicolette, had married a wealthy restaurateur and moved to Venice.

Aunt Estelle gestured for us to sit down. "It's so good to see you both. Natalie, how's your vacation so far? I'm surprised you came home just to follow up on a production."

"House of LaRue is important to me. I think about it all the time, even when I'm on vacation. Dad would have done the same, right?" I pulled out a chair for my mom and sat down beside her. "This trench coat collection is new, and I worry if our loyal customers will respond well."

"We're all worried about the status of LaRue, so it's natural for us to want it to succeed." Mom interlaced her fingers on the table.

Aunt Estelle sighed. "There's no need to worry. LaRue will continue to be loved by many. Once it sells—"

"It won't." I forced a smile on my face. "I won't let my family's legacy fall into the wrong hands. We don't know who these people are. They could be criminals, and that would taint our family's name."

"They're not criminals," she barked. "They're investors who are interested in helping us regain our status in the fashion industry. I don't understand why you'd be opposed."

"Eugene wouldn't have wanted this," Mom interjected.

"Eugene is *dead*, Charlotte." Her words fell like ice chips cutting into my flesh. "He can't help us. So *I* need to."

I'd never despised anyone as much as I did her. How could she speak about her brother in such a callous way?

"I'll do whatever I can to stop you from trying to sabotage LaRue—*your* heritage." Mom retorted.

"I'm the new CEO. You can't stop me." She looked at Mom and then me. The gleam in her eyes wavered between amusement, challenge, and suspicion.

Amused that anyone dared speak to her in that tone when she held the power to the company—which meant she thought she could cause trouble for me. If she could, she would've fired me already, but she couldn't.

"I certainly can," I said calmly. "I'm the heir to this company. You're just interim CEO until the board meeting is over."

She glared at me, and I sensed the wall of unspoken truth emerge. It had barbed wires that stabbed into my flesh. "You're still the same brat you were when you were little. Never does what she's told."

"How dare you speak about my daughter that way?" Mom asked, her patience thinning.

"Words don't hurt me, Mom. Aunt Estelle has an evil streak that's unraveling for the world to see." I glared at her. "It's natural to retaliate when someone bullies my family and me, right, Aunt Estelle?"

I was no longer a child full of fear. I was now an adult who could see the hatred in my aunt's eyes. She was on a mission to destroy the LaRue legacy. Why did she hate us so much?

"How much money is the Fontaine and Chalamet Group offering you for LaRue?"

"What the hell are you talking about?"

I couldn't hold back my suspicion any longer. "It makes sense. They must have offered you an irresistible deal. Money corrupts people just like the House of Gucci. They had family drama that dealt with betrayal and murder. Sometimes I wonder if House of LaRue is just like them."

I sensed my words drop like a pin to the floor, bouncing several times before lying still. The silence throbbed in the room as Aunt Estelle tilted her head at us. What was she thinking? Did my words insinuate her fear? Or was she too cold to even feel it?

A burst of laughter erupted from my aunt. "What is wrong with you? Are you accusing me of something? Are you *threatening* me?"

"Aunt Estelle, I wouldn't dare threaten you," I said in my most innocent voice. "I'm just a girl terrified she can't protect her father's legacy. And fear is mighty powerful."

A smile curved onto her lips. "I should have kept you locked in that closet back then. The little brat has grown into a big one."

"Right, just a little brat trying to catch up to you." Anger rose in my gut, but I tried my best not to show it.

I'd always considered myself a nice person, but at this moment, a monster formed in me. It had six arms with claws thrumming for violence, three eyes that shot out laser beams, and a giant mouth with rows of sharp teeth that could rip off her head in one swipe. The desire to reach across the table to kill her pulsed in me. But if I went to prison for murder, my mom would be devastated and alone, and my dad wouldn't get the justice he deserved. So I prayed to God to give me strength and patience.

Mom turned to me. "Did she lock you in a closet? When did this happen?"

Underneath the table, I placed a hand on my mom's thigh, comforting her. "Tell you later. Just know that I survived and I'm stronger and wiser because of it." I smiled at my aunt. "Thank you for that."

Survival meant seeing the positive in the negative. I had transformed from that event.

"So, are we done here? You obviously didn't come for an update on trench coats or new vendors."

"We're here for everything that has to do with LaRue. I want to make sure you're doing your job." I got out of my seat so I could walk around the room. "Did you know that there's a rumor Dad's plane crash wasn't an accident?"

I paused in my steps, watching her facial expression. No emotion, but her eyes revealed what her impassive expression tried to hide—fear. She was actually capable of that emotion.

"Is that right? Did you hear about that in the gossip rag that's always looking for its next headline? Why are you wasting time listening to hearsay? We have a company to save."

"I agree. We have to save LaRue. But I wonder if its demise was intentional." I shrugged and leaned against the conference table. "I want to know if my dad's death was an accident or murder. As his sister, I assumed you'd care and want to know too."

"Do I look like I have time for rumors? The next headline could be about me being a mistress to some prince in another country with triplets no one knew about."

"I'd believe that," I said and saw my mom smile.

Aunt Estelle's lips thinned, not finding the humor in my statement.

"Well, if that's all. I need to get going." She glanced at her watch and resumed typing on her computer.

"I've passed this information to the authorities. I'll let you know when they find something. If Dad's death was a murder, I'm sure the Fontaine and Chalamet Group won't be interested in acquiring a tainted company. Like you said, they're smart investors. A company that comes with bloody baggage isn't a wise investment at all. Wouldn't you agree?"

She stared at me, but the glint in her eyes and the shift in her seat showed I'd rattled her. What would she do now?

Inside my apartment, I sat on the cushioned window seat and stared out at the spectacular view of the Eiffel Tower. People came from all over the world to Paris—the city of love—for the sensual atmosphere it offered.

I could sense love in the air, but if you looked deeper—if you paused and listened—there was a darkness here as well. It slithered like the mist hiding in the crevices of the ancient architecture, hovering around the cracks in the cobblestones, listening to tourists' conversations, and clinging to the masks people wore to disguise their true selves.

Aunt Estelle always dressed like she belonged on a magazine cover, but the woman beneath the luxurious clothes and pricey makeup was a monster. What made her this way?

"Here." Mom offered me a warm cup of tea and sat down next to me.

"Thank you." The warmth of the teacup soothed my erratic nerves. I knew Mom had questions regarding me and the closet. Looking back, I'd been stupid not to share it with anyone. But I'd been terrified of losing my parents too.

After taking a sip, Mom looked at me. "Tell me about the incident."

Her face hardened as though she was trying to fight for something she didn't quite understand yet. Perhaps it was the lioness in her, wanting to protect her cub. Perhaps it was guilt knowing she hadn't been there for me when I needed her. Emotions billowed in her eyes, and I wanted to help her, letting her know I was okay.

The dam in me burst, and tears rolled down my face. I

couldn't have stopped them if I wanted to. I didn't even know I held so much pain in me.

Mom scooted closer and held me. "What happened to you, Natalie? Please tell me."

"Remember how you and Dad used to travel a lot for work? And you brought me to Aunt Estelle's?"

Mom stroked my hair like I was still a child. "Yes."

"Nicolette and I never got along. We fought one day. I defended myself and pushed her to the ground. She scraped her knees, and that made Aunt Estelle furious." I inhaled a breath. "She dragged me to the closet and locked me there until the next morning."

"In the dark?" Mom asked quietly.

I nodded and spared her the part where Nicolette played the horror movie. Mom was already in too much pain—I didn't want to add more pressure to her heart.

Mom tightened her arms around me, tears spilling from her eyes.

Her face strained when I told her about the threat. "She's an evil woman. I always had a feeling that she didn't love your dad the way he loved her. He was her big brother, so he got defensive whenever I said something bad about her."

Love blinded people, whether it was a family member or someone else. I was afraid to truly love anyone because of this. Was I seeing the truth for what it was, or was I seeing an illusion that could eventually hurt me?

Mom cupped my face in her hands. "My job is to protect you, Natalie. You should have told me." She dropped a kiss on my forehead. "Please don't ever keep anything like that from me again. No matter how old you are, you're still my little girl."

Nodding, I took my mom's hands in mine. "I will."

An uncomfortable knot twisted my stomach as I replayed the scene in the conference room with Aunt Estelle. I saw the hatred for my family in her eyes.

Mom had planned on meeting a few board members in the following weeks, hoping to sway their votes in favor of not selling LaRue.

Mom took my empty teacup, walked over to the sink, and washed it along with hers. "Now that you're not working at the City of Providence, do you want to come home?"

A hollow feeling formed in my stomach. I wasn't ready to leave Providence—leave Grayson.

"I still want to know why Dad bought me that building. The mystery around his death has widened with Camille's confession. Maybe the building is connected to his death? I feel like he wants me to find out. Otherwise, he wouldn't have sent the deed."

Mom dried her hands, leaned against the counter, and nodded. "You focus on that while I focus on the issue over here. I need to speak to my lawyer about this recent development."

I stood next to her. "Don't worry about me. I'll be fine. Grayson has been my support."

She placed a gentle hand on my cheek. "I'm so happy for you. You went through hell with Rafael. The engagement with him was a bad idea from the beginning."

"I was foolish."

"You were desperate to help your family, but I don't want that." Mom sighed. "House of LaRue is experiencing a transformation. That's part of business. I don't want its survival to be at the cost of my daughter's happiness. It's not worth it. Your dad wouldn't want it either. He'd rather the brand dissolve." She crossed her arms. "So, are things serious with Grayson? He's a fabulous architect. I googled him, you know."

I flicked her an amused look. "You did? And?"

"He's an interesting man. I'd rather not comment until I meet him in person so I can determine if he's a one-woman kind of man. My daughter doesn't share. She deserves the best."

Grayson's past had been splashed all over the internet. Images could paint an ugly story. Those stories cast him as a shallow playboy who changed partners like he changed his tie. I had thought the same, but the man I'd come to know had so much depth, I'd almost drowned in it.

It surprised me he hadn't gone after the tabloids for telling lies about him fathering a child with a social media influencer. But then again, I knew that once a lawsuit started, the paparazzi would only use the story for even more views. Gossip was a never-ending story.

A sense of protectiveness overcame me. "He's not like that, Mom. He's changed."

Her brows knitted in contemplation. "Sometimes love makes you see things differently. Keep *this* safe." She placed a hand over my heart. "A real man who loves you will protect you at all costs. He won't use you to gain anything."

Mom knew Rafael had wanted the LaRue name to gain access to more wealth.

I understood my mom's concern, which was why I was careful about revealing my heart to Grayson. I was in love with him. But I needed to keep that truth safe and tucked away for later.

Had I fallen for him because I needed someone during my weak moments? Or had I fallen for him because he was the only man who had opened my heart completely? I couldn't tell for sure. What if he didn't feel the same way? Dating someone and falling in love with them were different things. Love meant commitment. Was Grayson the kind of man who could commit to one woman forever?

I had to protect my heart. Safety held me in a protective cocoon, like a big coat keeping me warm. Unlike other men, Grayson had tugged on the sacred thread that kept me safe. The first kiss we'd shared was him yanking at the stitches, unraveling me like a garment opening at the seams.

Mom left for a spa treatment with some friends. I declined her invitation to join her. I wanted to take a warm bath at home.

My body ached, desperately needing a massage. I filled the bathtub with warm water, essential rose oils, and rose petals, hoping the self-care would relax me.

I stripped and stepped into the warm water, settling in. Leaning back, I stretched out my neck muscles, and my mind wandered to Grayson. What was Grayson doing now? I missed him so much. We'd only exchanged a few text messages since I left. I wanted to see him. In two days, I'd be back home.

Home in Providence. I considered it home already. What had been a temporary stay had turned into something more. Could I make it work? Living in Providence while overseeing LaRue?

Stop stressing. Focus on the bath.

A noise from outside the bathroom startled me. I stiffened, sitting up as my heart raced.

Who was in my apartment? I remembered locking the door when Mom left. As I prepared to get out of the tub to get my cell phone from the counter, the bathroom door swung open.

"Miss me?" Grayson stood in the doorway wearing dark jeans, a white button-up shirt with the sleeves rolled up to the elbows, and his dark hair all messy and sexy.

My heart rolled like a strawberry dipped in chocolate. It wanted to jump out of my chest and hop into his arms.

"What are you doing here? How did you get in?"

CHAPTER FORTY-SIX

GRAYSON

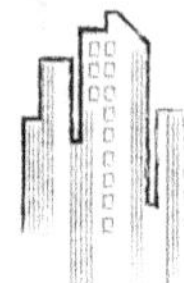

The past few days had been chaotic, and I'd never missed a woman the way I missed Natalie. After attending an opening ceremony for a building I'd designed for a movie producer in Los Angeles, I skipped the banquet and hopped on a plane to see my woman.

I walked over, sat on the bathtub ledge, and raked my eyes down her slick body, which was hidden by an abundance of red and pink rose petals.

Three candles flickered on a table beside the massive tub and gave off a sweet aroma. A book titled *The Discipline of Virtue and More* sat beside a bowl of crystals.

"My woman is reading the works of Descartes while naked in the tub. Makes me want to know what kind of kinky things she's thinking about."

Natalie cocked her head. "A woman needs to expand her mind to keep up with the ever-changing world ruled by patriarchal men who want to keep her down."

"I'm not those men. The only 'down' position I want you

in is where I can ravage you." I flicked my gaze to the spot between her thighs covered with petals.

Though lust swam in her eyes, she didn't retort, changing the topic. "How did you get in here? The door was locked."

Needing to touch her, I dipped my hand into the warm water, shoving away the petals, and my cock hardened seeing her bare body. She was so beautiful and all mine.

"I had a conversation with the security manager, telling him I was here to surprise my girlfriend. After checking my credentials, he let me in, and I gave him a generous tip. Money can solve a lot of things."

She'd only been gone for six days and it felt like it had been a year. This desperate yearning wasn't normal for me. Abandoning several multimillion-dollar projects so I could see her face was something new to me.

When I entered the apartment, I had expected her to be on the couch resting, but finding her naked in the bathtub had been a bonus.

"Seems I need to have a chat with André about letting in strangers."

The rose petals clinging to her body made her appear like a decorative appetizer, calling to me. My hand cupped her breast, kneading, and earning a delightful moan from her lips.

"We're not strangers, buttercup. I think we know each other pretty well." I teased her nipple between my fingers, and her eyes fluttered. "Did you think of me last night?"

Desire darkened her eyes. "Yes," she said in a breathy voice that also contained a plea.

My blood heated from the needy look on her face. My cock jerked with desperation. *Calm down, buddy.*

I wanted to jump into the bathtub that could fit three people, but seeing her facial expressions as I adored her with my fingers was more enticing at the moment. Every moan she released belonged to me.

"I missed you so damn much." Though I'd been working on leads about Derek and The Trogyn, I had to come to see her for several reasons. One was to make sure my love was okay. Two, to meet her mother, and three, to meet with a few people Rafael had mentioned to me.

But I'd keep the latter to myself because it would only give her anxiety. My intention was to protect her.

"What did you imagine?" I asked, loving the way her skin flushed from my touch.

Her chest rose and fell as I grabbed a rose petal and brushed it against one nipple, then the other. "You were here with me . . ."

"And."

"Doing all kinds of . . ."

"Hmm?" My eyes fixated on that sexy mouth, holding back what I wanted to hear.

"Sexy things . . . *sinful* things . . ." The blues in her eyes shifted to a different color. "*Kinky* things . . . to me."

Fuuuck.

"Well, I suppose I should be a gentleman and make your dreams come true." But there was nothing gentlemanly about the things I wanted to do to her.

Stripping off my clothes, I stepped into the tub. Warm water sloshed over my legs, disturbing the petals that probably hadn't expected a man to join them tonight. Who would have thought I'd be bathing in a tub full of roses and essential oils?

Who am I?

A man in love.

"Don't move." She got onto her knees and gripped my cock with a firm hand.

My body paused at her seductive command. Mischief flickered in her eyes, sending a thrill through me.

"One passion from the *Discipline of Virtue* is wonder, then desire. . ." She stroked me with perfection—a skill only a creative mind could master. I grew larger, harder. "I've been thinking about this marvelous stalk all day. Have you been kissed by a rose, *amour?*" She spoke to it as though it understood her.

My cock twitched in response as a rose petal brushed gently up and down my length. Each feathery touch blazed with potent fire that almost undid me.

A storm brewed inside me, threatening to rage from the decadent kiss of a rose petal, followed by sinful lips that made me the luckiest man alive.

Her mouth skimmed down my length, and I was bewildered by the beautiful face, that sexy mouth, and her dangerous tongue.

"Natalie, I think, therefore I am." My hand settled on her head. "I'm in fucking heaven."

She glanced up with amusement. "If you can think while I'm pleasing you, then I'm not doing a good job."

"You're doing an extraordinary job. I love it." I swallowed and licked my dry lips. "I'm just spewing nonsense about what I know about the philosopher . . ." A loud groan escaped me as her pink tongue tantalized my crown. "Logic isn't here right now . . ." I couldn't think when she took me into her wicked mouth.

Fucking hell. A bolt of sensation shot through me,

spreading fire to every part of my body. My abdomen constricted with her ravenous mouth and talented tongue.

"Baby, slow down. I want to be inside you."

She released me, her big blue eyes meeting mine. "I've been craving you."

"Same here." I nudged her back down to the tub. "Tell me about the sinful stuff you were thinking about before I showed up. It turns me on."

I braced a hand on the ledge behind her head, while the other hand skimmed along her elegant shoulder, moving down her body. She widened her thighs, welcoming me.

My mouth covered hers in a wild kiss. Her arms looped around my neck, pulling me closer. Tongues, teeth, and lips collided in a whirlwind of sensations. My hand found her center, soft, silky, and ready for me.

Drawing back, I smirked and teased her opening, earning several moans. "Tell me if this defines Descartes' meaning of existence to you, buttercup." I inserted two fingers into her, moving in and out.

"Not yet," she gasped, flicking me a provocative look belonging to a hellion. "More."

How could I resist a demand like that? Removing my fingers from her warmth, I drove into her, pounding like a madman with one mission: to please his woman. To see the sultry look in her eyes, to feel her muscles tightening around me, and to hear the alluring sounds, it all turned me into a damn philosopher at this moment.

Everything I felt for her defined my life.

"How does this feel now?" I nibbled on her earlobe.

She gyrated her hips, moving in a fast rhythm with me. Water and petals ebbed and flowed between us. "I think . . ."

I didn't want her to think. I wanted her mind empty of everything but me.

She cupped my face with her hands and looked me in the eye. Her body quivered, and I knew she was close to ecstasy.

I pumped harder, deeper, wanting more of her. She breathed with unsteady gasps as our wet bodies slapped against each other. I loved every sound that left her mouth, including the sated expressions splashing across her face.

"You . . . make . . . me . . . feel . . . worthy . . . of my existence . . . Grayson!" she cried out as her body trembled.

I sensed the orgasm ripple through her body and into mine. It was as though she gave me a part of her pleasure. Fucking glorious.

I crushed my mouth to hers as heat and need collided. The tension rose and exploded, sending me off the ledge. I saw stars as my body bucked from the potent force that blasted through me.

As the pleasure descended, I pulled out and shifted behind her so I could gather her into my arms.

"I didn't know French philosophers were so kinky." I kissed her head. "Descartes was a wise man, after all. By incorporating his philosophy, you took sex to a new level. This could be our new thing."

She laughed. "I didn't know architects were so pervy."

"Buttercup, I've become so many things because you arouse the hell out of me."

We spent another hour in the tub exploring the many ways to apply philosophy to sex. After dinner, we continued our exploration and discovered how Voltaire, Rousseau, Michelet, Confucius, and LaoZi made our bedtime stories irresistibly sinful.

To be honest, I never loved a woman in this way. It had never occurred to me that philosophy and sex were so hot together.

While she slept, I thought about the new revelation regarding her father's plane crash. The burden on her shoulders had grown, and I wanted to remove it for her.

CHAPTER FORTY-SEVEN

We'd been back in Providence for a week, and I jumped into working on my Momentum collection while waiting to hear from the French authorities regarding the plane crash. Mom's lawyer had requested an investigation into the accident, claiming that an anonymous tip had come to one of the victim's family about the plane's engine being intentionally sabotaged.

The lawyer had already received several phone calls from other victims' families voicing similar suspicions. One caller had received a text message from a family member on the plane minutes before the crash, saying his son had heard loud noises coming from the engine.

The tabloids were having fun with the headlines. I wanted them to splash the news all over the world. Perhaps the exposure would push Aunt Estelle to fear, and that would distract her, forcing her to make mistakes. Mistakes could lead to evidence.

What also settled my nerves was that Mom convinced the board members to postpone the voting. If my dad's death was part of a murder scheme, then the company could earn a substantial profit from the class action lawsuit and ultimately save LaRue. Aunt Estelle had asked the Board of Directors to move up the meeting, which became an inconvenience and had them questioning why.

Suspicion floated in the air like dust particles, and Aunt Estelle didn't like that.

There wasn't much I could do but wait. Things were set in motion, and I could breathe easier. I'd finished my womenswear collection and was now starting my menswear collection. As I sketched the designs, I envisioned Grayson as my muse. He didn't know I was creating a special accessory line for him. I hoped the factory could squeeze in the production for me. It was a late addition to the line, but once I saw the prototype, I knew it'd be successful.

I loved this man; I wanted to show him how I felt.

Another unforgettable thing happened in Paris: my mom approved of Grayson. We took her out for dinner on the evening before our return flight, and he completely charmed her. He was the first boyfriend to earn her approval from one sitting. Maybe he'd earned her approval because he wouldn't release my hand as we strolled with Mom near the Eiffel Tower.

Tonight Grayson was going to sleep at my place, and I'd be at his tomorrow. I'd made room for his belongings and he'd done the same for me. He'd asked me to move in with him weeks ago, but I wanted my own space to work on my collection. His enormous house had enough space for me. However, it was easier to design something secretive for him at my place.

After a few hours of designing and picking out trims, my

stomach growled. I glanced at my phone and it was a few minutes past noon.

I should have texted Grayson in case he was in a meeting, but I wanted to hear his voice and called him.

"Miss me already?" He answered on the first ring.

"Yup. Did you eat yet?"

"No, you?"

"Nope. Let's have lunch together. I need a break. I'll pick up something and meet you in an hour? Does chicken lo mein sound good to you?"

"Whatever you want, love."

"See you soon."

Love.

I wasn't sure if he meant it as a casual endearment—that was said on impulse, or was it a Freudian slip? He had never said those words to me, and nor had I. We were both careful with our hearts.

I loved him more and more each day. It frightened me. I'd never felt this way with anyone—this emotion that overwhelmed me with joy and hope. With him, I could be anything. Even when I was stressed, he made me feel everything would work out. No man had sat with me in the dark just so I could heal. That took time and patience, and I appreciated every moment with him.

These days I didn't need his companionship during the dark. I was getting used to seeing how the darkness offered me a sense of peace my body and mind needed. I hadn't experienced that until now. The complete silence was like looking at the starry night sky. The vast unknown could be frightening, but it could also be a lovely sense of wonder. I was seeing the darkness in a whole new way because of him.

How would he react if I confessed my feelings to him?

What if it scared him? I knew his heart had been fractured because of his uncle. What if my confession was too soon for him to accept? Maybe it was best to wait.

He'd been swamped with projects and the issue surrounding his uncle. I understood his anxiety because I knew my aunt had been involved in my dad's death. Grayson and I were two souls on a parallel journey.

After placing an order for pickup, I threw on a knit top and jeans and rushed out in sneakers. I parked in the lot beside the restaurant and got out of my car as a homeless man wearing a gray hoodie approached me.

"Do you have a dollar to spare, miss? I'm very hungry."

As I reached into my purse, strong arms grabbed me from behind. Another person appeared and slapped a cloth over my mouth and nose. I kicked and tried to scream as two men with ski masks hauled me away into a black van. The homeless man hopped into the van, tossing back his hoodie. I didn't recognize him. When the other two men yanked off their masks, I saw Paul, the city inspector. He met my eyes and smirked as he pressed the cloth firmly against my nose and mouth.

I tried to fight him, but the chloroform—or whatever it was—had gotten into my system. My vision blurred, and my body weakened as I lost consciousness.

CHAPTER FORTY-EIGHT

GRAYSON

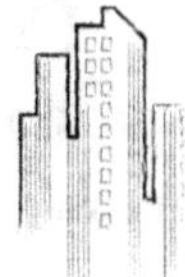

After my status meeting ended, I hurried back to my office. The meeting went on for an extra ten minutes, but it was necessary. We had a lot of projects on hand, and it was best to see where everything stood.

I had expected Natalie to already be in my office, but she wasn't. I'd be lying if I said I wasn't disappointed. What people said about love was true. I thought about her *all the time.* I understood why my friends acted foolish when it came to their girls. I used to make fun of them when they'd declined a party or dinner invitation to go home to be with their girl. Now I was in the same boat. I'd decline every invitation to be home with her.

Being in love gave me this innate drive to be better. A better architect, a better man, a better lover. All of it. I wanted to protect her, give her a comfortable life where she could do anything she wanted. I could imagine her telling me bedtime stories for the rest of my life.

How cheesy was that?

While I waited for Natalie to bring lunch, I logged into

my Level Three demo. It was almost finished, and I wanted to show her what I'd done with the attire she'd designed. I tweaked a few scenes with monsters and added a library where the player had to find clues hidden inside philosophy books to get more gems in order to access weapons and such. I smiled as I added Sartre, Descartes, and Voltaire into the mix. Natalie inspired this library.

My stomach growled, and I looked at the clock to see it was a quarter past two. Where was she? I checked my phone, and there were no text messages or voicemails. Unease stirred in my stomach. I called her, but her phone went straight to voicemail.

I paced the room and had the security guard from her building send me videos of all the entrances for the building. A few minutes later, I reviewed the videos and saw Natalie dressed in casual clothes, rushing out the door. Nothing appeared abnormal.

Something had happened to Natalie. I felt it in my gut. Fear tumbled inside me, gripping my heart. I called the PI and asked him to track her phone immediately. A minute later, he replied it was off the grid. The last known place was the Phoenix Dynasty restaurant, which wasn't far from my office.

I drove there and questioned the older gentleman with a head full of white hair. For a moment, I thought of my dad. If he were still alive, he'd have hair just like this man.

"Excuse me, sir. Did a pretty girl stop by to pick up a chicken lo mein order?"

He gestured to the bag from the back table. "No. I've been trying to call her, but she's not picking up."

My heart pulsed with apprehension as fear swirled into icy knots in my gut.

Natalie hadn't picked up the food, but she'd been here. So whatever had happened to her occurred nearby. I discovered her car and purse in the back parking lot. The lot had a camera in the guise of a fire alarm attached to the building. I only knew it was a camera because it was one of the new security systems I'd considered for some of my properties. At a glance, people would assume it was nothing more than a fire alarm.

Returning to the restaurant, I asked the man, "Can I please check your recording for the parking lot? My girlfriend is missing. She was supposed to pick up lunch two hours ago. Her phone showed she came here."

The man furrowed his eyebrows, probably not wanting to get involved. If he said no, I'd have the PI hack into his system anyway, but I wanted to review it *now*.

I spoke to him in Cantonese. "請幫我."

"Please help me" spoken in his native language, did the trick. He introduced himself as Jason and gestured for me to go to the back room, where I reviewed the recording. A cold chill ran up my spine as I saw two men shoving her into a van. The angle of the van made it difficult to see the license plate number accurately, but it was enough for the authorities to work with.

She'd been trying to help the fucking homeless man who had been one of the kidnappers. Rage soared and slammed into fear, making me want to kill them all. If these people dared touch her, I'd scour the world to track down each one of them. I'd skin them and make sure they suffered before their last breaths.

"We have to call the police," said Jason, the restaurant owner who watched the abduction beside me.

The police arrived quickly and took down the report of a

kidnapping for Natalie Chapelle. After checking her car for clues and finding nothing, they released it to me. I had my assistant drive it back to my house.

Who had done it? Rafael? I called him, but he denied having anything to do with her abduction. I believed him because he was working on something with me. He'd be stupid to blow up the multimillion-dollar collaboration with me.

Could it be the crime organization? But why? She had nothing to do with them. Were they getting to her because of me? What did they know about me? A thousand questions bombarded my head.

My phone continued to ring and buzz with calls and text messages. I sent a group text to my friends, letting them know I'd reach out as soon as I received more information. I knew they were worried, but I didn't have the capacity to talk right now. Too much noise wasn't helping me think at the moment.

Who the fuck had taken her? Was she all right? Did they hurt her? Every fiber of my body vibrated with worry, fear, and vengeance.

When I arrived home, it was around eight in the evening. I wanted to drive around the city looking for her, but I knew that would just make everything worse. Natalie needed my sanity to save her, not my insanity.

I felt detached from myself. My body felt like it was floating elsewhere while my brain and heart wanted to remain in one place.

My phone buzzed again. I glanced at it in case the PI or the police discovered something, but an anonymous number showed up. I clicked on the message that came with a link.

She's here. Use the map. Go alone. Be careful.

Normally, I'd never click on a link from an unknown number. But I knew in my gut this person was referring to Natalie. The link opened to a blueprint of The Prism—an underground map.

A part of me wondered if it was a trap for me, but intuition told me differently. I closed my eyes, shoving all the concerns aside. Who sent the text? Did I know this person?

Before I left, I sent the anonymous number and the link to the PI to trace. This person was involved somehow, and despite him giving me a clue, I didn't trust him. But it was the only clue I had of Natalie.

Even if this was a trap, I had to give it a shot. Natalie was waiting for me.

CHAPTER FORTY-NINE

I woke in a cold, dark room. Fear twisted my stomach as I remembered what had happened. A glow allowed me to see I was lying on a bed against the wall. No windows were in sight.

My body ached. I shifted and something poked my shoulders. The springs had punctured through the mattress, stabbing me. I pushed myself up. That was when I noticed where the light came from. I clasped my fingers over my red diamond pendant. Light illuminated from the gold setting around the diamond like a nightlight.

Tears flooded my eyes, knowing Grayson had created this light for me. I hadn't even noticed it until now. He probably didn't know I'd developed a friendly relationship with the darkness. Before he gave me the novel necklace, I'd sit inside a closet by myself, trying to mimic the childhood trauma. No panic emerged. Instead, what came was my remembrance of his presence and all the conversations we'd shared. He'd been right: the dark wasn't the core of my issue.

It was the combination of being mistreated, the threat

from my aunt, and being locked up that contributed to the phobia my mind had created on its own. The dark just became something tangible for me to blame.

I clasped my hand over the glowing pendant. Did Grayson know I was missing? Was he looking for me?

I scanned the room, and there wasn't much in it except a side table, a chair, and a bunch of cardboard boxes in the corner. So many questions pounded my head.

Who were these people? What did they want from me? How long had Paul been working with these awful people? He'd always appeared creepy, but I never imagined he would kidnap me.

Voices echoed outside. With caution, I approached the door, pressed my ear to it, and listened to a conversation.

"What are we going to do with her?" a man asked.

I pressed my ear closer. Was that Neil Allen, the mail guy from the DPW? What the hell was going on? Was anyone else from the city trying to hurt me?

"Ship her to Italy," Paul said.

"Why?"

"Stop asking questions. Just do the job, and you'll get paid."

"What about the women in the other rooms?" Neil sounded genuinely concerned. Or maybe it was my frightened mind playing tricks on me, hoping he was the nice guy I'd always considered him to be.

"What did I tell you? Stop asking questions."

"Well, I need to know so I can avoid mistakes."

Paul grunted. "Everyone is going to Italy. They sell for a lot of money."

"Being sold or already sold?" Neil inquired.

"Fucking Christ! You don't need to know these details. The less you know, the longer you'll live. Got that?"

"Okay. I was just curious how much a human goes for."

"Why did they fucking hire you?" Paul cursed. "These women are already sold. We're just delivering expensive products. That bitch Natalie is worth millions."

What? They sold me?

By whom?

To whom?

The fear in me twisted so hard that pain shot from my stomach down to my legs. I had to bite my bottom lip to stop myself from screaming.

"Oh. Wow."

"Give her something to eat, so she doesn't look malnourished."

Footsteps approached, so I limped back to the bed, removed my necklace and shoved it into the front pocket of my jeans. I lay back down, pretending to sleep, and prayed the cramp in my leg would subside.

The door cranked open, and the light flicked on. I could tell through my closed eyelids. I breathed slowly, trying to calm my heart rate and the tremor in my body.

Stay calm, Natalie. You've got to get out here alive. There are things waiting for you to do. Work on your new collection. Tell Grayson you love him.

I cracked my eyes to see Neil placing the bag of takeout food and a bottle of water on the side table. Why would he join the crime world? He'd always been kind to me, so this was a complete surprise.

The look on his face showed fear and regret. I didn't know if I could trust him, but at this moment, he was the only option I had. I didn't know how many men were out there. Even if I could escape this room, would I be able to get away safely? Where was I? Was I in another city? Another state?

Trusting my instincts, I pushed up from the bed, swinging my legs to the floor. "Why are you doing this, Neil?"

"I'm sorry Natalie. I didn't mean for this to happen. I didn't know . . ."

"Where am I? Am I still in Providence?"

"You're still in Providence, but underground." He looked at me. "How are you feeling?"

Underground? I had more questions, but I only had time to ask relevant things. My life could end any minute.

"I'm scared, Neil." There was no lie there. I hoped my admission would inspire him to help me. Was that too hopeful? "Are you going to kill me? If you are, at least give me the reason." I didn't want him to know I'd listened earlier.

"You're not going to die. They're selling you to some rich guy in Italy."

"That's death to me," I said.

Anguish flashed over his face, and his voice lowered to a whisper. "I didn't know I'd be kidnapping you. I'm sorry. I needed money and took a side job, but I had no idea I'd be trafficking people. Paul introduced me to people he knew, and they hired me for 'miscellaneous' tasks. I should have known money couldn't be made easy."

"Can you help me escape? Please?" I begged. "I don't want to be someone's sex slave."

"You've always been nice and respectful to everyone at work. I liked that about you." He pointed to the corner of the room covered with cardboard boxes. "After I leave, move the boxes aside. Use the tunnel to crawl out of this room. It'll take you to a wider passageway that will lead you to an adjacent building's lot. Stay close to the wall. If you hear a sound, don't move. Most of the guards are on this side of the building tonight. Get out as fast as you can. There are no cameras in this room. There are armed men lurking around, but they don't know about this tunnel." He jerked his chin toward where I was supposed to go.

"How do you know about it?"

"I was part of a team who worked on miscellaneous jobs for extra money. They said it was a city job. It wasn't. But I kept my mouth shut for the money."

"Who are you working for now?" I asked.

"Paul works for men who are linked to a crime organization. I don't know them. Paul is the one who pays me." He glanced over his shoulder at the door. "Shit's going down soon, and I need to get out of here."

He cleared his throat, signifying the change in conversation.

"Eat." His voice grew loud, as though he wanted everyone to hear.

"Okay," I said.

He offered me a nod and left.

Neil didn't need to share all that information with me, but he did. Right now, he was my ticket to safety. I had to trust him.

Despite that, I didn't eat or drink anything. What if the other people had put something in the food or the drink to subdue me? I couldn't risk it.

I waited about five minutes before easing the boxes aside. I tried my best not to make a sound. A metal grid greeted me. It hung loose by a single screw. My heart hammered as I removed it and put my necklace back on again. It would be my guiding light in the darkness.

I'd seen movies where victims crawled through tunnels or vents to escape their enemies. I never imagined it would be me.

On all fours, I fit through the tunnel and made my way slowly. My knees and palms pressed into pebbles as I advanced deeper into the dark tunnel. The smell of moist dirt surrounded me. I also heard faint noises somewhere.

What if they could hear me? Fear made me stop for a few seconds.

Keep going. Grayson needs to hear your words.

The small tunnel came to an opening that was blocked by a box. I assumed it was another cardboard box, similar to the ones I'd removed earlier. Voices echoed in the distance, but then I heard footsteps nearby. I curled my fingers, stopping myself from pushing at the box that separated me from freedom.

What if Paul or another criminal was on the other side?

I had to wait until I couldn't hear any more footsteps before pushing my way out.

CHAPTER FIFTY

GRAYSON

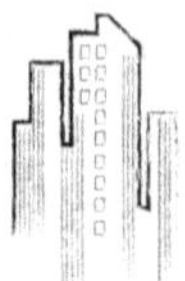

With adrenaline pumping through my blood and fear gripping my heart, I made my way to the back of The Prism and found a door with a busted doorknob. Could it be my luck? This was looking more like a trap, but I couldn't dismiss my only chance of rescuing Natalie. If she was here, I'd be here.

Who had broken the doorknob? Was there another intruder already inside?

Regardless, I wasn't going to leave without her. With caution, I pulled out my gun, cocked it, aiming downward as I yanked the door open and entered.

A dark hallway greeted me, and I turned on my phone flashlight, illuminating my path. I walked down the hallway, making my way to the main hall. From the blueprint I received, I knew the underground layout of the building. Who had created these passageways? For what purpose?

The blueprint showed hidden rooms and tunnels built into this building, making it even more invaluable than I initially thought. Perhaps this was the reason Natalie's father had purchased it. The property was supposed to be empty, but apparently someone had broken in, occupying the space.

I crept quietly down another hallway and found a maintenance storage room that had several metal racks of tools and supplies. Cobwebs stretched across the racks. My heart pounded as I imagined what Natalie was going through. Was she safe? Had they hurt her?

Anger boiled in me. I'd kill every last one of them for touching her.

I should have reported this recent development to the authorities, but I didn't trust them. The crime organization had infiltrated the government, even the City of Providence. Whoever had sent the text probably knew that as well. I could have asked one of my boys to accompany me, but if this was a trap, I didn't want them to go down with me. Remi had Audri to worry about, and Royce had Michelle. They were family to me.

A wooden display of paper towels and tissue boxes sat too far from the wall. I pushed it aside and discovered a door that led me down a stairwell with one dangling light bulb.

Holy shit.

I came to a wide passageway that could fit a truck. Most of it was made of dirt, but portions of it were made of brick and concrete. Gravel covered the ground, and unlit sconces were fixed to the ceilings. I searched for footprints and found none. The dampness and darkness made for an uncomfortable atmosphere.

Was she in the dark? *Fuck.* She'd been doing so well with her fear. I prayed she was okay.

As I moved cautiously, I studied the structure of the tunnel. What did they use this tunnel for? Where did it lead?

A memory surfaced. Derek had mentioned a tunnel that connected to the crime organization. Was this it?

I'd figure that out later. Time was of the essence right now. Voices rose in the distance, and I leaned my back against the wall, trying to listen. I couldn't tell what they were saying. It sounded like an argument.

Was Natalie there?

Making my way toward the sounds, I stayed close to the wall, searching for any hidden cameras. I stopped in my steps for a few moments, trying to listen to any sounds that could lead me to Natalie.

I was about to move ahead when a nearby scraping sound caught my attention. I turned to the right, and the flashlight revealed boxes on the ground. Several boxes thudded aside, and a woman crawled out from behind them. A light dangled around her neck, swaying back and forth. Hope erupted in my chest, and I rushed over to my girl.

I wrapped my arms around her. "Buttercup, you okay?"

"Grayson?" She touched my face. "I'm not hallucinating, am I?"

"No. You're not. It's me." She looked fragile and frightened.

A loud scream erupted somewhere down the hallway.

"There are other women trapped here."

Something exploded, and dirt rained down on us.

"Let's get you out of here first." I wrapped an arm around her, guiding her back to where I had come from.

A shot rang out, and someone shouted, "Get them!"

Bang! Bang! Bang!

I returned fire, shifting my body to shield Natalie as we moved to the exit. As I neared the stairwell, Forrest and Royce came through the door wearing bulletproof vests.

"Go! We got this!" Forrest gestured to the stairs.

I didn't know how they knew I was here, but I was grateful for their assistance.

More blasts boomed as I took Natalie toward my car on the other side of the street. Sirens wailed in the distance just as a massive explosion occurred, taking out portions of the building.

"Oh, my God! Royce and Forrest!" Natalie clamped a hand over her mouth, while her body shook.

"Don't worry, they're fine!" I pointed to my friends, who were rushing toward us. "Get out of here. I'll deal with the cops."

As they darted into the shadows, I brought Natalie farther away from the burning building. The devastation on her face crushed me. It was as though I could see her crumbling inside while the structure of her building collapsed. Like the angry fire, the turbulence in me wanted to destroy everything in sight for putting her through this, but I remained calm for her. She didn't need another violent storm.

Somehow, my gaze darted to a silhouette leaning against a truck, watching the inferno unfold. He didn't seemed distraught or shocked like us. His casual stance made him stand out against the raging flames and explosive noises. When the police cars and fire engines arrived, he disappeared into the shadows. Who was he?

"It's gone," Natalie cried as another explosion erupted.

I tightened my arms around her, letting her fall back into me. This property had been a gift from her father, and it had crumbled in front of her eyes. I'd recently received information about The Prism from the PI but hadn't had time to review it yet.

As I held Natalie in my arms, I knew the danger surrounding me would get to her. No woman had mattered to me more than her.

When I saw the abduction video, my world fell apart like The Prism. All the pieces that kept me intact disassembled in slow motion. I felt hollow and scared.

What if I had lost her forever? I loved her so much. I could let her know right now, but I feared my confession would only make things worse later.

Derek's warning came to the forefront. If I wanted to destroy this crime organization, limb by limb, piece by piece, I had to keep what mattered most to me far away.

After speaking to the police and taking a trip to the hospital where they examined and cleared her, I brought Natalie home. She'd mentioned that Neil Allen had showed her the escape route. Paul Brooks had died in the explosion. If he hadn't, he would have died by my hands. Five other guards and two women perished in the fire. But the fire-fighters rescued three women.

I knew these passageways were used to conduct illegal business. For now, I pushed all these things aside to take care of Natalie, who still looked terrified and exhausted.

CHAPTER FIFTY-ONE

GRAYSON

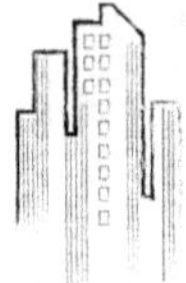

Once I tucked Natalie into bed, I walked into my office and had an urgent conference call with my friends.

"Thanks for having my back." I nodded at Forrest and Royce.

"You should've told us," Remi said with furrowed eyebrows.

"I didn't want you guys in danger."

"You don't trust us," Arrow said flatly.

Arrow and Remi had been monitoring Royce and Forrest from inside a nearby car when they were in the tunnel.

It wasn't like that, was it? Trust was something I'd been struggling with. It was still difficult at times. What they said was the truth, even if it wasn't about them. It was about me and my issues in general. Would they understand?

"I've got shit going on, and I let it cloud my judgment," I replied.

"We know, so we're good. We got you . . . *asshole*." Arrow shifted in his seat and stared at me.

"Next time, tell us, even if it's in the middle of the night," Forrest added.

This was why I loved them.

"Thanks."

"Is Natalie okay?" Forrest asked.

"Yeah, she's sleeping. How did you know I was there?"

"An anonymous text message with the location and a blueprint of the building," Remi said.

"Me too," I replied. "He told me to go alone. So he knew help was coming."

Remi pursed his lips, thinking. "Someone's aiding us."

"We have to be careful. We don't know who this guy is. Maybe he's trying to deter us from something else." Arrow drank from a water bottle.

"There was a guy watching the building burn. Did you see him when you arrived?" I looked at Royce and Forrest.

"I didn't see anyone," Royce said.

"Neither did I."

Remi crossed his arms. "This guy had to know we were friends."

He also had to know me and my relationship with Natalie. Who was he? "We're being monitored."

We spent the next hour discussing how we could protect our loved ones. Because this could be the work of The Trogyn. Maybe they finally discovered something about our drone recordings. We weren't sure, but we didn't want to risk our women and our families.

The more I spoke with them, the more I suspected something was going on with the man I saw that night. Did he *want* me to see him?

I decided to take a leave of absence from my company,

deferring everything to my team. They had never failed me, and I had to trust them again.

I relayed information about Derek to my friends regarding The Trogyn. We all agreed this crime organization would eventually come after us, so we'd cut off their limbs one at a time. It would take our collaboration and careful steps to succeed.

What wealthy men hated most was losing money. Money meant power and status. Some people lived for only those things. We had to attack from that angle. So, though I didn't know these members, I knew one way they made their money—elite clubs. And if my friends and I could start destroying pieces of that colossal conglomeration, it would eventually fall.

"You get some rest. We'll do some research on the various clubs around the world and catch up soon."

"Forrest, I need to consult with you on a medical matter."

Forrest remained on the screen after the other guys logged off. "What's up?"

I described a plan that needed his medical expertise. "I don't advise you to do that, but I understand your situation. As a doctor, my vote is no. As your friend, I'll leave that up to your discretion."

Forrest didn't know I'd already decided. Getting his medical opinion was just extra caution.

After our conversation, I compiled an email listing all the tasks for the management team. I'd want weekly updates, but I'd only chime in on urgent matters. Otherwise my focus was on two things: Natalie and the crime organization who wanted to sell her.

I went into the bedroom to check on Natalie. She stirred, opened her eyes, saw me, and pushed herself up. "Hi."

"You should go back to sleep, get some rest." I gathered her into my arms.

"I was so scared I'd never see you again." She placed a hand on my heart. "I love you, Grayson."

My heart jolted and then swelled, filling my chest with so much warmth I didn't know what to do or say. I tightened my arms around her and kissed her head.

I knew that I *should* say those sacred words to her, but I couldn't. My words would make her happy now, but it would only make the situation worse later. I had a plan, and I had to stick to it. So I sealed my lips and embraced her, rocking her back and forth like a baby.

"I want you to rest. No more thinking about anything, okay? You *matter* to me more than you know, and it hurts to see you injured. I want to kill every last one of those dogs."

Her fingers came to my lips. "No. I don't want blood on your hands because of me. Who am I going to tell bedtime stories to if you're in prison?" She smiled.

God, I loved her so much.

"You got me there. Your bedtime stories are only reserved for me."

Ten minutes later, she fell back into a deep sleep.

She told me she'd been sold to someone in Italy. Who had sold her? The buyer would hear from me soon enough.

Brushing a hand over her forehead, I whispered, "I love you too. Sorry, I wasn't there to protect you."

I stared at the woman who held my heart—the woman who had rebuilt it. Memories of our meeting came flooding back. Our encounter had started off on a rough patch. She was the irritation that turned my heart inside out. She made me feel alive again, allowing me to see and trust my heart. Right now, my heart was showing me a way to keep her safe. Though nothing was certain in life, I knew I could never love another woman the way I loved her.

I was a man who knew how to construct innovative architecture. A building was nothing without the structure that supported it. Natalie was my structure and my foundation. Without her, I didn't exist.

So how could I not protect her at all costs?

Before washing up to get ready for bed, I texted the PI.

Grayson: *The Prism got destroyed today. I need all videos from the surrounding streets.*

PI: *Will do.*

My phone rang with Remi's number. I hated receiving calls this late in the night because it always meant bad news.

"What's up?" I asked.

"There's been an explosion at Derek's prison. Heard there are multiple casualties. He might be at the hospital. Just wanted you to know."

"Thanks, man."

Could anything else go wrong today? Derek had information about the tunnels. Was the prison explosion linked to the one that had occurred at The Prism?

I'd pay Derek a visit when I had more energy. If I went now, what could I do? What would be my reason? He didn't deserve any emotion from me.

My head was going to burst if I didn't get some sleep.

CHAPTER FIFTY-TWO

The next few days consisted of Grayson giving me self-defense lessons and me calming my mom about my abduction. She wanted to fly over to check on me, but I told her not to.

I was fine. Mom was overseeing House of LaRue. Aunt Estelle had disappeared after the heightened publicity regarding the plane crash. She'd cleaned out her bank accounts and stopped coming to work. Even her daughter hadn't heard from her. This proved to me she was involved in my dad's death. Who had helped her?

I should be thankful she wasn't around to cause trouble for the company. But I didn't like the reality of it either. My aunt had hired someone to kill my dad. Was it all because of money?

I hoped she'd get the punishment she deserved.

Everyone knew about the Gucci family drama. I never imagined my family would share the same fate. I didn't want a cloud of shame hovering over the LaRue name.

Grayson had been busy with work and concern for his

uncle, who had gotten injured in an explosion at the prison. Not wanting me to worry, Grayson didn't share a lot of details with me. Today, he was visiting his uncle at the hospital.

Needing to do something that wasn't stressful, I stayed at my apartment to work on Momentum. I followed up with the vendors producing my garments. Everything seemed to flow nicely with no delivery issues.

The girls wanted to meet up to see if I was okay. I appreciated their concern, but I wasn't in the mood to socialize. I didn't know why, but something was still bugging me.

Liar.

Was it wrong of me to want Grayson to say those sacred words back to me? Was I being petty for overreacting? So much was happening around us, so I should have given him more time, been more patient. Men didn't think like women. We needed things to be clear.

But what if he didn't say "I love you" back because he didn't feel the same way?

Stop depressing yourself.

If I met with my friends, they'd see the concern on my face and inquire. I didn't want to discuss my relationship, the abduction, my family drama, or the mystery around my dad.

I just wanted to escape and design from a place of no distractions or expectations. Closing my eyes, I pretended I was on some tropical island sitting on the white sand, sketching. Grayson napped beside me, and the ocean waves ebbed and flowed in front of us.

Yes, that would be lovely.

Opening my eyes, I studied the blank page on my sketchbook. Inspiration tugged at me as I thought about my friendship with Audri, Michelle, Kiera, and Vivian. Each of them embraced intelligence, grace, creativity, independence, beauty, and strength. I wanted to create a line of purses that represented these sacred feminine attributes. What girl didn't love handbags? I had too many from various designers. But I wanted my own collection.

Creativity should be limitless and not based on the demands and restrictions of society. Sometimes the best-sellers often lacked character and were only based on what celebrities wore. Like other businesses that needed to make money, they hopped onto the trend in order to survive. There was nothing wrong with that. It was often necessary to adapt to trends.

Joy burst in me as I sketched my designs and created spec and trim pages to send off to the vendor. My friends would be the perfect support group to advertise this new accessory line.

My brand Momentum was an ever-growing collection of sacred moments in my life—tidbits of love, fear, motivation, and so on. They were all beautiful moments that made up life. I'd weave charming trims to accentuate the handbags. Like life, the handbags would embrace the rough and smooth textures of the materials, the sharp edges and the perfect bend around the corner. Some designs would be adorned with shiny zippers and distinctive buttons, while others would be more subtle, yet still graceful and eye-catching.

A sound came from the door, and my heart leaped, knowing it was Grayson. He entered with a bag of pastries, looking exhausted.

I got up from the dining table where fabric swatches were scattered around my laptop and placed a hand on his cheek. "You okay? Did you sleep last night?"

"I'm fine. Want some pastries?" He offered me the bag with macarons and cake.

"Thanks." I took the bag and placed it on the table. "How's your uncle?"

"I don't think he'll last the week." He went over to the couch, dragging me with him.

Squeezing his hand, I said, "I'm sorry to hear that."

"Karma catches up to you. He would've had to pay for his sins eventually." Sadness tinged Grayson's voice. He still had this love for his uncle, which I understood. Derek had been a father to him for most of his life, so despite what he'd done, Grayson still remembered the good times they'd shared.

"Your aunt will have to pay for her sins too." Grayson looked at me.

"Our situation is similar. Your uncle ruined your family, and my aunt ruined mine."

He nodded. "Our lives are parallel in some ways."

"The big difference is that your uncle loves you. My aunt never loved me." There were no harsh feelings. She was a veritable stranger to me. "Thank you for everything. For speaking to the board members and investing in LaRue. I don't know what to say."

"You don't have to say anything. I invest in businesses with great potential." He gripped my chin. "*You* have great potential, and I'm investing in *you*, buttercup. There's one more thing you need to know."

My heart thudded rapidly. "What is it?"

"The paperwork to invest in House of LaRue is finalized. It's a done deal."

I threw my arms around him, holding him tight. "Thank you."

House of LaRue was no longer in financial distress. I'd been waiting to hear about the finalization before I could truly celebrate. Not only was Grayson an investor, but all his friends were as well. That was one reason I didn't need to return to Paris so soon. Mom could take care of the rest.

I drew back and looked at him as tears blurred my vision. "You don't know how grateful I am—" I choked on my emotions. I thought I could hold them in, but the sincerity on his face, and the love in his eyes—the love he couldn't tell me —were too much for me.

"You'd do the same for me."

It wasn't a question. He knew I would.

"You own part of a fashion brand now. Do you want to go out to eat? It'll be our little celebration."

He yawned. "Sorry, I've got a conference call with an overseas vendor in a few hours. I'm too tired."

"Okay." Disappointment squirmed in me.

Our conversation continued about random things, but then I heard him snoring and glanced over. His head had fallen back onto the couch.

What had he been up to? Exhaustion had weighed on him the past few days. Every time I asked him, he told me it was just work, but why didn't I believe him?

CHAPTER FIFTY-THREE

GRAYSON

A week later, Natalie came over to my place with a silver box. "Don't open it yet."

"Why? What's in it?" I studied the box measuring about eighteen inches by eighteen inches, with a height of about eight inches. I stared at the handwritten note taped on the top: *Do not open until Natalie says so.*

She flicked me a glance. "Follow directions, and you'll be rewarded."

"I always follow directions." The more she told me I couldn't do something, the more I wanted to. That was human nature, right?

But I respected her wishes.

"I need to hide this in your dressing room so you can forget about it." She smiled at me. "Be right back."

I loved seeing the smile on her face, but I had information that might erase that joy today. The folder on the table held the information she'd been waiting for. Sometimes the truth hurt, but it was better than a lie. Natalie had sacrificed her comfortable lifestyle to take a job with little pay so she could uncover the truth about her father and The Prism. That showed dedication, love, and courage. She'd taken a leap of faith without knowing she'd find anything.

I admired her courage and persistence. She never gave up on hope. It was this persistence that had brought us together—her constant hounding at me had gotten my attention.

When Natalie appeared in the living room, I patted the cushion next to me. "Come here."

Concern splashed on her face. By now, we knew each other's facial expressions. The slight tension between her eyebrows, the twitch at the corner of her lips, and the worry darkening her eyes were aspects of her that seeped into my memory.

She sat down beside me. "What's going on?"

"First, I want to give you the good news that I found the pilot who flew the plane. He's alive and well."

"What? How?" Her eyes widened in disbelief.

"It's a long story, but all you have to know is that he's been arrested and he's come forward to work with the FBI and the international authorities. There's now an international manhunt for your aunt. She paid the pilot a lot of money to compromise the engine. He already had an escape plan on that day and jumped out before the plane went down."

"How did you find out all this information?"

I'd been working overtime regarding many things. This was one of them. Natalie needed closure, and I wanted to give her that so she could move on.

"Money can buy a lot of things. One of those things is information. I have a wide network of people who help each other out when needed. The right questions usually yield the right answers. I pat your back, you pat mine. A lot of people owe me favors, and I just redeemed a few." I smiled at her, not wanting her to inquire further.

"Thank you," she sighed. "Aunt Estelle must be hiding in another country."

"The guy who 'purchased' you from your aunt is dead."

Natalie gasped, placing a hand over her heart.

"He's an Italian billionaire who had ten mistresses and twenty children. He abused them and held them in cages behind his villa."

Her mouth dropped open, probably seeing herself in their shoes and realizing how lucky she was. She didn't ask how he died. She searched my eyes and probably knew, but she never asked.

I wouldn't tell her, anyway. Filth like him didn't deserve to live. I did society a favor by eliminating men like him.

She swallowed. "I'm certain they cheered for his death."

She was right. I met with the oldest mistress who cried in gratitude when the assassin I'd hired sniped him while he was beating her. The sharks fed on his body. But I kept all the dark stuff from Natalie. I didn't want her tainted by my deeds.

"I have more to tell you," I said. "The reason your father was in Providence was because he bought The Prism for you to start your own fashion label. He wanted something that truly belonged to you."

CHAPTER FIFTY-FOUR

NATALIE

My heart bloomed with joy and sadness. I was so thrilled to hear my dad had noticed my passion, took it to heart, and tried to make my dream come true. But I was sad he didn't get to witness what I'd done with that dream. I created my own fashion label.

Dad knew I'd always wanted to explore other designs, but my duty was loyalty to my family's name. To know that he'd bought the property specifically for my dream meant the world to me.

Tears spilled down my face. I wiped them away with the back of my hand. "How could you possibly know this?"

Was this why he'd been working and traveling so much?

"Time, patience, and luck." Grayson peeked at his watch. "Someone will be here to explain things to you."

He handed me a folder. "This is the reason your aunt isn't fond of your family."

The emotions that filled my heart today ranged from shock and sorrow to love and hope. There was nothing left to surprise me.

But when I opened the folder, my heart skipped a beat, and I gasped at the copy of the birth certificate. "She's not a LaRue."

"No, she's a Hickson. Her father was a Navy officer."

Grayson told me about the affair. Apparently, he met Andrew Hickson's widow, and she confirmed he had an affair with a French woman—my grandmother. Aunt Estelle had paid the widow to keep quiet with threats of consequences if she didn't comply. The widow didn't like threats and had reached out to my dad. He discovered the information two years ago.

"But he said nothing to the family."

Grayson lifted a shoulder. "Maybe it didn't matter to him. Maybe he loved his sister because he grew up with her."

"She didn't love him."

"I think she wanted something she couldn't have. It turned her into a bitter woman who wanted to eliminate your father so no one knew about her bloodline. She wanted House of LaRue, but the truth of her lineage threatened that, so she wanted to sell it."

I sighed, trying to absorb the family drama.

"Also, your dad never had any affair. I think your aunt fed that information to the media."

I could see that.

"He was meeting an acquaintance here in Providence regarding the building."

The doorbell chimed, and Grayson went to open it.

Nerves stirred in me. I stood up from the couch, following him to the door. But I stopped in my tracks when none other than Dolores Kennedy stepped into view.

"Sergeant Kennedy, what are you doing here?"

"You can call me Dolores. 'Sergeant Kennedy' is my alias

at work." The stern face she usually wore at work softened on me. "Yes, I know what they say about me behind my back, but I don't care. Someone needs to maintain law and order in there."

"You sure do," I said.

"We all miss you in the office."

"Please send my best to everyone."

I'd never received so much information in one day. It overwhelmed me. I didn't know which news I should try to absorb first. It was as though the universe was dumping everything all at once to prepare me for something else.

Or maybe it was because my prayers had been answered —I was finally getting the closure I deserved.

"How are you feeling, Natalie?" Dolores asked. "I heard about the abduction, and I'm so glad you're safe."

"I'm okay. Please have a seat."

"Do you want something to drink?" Grayson asked us.

"Wine. A big bottle, please." I needed something to soothe my nerves.

Sergeant Kennedy laughed. "I'd never say no to wine. Give me your best wine, boy." Her gray hair had grown longer, and she wore it in a braid. She paired a brown jacket over a flannel top with jeans.

Grayson poured three glasses of wine and sat beside me.

Dolores sipped and placed her glass on the table. "This is fabulous."

"It better be. I paid thirty grand for that."

Dolores blinked and grabbed the glass again, downing it. "Then I better make sure it doesn't go to waste."

I laughed and agreed the wine was fantastic.

"I volunteer at RISD because my husband was a film and animation professor there," Dolores began. "When Sam passed, I continued volunteering. I met your father at one of the fashion show presentations. He loved one of the indie films Sam had worked on. We started chatting, and I told him Sam left a property to me, but I didn't know what to do with it."

Grayson rubbed circles on my back.

"Your dad told me you're very passionate about your work, but family responsibility trapped you. Restricted your creativity."

Tears welled in my eyes. Dad knew me more than I thought.

"He wanted The Prism so you could start your own company here in the States. No one would know your connection to LaRue. Even if they did, it would be two separate entities. You could do whatever you wanted with your own label."

Grayson offered me a tissue.

"Thanks." I dabbed my eyes. "Were you the one who sent me the deed and his pocket watch?"

Dolores nodded. "He mentioned about his sister. Though he didn't say much, he asked me to keep the property private until he resolved some financial issues at LaRue. He also gave me the watch. Maybe he sensed something was wrong and needed to prepare. He'd speculated his sister had gotten the company into financial hardship on purpose, but needed proof."

I'd always wondered why House of LaRue suddenly had financial issues. Now I understood the reason she never offered Mom or me straightforward answers.

"Why weren't there any keys to the property?" I asked.

"Sam had so many keys, and I didn't know what set belonged to which building. He wasn't the most organized individual, but I loved him. I gave your dad several keys, hoping they'd work. Maybe they didn't, and he never got the chance to get new locks and keys."

Even if I had the keys, the crime organization that took over the passageways would have changed the locks anyway.

"The timing of the plane crash didn't sit well with me," Dolores said. "So I hid all the information about The Prism from the City of Providence. I'd been employed there forever. No one questioned me when I gave them an answer." Her eyes sparkled. "When I saw your resume, I knew it was Eugene's daughter in disguise. I'm on the hiring committee, and I vouched for you."

"And here I thought I got hired for my credentials."

"Sweetheart, your resume was fine, but there were other candidates who were more qualified because they had municipal experience. You had none, and the jobs you put down were fake. People on the hiring committee do their research, but I took your resume and told Commissioner Conner that you'd be a great fit for him."

I reached across the table for her hand. "Thank you for helping me."

"You're welcome."

<hr>

After Dolores left, I stayed on the couch and finished another glass of wine. Dolores took the bottle home, promising she'd finish it when she got home.

Grayson didn't believe her and decided to drive her home.

Information bounced around in my head. Dolores had given me the closure I needed. She didn't know about the tunnels under the property. The Prism was destroyed, but now I knew why Dad had given it to me to do as I pleased, a lightness surrounded my heart. I could now sell the land without feeling guilty.

I wanted to sell it to Grayson to be part of Three Point Park. If anyone could rebuild it to something iconic, he could. I didn't care if he kept the same design or created something new. The reason my dad gave it to me was because he wanted me to start fresh. No other man could help me with that better than Grayson. I wanted him to have it.

As far as my fashion label went, I was content moving at a slow pace. I didn't need a large building. When the time was right, I'd consider it, but right now I preferred keeping Momentum on a manageable scale so I didn't stress myself out.

I'd tell him my decision when he returned.

CHAPTER FIFTY-FIVE

GRAYSON

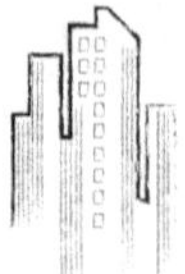

On my way home from Dolores's, I received a call from the nurse at the hospital where Derek had been staying and rushed over.

"Where is he?" I asked Nurse Carol. I'd paid her a bonus to monitor him and to alert me if someone suspicious visited him. The guard I'd hired would have kept him safe, but I wanted an extra set of eyes.

She shook her head, and my heart dropped. "I'm sorry. He didn't make it. His injuries were too severe. He could speak a little in the last few days and left this for you." She handed me a flash drive.

"He wanted to be cremated and asked if you could send him to the ocean, so he could apologize to his brother."

For the first time since my dad's death, a tear slid down my cheek. Dad and Uncle Derek used to love fishing. I'd accompanied them a few times. They told me stories about the ocean connecting people after death because water could flow from one realm to another. Death had finally released Uncle Derek from his sins and the crime world.

After signing papers and organizing the cremation, I went into my car, grabbed the spare laptop I kept there for emergencies, and reviewed the flash drive.

A video popped up with an apology. He'd recorded it in his prison cell.

"Grayson, I know you'll never forgive me. And I don't want you to. I deserve your hatred, but I want you to know I regret everything I've done. My time is up. The Trogyn have placed their men as construction workers renovating the prison. They want me dead because I know too much. I'm running out of funds, so I can't pay the people who were keeping me safe. They're just as powerful as The Trogyn. Money talks in the corrupt world. Here's a list of clubs you can start with."

He named the clubs, and I typed them into an email ready to send to my friends.

"These are the ones I know about. There are more out there. Some might go by different names to hide the club's true identity. If you can get into the club, someone will ask you strange astrological questions like: who is Salacia Neptuni? The answer is: Neptune's mermaid wife. She represents the sparkles of sunlight and moonlight on the surface of the sea."

I'd never heard of that name before.

"Another question might be: what's the asteroid that changed the sea? The answer is Asteroid Sedna. It's an Inuit myth where her father chose some men for her to marry. She didn't like them and rebelled by marrying a dog. That made him angry, so he brought her out to the sea in a canoe and tossed her into the water. She clung onto the edge of the boat, and he cut off her fingers. She became the goddess of the sea, and her fingers became the whales, dolphins, and turtles."

That was a wild story, and I would never have known any of it. Who thought of these odd questions?

"There could be other questions, but these are the ones I've encountered." He paused a moment and looked into the camera straight at me. My skin tingled from his stare. *"I'm very proud of the man you've become. This is from one man to another. You've become the man I could never be, and I know your father would be just as proud of you as I am."* He pressed his lips into a thin line. *"I've given you video clips of other crimes I've witnessed in the organization. Maybe they'll be useful to you and your friends. Take care of your sister and your mom for me."*

The video went blank, followed by a series of clips that would definitely be useful later. I sat in the car for a long time, trying to process my emotions.

CHAPTER FIFTY-SIX

NATALIE

After Grayson scattered his uncle's ashes at sea, he focused on work, flying back and forth between the East and West Coast. I'd hardly seen him in the last three weeks. When we saw each other, he wouldn't look me in the eye. Or was that my imagination? It seemed like he was avoiding me. But why?

He thanked me for The Prism and promised to make it even better than what it was. I didn't doubt that.

With the money from the sale, I created a fund to help students in financial need at RISD. Dolores Kennedy was happy to assist me in managing that fund.

I didn't have anything scheduled for the rest of the day, so I wanted to go shopping to clear my head. Maybe I could browse the commercial properties in the area for a potential retail space that would suit my future store. The reality of it wouldn't happen anytime soon, but I loved the mindset of living the dream as if it had already happened.

Grayson wouldn't be back until tomorrow. Perhaps I

could buy some new lingerie to entice him. Something was going on with him, but I couldn't pinpoint what. Maybe it was Three Point Park that was stressing him out. I was hoping he'd share more details on his plan for The Prism, but he hadn't said anything.

I stopped saying "I love you" to him because I didn't know if it meant anything. He hadn't said those words back to me. If I kept saying them, it might make him feel awkward. I only wanted those words from him when he was ready and not because I pressured him. I didn't know. Maybe I was overthinking things. This whole thing unsettled me.

Should I confront him? But he'd been busy, and I didn't want to add more stress onto his plate.

Shopping had solved a lot of issues for me in the past. Maybe it would solve this one too. I loved the late October weather that called for a light jacket over a sweater and long boots. I entered a boutique in downtown Providence called The Style Palette and browsed the racks. The quaint shop carried unique collections and supported local designers. I loved the atmosphere where you could find novelty styles.

Not that I didn't enjoy going to the big shops with all the big brands. I loved it, but I was used to that world already. Enjoying the little shops and discovering new designers held a different kind of allure for me. Newly discovered designers didn't have barriers. They could be wild and free. Once they became popular, there was this stigma that they had to stay in their lane so people could pick them out of the crowd.

I felt like I was one of these up-and-coming designers, even though I had years of experience in the fashion world. My new collection was limitless. I didn't care about barriers. I'd been there and knew what it felt like. Also, I didn't need the financial support that most designers required to start their career.

Though I had experience, I still feared failure. As an artist—as a designer—criticism poked my skin, no matter how thick it was. I was pouring my heart and soul into this collection. I was showing the world a part of me that no one had seen before. This was me turning myself inside out, so it was natural for me to fear people's reaction. What if no one responded well to my collection? What if the press wrote a bad review and no one bought my designs?

Stop sabotaging yourself. It doesn't matter what others think as long as you love it.

I had to succeed for myself, for Grayson, and for my dad. These men believed in me, and I didn't want to disappoint them.

I found some nice pink lingerie hanging on the rack. Maybe Grayson would like another lap dance with me in this outfit. After paying for my items, I left the shop and walked toward a takeout place. I was in the mood for sushi.

Someone bumped into me, shoving me right into the wall of the apartment building. I turned, and my heart hammered at the woman wearing a hooded jacket.

Aunt Estelle held a gun to my stomach. "Come with me. We need to talk."

I should have screamed, but I was curious about what she had to tell me. The world was looking for her.

One look in her eyes revealed a crazy woman at the end of her rope with nowhere to go. She'd shoot me without qualms. That was her personality. She always had to have the last word.

I could let her talk because I had things to say to her too.

I also wanted to test my self-defense skills on her. Not that I was good or anything, but my anger toward her needed an outlet. From the few self-defense classes and lessons with Grayson, I'd learned some moves.

She nudged me into an alley beside the apartment building and pushed me against the wall. I dropped my shopping bag.

"There's a manhunt for you. I can scream, and the authorities would be here. What do you want, Estelle?" Her name stung like poison on my tongue, and I understood why Grayson had addressed his uncle the way he had. She had lost the privilege of being my aunt.

"You ruined everything, bitch."

"Me? You murdered my father and fifty other passengers because you feared he'd reveal your true identity. You don't deserve to be part of the family. Dad accepted you even when he knew your identity. But you killed him."

"House of LaRue should've been mine! Your father was an incompetent man. He couldn't take LaRue to the next level. Every time I asked him to collaborate with investors, he turned it down. LaRue could have been the most valued brand in Europe, but he chose not to see its potential. What kind of business owner rejects an opportunity to advance? Stupid idiot."

"A businessman who values family and knows that quality doesn't mean how big it is in Europe. That makes him smart. It makes you an evil woman who's been working with criminals. What kind of person sells her niece to some sick man?" My hands curled into fists.

"You're not my niece. I put your picture up for auction, and several men placed obscene bids on you. I'm a businesswoman, so I'm not stupid enough to let that golden opportunity slip away."

"Just so you know, that Italian guy you paid is dead."

She blinked. "You killed him?"

I didn't reply and only smiled. She could interpret that statement however she liked.

"Bad people always pay for their sins. It's God's punishment. Yours is coming."

"You don't have the guts to kill anyone," she seethed as her hand trembled uncontrollably.

I took the opportunity and shoved her away, picking up a shard of glass from the ground. "Try me."

Her body quaked and a glaze formed in her eyes. Was she on drugs?

"Even your daughter doesn't want to have anything to do with you. She told the press her mom was dead to her. Did you know she's pregnant? Do you think she's going to want her child associated with a *murderer*?"

"You—"

I chopped at her hand with my forearm, and the gun clanked to the ground. I kicked it aside and used my body to block her attack. She pulled my hair, and I slammed a fist into her face and chest. She screamed and attacked me with her hands, which I blocked.

Someone pulled her away from me, and she shouted, "Let me go! Do you know who I am?"

"You're wanted for murder. The cops are here for you." I looked up at a stocky man holding a gun to Estelle's chest. He turned to me. "Ms. LaRue, are you okay?"

I nodded. "Yes. Thank you."

When the police arrived, I told them everything and discovered the man who helped me was Andrew Summers, a bodyguard Grayson had hired to keep me safe. Grayson had feared Estelle would come after me unexpectedly.

Why hadn't he shared this information with me? He was keeping too many things from me. We didn't talk like we used to. I didn't like how we were drifting further apart.

CHAPTER FIFTY-SEVEN

NATALIE

Grayson didn't come home for the next few days, saying he had urgent meetings. I assumed he'd want to see me after my frightening encounter with Estelle, but we'd just talked over the phone. I missed him.

My heart felt like a shoe with a broken heel. It wobbled back and forth as I sensed my relationship with Grayson falling apart. He'd been stressed, working late, and avoiding me. It was unlike him. Or was this the real Grayson I hadn't gotten to see until now?

I was so confused. He'd done so much for me, so I should be more understanding of his schedule. Yet, my inner voice kept whispering doubts to me.

Shoving my anxiety aside, I uploaded my entire collection onto a rendering software. It allowed me to see the apparel designs on three-dimensional figures. Excitement filled me as I reviewed and fell in love with the ten designs I'd chosen for my Momentum debut.

I kept this first collection small and manageable. Each one told its own story instead of the twenty or thirty designs I could've created. When I received the new forecast on fabric trends, I incorporated them into my collection. Concentrating on materials that were new to the market and Earth friendly was important to me. I was proud to be a member of Nature's Innovation Society, an association that researched new techniques in wearable materials. I didn't want to dump hazardous dyes into the land or the ocean. My preference was to use as many organic materials as possible.

Success came with responsibility, and House of LaRue had been part of Nature's Innovation Society since its inception five years ago. It was crucial that the environment I lived in was safe, clean, and healthy for me and my children. Yes, I hoped to start a family someday.

A smile danced on my lips as I wondered if Grayson wanted kids too. What would our children look like? They'd be a beautiful blend of cultures, aspects of him and me, and our unique creativity.

He was the first man I'd ever considered having kids with. My history with men hadn't been successful, and I had thought something was wrong with me. Or that I was just unlucky with men.

Every mistake led me one step closer to the man I was meant to be with.

I wanted to share my new designs with him. He'd be thrilled because he knew how much this meant to me. This was my breakthrough—a dream I didn't think would happen.

Feeling a little better about myself, I texted him.

Natalie: *Hi! Are you busy?*

Grayson: *Yup.*

Natalie: *Oh, okay.*

Nausea stirred in my stomach.

Grayson: *What's up?*

Natalie: *Nothing. I just miss you.*

I didn't want to interrupt him if he was in a meeting or doing something important.

A long moment passed without a reply. The construction for the two buildings for Three Point Park was almost finished, so I could only imagine the stress Grayson was dealing with. The construction for The Prism was last on the list because it started after the other two buildings.

He and I were on similar journeys, both working toward our dreams. We understood the artist's struggle, the emotional rollercoaster of self-doubt, and the courage and patience needed to continue despite those struggles.

I fell for him because I understood him. Did he understand me the same way?

With Derek's death, Grayson could now start his healing process. Though Derek was a bad man, his love for Grayson was real. That proved to me that a dark heart could learn to love. That there was hope for everything.

The human heart had immense power, but it was also a mystery that no one truly understood. Perhaps that was its beauty and its curse.

Grayson: *Gotta run to a meeting. Won't be coming home until next week.*

I couldn't shake this odd feeling that a storm was coming and there was no umbrella wide or strong enough to protect me.

CHAPTER FIFTY-EIGHT

GRAYSON

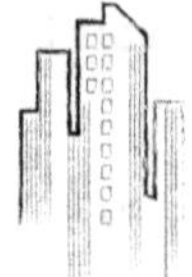

Inside my hotel room in New York City, I stared at Natalie's text messages. She was hurt, and I'd done it. I could feel her pain searing into me from the screen.

This was the only way to ensure her safety.

CHAPTER FIFTY-NINE

NATALIE

Grayson arrived in Providence yesterday, but was too tired to visit me. I'd been working all morning, and it was now lunchtime. I missed him and sent him a text.

Natalie: *Will you be home for dinner?*

Grayson: *I've got a lot on my plate. Not coming home for dinner.*

Natalie: *You need to eat so you have energy.*

Grayson: *I'll order something. Is that all?*

My heart cracked from the bitter tone.

Natalie: *I'll let you get back to work.*

Why did I feel like I was just pushed aside?

He was probably stressed with Three Point Park. Anxiety took a toll on a person, so I was trying to be an understanding girlfriend. But I wasn't sure how much longer I could tolerate his dismissal of me.

The following day, I went to his place after work and found him in a sweatshirt and pants inside his office, slouching in his chair, drinking from a bottle of whiskey. He'd never done this before. What the hell was going on?

I yanked the bottle away from him. "Is everything all right? Why are you drinking?"

"Having a good time."

"Did something happen at work? Why are you acting like this? I'm worried about you."

He grabbed the bottle back from my hand. "This is how I was before I met you. Stop trying to change me."

That comment stung, but I shoved it away.

"I'm not trying to change anything. What happened to the architect I fell in love with? What happened to the joy I used to see in your eyes? What's going on with you? How can I help if I don't know?"

"I'm not interested in your help. I like variety. If you haven't noticed, open your eyes."

What did he mean by that?

"What are you talking about?" Nerves stabbed my insides.

"It's been fun, buttercup. But I need more variety. More *spontaneity*. You're too . . . simple for my taste."

I didn't know what people meant when they referred to the heart dying. How could it die when they were still breathing? But at this moment, I finally understood what it felt like to have my heart deflate in slow motion like a balloon losing helium. My bodily systems detached from themselves, disabling my emotions and my senses. I felt like an empty shell standing before him. Like a fool who had just realized she'd been defeated.

Don't cry.

Don't show him how shattered you are.

"Is that why you haven't been home?"

He let out a laugh. "Did you think I was working? I was

craving variety in lap dances . . . happy endings. Yours were good, but not that good."

His words cut into my heart like sharp shears snipping it to pieces that fell to the ground. As they fell, the raw edges came apart, making my heart unsalvageable, as though it was a garment that could no longer be repaired. My body trembled like a spool of thread being yanked by its last strand. There was nothing left for me—nothing left for us.

Don't crumble.

But he's drunk. Could he mean those words? *People usually tell the truth when they're drunk.*

I dared not collapse in front of him. That would give him too much power. I was too shocked and devastated to think clearly, but there was one thing I was good at—maintaining my integrity. If he only saw me as one of his many women, that was his loss.

I knew why he never said those words to me. He'd never loved me. Had he laughed at me every time I poured out my heart to him? He was always the player the media claimed him to be. A tiger didn't change its stripes. I should have known better.

I was a fool for believing he was different.

"I guess this is it for us."

He could drink himself to death. I didn't care.

A sigh escaped me as though it were the last breath in my heart for him. My shoulders caved along with my chest as I made my way out of his house with no intention of returning.

As I drove away, tears stung and blurred my vision, forcing me to pull over to the side of the road. My heart hurt so much. I didn't know what to do. I thought what we had was precious.

Why was I so stupid? I let myself cry until I used up the entire tissue box.

CHAPTER SIXTY

NATALIE

Grayson never called me after that night, and I never called him either. It was over. We'd broken up and left our belongings at each other's homes. He could toss out my stuff. I didn't need it. I could start fresh by buying new stuff.

A stupid part of me wanted him to call or text me. At least that showed the relationship had meant more to him.

I was so done with men. I texted my girls.

Natalie: *You guys want to go out for drinks? I'm pissed.*

Audri: *Yes. Come to Krazee Tavern. I'm already here.*

Kiera: *Meet you there in fifteen.*

Michelle: *See you soon.*

Vivian: *Still in CA. Update me later, please.*

Natalie: *Okay, Viv. Don't worry.*

Twenty minutes later, we gathered around a table. The girls ordered some appetizers and drinks. I got a bottle of white wine—the most expensive bottle the restaurant had in stock.

"I'm paying for this. Don't write it off." I glared at Audri as I refilled my glass.

"Okay." Her expression softened. "What's going on? Did you have a fight with Grayson?"

I laughed. "It wasn't a fight. We broke up."

"What?" Kiera, Michelle, and Audri exclaimed in unison.

I gulped my wine and refilled the glass. "Yup. He told me he wanted variety, and that I was 'too simple' for him."

Audri furrowed her eyebrows. "He said that?"

I nodded as tears welled in my eyes. "I thought he'd just been working late, but it turns out he's been seeing other women."

"I'm going to kill him!" Audri said.

"Oh, honey." Kiera pulled me into an embrace. "Men are jerks. I'm so sorry."

"I thought we had something special," I cried and finished another glass of wine. Reaching for the bottle, Michelle swatted my hand away.

"I want some wine too. Don't drink it all." Michelle poured herself a full glass and gave me just a little. "Anyone else want some before Natalie drinks it all?"

Kiera lifted her hand even though she hadn't touched her Cosmopolitan.

"Bitch, stop hogging it," I said with a laugh, my words slurring. *Shit.* Was I already drunk? "I only had two glasses of wine. Why do I feel all woozy?"

"You had four glasses," Audri said.

"What . . ." I buried my face in my folded arms on the table and cried, "I feel so stupid."

"You're not," Michelle said. "He is."

"I can't believe him. I'm going to kick his butt for you," Audri said.

I sat up. "Okay."

Kiera pushed a glass of water in front of me. "This is going to help prevent the hangover you might have tomorrow."

"I'm not drunk."

"Yes, you are." Kiera smiled.

"Maybe just a little." I placed a hand on my throbbing head. I wasn't used to this much wine in one sitting. It was too much for me, and my body didn't like it. "I have a favor to ask you." I drank the glass of water and prayed I'd be fine when I woke tomorrow.

"You don't have to ask. We're here for you." Michelle clasped my hand and squeezed.

"I have a new handbag collection I would love you to help me promote."

Audri gasped. "Do you have a marketing campaign already? If not, I'd love to help out."

"I don't have anything yet. I plan on staying in Providence to promote Momentum. Maybe look for a retail space."

"That's the label?" Kiera asked with wide eyes.

"I thought I already told you?" A hand went to my forehead.

"Nope. You've had a lot going on with the abduction, the mystery around your dad's death, and now this. We understand." Michelle sipped from her wineglass.

I narrowed my eyes at her, knowing she'd taken the wine so I couldn't drink more.

"You don't need to go back to Paris to help with LaRue?" Audri asked.

"I can help them while I'm here. My mom has it under control, and they promoted a designer to take over my role so I can dedicate more time to Momentum."

"Count me in." Michelle smiled. "I'll do a bunch of blog posts on your bags and clothes."

"I'll be your fashion photographer. If you have samples, I can give them away to supermodels to promote. If they know you're the designer for LaRue, they'll be all over it."

"Please don't tell them. I want to do this with no ties to LaRue. I need to succeed on my own."

"Okay, no worries," the girls said in unison.

I didn't remember driving home or getting into my apartment. Somehow the girls must have tucked me into bed. The last thing I remembered was thanking them for being my friends and imagining Grayson as the dummy in my self-defense class, where I kicked and punched him until his limbs fell apart.

CHAPTER SIXTY-ONE

GRAYSON

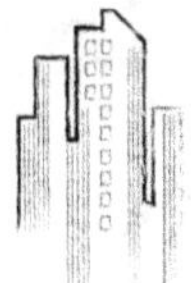

"What is wrong with you?" Audri yelled at me over the phone.

"What are you talking about?"

"You and Natalie. You've been cheating on her."

I didn't reply to her statement.

"Why?"

"That's none of your business."

"Well, she got drunk last night with us. You broke her heart. I've never seen her so devastated. I can't believe you!"

"She was drunk?" Guilt speared through me.

"Yes. But she told us she was staying in Providence to promote her new fashion label. We agreed to help her."

"What? She's *staying* in Providence?" Fear tumbled in my stomach. This wasn't how it was supposed to happen. This wasn't the plan. She was supposed to leave me and go back to Paris, where she could be safe.

"Why do you sound so surprised?" Audri asked.

"Well, if she's around, then she'll see my new girlfriend. It'll be awkward."

"You're such an asshole. I thought my brother was better than this. Stay away from all my friends!" Audri hung up on me.

I'd managed to piss her off too.

My heart ached, knowing Natalie was in pain. What she didn't know was I hadn't been drunk that day. Each word I told her had cut into my heart as well.

She couldn't be here in Providence—close to me—where danger lurked in every corner.

Plan A didn't work as I had hoped. Now it was time for Plan B.

I made a call to two women, but neither of them were Natalie.

CHAPTER SIXTY-TWO

GRAYSON

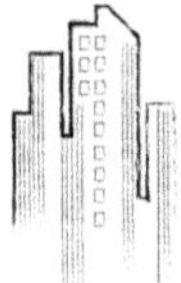

A few days later, I sent Natalie a text hoping she'd meet me.

Grayson: *Can we meet up?*

Natalie: *Why?*

Grayson: *I have your belongings.*

Natalie: *Fine. I have yours too.*

Grayson: *I'll swing by in an hour?*

Natalie: *Fine.*

I picked up dinner and arrived on time. She opened the door, and her expression appeared impassive. She had on makeup and looked like she'd just gotten back from an evening out. I wanted to ask where she'd been and who she went out with, but I couldn't.

I left a box of her belongings on the kitchen table, along with the takeout dinner and two bottles of water. I didn't give her back all her belongings. When I missed her, I'd want something tangible to remind me of her.

She gave me a box of my stuff with *everything* in it. My toothbrush, razer, shaving cream, and other toiletries sat on top of clothes.

"Thanks," I said.

She stared at me. "Are you done? You can go now."

Her words pierced through my heart and out to the other side. "Do you want to have dinner with me?"

She snorted and made a disgusted face. "Don't play games with me, Grayson. You ripped my heart out and stomped on it. And now you want to have dinner with me? What planet are you from? Because women on Earth don't approve of assholes treating them like shit." She crossed her arms.

"I know you're mad at me, but I still consider you a friend. Do you want to know how the Three Point Park project is coming along? Just pretend I'm an acquaintance."

She considered me for a moment and sighed. "No, thanks. I'm sure it'll be wonderful. I'm tired. I need to rest." She gestured to the door. "You can go now."

Ignoring her, I asked, "Why aren't you back in Paris?"

"Why do you care? Am I an eyesore around here? Am I interrupting your various dates?"

"No," I said too quickly. "I was just curious how LaRue is doing."

"It's fine. Anything else?"

I shook my head and walked to the door. "Enjoy the dinner. I got you sushi." I left with my box of belongings and sat in my car until one in the morning.

This was my property, so I could enter whenever I wanted. I still had access to her apartment. She'd forgotten to change the code, but even if she had, I'd know it.

For Natalie, I'd done so many things that baffled me. I'd never broken into a woman's apartment before, but there was no other way. My stubborn woman refused to leave Providence. What choice did I have?

Quarter past one arrived, and I stood in front of her apartment. Pressing my ear to the door, silence greeted me. I used the master key along with the code and entered the dark apartment. I checked the kitchen table and didn't see the food or drinks I'd left. Pulling out her trashcan, I saw the empty sushi container and one empty bottle of water where I'd crushed a sleeping pill and mixed it with the liquid.

I walked into her bedroom and found her sound asleep. A cute snore escaped her. The other water bottle I'd brought was beside her bed on the nightstand, unopened. I gathered her purse, her laptop, the charger, and a few clothing items, shoving them into a luggage case I got from her closet. Then I carried her to my car first. The second trip was for her luggage. Next, I drove to a private airport where a plane was waiting for me.

I brought her into the plane, and Mom greeted me in a sweatshirt and matching pants.

"I can't believe you're doing this." My mom helped situate Natalie in the reclined seat and covered her with a blanket. "She's going to hate you."

Natalie let out a whimper and snuggled into the roomy seat.

"I know. But she'll be alive."

"Grayson." Mom placed a hand on my cheek. "Are you sure this is the only way?"

"It is, Mom. Thanks for helping. Mrs. LaRue will be at the airport in Paris to pick her up."

Shaking her head, my mom sighed. "Okay. Go home and rest. I'll text you when I've delivered her safely to her mother."

"Thank you." I stayed in my car and watched the flight take off.

I remembered when I first asked my mom and Natalie's mom to help me with this plan. They both had declined vehemently. But I reminded them about her abduction and the danger that surrounded me and the crime organization. I briefly told them something dangerous was happening, and I didn't want Natalie hurt. If I wanted to destroy this organization, then Natalie had to be far away from me. No one could know I loved her.

Her mother agreed. She'd already lost her husband; she couldn't lose her only daughter too.

To keep Natalie safe, I had to break her heart. But I feared this sacrifice was taking too much from me. What if I could never have her back?

I didn't want to think about it. Right now, I had to follow through with my plan.

Tomorrow, I'd be meeting the person who helped me locate Natalie when she'd been abducted. I needed to get home to continue my research on Club Diablo to prepare for an imperative meeting with my boys. We had to analyze every detail about our attack on this crime organization. Sending Natalie away was a huge sacrifice for me, and I had to ensure I survived to ask for her forgiveness.

The following week, I'd be entering Club Diablo in Cranston, Rhode Island, courtesy of Rafael. He'd gotten me tickets to the members-only club, where wealthy men came to gamble. To enter, a member had to refer you. Rafael's referral, his statement to the FBI about Natalie's aunt hiring him to deliver her to a buyer in Italy, and all the information he had about the crime organization earned him immunity from the authorities. They needed his cooperation to get more details about the secret society.

As long as he stayed out of my way and left Natalie alone, I'd make sure he could continue to breathe and enjoy his comfortable life.

CHAPTER SIXTY-THREE

NATALIE

I woke to sunlight blasting into the room and realized I was in my bedroom in Paris!

I bolted up on my bed, whipping my head around. Was I dreaming? I pinched my cheek, and pain bloomed. I glanced down at my matching pajama top and bottom. They hadn't changed.

What the hell was going on? I flew off the bed and paced around my bedroom. My purse was on the armchair and my phone was on its charging station. I peeked out the window, and yes, I was in Paris. But how had I gotten here? Had I been sleepwalking?

Even if I had, how had I gotten through the security checkpoint? This was bizarre. The last thing I remembered was showering and feeling exhausted, which led me straight to bed. I didn't want the sushi Grayson had brought over to go to waste, so I ate it. I was mad at him and not at the food or water bottles . . .

Was something in the food or in the water bottles? Had Grayson drugged me? The fucking asshole! Oh, my God, I could have killed him. I was so furious, my body shook. Was this some kind of joke? Did he think he could toss me out of Providence just like that? He didn't own me.

I understood he didn't want me there, but this interference in my life—my body—was beyond that. It was illegal.

Breathe, Natalie. Breathe.

Anxiety tightened my muscles, and I felt sick. Sick in my heart, sick in my mind. Just because he had money and power didn't mean he could drug me and discard me like trash.

Noises erupted from the kitchen, and hope sparked in me. Was he here so I could kill him with my own two hands?

I strode out to see my mom preparing breakfast. "Morning, sunshine."

It was stupid to think it was him. Grayson didn't want me. Why would he be here?

Get over him. You don't need him.

A numbness overcame my body, and for a moment, I couldn't feel anything. No anger, no resentment, no love . . . just nothing. Was that worse? I didn't know emptiness could make me so lost.

I didn't reply to my mom. She walked over, grabbed my hand, and led me to the kitchen table. "Let's eat."

I sat down and stared at the scrambled eggs. "How did I get here? Why are *you* here?"

Mom sighed. "I brought you home from the airport last night. Grayson said you're safer here in Paris."

"And you believe him?" I stabbed the eggs with my fork, pretending they were him.

"With all that's happened with your aunt and his uncle, I think it's best you spend some time here. Let the dust settle."

"Mom, Grayson and I broke up. It'll take me a while to

get over it, but what he just did was beyond that." I placed down the fork. "Did you ask how he got me onto the plane?"

Mom didn't say anything.

"He drugged me! That's breaking all kinds of relationship rules, not to mention it's illegal. He's not a doctor. And even if he was, he can't put sleeping medicine—or whatever it was—into my drink without my consent." Anger rose in me. "He *violated* me."

Would I have gone to Paris willingly if he'd asked? Absolutely not. But that was my right and my decision to make. He couldn't take my choices away from me. This emotional roller coaster was too much.

Tears streamed down my face.

"He told me what he did," Mom said. "I agreed."

"Mom! How could you?"

Now my mom cried. This situation was a fucking mess, and I hated him for it.

"I wanted you safe. You can work on your collection here. Give it a few months, then you can go back."

I had so many questions. How long had she known about his plan? What kind of spell did he put on my mother to make her agree to this insane scenario? What could happen in Providence that meant I needed to be in Paris?

"He wants me in Paris, so I don't interfere with his womanizing. He's been cheating on me, Mom. Whatever excuse he told you about my safety, it's a lie." I got up from the table. "Thanks for breakfast, but I'm not hungry. I'm not in the mood for company. The door will lock itself when you leave."

"Natalie . . ."

I just kicked my mom out of my apartment and my heart

hardened as I retrieved my laptop and concentrated on Momentum.

It didn't matter where I was—I could make Momentum succeed. And I'd have a fashion show in Providence just to shove it in his face that I was back.

Perhaps the distance would be good for me. I sensed a gloom rising from within me. Or was it depression clawing its way up my body, making me angry at myself? I couldn't tell anymore. I was a mess, but I didn't want to give him the satisfaction of seeing me defeated.

What he'd see would be a smiling woman enjoying life as though I'd never met him.

CHAPTER SIXTY-FOUR

GRAYSON

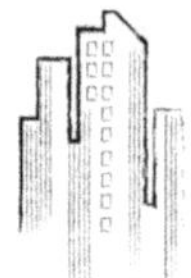

I leaned against my car, which was parked in front of the lot filled with construction vehicles and equipment. I had started the foundation and framework for The Prism. Natalie had sold it to me at an affordable price. She wanted The Prism to be part of Three Point Park, and that meant a lot to me. Rebuilding The Prism was a privilege, so I needed to make sure it represented something beautiful for Natalie.

Her mom had texted me saying Natalie was furious, but safe. She'd thrown herself into work, and that was what I'd wanted for her. She was with her family, and I didn't have to worry about her.

Maybe one day, Natalie would forgive me. It appeared she'd hate me forever. I had violated her body and her rights as a person. I'd never drugged anyone in my life, and it felt like shit doing it. When I first asked Forrest for his opinion, he flat-out told me not to do it. He was a doctor, so honoring a patient's rights was part of his code of ethics.

I wasn't a doctor, and she wasn't my patient. I was a man

deeply in love with a woman, and I'd do anything to protect her, including breaking the law.

What I wanted from Forrest was information on sleeping pills, like how many I should put into the water bottle. He cursed at me, but I explained my reason. He understood and also told me that Natalie would have my face on her dart board for the rest of her life. After the chat, he prescribed a sleeping aid where I only needed one pill to do the trick.

My friends and I had walked a thin line between right and wrong. That line often shifted because nothing was truly black or white. We had to do what was necessary, even if it was questionable. I didn't want to drug Natalie, but in order to keep her safe, I had to.

There was no doubt The Trogyn would target her if she were here. She was my weakness—*my everything*.

So I convinced myself that her hatred and anger toward me were side effects that came with the medication. Hopefully, they'd fade over time.

I pushed myself away from the car and walked toward the fence that secured the lot for construction. I'd renovate the tunnels under the property soon. Several explosions had occurred on the first floor that night, which left me wondering if the person who had detonated them knew about the passageways.

I'd incorporate the passageways into the new building, but few would be privy to that knowledge. Where did the tunnels connect to? Were there more in the city? These were questions that had to be analyzed later.

After the explosion, this area became an empty lot. Like a blank piece of paper, it could be anything. How would Natalie imagine it? I wanted this building to be a gift to her. A reminder popped into my head. She'd left a box in my dressing room, asking me not to open it until she said I could. That wasn't going to happen soon. I'd open it when I got home.

A cat scurried past my leg as a gray SUV pulled up behind my car. The driver exited the SUV wearing a leather jacket, slacks, boots, and dark glasses. He walked toward me, giving me a fist bump. My old friend had grown older with long silver hair tied back with a band.

I had my suspicions regarding the man who had been providing me information all along. This man should have been dead, but he was now smiling at me.

"How've you been, amigo?" Slash asked.

I was forever grateful he had given me and my friends a second chance at life on that fateful day at the abandoned church.

"I should ask you that question." I studied his face. The long slash that ran from his forehead across his cheek down to his neck remained the same. But there were burns on the other side of his face. "We all thought you'd died."

"I did die." He grinned. "How about we sit in your car and chat in case someone's driving by? I'm supposed to be dead, remember?"

Once we settled inside my car, I said, "How did you fake your death?"

"I had intel that the organization was sending someone to kill me. These people won't stop until the deed is done." He looked out at the street where two teenagers rode their bikes on the road. "They attacked faster than I expected. I almost died, but I'd been working with my friend Viktor— Royce's father—behind the scenes. He got me out and replaced me with a dead from the local morgue. The dead body wore my clothes."

Royce's father had been undercover with the organization trying to reveal who the elite members were, but he hadn't been successful. Now, Royce's parents were living a peaceful life in another country under different aliases.

I remembered Remi saying Slash had left a note requesting no one show up at his funeral because members of the organization would be present.

"Did you even have a funeral? Did your wife know about your fake death?"

He looked at me with regret in his eyes. "I couldn't tell Maria. They were watching her too. She had to show her raw emotions. My poor baby was devastated. When things settled, I reached out to her. It took time for her to forgive me, but eventually she did. Thank God." He pressed his palms together in prayer.

"How long did it take?" I asked, wondering when Natalie would forgive me.

"Six months of me showing my dedication and devotion."

There was hope for Natalie and me.

"What did you do that needs forgiveness, amigo?"

"Something unforgivable."

Slash waved a hand. "Anything can be forgiven if you do it right. You need to show your heart." He tapped his chest. "Words mean shit. You need to prove what you want."

The difference between him and me was that he'd been married for a long time, so he and his wife had a long history. Natalie and I were just embarking on a new journey, and I had crushed her. So her forgiveness might not happen.

Returning to the task at hand, I said, "Thanks for the intel on Natalie's location. How did you find out?"

Slash placed an elbow on the armrest. "A dead man is

like a ghost who can get things done better than one who's alive. The person who ratted me out to the organization was Natalie's aunt. Estelle LaRue is a ruthless woman, moving up the ranks. She asked me to kill someone for her. I told her I was busy with something. She didn't like people saying no to her, so she complained to the organization, claiming I wasn't loyal to them. She was right, but I wasn't sure if she knew about my business outside of the organization or was making shit up because I didn't do what she'd asked."

I told him her real identity.

He shook his head. "She was trying to find her place in a crime world ruled by powerful people. No one is your friend, no one is truly loyal. It's all about the money. If you make money for them, you're valuable—to an extent. I'm happy to hear about her punishment. But they'll get to her before she starts her prison sentence."

I wanted to say that Uncle Derek had lasted longer than expected, but he'd had money stashed away and paid another organization for protection. I didn't think Estelle was that prepared.

"I killed Adonis," Slash said casually. "The guy was on steroids and other shit. He was lurking around your building too many times."

He'd been aiding me from the shadows. "Thank you. You're responsible for the collapse of The Prism?"

Slash nodded. "They'd been using parts of the building for their crimes. It had to go."

I told him that the real estate now belonged to me.

"Good. Resurrect it. Clean it up. Make it better, amigo." He looked at me with curiosity. "So, what's your plan?"

"Club Diablo."

"Ahhh . . . Yes, start there. How did you know to start with the clubs?"

"Uncle Derek."

Slash nodded. "He came through at the end, didn't he?"

I nodded, coming to terms with my feelings about my uncle. "He said the organization discovered videos of us flying drones that day. He'd deleted them. I don't know if there are other videos around."

"I deleted the ones I knew about," Slash said. "I still have connections to the organization in ways they'd never know."

Relief settled in me. "Good to know."

"I can help you with whatever you need. Just call or text me." Slash handed me a phone. "Use this to contact me. I want to remain a ghost, so it's easier to help you and your friends."

"Does Remi know you're alive?"

"He will. I plan to meet up with him and the other boys soon." Slash looked at me. "You need bombs? Like the ones used to blow up that building?" He jerked a chin toward the construction site.

"How many do you have?"

"How many do you need?" A sly smile crept onto his face. "I've been to Club Diablo a few times before. I assume the layout hasn't changed. You only need a few bombs to go off at a certain time—when the gambling 'kings' play at the golden table. It's literally gold. It's hideous, considering all the money they have. Just my opinion."

I had planned to destroy the club, but wanted to check out the layout first. The blueprint I'd gotten from the City of Cranston showed a very simple layout of a restaurant. But the image I got when I drove by the other day revealed a much larger space. I couldn't trust the information the city provided.

"How soon can you get me the bombs?"

"When are you going?"

I told him my plan, and he promised to deliver them in time.

"They're high-tech ones. You can hide them in your socks."

I winced, imagining the various ways I could lose my feet.

Slash rolled his eyes as though we were shooting the breeze at a football game. We were talking about bombs, for fuck's sake.

"They won't go off. Each one is scheduled to detonate at a certain time. You'd want it on the day when innocent civilians aren't eating in the restaurant on the top floor. Their people monitor the basement, so if they all die, that's fine with me." He shrugged.

Agreeing with him, I scrubbed a hand over my face, realizing how real the danger was. What if I got caught? I could only imagine all the horrendous ways they'd torture me for information.

"Okay. I'll be in touch."

CHAPTER SIXTY-FIVE

NATALIE

When the samples for Momentum arrived, I hung them on a rack in my living room. A male and a female dress form stood staring at me, waiting to get dressed. I took a gown and pulled it over the female form and added a cropped jacket. Then I stepped back, surveying the outfit. The ensemble needed something else. I added a necklace and a leather belt.

Too much, I thought. So I whipped the belt off, tossing it aside. I had to compile the perfect ensemble for the fashion show. I had plenty of time. So much time that I was already working on the upcoming collections for next spring and fall. The designs could always be tweaked, but at least I'd have the staples for the selection completed.

Life had been interesting for me. Sometimes I didn't know what I was doing. I felt like a machine that was programmed. I'd wake up, eat breakfast, check my emails, and work on my collection. Sometimes I broke for lunch, other times I skipped it. I declined lunch with friends because I didn't consider these girls my true friends. They were acquaintances. I was done with faking my feelings.

Audri, Michelle, Kiera, and Vivian called and said they wanted to visit, but I wasn't ready for them either. I wasn't avoiding them. I just needed time to heal. My heart was still fractured, and I didn't know when it would mend itself.

Could it heal after an agonizing rupture like that? I'd fallen in love and opened my heart and soul to him, but he wrecked it all, making me feel foolish and unworthy. Even though I knew I wasn't foolish or unworthy, self-doubt had a sharp edge that sliced into me. When the person you loved— the man who was supposed to protect you—took your heart and tore it to shreds in front of your face, how were you supposed to react?

I decided a walk, and fresh air would help me breathe easier. It was mid-January, and light snow had fallen, making the city appear peaceful. I put on a coat, scarf, knit hat, gloves, and boots and braced for the cold weather.

The chill kissed my face, and I looked up at the falling snowflakes. I let them land on my face, appreciating the beauty of them. Each snowflake that dropped onto me was like silent words from the universe.

Be strong.

It will pass.

Your heart will be whole again.

I opened my eyes, and a snowflake landed on my dark glove. I used to love walking in the gentle rain, letting the raindrops kiss my face. There was something soothing about it. The snow flurries had the same effect. I stared at the snowflake as it melted on the surface of my glove and couldn't help but compare it to my heart. Though my heart was disappearing, aspects of it still lingered, reminding me of the pain.

He didn't love me, so I should be able to forget him easily. But why couldn't I?

Maybe I should start dating again. Perhaps that would help me forget him. Grayson had seeped into my blood, and I didn't know how to get rid of him.

Mom told me to give it time. She made no suggestion for me to see other people. Her support for Grayson baffled me. Most mothers would want their daughter to move on, but somehow Grayson had charmed her. I didn't understand it.

Tears filled my eyes, but I blinked them away. I went on a walk to clear my mind, not to cry in public.

Cars honked and a group of tourists came out of a restaurant, filling the silence with chatter and bringing out a different energy.

I took out my phone and snapped a photo of another snowflake on my glove and posted it to ChatNow. It was my second photo on that platform with one statement: Beauty is momentary. Capture it before it disappears.

More people strode by with cups of coffee warming their hands. A couple walked toward me, the man with an arm around the woman, pulling her close to keep warm. My chest tightened, remembering how Grayson used to make me feel safe and warm.

Stop thinking about him.

I went into a café, bought a cup of coffee, and continued walking. I had no direction to where I was going and kept walking and turning down streets. Eventually, I came to the building that held my first auction—where Grayson had purchased my sweater.

Had he worn it yet? Or had he tossed it out?

My heart lurched, imagining him throwing it out. That sweater meant so much to me. I had been terrified when I knitted it, and even more frightened when I submitted the piece to the auction. After it sold, I felt validated—someone loved it enough to pay that much for my sweater.

I hoped he'd donate it to RISD, MassArt, FIT, or even Pratt. A fashion school would be happy to receive it.

Sighing, I continued walking away from that building and headed down another street and another. A ruckus sounded in the distance, and I was about to head over there, but a voice spoke up near me.

"It's not safe over there. Too many drunken men in the streets."

I turned to Andrew—Grayson's bodyguard—standing beside me wearing a thick coat and a paperboy hat. He gripped a cup of coffee in his hand. "It's safer that way." He gestured to where I had just come from.

I remembered how he'd come to my rescue when Estelle attacked me.

With furrowed eyebrows, I studied him from top to bottom. "Did Grayson send you to Paris?"

He didn't reply, but his smile and his eyes told me enough. How long had Andrew been following me? If Grayson didn't care about me anymore, why would he send his bodyguard to watch over me? Had he made some deal with my mom?

I could take care of myself. I didn't need Grayson or his bodyguard.

There was no anger in me. I was too tired for that and sighed. "Andrew, it's very nice to see you here. I hope Paris is treating you well, but please tell your boss I don't need or want you following me around. He can save money and put it toward something else. I'm certain he has a lot of job openings more suitable for you. It's boring following someone who rarely goes out, right?"

Andrew smiled, but didn't reply.

"Have a good evening. Don't stay out too late. I heard more snow's coming."

"You as well, Ms. LaRue."

Grayson said he still saw me as his friend during our last encounter. How many of his other female friends had a bodyguard following them around? Maybe all of them.

I returned to my apartment and threw myself into work, forgetting about Grayson.

CHAPTER SIXTY-SIX

GRAYSON

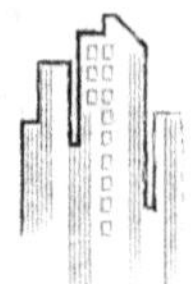

I hadn't slept well in days, keeping myself busy with the upcoming visit to Club Diablo and the Three Point Park project.

Inside my office, I sat and mapped out what I needed to do in the next few days. My phone rang, and I ignored it. It rang again.

Cursing, I picked up the call and barked. "What?"

"You okay? Just wondering if you want me to swing by with dinner later?" Forrest asked.

My boys and I were supposed to go over the attack plan for Club Diablo. I'd almost forgotten about it.

"Sorry. Anything is fine. I don't care."

"You need a break? We can reschedule the meeting for tomorrow if that's better for you."

"No, tonight's good. The sooner we get the strategy outlined, the better I'll feel."

"Agreed."

After I hung up, I headed into the kitchen and made myself a cup of coffee. Just the scent of the coffee gave me the boost I needed. My mind had to be alert for my friends. Details mattered for this kind of intricate plan. Things could go wrong, and we had to cover all the bases. If someone caught me, I was certain they would torture me until I gave them the information they wanted. I'd rather die than give them what could hurt my family or friends.

So yes, this coffee was my lifeline. After the meeting, I'd be able to crash.

Last night, I received a text message from Andrew saying Natalie had a conversation with him and requested he stopped following her around. There was no way I'd pull Andrew from his important post. He had to be more discreet, so she didn't spot him. Someone had to be there to protect her because I couldn't.

Andrew had sent me some pictures of her wandering the streets. She looked sad, yet hopeful. I wished I could give her a hug.

When this incident at Club Diablo ended, I'd apologize and pray our relationship could resume. But something told me it wasn't going to happen.

Remembering her gift box, I finished my coffee, walked into my dressing room, and retrieved it from the top of a drawer. I removed her note, setting it aside. Lifting the lid off the box, I took out three elegant ties in red, navy, and silver. Each had geometric designs that looked like textures I'd used in my buildings and decorative accents. They were simple designs that suited me perfectly. She knew me well.

I opened the small envelope and pulled out a card.

*Three reasons **knot** to forget me.*

I'm putting a label on this relationship with care instructions on the back.

I didn't know how to tie a Natalie knot the way she did.

She'd have to come back and show me. Would there even be a chance? With the box of ties in my hand, I dropped into the armchair and examined each tie carefully. I flipped it around, checked out the care content, and my heart expanded, filling my chest with warmth.

100% Love

Only For You.

Forever and Ever.

Underneath that customized label was the real care content stating, "100% Silk, Dry Clean Only. Steam, Not Iron. Do Not Bleach."

I sat for a long moment, absorbing her words and the care she took to make these for me. After an hour—I'd lost track of time—I placed the ties back into the box, planning when I'd wear them. My eyes went to the sweater I'd bought at the auction.

Removing my sweatshirt, I put on the novel sweater, snapped a selfie, and posted it to ChatNow. I saw her snowflake image, and my heart ached, missing her. My house still carried her scent. Or maybe that was me remembering her everywhere. I was going to like her post, but then she might block me, so I didn't. On the post, I typed the caption: keeping warm with love.

After that, I went to work on The Prism's blueprint before my friends' arrival. I knew what I'd design for the interior of the building now.

All my boys arrived on time, which was a miracle. Someone was usually late. Maybe Forrest told them I was tired and needed to get shit done so I could sleep. Whatever it was, I was glad I didn't have to wait for anyone.

Arrow pointed to the strategy he'd laid out on the table. "Based on the rough sketch Slash provided, I assume one of the best places for you to hide the bombs would be at the bar."

Royce reviewed Club Diablo's layout. "Another could be over here, assuming that's where the gold gambling table is. Are you playing?"

"No. Only seasoned members are invited to play. New members can watch. I'll use the opportunity to browse the area with Rafael."

"He's coming too?" Remi asked from across the round table.

"Yup. It's his last deed before I help him with a business that could make him money. I'll profit too. But he doesn't know that yet."

My generosity had its limits. I wasn't going to help Natalie's ex-fiancé without getting something back. He'd put his hands on her and threatened her. How could I forget that? At one point, I'd wanted to kill him, but he was more useful alive than dead.

"Do you have your audio equipment ready?" Forrest asked, rummaging through the box of electronics on the table.

I jerked my chin at a smaller box. "They arrived yesterday. These are tiny and have better reception. You guys should be able to hear everything."

"We got you something." Remi handed me a box.

"It's not my birthday."

"Just open it." Forrest slapped a hand on my back.

I opened it, pulling out a gleaming Rolex. "I already have one, but thanks."

"This one has a camera in it. The clarity and audio are fantastic. It's a limited edition." Remi pointed to a tiny dot signifying the camera.

"Cool. This will be useful."

"Where's mine?" Royce teased, looking at Remi.

"I knew you'd ask." He went to the couch and brought over a bag. Each one of us got a slightly different Rolex, including Remi.

"You went shopping." Arrow put his watch on. "Thanks, man."

"I stopped by the shop to pick them up when I dropped Audri, Michelle, and Kiera off for their Hawaii vacation. They'll be there for two weeks. Audri doesn't know what's going on."

"Neither does Michelle," Royce added.

Forrest cut me a look, and an understanding passed between us. My boys were worried about their women too. They'd sent them off on a vacation. I infuriated mine, drugged her with sleeping pills, and forced her to stay in Paris. It seemed severe compared to what Remi and Royce had done.

But my situation was different. Natalie had recently been abducted, so she was already involved. In addition, her aunt had ties to the crime organization. It was too risky to have them link her to me.

After we reviewed the plan, they all went home. I hopped into the hot shower to clear my head and prepare for tomorrow. When I slid into bed, nerves churned in my stomach. Tomorrow was the turning point. Things would go well or turn into a disaster. I had to prepare for both.

CHAPTER SIXTY-SEVEN

GRAYSON

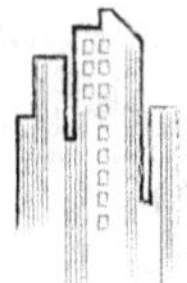

Dressed in a black suit with the red tie Natalie had given me, I strode into Club Diablo with Rafael, who wore all black, including his tie. The host had scanned our tickets, which were sent to our phones.

"Where did you get that? The red is fantastic." Rafael gestured to my tie.

I could be an ass and say Natalie made it for me, but then I'd be dragging her precious name into this club, a den of corruption. My buttercup deserved better. Besides, talking about her would only prompt Rafael to ask more questions, and my mind didn't have room for anything other than finding the appropriate locations to place the bombs.

I didn't tell Rafael about the bombs. He only knew I wanted to survey the club for elite members of The Trogyn, which was true. The less he knew the better off he'd be.

Most everyone in the club wore black suits. The few women who accompanied the men were decked in colorful dresses. I didn't recognize anyone. Maybe one of my boys would know someone. They were my eyes and ears as well.

The ambiance inside Club Diablo was similar to the elite men's clubs I'd visited before. Dim lighting and fancy sconces decorated the ceiling and walls. Sleek wooden furniture with luxurious couches adorned the lounge area. The burgundy rug made it seem like I was standing on a sea of blood.

The dark environment made me wonder if I was inside a nest of vipers. Were there eyes on me? I scanned the area, searching for cameras, but didn't see any. They probably had them hidden somewhere. Or did they assume no one would dare enter their turf to cause trouble? Maybe they thought everyone in the club had already passed the requirement with the size of their wallet.

Everyone who came here had money to play. And money was God.

Still, nerves and uncertainty prickled my skin. Things could go awry. I couldn't help but imagine there were multiple eyes scanning my every move.

A hostess wearing a tight black dress brought over a tray of champagne and wine. I took the wine glass and tipped her well. "Thank you." I made sure to hold the wine glass with my left hand so the Rolex could capture more videos.

"You're welcome. If you need anything else, let me know." She winked at me.

Rafael elbowed me. "That's an invitation for the back room, man." He smiled and jerked a chin toward the hallway past the bar. "I'm getting a whiskey on the rocks. Want anything?"

"Maybe after the wine, but I'll check out the bar with you." I didn't want my usual Martini stirred because everyone knew that was how I preferred my drink. It was best to separate the true Grayson from the one lurking in this club.

There was nothing peculiar about the bar that stood out to me. Two bartenders also dressed in black served two gentlemen in front of Rafael. I leaned on the counter, looking around at the five poker tables and spotted the golden table.

Holy shit, it's ugly.

I stared at the giant golden legs that supported a thick slab of gold. The slab was probably some granite painted in gold. Above the table hung a chandelier that reflected on the table. Shaking my head, I sipped my wine.

"It's a unique table, don't you agree?" A woman in her early forties wearing an elegant black dress stood beside me, holding a Mojito. She had dark brown hair that framed her oval shaped face.

"It's very . . . *shiny*," I said.

Her light green eyes sparkled. "Indeed. I always wondered how they could concentrate sitting there." She raked her eyes down my body and looked at my watch. "What's the asteroid that changed the sea?"

Fuck.

That caught me off-guard, and I flipped through my memory, trying to remember what Uncle Derek had said. It was the weirdness of the question and the answer that helped me remember.

I lifted my wine glass to her. "Asteroid Sedna. She's quite the character."

"She is indeed. What do you know about her?"

I told her what I remembered. "She didn't want to marry the man her father chose for her, so she married a dog. Furious, he took her out to sea in a boat and tossed her overboard, but she clung on. A woman who knows what she wants doesn't give up easily, right? He cut off her fingers and she became the goddess of the sea. Like the sea, she could be gentle or disruptive. I'm sure the sea embraced her." I finished my wine and placed it on the counter. "What's your name?"

"Linda Conner." She smiled. "You're well versed in myth and astrology."

"Not really." I let out a laugh. "But they fascinate me."

"I know you." A smirk appeared on her lips.

"You do?"

"My husband knows you too."

This conversation was getting interesting. Rafael went off to gamble after seeing me chat with Linda.

"He's over there, getting ready to play at the god-awful golden table."

I saw three men already seated at the table, but my gaze fixated on the man I never imagined would be here. "Robert Conner, The Commissioner for the City of Providence DPW, is your husband?"

"Isn't he handsome?"

I studied her. "I've never seen you before."

She sipped her drink. "It's because I travel for work between Texas, California, and Rhode Island. He's needed here in the city. We don't get to see each other often."

I'd always enjoyed working with Robert, but then again, people wore masks. And he wore his well because this was a complete surprise to me.

If anyone else had asked me that secret question, I'd still be looking for the elite members. But Linda Conner asked me, and in doing so, she gave me the answers—she and her husband were two of the elite members.

The other gambling kings at the golden table were probably part of The Trogyn too. People who could afford to gamble at that table had a lot of money. I didn't know Robert Conner was a wealthy man. He didn't come off as one. Perhaps it was his wife's money. It didn't matter. He was one of them.

"Nice meeting you. Enjoy your evening." Linda excused herself, walking over to a couple who had wandered in.

Did she suspect me? She had no reason to. I was a wealthy man visiting a luxurious club. I didn't know they frequented this place, and they didn't know about my visits. Perhaps this was a surprise to us both. Robert didn't even glance my way as he was concentrating on the players at this table.

Finishing my wine, I turned to the bartender and asked for a Kamikaze. Then I asked to use the restroom.

After placing a dime-sized bomb into toilet paper rolls inside a cabinet, I made my way to the back room, hiding one there as well. Slash had provided extra bombs, and this was my opportunity to use them.

On my way back, the waitress who had "invited" me to the back room earlier held a tray full of drinks, heading out from the bar. Pretending to look at my phone, I bumped into her. Her tray crashed to the floor, spilling drinks everywhere.

"I'm sorry," she said, looking horrified as she cleaned up the mess.

"No, I'm sorry. I should have paid more attention." I picked up the tray and a few glasses, bringing them behind the bar to the counter.

"Are you okay, sir?" the bartender with the short hair asked, looking at my stained jacket and pants.

I waved a hand. "It's fine. Do you have napkins I can use?"

He offered me a clean towel and went to serve three customers.

I bent down to wipe my pants and hid a bomb under the liquor cabinet. Once I was done, I got my Kamikaze and walked around several gambling sections, making sure the Rolex got various angles.

One table had three women chatting. They weren't playing cards or anything. I wanted to put a bomb under the golden table, but there was no way I'd get close to it without being questioned. So the next option was to find something close by.

These women were probably with the men gambling with Robert Conner.

"It must be nice to be playing at that shiny table." I gestured to the empty seat. "Is anyone sitting here?"

"Go right ahead, handsome. I've never seen you here before. I'm Bridgette." She had long, red hair and looked like she was in her twenties. Younger than the other two ladies.

"I'm Shauna," said the brunette with the puffy black dress.

"And I'm Crystal." She had curly black hair and blue eyes, but not as beautiful as Natalie's.

"It's lovely to meet all of you." I offered them a nod. "I'm Grayson."

"I haven't seen you at Club Diablo." Bridgette surveyed me.

"I've been traveling in Europe and recently returned. I needed a break so I decided to accompany, Rafael, tonight."

They looked over at Rafael who was winning something from the look on his face.

"Oh, you're with Rafael. He's adorable." Crystal's eyes sparked, revealing that she and Rafael had some kind of relationship I didn't want to know about.

"I'll definitely return more often." I slid my hand under the table, trying to find a groove for the bomb. Finding one, I carefully inserted it into the tiny groove, and my body relaxed back into the chair. "How often do you ladies come here? Are your men playing at the golden table?"

The conversation with these women revealed more than I anticipated. Robert and Linda Conner came to every event. Linda Conner was the heir to some oil mogul in Texas. She came from money and was probably the direct link to the organization.

Ten minutes later, I excused myself to use the bathroom and escaped out of the club, walking up past the first-floor restaurant and into the parking lot. Rafael came in his own car, and he knew I'd be leaving without him.

As I drove away, I chatted with my friends on the phone.

"Did you recognize anyone there?" I asked.

"Only Robert Conner," Remi said.

"Where the fuck did you pull that story about some sea goddess?" Arrow asked.

The other boys laughed.

I told them Uncle Derek had given me a couple of secret questions.

After a few more minutes, we ended our conversation, and I headed home to review the videos to see if I missed anyone suspicious. The bombs were set to explode tomorrow around the same time. The restaurant would be closed for the club's special gambling event.

I didn't know how much damage the bombs would cause,

but it would sow some chaos and have the organization wondering who was fucking with them.

Perhaps this attack would force them to retreat a little, giving me and my friends more time to destroy them.

I reached out to the PI, asking him to remove all videos of me around Club Diablo, including all the street cams within the vicinity. It was probably safer to go beyond the nearby streets. I didn't want to leave any breadcrumbs for these people.

CHAPTER SIXTY-EIGHT

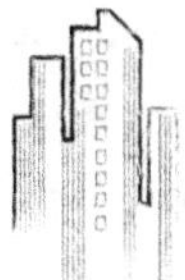

The next day, as I waited patiently in my office for the signal alerting me the bombs had gone off, I worked on The Prism. Three Point Park was coming together nicely, and the other two buildings, which I'd named Dream Key and Freedom Heights, were close to completion. Each of the buildings possessed forty-four floors.

As I worked on the designs for each floor of The Prism, I paid attention to the details. Floors forty-one, forty-two, and forty-three were designated to Natalie. Those three floors would have the best high-tech window panels on the market that also generated electricity. These acted like solar panels, but on a more advanced level.

I got lost in my work, forgetting about everything, until my phone rang and buzzed. I picked up Remi's call. "What's up?"

"Did you see the news?"

Realization dawned on me—I'd been so focused on The Prism that I'd forgotten about the bombs.

"Not yet. Did the bombs go off?"

"They did," Remi said with a joyful tone.

Turning on the TV, I watched the news.

The reporter wearing round eyeglasses described the situation. "A massive explosion occurred at Club Diablo just minutes ago. The restaurant has been completely destroyed. Authorities were shocked to find an underground gambling club beneath the restaurant. As of right now, there are no survivors, including the owner, whom the authorities wanted to question. In addition, Robert Conner, the DPW Commissioner for the City of Providence and his wife, Linda Conner, are among the deceased. There are so many unanswered questions. Why were the commissioner and his wife at an illegal establishment? Who else was there? The City of Providence and the City of Cranston are working with the FBI to sort this out. We will keep you updated as we receive more information."

A heavy sigh escaped me. This was exactly what I'd wanted. A big blow to The Trogyn. They had been responsible for my father's and uncle's deaths, as well as Royce's sister's. Not only that, they had also kidnapped my love and *sold* her. So this vengeance was well deserved.

This attack was just the beginning. My friends and I had to stop this organization from expanding. What would happen if they went unchecked?

A concept sparked in my mind. "Yo, I have an idea."

"I'm listening."

"We have video clips of Club Diablo, along with what Uncle Derek provided me for their other crimes. Let's incorporate the clips into our video games. We'll stylize them to work with our games. We could add them as images within a portal or something random like an Easter egg. Once Water-

Fyre Rising goes out into the mass market, everyone playing our games can see the evidence of The Trogyn's crimes."

"That's brilliant!"

A surge of hope rose in me like a sun rising after a stormy day.

"I'll upload the clips I have onto the shared drive for all of us to use."

"We should also incorporate videos we got from our drones," Remi added.

"Let's put everything we have on them in the game."

Our conversation ended. I sat back in my chair and allowed the excitement to fill me, knowing my friends and I had another way of protecting ourselves.

That night, I sat in my bedroom staring at the ties Natalie had given me. My hands shook as I prepared to send her a text message. This was scarier than entering Club Diablo. Natalie was everything to me. Her rejection was highly possible. What kind of woman would want to restart a relationship with a man who'd crushed her and made her feel like shit?

Despite the fear, I had to try.

Grayson: *Hi. Can we chat?*

A long pause with no reply.

Had she seen it and ignored me? Or was she busy?

Natalie: *Why?*

Grayson: *I want to apologize.*

Natalie: *It's too late for that.*

Grayson: *What do you mean?*

Natalie: *I don't want you in my life.*

A knife pierced through my heart and twisted.

Grayson: *I want to explain.*

Natalie: *No need.*

Grayson: *I'll wait until you forgive me.*

Natalie: *That will be a lifetime, and words mean nothing to me. Need to go. I'm busy.*

She didn't realize that I wasn't the kind of man who gave up easily. I knew I'd hurt her, and I'd do whatever it took to regain her love again.

CHAPTER SIXTY-NINE

NATALIE

To see my entire collection together was a thrill like no other. In the back room of a boutique gallery hosting my show, I stared at the rack of clothing in various colors. I only had ten main designs, but they came in various colors and patterns. There were twenty ensembles in total.

Momentum's show wasn't huge compared to the House of LaRue or other well-known brands, but this was my baby coming to life, so any exposure was worth it.

"Hey, beautiful!" Kiera's voice boomed in the room.

I'd invited the girls to my show in Paris. They'd be spending a few days with me at my apartment so we could catch up.

Audri, Michelle, and Vivian joined in for a massive group hug.

"I missed you all so much. You look beautiful, as always."

"We wanted to let you know we arrived safely." Audri glanced around. "Do you need any help?"

"No. You go out and take your seats or enjoy the art in the gallery. The show will start soon."

"You're even more gorgeous since I last saw you," Vivian said. "Must be all the hot European men surrounding you?" She ran a hand down my teal dress. "Love this."

"I'll get you one." I winked at her and the other girls. A memory sparked in me. "Don't go yet. I have something for you."

I rushed to the desk with all my stuff and brought over four bags with names on the tags.

"These handbags are part of my Friends Forever line. A bag is named after you. I appreciate your friendship more than you know." Tears blurred my eyes.

"Oh, my God. Look at this Audri bag! It's gorgeous!" Audri cried and gave me a one-arm hug. Her bag was baby blue with gunmetal trim.

"This is the most unbelievable Michelle bag! I love the lilac. There's so much room in it too. You're amazing."

Kiera almost knocked me over with her embrace. "No one has ever named a bag after me. It's stunning! The mossy green is perfect."

"Natalie, I don't know what to say." Vivian hugged me for a long moment before releasing me. "The pale yellow with lilac accents is so graceful. I love the extended strap."

I hadn't expected such emotional reactions from them. It made me cry even more. I didn't know why I was so sensitive today.

"The bags will be sold worldwide." I beamed. "I just got confirmation of a massive order for delivery in a few months."

"We're so happy for you." Michelle opened her arms for another group hug.

"Let's go show off our bags, ladies. See you soon." Kiera waved at the girls and headed to the front of the show.

Fifteen minutes later, the models showed up and my assistants helped get them dressed. Organized chaos flowed around the back room. I loved the energy during the fashion show. All the hard work came to this moment when the world got to see glimpses of your heart and soul. Though they couldn't see the work it took to create the ensemble, they could appreciate the finished products. I went to my desk, sat down, breathed, and sipped from my water bottle. As I checked myself in the mirror, I noticed a face in the reflection.

My heart thudded and a wave of emotion came over me. It had been two months since he texted me, asking for my forgiveness. I thought he'd moved on.

I turned to face him, and all the chaos in the room fade away. He leaned against a cabinet with his arms crossed. The space had just gotten smaller.

"What are you doing here?" I asked.

"You're in Paris. I'm in Paris. This is your first fashion show. Congratulations."

Grayson wore a dark gray suit with my silver tie. My feelings for him hadn't gone away no matter how much I'd tried, but I couldn't let him know. There was this barrier between us, and I couldn't remove it. He looked thinner, tired, and contemplative. Despite that, he still made my heart pitter-patter like no other man.

Exhilaration had burst in me when I saw the photo of him wearing my novelty sweater. He hadn't tossed it out. I'd wanted to comment on how perfect it had looked on him, but I didn't want him to know I was spying on his profile. Had he been stalking my profile too?

I traced the outline of his square jaw with the five o'clock shadow that made him look hot and exhausted at the same time. My body shivered, remembering how that rough face felt against my neck and inner thighs.

"Don't you have work to do? Who's running the business?"

"A business means nothing when my heart is unstable. I'm here to support the person who could stabilize my heart."

Every time he said those words, my heart melted, but I was cautious.

"Don't you have other women stabilizing you in Providence?"

I knew he didn't have a girlfriend because I'd been searching for him on the internet. There hadn't been any new pictures of him with anyone. Maybe he had someone but kept her hidden. I'd never know.

Men with money and power could buy anything.

The more I tried to forget him, the more I thought about him. Everywhere I turned, I saw Grayson. He was in all the buildings I passed—the texture of a garment, on the trees, and on the streets. He consumed me.

Standing so close, his musky scent urged my body to move closer, but I refused.

"There's no other woman in my life. You're the one I want."

Pierre, the male model wearing a button-up shirt with unique pockets, intruded the space. "Just wanted to say this shirt is exceptional." He made my menswear outfit look fantastic. "Are you available for dinner after the show?"

Grayson turned his head in a slow motion that mimicked a cobra surveying its prey. I sensed the animosity pumping off him.

I shook my head slightly. "Sorry, I'm busy."

Pierre met Grayson's eyes, understood, and left.

I hadn't dated anyone since Grayson, but that was my choice. My heart wasn't ready to see anyone.

Grayson stepped closer and gripped my chin. His touch sent a zing through me, reminding me of all the wonderful things we used to do. He lowered his lips but didn't kiss me. Instead, he ran his thumb over my bottom lip. "Congratulations again. I meant what I said, Natalie. You're the woman I want. Can we start over?" A pause that thrummed with anticipation. "Please?"

"Grayson, I'm not ready."

With his lips pressed tightly together, he nodded. "I'll be here when you are."

A month later, I had a show in Milan, and Grayson showed up to support me.

"You're in Milan. I'm in Milan. Wherever you are, I'll be there." he said when I questioned why he was present.

We had dinner and chatted about Three Point Park and The Prism. He did this for my following three shows. I was getting worried about him. Every time I saw him, he seemed more exhausted.

I'd never seen the fatigue in his eyes or how it weighed on his body. I sensed the weariness in him. "What have you been up to? Why do you look like you need to sleep for a month?"

"I'm working on fulfilling a dream."

CHAPTER SEVENTY

GRAYSON

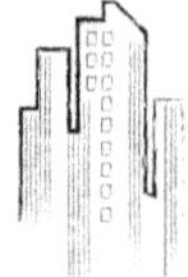

I'd been focusing on the construction of The Prism while my team concentrated on the interior of the other buildings. My schedule had been hectic because I followed Natalie's schedule and made sure I was there to support her dreams. After her shows ended, I'd rush back and continue with work. I wanted to ensure Three Point Park would be complete for October. After I added the trim to the arched doorway in her office, I wiped my hands clean and reviewed my work. Everything was moving along nicely.

Natalie didn't know I was part of the construction team nailing in the support beams, hanging drywall. I even painted them. I wanted to do the work on the three floors reserved for her. If she refused them, I'd leave them empty, waiting for the day she'd come back to me.

Working on this building every day for the past six months and flying to meet her had been difficult, but it was worth it. Every time I saw her, she gave me the boost I needed to continue. My love for her was the driving force behind everything.

I kept tabs on her via the French tabloids and searched up the men she took photos with—European models. Damn them all.

I had no right to claim her as mine after hurting her the way I had. But she was mine. These men needed to stay away from her.

Footsteps sounded, and I looked up to see Remi approaching with a bag carrying my lunch. "Yo. You need to sleep. You've got dark circles under your eyes."

"I'll sleep on my flight to Paris tonight."

Remi dropped the lunch bag on the table. "Does Natalie know what you're doing?"

"No. Don't tell her."

He shook his head. "Want me to help? The boys can all chip in, and we'd finish the three floors faster."

"No. I need to do this myself."

"If you keep this up, you won't *live* to see the completed project. She can't appreciate a dead person."

Those words hit me hard as I dropped into a chair. "The rest of the building is all set. I'm just working on these three floors. They'll be done this week for next month's ribbon ceremony."

"Did you invite Natalie?"

"No."

"Then how is she going to know about it?"

My body ached, and my muscles screamed for sleep. "I plan on giving her a tour at the right time." When she comes back to me willingly. Not because I asked, but because she wanted to.

Remi shook his head, not understanding my logic. But there was also a smile on his face.

"Are you here to bring me lunch or harass me?" I asked, my patience running thin.

"Both." Remington punched me lightly on the shoulder, taking the seat in the empty chair beside me. He watched me devour the steak and cheese sub he'd gotten me. "Love makes you do some crazy shit. You're going through that phase right now."

I didn't disagree, but I didn't comment either.

"There's a video game convention in two months. You going?" Remi asked.

I nodded. "What do you think about the demo I sent?"

"It's great." Remi smiled. "You're experiencing a phase of insanity, and that's pushing your creativity to new heights. I love how your world flips upside down and sideways, depending on which portal I choose."

Natalie had inspired that, but I wanted to keep that knowledge to myself. There was something sacred about keeping this truth in my heart instead of making it public knowledge.

Remi and I continued our conversation about the video games. Apparently, my friends were having fun incorporating the video clips into their games. Remi's phone buzzed, and his smile revealed it was Audri calling him.

He got up from his chair. "Got a hot date. See you later." As he walked off, he picked up the call.

Two hours later, I showered and prepared to head over to the airport, where I'd purchased a private jet to be at my beck and call. It was the only way to get me everywhere I needed to go in a timely manner. I had to be present at all of Natalie's events so that any man who wanted to ask her out would know she was with me, even though she wasn't.

Before I got into my car, my phone pinged with a text message.

Remington: *Got a crazy idea for you. Dare to try it?*

They knew how competitive I was.

Grayson: *I never back down from a dare. What's the wager?*

Remington: *1992 Screaming Eagle Cabernet. Worth over 500K. You game?*

Grayson: *I never say no to rare wine.*

Remington: *You haven't even heard the dare.*

Grayson: *Dude, what is it? I'm tired, and I'm getting ready to hop on a flight.*

My brain was exhausted, and I just wanted to land in Paris, get to my hotel, and sleep so I could escort Natalie to her event the next day.

As I drove to the airport, Remi called to explain his idea. Man, my friends were nuts.

I wanted to back out. "It's too much work."

"We got you. We'll all help."

"Don't you have better things to do?"

"Nah. This is more fun," Remi said. "To see my boy happy makes me happy."

I snorted. "Did Audri teach you that line?"

"And?"

I laughed for the rest of the ride, wondering how this dare would pan out.

CHAPTER SEVENTY-ONE

NATALIE

Grayson had accompanied me to my events for the last few months. Today, he didn't need to be present for a promotional event with a fashion magazine. But he stood in the studio watching me and the models . . . especially the male models.

He walked me to my apartment because the photo studio was just a block away. We stopped by a bench and he pulled me to him, wrapping his arms around me. The dark circles under his eyes had worsened. He hadn't shaved in a few days. It sounded strange, but I could *feel* the fatigue in him.

"Are you sick?" I asked, touching his face. "You look exhausted."

"Does lovesick count as an illness?"

A small smile curved my lips. He had been true to his words, showing up at all my events. The wall that had stood between us crumbled brick by brick. I was letting him back into my life again. In actuality, he'd never left. But I feared this could be another mistake on my part.

What if starting over meant opening myself to heartache

again? I was in a good place right now. There were no expectations, but there was also no love. Though I loved him, the magic was lost when it wasn't reciprocated. To pine over someone who didn't feel the same about you was painful and exhausting.

"I think you need to go home and rest. You don't have to come to every event. I appreciate—"

"I love you, Natalie." He tightened the embrace, kissing the top of my head.

My heart blossomed, and the velvety petals flowed around my stomach. I let him hold me because if he hadn't, my body would've collapsed in shock and elation.

He veered back, looking into my eyes. "I'm so sorry for hurting you the way I did. Please know that I wanted to keep you safe. I meant none of those things I said to you. I had to push you away so you'd run back to Paris. When you didn't leave Providence, I recruited our mothers to help with the sleeping medicine—which I promised to never do again without your consent."

"Wait." My eyes widened. "Your mom and my mom worked together?"

He nodded. "I even asked Forrest about the dosage and the side effects to ensure your safety."

I couldn't believe he did all that just to get me to Paris.

"You did all this because you wanted me away from Providence? Why exactly?"

He told me about Club Diablo and Robert Conner and his wife. I couldn't believe the things he told me. I'd worked with Robert and found him to be a decent man. But I supposed you could never truly know someone.

Grayson did all that because he didn't want the organization to get to me. I was his weakness. My throat tightened.

"Why didn't you just tell me?"

"Would you have gone home if I told you the risk I was taking?"

Absolutely not. I would have stayed with him no matter what. What if he hadn't made it out of Club Diablo? Just thinking about the terrifying scenario made me shiver.

He placed a hand on either side of my shoulders. "I'll show you how much I love you. Will you give me the chance to prove it?"

How could I say no? I'd been waiting for this moment.

Tears misted my eyes. "Okay."

His eyes gleamed from that one word, and the fatigue on his face disappeared.

"I've got to head back to Providence. I'll see you soon." He kissed me lightly on the lips and strode away.

I stood in place for a few minutes, trying to replay the magical moment. Everything around me suddenly appeared brighter.

As I entered my apartment building, the adorable receptionist named Annette gave me a silver gift box. "Mademoiselle LaRue. You have a package."

"Thank you." I removed the lid and pulled out a wooden ruler. A notecard in Grayson's handwriting read: *I don't want to fall short with you.*

Smiling, I brought it up to my office and placed it with all my favorite sketching supplies.

The next day, Annette called me to let me know I had another package in a silver box. This time, it was a calculator with the message: *I want this relationship to count.*

The following day, another package came. Annette smiled. "I think you have a secret admirer."

"Yeah. He's crazy." I couldn't help the grin on my face.

"I want someone to be crazy about me like that," Annette said.

The package had a compass and a note that read: *I don't want to ever lose you again.*

That night, I gathered all his gifts onto my bed and stared at them. From my quick search on Three Point Park, it was due to finish in October, just next month. Grayson never invited me to the ribbon ceremony. Maybe he assumed I was busy or that I wouldn't come.

I'd been waiting for this day so I could see the Three Point Park project that had initially brought us together. I also wanted to see what he'd done with The Prism.

My brand was growing, but I didn't want to decide in haste. I was still deciding if I wanted to be based in Providence or Paris. Once I narrowed down the location, I could focus on the expansion.

House of LaRue didn't need me except for design approvals whenever a new collection was ready. I'd review it with my mom and the new designer, Elyna, who was fabulous. But that process could be done via video conference. So I didn't need to be in Paris.

My heart already knew the answer. However, I'd been afraid to go back to the city that held so many memories. Providence had given me happiness and sadness. More importantly, it had given me love and hope.

The man I loved was there. He'd finally confessed his love to me, and I couldn't be happier. No man had ever made me feel and want so much.

Time away from Grayson had allowed me to dive deep into my imagination. I'd imagined all the joyful times we'd spent together. Even all the fantasies I'd made up to make myself feel better. Imagination was powerful; it was a force of perseverance for me. It helped me heal when I didn't know how. I could flow with the moments because of it.

Had he tapped into his imagination when he tried to earn my forgiveness? In my heart, I knew he did. Our creative hearts understood the imaginative language.

What Grayson didn't know was that I had already forgiven him. Each time he came to support me, he'd erased a little stain from my heart. When he told me about why and what he'd done to keep me safe, my heart was renewed—all the stains had dissolved like some kind of metaphysical activity that strengthened my heart.

Still, I wanted to see what he meant by showing me his devotion. These tools meant the world to me. The ruler, the calculator, and the compass were aspects of him making a promise to me.

By the end of the night, I'd packed my belongings and booked a flight back to Providence for the following day. My apartment was still there, waiting for me.

CHAPTER SEVENTY-TWO

NATALIE

I'd been back in Providence for a week and fell into my routine as though I'd never left. I'd met with the girls two nights ago, and we had a blast.

My phone rang with Royce's number flashing on the screen. Something twisted in my stomach. Royce didn't usually call me.

"Hey, Royce. Is Michelle okay?"

"Michelle's fine." Royce's tone made my blood turn cold.

"What's wrong?"

"It's Grayson. There's been an accident."

An iceberg the size of Europe dropped into my stomach. "What happened? Where is he?" Awful scenarios of what could've happened filled my head.

"He's currently at Vitality Health Clinic." Royce gave me the address and nothing more.

Why wasn't he giving me more details about the accident?

Because he doesn't want you getting into an accident while driving to see Grayson.

"Okay, I'm on my way." My body shook as I grabbed my purse and hurried to my car.

My heart deflated as though someone had poked it with a needle. The slow deflation made it difficult to breathe. I hated the way stress took over my body.

Inhaling a deep breath, I gripped the steering wheel and drove off.

Dear God, please let Grayson be safe.

We were supposed to meet tomorrow. What if—

Stop thinking negative thoughts!

I wanted to start a new life with him. I wanted to hear him say he loved me every day.

Tears slid down my cheek as I thought about how much time I'd wasted by not forgiving him sooner. I zipped into the parking of the medical clinic, whipped into the spot closest to the front door, and darted inside toward the receptionist wearing a colorful dress and a nametag that read Patty.

Patty glanced up from her desk, smiling as though there were nothing wrong in the world.

"Hi, I'm looking for Grayson Wu." I curled my fingers into a tight fist so my hand wouldn't shake.

Patty pointed down the hall. "He's in the last room."

I nodded. "Thanks. Is he . . . is he okay?"

"He'll be okay," she said with a smile.

That was good news, right?

Grayson didn't need to see me all worked up. That would only stress him out. I had to be strong for both of us. We could get through this hurdle.

I reached the last room, stopped a moment to breathe and gathered myself to be presentable. With the back of my hand, I wiped the tears from my eyes, opened the door, and entered.

"*Oh, my God.*" I rushed in, tossed my purse onto the armchair, and went over to him. "How did this happen?" I placed a hand on his cheek, afraid to touch him elsewhere.

A cast covered his left leg, another one protected his arm, and several layers of gauze wrapped around his neck. He had a bandage on his forehead with a fat stain that looked like dried blood.

Tears stung my eyes, but I pushed them back. He didn't need to see me cry right now. "My poor baby. Are you in pain?"

He nodded and looked at me. "But not anymore, because you're here." He let out a groan, followed by another.

"What happened?"

"I was working on The Prism." He released another groan.

"Grayson." I sighed. "I asked you to leave those tasks to the contractors. Just because you know how to build doesn't mean you have to show off your skills. Look at you! You should think about your future. About me." I placed a hand over my heart.

"I wanted to show you how much you mean to me. Each brick I placed in that building has my love, sweat, and effort embedded in it. I designed and built it for you."

Tears streamed down my cheeks. "You're so stubborn. What am I going to do with you?"

"Love me forever." Another groan escaped him, followed by a wince.

My heart quickened as the window to my soul opened for him. I'd never stopped loving him. He was the sacred thread that stitched my heart and soul together as one.

"I already do," I said.

A goofy smile appeared on his face, and he didn't look as ill as he should have.

"How long do you need to keep the cast and gauze on? What happened to your forehead and your neck? Did you lift an entire floor?" I reached for the bandage, wanting to touch it, but he shifted away too fast, making me stare at him suspiciously.

Guilt—like a kid being caught doing something he wasn't supposed to—splashed across his face.

I got off the bed and walked around, surveying his body. Narrowing my eyes at him, I played along. "Your bandage needs changing. The blood has seeped through. Have you been resting well?"

He shook his head and offered me a groan that I could now confirm was fake.

"Let me get the nurse to give you a shot." From where I stood, I could see the awful way the gauze had been wrapped around his neck. It looked like a first-grader had done it. The bandage looked like ketchup had been carelessly squirted on it. A few spots appeared like fingers trying to smear excess ketchup away.

"I'm not feeling well," he said, trying to see what I was looking at.

"They have these new shots to treat Asshole-itis." With a swift movement, I yanked the bandage off.

"Ow." He sat up, removed the casts from his body, and tossed them onto the bed. "I knew it was a dumb idea."

I crossed my arms and glared at him. "And whose idea was that?"

He walked over to me and took me into his arms. "The boys. They knew I was waiting for you to take me back and thought this dare would prove you still love me."

His eyes bored into me.

"Grayson, if you want to know if I still love you, all you have to do is ask. Not think of this ridiculous scenario that scared the shit out of me. You can't even act."

He laughed. "I know. It's not my talent. So . . . Do you forgive me?"

"Yes, I do." I smacked his chest playfully. "But if you pull off something like this again, I'll have to reconsider."

"Did you pay the clinic and the receptionist to play along?" I asked, glancing around the room that looked too real to fake.

"The clinic belongs to Forrest, and his receptionist is in on it. How could she not be? There were four men cursing up a storm in here, trying to put me in a cast and stage the scene correctly. Royce almost squirted ketchup in my eye twice."

I grinned. "How in the world did your friends convince you to do something like this?"

"It was a dare that earned me a 1992 Screaming Eagle Cabernet. It's worth over five hundred thousand dollars. We can try it tonight."

He wiggled his eyebrows, and I got my McDimple back again.

CHAPTER SEVENTY-THREE

GRAYSON

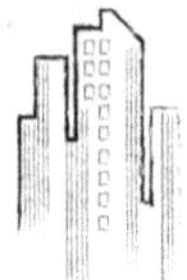

In early October, I sat on a chair behind the podium in my dark suit and red tie. Beside me were the city manager, mayor, and governor. I looked out into the audience, and gratitude filled my heart as I scanned the familiar faces.

Sitting in the front row, Natalie smiled at me. She wore a light gray jacket over a wine-colored dress with long boots, looking more beautiful every day. She sat beside my mom. They'd spent time together in the last few days and planned on meeting up with Natalie's mother for a shopping trip in New York next month.

To see the woman I loved get along with the woman who gave birth to me stirred my heart. Maybe it was this special day with the autumn leaves brightening the sky that made me sentimental. Or maybe it was seeing all my family and friends filling up Three Point Park that made this day unforgettable.

The City of Providence had gotten an interim DPW Commissioner named Jordan Stokes. He took over for Robert and had ensured nothing delayed my Three Point

Park project. I was still suspicious of people, but mostly those I didn't know. I considered that trait a detective's skill. Everyone had an agenda, and if theirs didn't harm me or mine, then all was well. Caution could be beneficial if you learned how to trust your heart.

Jordan introduced me and I got up, walking to the podium.

"Thank you for the warm welcome, everyone. Today is a special day for the City of Providence. Three Point Park has been a dream of mine for a long time. I'm happy to have the city join me in this celebration of the park that will attract an abundance of tourists from all over the world."

The massive TV screen on the side showed stills of my buildings, The Prism, Dream Key, and Freedom Heights.

"Three Point Park will create new jobs and expand businesses, therefore creating revenues for the city. This is *my* city, and also *your* city. We must protect its integrity at all costs. Let truth and beauty shine. Don't let greed consume our city the way it has done with other cities in this country."

I wasn't sure who was listening, but if any members of the organization were, perhaps they'd read between the lines. Maybe they'd assume I was a billionaire saying one thing and meaning another. Maybe they'd approach me for a business collaboration on that assumption. But I hadn't intended for any collaboration. My words were a promise to protect what was mine at all costs.

I was speaking the truth regardless of who was listening.

I gestured to the TV screen again. "Office and retail spaces are available for lease. We welcome the arts in all forms. Creativity is how we solve problems."

After my speech, the governor, mayor, and city manager

all took their turns speaking and applauding Three Point Park.

The media had some questions for me regarding The Prism.

"This architecture is mesmerizing," said a female reporter from Channel Five News. "Did anyone inspire you to design The Prism?"

Natalie met my gaze and smiled. My heart overflowed with love.

"Yes. Someone inspired it. We all know the inspiring story behind the Taj Mahal, where a king built a castle-like mausoleum, dedicating it to his wife after she passed while giving birth to his child. He wanted to show his devotion to her." I swallowed, preparing to share a small piece of myself with the world. "I built The Prism because I want to dedicate it to my love. Devotion after death is beautiful, but devotion to her while she's alive and can appreciate it is even more beautiful, don't you agree?"

The crowd erupted in applause, and more questions boomed.

Tears streamed down Natalie's face. Mom, Audri, and her friends were also in tears. Remi and Royce joined in the applause. Forrest and Arrow exchanged a teasing glance. *Assholes. Just wait until you fall in love.*

My family and friends went home after the ceremony. Natalie and I stuck around and walked Three Point Park hand in hand, enjoying the cool, crisp weather.

"Thank you for the lovely dedication," she said. "I don't know what to say."

"You don't have to. Just keep it here." I placed a hand on her heart.

Nodding, she looked ahead and gasped, dragging me to the wishing well. "Oh, you built a centerpiece for the park."

"Yeah, I figured it needed something simple that didn't take away from the buildings." I glanced inside and saw a handful of coins at the bottom of the well.

Natalie dug into her purse for change and gave me a quarter. She held one in her hand, then closed her eyes and tossed it in. Then she looked at me. "Go ahead. Make a wish."

"I don't have anything to wish for. I already have everything I need, but for you, I'll make a wish." Closing my eyes, I wished in silence.

Make Natalie's dream come true.

CHAPTER SEVENTY-FOUR

NATALIE

He stood with me by the wishing well, and I grabbed his hands, studying them. They were rougher than when I first met him. More calluses and scratches covered his palms and fingers—the result of him working day and night on The Prism for me.

"I truly appreciate what you've done for me, Grayson. The Prism is spectacular. It's better than I imagined." It looked like a modern version of the old building—a rectangle shape with a gray façade and window panels that were wider and more reflective.

I kissed his hand and touched his cheek, which wasn't hollow anymore. He'd been sleeping and eating better since the completion of Three Point Park. He didn't have to fly around the globe to support me, looking like a zombie.

"You're welcome. Building those floors for you was like building up my heart again. When we first met, my heart was in pieces. You're the architect of my heart, rebuilding me from within."

My heart bloomed like a giant rose, and I felt each petal

unfurl inside my chest. I didn't know my heart could expand that large. I didn't know I could fall more in love with him, but here I was, diving into the depths of love.

"Being loved by you is like walking in a gentle drizzle while having pink raindrops kiss my face." I had no idea why I was being so poetic, but the image popped into my head and I had to let him know.

"Pink raindrops? Is there such a thing?" he asked.

"Of course. It comes from having an open heart and an open mind. When those two things are free, anything is possible. Your love opened me to possibilities. My world is painted in unconventional colors because of you."

I embraced him, wrapping my arms around this stable form that had always offered me protection. An orange autumn leaf with red specks detached from a nearby tree branch and floated in front of me, falling beside my boot.

The simple moment helped me pour out my soul to him.

"When we met, I was living a life full of dissatisfaction, instability, fear, and losing faith in love. I felt like I was trying to catch up to the world and failing miserably. House of LaRue was unstable, and I had to sacrifice my dreams to maintain my family's legacy. I was afraid that if I dared go after my passion, it would backfire. But then you bought my first design, sat with me in the dark, and showed me the meaning of love. You proved to me that something can emerge from nothing." I bent and picked up the autumn leaf. "Like this leaf, I've let go of all those things that once attached me to fear and unhappiness. I'm now *free*, Grayson. You showed me how to do that with your love." I kissed him lightly on the lips. "Thank you."

His eyes beamed with warmth. "You've freed me too, buttercup."

Hand in hand, we walked to Dream Key and Freedom Heights before stopping at The Prism.

Standing on the ground, I glanced up. "It's magnificent, Grayson. You brought the building to life. My dad would've been so proud to see what it has become."

Grayson embraced me from behind, pointing up at the building. "See those three floors with the colorful, reflective glass?"

"Yes." How could I miss them? The way the evening sun touched its surface made it seem like the building blushed on contact.

"Those are yours."

I turned and gaped at him. "Mine? What do you mean?"

"I own the building so I can do whatever I wanted with it. The Prism was yours before it became mine. I want it to be *ours*. I think that would've made your dad happy. I built those top floors for you to do as you please. I didn't work on the other seven floors. It would have taken forever, and I'm not that patient."

Tears misted my eyes, but I blinked them back.

Cupping his face in my hands, I gave him a big, fat, sloppy kiss. "I suppose that makes us an official couple again?"

Confusion twisted his face. "Buttercup, I thought that was a given when you moved back to Providence."

"We never discussed it. I assumed, and you assumed." I poked him in the chest playfully. "I don't want to assume. I like facts."

He grabbed my ass in public and squeezed it hard. I yelped with laughter.

"That's your confirmation." He offered another squeeze. "You're mine. Period."

"Okay." My eyes sparkled. "When can I see the three floors?"

"It's getting dark, so you won't be able to appreciate its beauty. We can see it tomorrow. I've got plans for you tonight."

"What kind of plans?"

"Plans that involve you moving all your stuff into my house. I made plenty of room for you. What do you say?"

I ran my fingers along his square jaw that he'd recently shaved. "Well, since you made this building for me, I suppose I could comply and *obey* you." My hand slid under his suit jacket, stopping at the top of his waistband. "I've got some new creations for you too. I wrote a few bedtime stories during our breakup that you might enjoy." I pressed my fingers to his lips.

"Like what?" he asked as we walked back to the parking garage at City Hall.

"Like where I obey your every command," I purred.

"And?" He walked faster, pulling me along.

I laughed at our speed walking, my joy echoing all around us.

"I also learned some new lap dances."

He scooped me into his arms and ran toward the parking garage. "We need to get home now!"

With his powerful arms carrying me and the beating of his heart speaking to mine, I became the luckiest woman alive.

Grayson

On a warm April afternoon, I went to get sushi to bring back to The Prism for Natalie. Work had resumed for me, but I kept a light schedule so I could help her acclimate to her new office space.

The headquarters for Momentum took up the three floors I'd reserved for her in The Prism. For the past several months, she'd been designing the interior space, picking out paint colors for the walls, choosing the flooring, ordering light fixtures, reviewing office furniture, and so on. I enjoyed seeing her add little details to make the space her own.

Remi leased out a floor for Audri's Epiphanii jewelry line. She loved the location and the idea that she could visit Natalie for creative discussions. I would've let Audri use the space for free, but Remi wanted to keep business separate from family matters.

Insurance companies, media groups, and law firms occupied several floors. The rest of the building was composed of luxurious apartments. The top floor of The Prism was reserved for me. I didn't know what I wanted to do with it yet. Right now, it was another office space, allowing me to visit Natalie whenever I wanted. It could also be a potential meeting area for WaterFyre Rising discussions with my friends. I was in no rush, and I wanted the view of the city from the top.

With the lunch bag in my hand, I stood on the sidewalk in front of Momentum's flagship store, which was scheduled to open before the holidays. The retail space took up three-quarters of the ground level and Audri's jewelry store took up the rest. She didn't need as much space as Natalie's apparel and accessory line. Everything worked out beautifully.

Looking at the clothing fixtures and mannequins that were lined up against the wall waiting to be assembled, satisfaction spread in my chest. My woman and my sister were displaying their hearts and souls to the world, and I was glad to be part of that.

I saluted the three men installing the light fixtures at the sales counter.

The passageways under the building were also renovated to be more functional. It was closed to everyone except me and my boys. Natalie saw what I'd done to the space and approved of the renovation. It looked nothing like the place that had imprisoned her. That room had been transformed into an office space for future use.

The tunnels led to one main channel guided us to an empty warehouse by the river. The warehouse had been owned by someone who had died at Club Diablo. I bought the property from the city when they took it over. The city had no clue about the tunnel, and I had no intention of sharing that detail. I wasn't sure what I'd do with the warehouse yet. There was no rush.

I walked into the main entrance and took the elevator up to Natalie's floor.

Natalie got three floors in The Prism. Floor forty-one was reserved for her office. She had the entire floor to herself, which included a conference room, design area, a lounge area with a reading nook, and open space for whatever she wanted to do. Floors forty-two and forty-three contained design studios, employee offices, showrooms, storage, a swatch and trim library, and anything else she wanted.

Walking on the hardwood floors, I made my way to her office, which had a nice setup already. Simple furniture adorned the open space. I'd sectioned off an area for a spa if she decided to have one on her floor.

I heard her talking on the phone and made my way over.

"We'll get together before your trip, Kiera. I'm sorry to hear about your mom. If you need anything, let me know. We're here for you. We can help."

Natalie's voice was like a dose of joy for my body. I sounded sappy, like some of my friends, but I guess that was the beauty of being in love. It changed a man, smoothed out his edges, allowing him to see beauty in places it had once been lacking.

I strode over to her design table, a massive block of stone I'd gotten from a European vendor. Placing the takeout bag on a side table, I met her smiling eyes as she continued her phone conversation.

She quickly adjusted the black fabric covering the display. "Okay, see you tomorrow night." Placing her phone on the table, she beamed at me.

"Everything okay with Kiera?" I asked.

"Yeah. The girls and I are meeting tomorrow before she goes to Texas for her next photoshoot. Her mom's in the hospital, so she's stressed. I told her we'd visit Mrs. Ford so she could focus on work. Mrs. Ford lives just outside of Providence."

"That'll give Kiera peace of mind."

Nodding, Natalie moved in front of the display as though she didn't want me to inquire, but her suspicious gesture made me curious. Her excited expression made me want to yank off the cover.

Sunlight streamed in through the reflective glass and cast a shower of golden rays onto the walls and the floor.

She walked up to me, and beams of sunlight radiated around her, illuminating her face and making her hair appear gold. Or rather, *she* made the sunlight brighter.

Sunlight without her was just sunlight. Sunlight *with* her transformed into this metaphysical or cosmic ray that I couldn't explain. It was like a photonic light that came from a different place that was so unique—so perfect.

I yanked her to me and turned her around to face the windows.

"This is the beauty I want you to see." A flock of birds flew by and broke through the sunrays while casting moving shadows on the floor and walls.

"I love how the sun illuminates my office. It's magical the way the building comes alive with the light."

She turned to face me, the blue of her eyes like glittering gemstones.

"You make it come alive." I tucked a strand of hair behind her ear. "I used to think I knew everything about architecture and creativity, but I was wrong."

A crease appeared between her eyebrows. "What do you mean? You're an extraordinary architect. My *favorite*."

She had no idea the profound effect she had on me, or how much she had changed me.

"Everyone knows the sun gives life to everything. The initial reason I was drawn to The Prism was because of the way the sunlight hits it. But since I met you, I learned something new." My fingers skimmed her cheek. "The sunlight didn't know it existed until it touched *you*. You gave it meaning." I heard her gasp as emotion filled her eyes. "The moment the sunlight hits your face, it realizes its purpose."

Tears glistened down her face like rivers of diamonds.

"You gave me purpose, Natalie. I love you." I ushered her over to the window, placing her hand on the panel with mine. "Windows are my signature feature. They let me see everything in the world. You're everything I see, everything I feel, and everything I dream of."

"Stop making me cry." She buried her face in my chest.

Smiling, I grabbed her a tissue from the desk.

Once she dried her tears, she embraced me, pressed her face into my neck, sniffed, and sighed as though she wanted to absorb me.

"You've changed me too, Grayson. Your brilliant mind makes you an innovator who creates profound things. I admire what's in here." I tapped his head. "And here." I placed my hand over his heart. "Let me show you how you've inspired me."

Natalie

. . .

His unique scent was kissed by the sun, chilled by the snow, and pressurized in a container of aged wine, organic wood, and rustic metal. He was masculine, and he was all mine.

I never knew what it felt like to matter so much to someone. Grayson made me feel like I was the reason for his existence. Standing beside him, my heart overflowed with love and gratitude.

I broke free from his addictive scent and interlaced my fingers with his, steering him toward the concealed display. "I dedicate this to you—a man forever tied to me."

He arched a curious eyebrow while walking around the concealed display case.

My heart thudded, unsure if he'd like what I'd created for him. He'd seen three of them before, but now he had the full spectrum of colors and designs.

His eyes sparkled, trying to guess. "What is it?"

I gestured to the black fabric. "The honor is yours. You can reveal it."

In one swoop, Grayson yanked away the fabric, revealing a tie collection with the label Forget Me Knots. A massive smile stretched across his face as he looked at all fifty ties.

"There are so many colors. Forget Me Knots is the only brand I'll ever wear from now on." He picked up a light blue metallic tie with a cool print. "Isn't this an abstraction of The Prism?"

"It is." I'd created a print for each of his buildings. I pulled out a mint green tie. "Guess what this is?"

He examined it. "The Fortress looks fabulous." He looped the tie around his neck and created a messy Natalie knot.

I made a mental note to teach him the steps again. The tie looked adorable and silly over his knit top.

"Thank you, buttercup. I love them."

"This tie collection will be available in stores worldwide. I want the world to wear Forget Me Knots. Every time a woman buys a tie for her man or a man wears the tie, they're appreciating *you* the way I do."

"I don't need the world to love me, Natalie. Only you."

I wound my arms around his neck and felt his throbbing bulge. "Do you know the story behind the little black dress?"

"No. Should I?"

"Coco Chanel made the little black dress famous. When her lover died, she mourned for him and created the dress. She wanted the world to mourn with her. It's a beautiful and morbid love story." I stretched up to kiss him lightly on the lips. "I don't want to show my appreciation to you after death. I want the world to know how much I love you *now*."

"Natalie—"

I crushed my lips to his, silencing his words. For a long moment, we showed our appreciation for each other with our mouths and tongues.

He veered back, his eyes glinting with mischief. "There's something we haven't done to this building to make it more magical."

"What is it?"

"Christen this floor with our love." He grinned.

"What about our cold lunch?" I asked, even though I wasn't hungry for food.

"We can go out for a bigger meal later." Lust darkened his eyes. "Then we can bless your other floors. Let's start in your office. Your employees won't start until next month. We have plenty of time to check out all the buttresses, corners, and *angles*. I want to see you wearing nothing but my tie."

I laughed as he whisked me away into my office and loved me.

Thank you so much for reading Natalie and Grayson's story!

For Kiera and Forrest's romance, order **The Inquisitor** (Book 3) now!

https://nadiahan.com/books/

Read Natalie and Grayson's **bonus scene here** or scan the code below. She has a new bedtime story for him!

If you enjoyed The Innovator, I would appreciate a review on your chosen platform(s). With your support, I can continue to write more stories.

For exclusive content, new releases, and giveaways, sign up to my newsletter.

https://nadiahan.com/newsletter/

. . .

Join my **Facebook reader group** for bonus features and exclusive giveaways!

https://www.facebook.com/groups/nadiahanselitebookworms/

Stay in touch with me! You can scan the code for easy access to me.

Instagram: https://www.instagram.com/authornadiahan/
TikTok: https://www.tiktok.com/@authornadiahan
Pinterest: https://www.pinterest.com/authornadiahan
BookBub: https://www.bookbub.com/authors/nadia-han
FB author page: https://www.facebook.com/authornadiahan
Goodreads: https://www.goodreads.com/author/show/
22312698.Nadia_Han

ACKNOWLEDGMENTS

With every book, I'm more grateful to those people in my circle. The Innovator has increased the size of my heart. It is full of gratitude because of you!

Anna, thank you for being the extraordinary editor that you are. You know my voice and my style like no one else.

Lindsay, thank you for the wonderful copy edits that trim my manuscript like a cardio workout.

Violet and Melissa, your proofreads are truly spectacular. I'm always amazed by what you find.

Sharon, thank you for always asking the right questions that make me a better writer.

To my wonderful PA, Carissa. Thank you for helping me with everything so I can focus on my writing.

To all the readers on my ARC team. I am truly blessed to have you on my side. Thank you for reading and posting about my books.

Thank you to my husband and children for acknowledging my dreams. Because of you, I'm learning how to create my own stars in the sky.

ABOUT THE AUTHOR

Nadia Han is a dreamer, a visionary, an artist, and a believer in karma and kindness. She lives in New England with her family and spends most of her time crafting stories. When she's not writing, she practices yoga, reads, creates art, explores nature, and eats all kinds of foods.

facebook.com/authornadiahan

instagram.com/authornadiahan

bookbub.com/authors/nadia-han

amazon.com/author/nadiahan